SPIRIT HORSES

SPIRIT HORSES

a novel

ALAN S. EVANS

Oceanview Publishing
IPSWICH, MASSACHUSETTS

This book is dedicated to all those involved in protecting and insuring the future of our American wild mustangs. These fascinating creatures should always be recognized as irreplaceable living symbols of our nation's strength and resilience.

Acknowledgments

It would have been an impossible task to bring this book to publication without the help of so many fine people who believed in me and pushed me beyond my own doubt.

Thanks to my wife, Carlie, whom I bounced more ideas off than anyone should have to endure. To Margie and Bill Evans who became my first unofficial critics and editors. A big thank you to Dot Whittle whose honesty, expertise, and time helped me shape a roughed-out story into a manuscript worthy of exposure to literary professionals. Thanks to Lynn Guelzow and Lisa Maier whose interest and connections must have been God sent. I have a special appreciation for Drs. Pat and Bob Gussin of Oceanview Publishing. Their investment of time, money, and faith means more to me than I can express. Last but not least, to the entire team at Oceanview, thanks for your professionalism, enthusiasm, and creative energy that shows well beyond your desks and computers.

SPIRIT HORSES

Prologue

An intense heat simmered over the fairgrounds located just south of the small town of Douglas, Wyoming. The light gray clouds lingering high overhead, showed no real threat of rain, but were casting some welcome shade on this hot summer afternoon. The annual event, just beginning its final weekend, was in full swing, bustling with a record crowd.

Among a large group watching a demonstration in the livestock arena, were two men who had never met. The strangers, both wearing faded jeans and worn boots, soon struck up a conversation while leaning against the grandstands.

They had come to see the talented young horseman that had been so heavily advertised around town. The guy they were watching was just beginning to work with a nervous two-year-old black colt in a round pen.

The older of the two men threw his half-smoked cigarette on the ground, stepped on it with the toe of his boot, and asked the other, "Who is this guy, where's he from?"

"I don't know," the younger man answered, "but I heard he's an Indian."

A third man sitting in the stands just above looked down and commented. "No kidding, if you ask me, he looks like a boy just off the reservation." They all laughed a little under their breath. A few minutes later he glanced down again, "I had a chance to watch this guy during yesterday's show, and I'll tell you this, that kid's damn good with a horse."

The young horseman's name was Tommy and he was "right off the reservation," the Wind River Reservation in Wyoming. Tommy was nineteen years old and a pure Shoshone, who was starting to build a name for himself on the horsemanship clinic tour. He traveled around working with young horses that were often rank and too dangerous for their owners to train. He would hold these demonstrations in front of large crowds, showing them how easy it could be to start young horses under saddle, with the right knowledge and experience. This audience had paid to watch him and they expected to be impressed. He didn't let them down. The frightened black colt was soon calmed, and eventually accepted a saddle and a rider for the first time in its life.

"How did he do that so quick and easy?" the older man asked out loud.

"I don't know, it must be some kind of Indian voodoo," the other answered half jokingly.

After the clinic was over, Tommy headed toward his trailer to put away his gear.

A lanky, older man, wearing a cowboy hat, approached him from the distant crowd. "Hey kid," he hollered from a few feet away. Tommy kept his eyes down and continued packing his equipment, not responding to the man's loud, rude beckoning. "Hey!" the man repeated, "I have a horse farm nearby and I could use a guy like you to help break in my colts."

Tommy, having no interest in the job, slowly looked up and replied, "I don't break horses mister, I *start* them . . . and I already make a good living doing my clinics. But thanks for the offer."

The cowboy looked put out for a moment, then scratched his head and accepted the answer before asking, "Where the hell did you learn to get along with a horse like that, son? Is that some kind of ancient Indian shit you do?"

Tommy smiled and said, "No sir, believe it or not, what I do, I learned from a white man."

Chapter 1

Well beyond his prime, the old Native American slowly makes his way through the familiar lush green forest. Finally reaching his destination, he sits on a large flat rock to catch his breath. After a short rest, he looks up toward the snow-capped mountaintops and whispers the Indian word, *Tahotay*. Then with outstretched arms, he raises his open palms to shoulder height and begins a chant that is old as time itself.

He is a highly revered man among his people, the last in a centuries-old line of true spiritual shamans. He prefers the old ways, often speaking his native tongue, and living by the ancient beliefs and traditions that he fears will one day be lost to his tribe. It's this particular sacred spot where he often comes to meditate and seek answers. Just as his father had done, and his father before him.

A red-tailed hawk circles high overhead in the cloudless, blue sky, screeching its piercing call. To the aging spiritual leader of his tribe, this is a sign that his ancestors are near. He closes his eyes, lowers his arms, and drifts into a trance. Soon, a tear runs down his face as a vision, which he has seen before, reveals a dark future for his people and their ancestral land.

Little does the old Shaman realize that events that would deeply affect his fate were beginning to unfold fifteen hundred miles away, and a world apart in northern Tennessee.

*   *   *

The morning was beginning like many others on the farm. It was
6 a.m.; Shane Carson had already fed the horses and was now relaxing with a cup of coffee on his front porch. The hired help would
be in soon to start setting up for the long hours of training that lay
ahead. This was one of Shane's favorite times of the day. With his
family still asleep, he looked forward to these early mornings alone
on the porch. It gave him a chance to plan out the day's progress he
had in mind for each horse while watching the first rays of light
slowly dance across his farm.

Shane carried a deep admiration for his land. To him this place
was much more than just a monetary asset. He saw the real treasure
in the countryside itself, with its ageless, tree shaded, grassy hills and
their whispered surroundings. Here he had plenty of room to stretch
his arms and raise his kids without the congestion and problems of
more populated areas. Shane felt fortunate for this lifestyle, but taking care of his land and the valuable animals entrusted to him re-
quired a tremendous commitment involving timeless days of hard
work.

It was early November in Cheatham County, Tennessee, and
there was a light frost on the grass. This was the first cold morning
of the season, so the horses were feeling frisky.

Shane took another sip from his cup of coffee as he admired the
bright waning moon still hanging low over the horizon, soon to trade
places with the rising sun. Off in the distance he heard one of his
broodmares whinny for her foal. He knew which one it was by the
sound of her call. He knew all of his horses that well. Following the
mare's call, he heard the sound of thundering hooves in their field
located on the back side of the property. There were eight broodmares in that field with eight babies by their sides, and all sixteen
were soon caught up in a playful stampede around the large, rolling
meadow. This was not a rare occurrence on the farm, but the cool
morning's nip seemed to be adding to the herd's enthusiasm.

By the time they had made their second lap around the field, the
yearlings in the next pasture over had joined in the fun. With all

the heart and strength they could muster, each animal desperately tried to outrun the others. This playful madness quickly launched an unstoppable chain reaction that continued on to the two- and three-year-olds in training, which were kept near the barns on the front of the farm. Then, just as suddenly as it all started, the herds began to settle. The horses, one by one, exhaled a last snort, dropped their heads, and began to graze quietly.

Witnessing all this brought a smile to Shane's face. He knew how important it was for these animals to grow up like this; being able to interact with each other in a large group was only natural for them. Providing this kind of environment helped them become secure in mind and strong in body, both of which would serve them well later on when they became work or show horses.

His business included training and selling the young horses he bred and raised, as well as training the ones his many clients sent him. All the horses he worked with were well pedigreed, expensive animals. Once they were finished and had proven themselves, these young potential champions would be given a life of envy. They were fed, groomed, and schooled on a daily basis, all of which cost their owners a substantial amount of money.

Shane sometimes joked about what aliens from another world might think if they were to observe a human's relationship with his horse. Watching the care, time, and quality of life afforded these animals, it would probably appear to the aliens as if the horses were the masters and people were their beasts of burden.

His methods were different than those of most trainers. They had been taught to him by a couple of special old mentors who had died years ago. At this point in his career he could do just about anything with a horse. He could start 'em, fix 'em, and also put a finished handle on one that would impress his clients as well as his professional peers. It was said by many that he had some kind of magical power over these thousand-plus-pound animals. Others claimed that he'd learned to hypnotize horses in order to tame them so easily. He knew differently. Hard work and knowledge had earned him this level of mastery.

He was well paid for what he did, and he loved his work, but Shane was no longer a young man. Now in his forties, every morning his body, abused by his occupation, reminded him of this. You couldn't be as good as he was without also physically accumulating the miles and injuries he had endured. But it was all worth it to him, and to do anything else for a living would be unthinkable.

The only thing that meant more to him than his work was his wife, Jen, and their two children, eight-year-old Jacob and Tina, who was six. The kids were now old enough to ride, and they begged daddy every day to put them on a horse. These were good times and Shane loved every minute he spent with his family.

With his cup of coffee now empty, Shane stood, stretched his sore back, and ambled toward his day's work. His assistant trainer, Terry Adams, was waiting when Shane arrived at the main barn. As usual, the dependable Terry had the first horse saddled and ready.

"Mornin', boss," Terry said as he handed Shane the reins. "Your first victim is ready for you." They both grinned.

The morning was going well, and by 9:30 they were already beginning to work with their third horse. This one was the young bay gelding he had ended with yesterday, one that had been started in a bad way by a rough trainer.

"You want me to saddle him, boss?" Terry asked as he led the trembling, wide-eyed young horse out of the stall.

"No, I need to put him in the round pen and try to get him to relax first. I'll wait to saddle him in there when's he settled."

It was only his second day with the gelding and the horse didn't trust Shane yet, but that would soon change. Shane knew it was going to take more than a kind word and a pat on his head to change how this horse felt about people now. He carefully led the scared gelding out of the barn, "Come on buddy, let's see what we can get done with you today."

Shane began his work in the round pen by allowing the gelding to run free. The round pen, which Shane often referred to as his office, was a circular enclosure that measured sixty feet across with a strong seven-foot-high wall. This design allowed a horse freedom of movement without the possibility of being able to jump out. It was designed and built for just this kind of foundation work. By staying in the center of the pen and allowing the horse to move around him on the perimeter, Shane was in a position of control without the horse even realizing it. From here he could skillfully apply and re-lease pressure as he needed to, in order to get the desired response.

Within thirty minutes, the colt was already making some positive changes. He could now see that this was a nice responsive animal who was very willing once he understood what you wanted from him. It would take more sessions before the horse would retain this attitude, but Shane was confident that each day he would become a little more trusting. He rubbed the colt affectionately on his neck as he spoke. "You keep trying for me like you did this morning, and I'll eventually make a nice horse out of you."

Shane looked toward Terry as he led the nervous gelding back into the barn. "Luckily, the idiots that tried to break him before didn't totally blow his mind. With a little time and patience, I think he'll be okay. We ought to be able to saddle him up and swing a leg over him soon."

"Who's next?" Shane asked.

As they continued to work, the cool morning slowly gave way to the warmth from the rising sun making the remainder of the day quite pleasant. By late afternoon all fourteen horses in training had been ridden and were now grazing lazily in their paddocks.

Tired and sore, but not complaining, Shane began the short walk from the barns to the house, leaving the feeding to the hired hands.

As he headed away from the main barn, Shane noticed out of the corner of his eye a shadowy figure following him from just inside the four-board fence. He realized it was the same bay gelding that he had worked with in the round pen earlier. The horse was keeping some distance, but was showing a curious interest in him. Shane didn't react to this at all, not even turning his head to look. To do so might cause the inquisitive bay to shy away, and he definitely wanted to leave the horse with this mind-set for tonight. "Looks like I got in your head a little today after all," he noted as he walked on.

When he got closer to the house, he heard a sound coming from behind the familiar old oak. It was a quiet giggle and then a stern, "Shhh!" Shane smiled slightly but pretended not to notice. He knew his two kids were trying to sneak up on him. Suddenly, they charged, screaming playfully. Jacob grabbed his left leg while Tina wrapped her arms around his right.

"Oh, my gosh!" Shane yelled, "You got me again."

The kids held onto his legs with all their might, knowing that the dreaded tickling would be their dad's predictable defense to the ongoing assault. Shane grabbed Jacob first. He knew right where to get him the best. The boy burst out in an explosion of laughter, and then let go to retreat. Shane then reached for Tina, who had already turned him loose and was now racing toward the house as if her mere survival depended on it. They scrambled noisily inside, slamming the door behind them, cutting off their dad's loud, jovial pursuit.

"Hey, easy guys!" their mom shouted from inside her office. "I've told both of you a thousand times not to slam the door!"

"Sorry, Mom," they yelled as they dashed by. "He's after us and we've got to hide fast."

As the two dove into their best hiding spot, they could hear the front door opening. "Oh, no, here he comes," Tina blurted.

"Shut up," Jacob whispered, "you always make too much noise."

"All right you guys," Shane's deep voice carried through the house, "I'm coming to get you, and when I find you there'll be hell to pay!"

Jen grinned and shook her head as she watched this familiar fiasco from behind her desk. "You have to remember to watch your language around those two," she said as he walked by her office. "Tell them to come out and get cleaned up. Dinner will be ready soon."

Jennifer was a few years younger than Shane. The couple had met at a training clinic he was putting on in Texas twelve years before. They'd been introduced by a mutual friend, and there was an immediate attraction between them. Although neither was looking for it, soon after meeting they both realized that life would never be the same.

Now, a dozen years later, they still shared a powerful love for each other, as well as for their family and farm. Jen was a good organizer and business woman who handled most of the bookkeeping, bill paying, and scheduling for the training and breeding business. Although sometimes her cooking left something to be desired, she was a great mother and anchored the family. She had kept her slim, well-built figure even after having the two children, and could still turn many a man's head.

The temperature was beginning to drop outside as the family sat down to eat. By now the horses were all standing in their stalls, finishing their evening hay. Shane looked up from the sawing motion of his steak knife as he cut a piece of meat. "It's dipping into the mid-thirties tonight; the horses will need their winter blankets for the first time this year. That's a sure sign that the nice fall weather is over and done with."

Jen took a sip of her iced tea and raised her eyebrows, "You always said you'd rather work in the cold of winter than through the heat of summer."

Shane shrugged his shoulders, "Sure wouldn't mind if it could just stay fall or spring all year long."

"Hey, Dad, can we ride tomorrow?" Jacob rarely let a day go by without asking.

"If you guys get your homework done, you and your sister come out to the barn about five o'clock, and I'll let you take ole Tory for a little spin."

Tory was a great old horse for the kids. He was what you would call a babysitter, and was as safe and dependable as you could get. At fourteen, he was still sound and would give you plenty of motor when you asked for it. Tory was one of the horses Shane had hauled all over the Midwest and eastern states when he was putting on horsemanship clinics.

Before he had a family, these clinics were his bread and butter. After twelve years of this kind of life on the road, he was ready to settle down. That's when he met Jen, got married, and purchased the farm.

During his traveling years, he built a reputation for being an extraordinary horseman and clinician. His methods and theories were featured in many national equestrian magazines. He also had several very popular videotapes on the market covering everything from starting a young horse to fixing specific problems that the general public would commonly have with their horses. All this had earned him a certain amount of notoriety and fame in the industry — which Shane would downplay if you asked him about it today. Shane looked back on those years with fond memories of the places he'd been and the people he had met. His time as a clinician had paid him well; therefore, with the money he made he'd been able to buy this beautiful ninety-acre farm in Tennessee, starting the life that he now knew.

The next afternoon Jacob showed up at the barn. "Hey, Mister Terry, where's my dad?"

"He's on his way back from the quarantine paddock. He'll be here in a minute."

"What's he doing over there?"

"Some lady brought in a young mustang mare. The woman said she couldn't keep it and asked your dad if he wanted her. The poor thing looks like she's been through the war. Your dad thought maybe he could save the mare and find her a home. But he didn't want her around the other horses until we had Dr. Tolbert check her out to make sure she's healthy."

A few minutes later Shane drove up in his truck. As he walked into the barn, Terry looked up from a horse's shoe he was tightening. "Do you think she'll be okay?"

"She's pretty scared. I couldn't get real close to her. She needs a good deworming, a lot of feed and hay, and her feet are in bad need of a trim. She should be fine, but we'll have Doc check her out tomorrow to be sure. Did you notice that strange brand on her hip?"

"No, I couldn't see through all that dried mud on her," Terry answered.

"She's a mess for sure," Shane muttered. "We'll give her a chance to settle in tonight. Hopefully we'll be able to catch her and clean her up in the morning before Doc gets here."

"Dad, can I go see her?" Jacob asked, "I've never seen a wild mustang before."

"You can walk out there nice and slow, but don't get too close to the fence; she might kick out. Go get your sister and take her with you. I know she'll want to see her, too."

Jacob sped off to get Tina.

Back at the barn Terry asked, "So what do you think about that brand you saw on her hip?"

"I've never seen one like it. It looks like a broken arrow to me. The lady who dropped her off said all she knew was that the mare was a wild horse, and came from somewhere out west. Maybe I can get Jen to research the brand on the Internet."

By now it was late afternoon. Shane took a deep breath, "Let's get these last two horses ridden. I'm ready to call it a day." He wanted to finish by five o'clock, which would allow him time to let the kids ride Tory as he had promised.

The next morning went smoothly, and by noon about half the horses were done and out grazing in their paddocks. Terry and Shane headed back to try to clean up the little mustang. Terry wondered, "Do you think we'll need to set up some stock panels to make a catch pen for her? There are some panels out there if we need 'em."

Shane shook his head. "Let's try to get our hands on her without them first."

It was about a five-minute ride on the golf cart to the back paddock. On the way the two men talked about Terry and his wife expecting their first baby.

"Are you ready for your life to get turned upside down?" Shane asked as he gave his coworker a grin.

"I've never been so scared, and excited all at the same time."

"You'll never forget the day your kids are born. I hope you don't have a weak stomach. You are going to be in the delivery room aren't you?"

"I've got no choice about that."

"I'll tell you one thing," Shane said, "you've probably never known another human being who you would, without hesitation, step in front of a runaway locomotive for, if that's what it took to save 'em, until you hold that baby in your arms for the first time. I really wasn't prepared for how much it affected me."

Terry peered at Shane from under his cap. "Boss, are you just trying to scare the hell out of me, or what?"

Shane shook his head and laughed.

As the two arrived at the back pasture, they found the little mare standing in the middle of the paddock with her nose to the ground. Shane walked over to her feed trough and saw that she'd eaten her morning grain.

"I put some salt in her feed so she would drink plenty of water," Terry said.

"Yeah, she doesn't look quite as drawn up in her flank as she did last night. I was worried about her getting colicky if she didn't get some water soon."

Terry nodded and replied, "As stressed out as she looks, we should still keep a close eye on her."

Shane had Terry wait outside the gate as he walked into the field. The little mare immediately snorted and ran to the opposite corner. On the positive side, this was not an aggressive move, but the mustang was sending a clear message that she wasn't interested in making friends.

"You want to set up a catch pen, boss?"

"No, the poor thing has probably had some pretty scary experiences being trapped in pens. I think she's had enough of that kind of stuff. Let's tell Doc to wait a bit before he comes to check her. That'll give her a couple days to get acclimated. Maybe this weekend I'll have some time to work with her. As long as she's eating and drinking it's not critical that we get our hands on her right now."

Terry nodded. That was one of the things that impressed him about Shane; he never rushed a horse and was always willing to spend hour after hour with one if that's what was needed. In all the years he had spent working with him, Terry had never seen Shane lose his patience with one of these animals. He had seen him lose his cool with people, but not with a horse.

The rest of the afternoon seemed riddled with minor problems, and it was much later than usual when they finished at the barn. When Shane returned to the house, Jen had his dinner warming in the oven.

"Sorry, Dad, we got hungry so we went ahead and ate," Jacob said over his shoulder while he helped his mom dry the dishes.

"That's fine, we finished a little late today, then I went back to check on the new mare before I came in." Shane sat and dug into his meal.

"Do you think she'll make a nice horse?" Jen asked as she poured him a glass of tea.

"I don't know, she's pretty spooked right now. I'll have a better feel for her temperament once I've spent some time with her."

Jacob looked at his dad, "If she turns out okay, can Tina and I have her?"

"We'll take real good care of her," Tina added.

"Don't get your hopes up, you guys. She's a long way from making a dependable horse; besides you have Tory to ride."

Swallowing a drink of his tea, Shane looked at Jen and told her, "I got a good look at her brand this evening. If I draw a picture, do you think you could research it for me online?"

"Sure," she answered as she cleaned up the rest of the table around him while he finished eating. "Not trying to change the subject, but how's Terry's wife doing with her pregnancy?"

"She's fine. Terry's the one who's freaked out about it." The two smiled as Shane stood to place his empty plate in the sink.

Later that night after the kids were in bed, Jen took the drawing of the brand Shane had sketched and sat down at her computer. The woman who gave the mare to them didn't know much about where she had come from. Jen sighed as the thought occurred to her that this search was not going to be easy. It wasn't long before she found out that the Bureau of Land Management never used a brand that resembled a broken arrow on any of the mustangs who went through their system.

The BLM was the government agency in charge of controlling the populations of wild horses through their capture and adoption programs. These programs were necessary to keep the wild herds scattered throughout the western part of the country at a healthy number. Since the one thing they were sure of was that the little horse was from a wild herd somewhere out west, Jen decided that the BLM was probably still a good place to start. She faxed them a letter along with a copy of the brand. Who knows, she thought, we could get lucky and maybe someone there will recognize it.

By Friday afternoon, Shane and his staff were ready for a break and looking forward to the weekend. When he walked in the house, he found Jen leaning over the fax machine. She smiled and waved a paper at him. "This is from the BLM office. Looks like the little mustang mare has an unusual background. Her brand is from a private wild herd owned and managed by the Shoshone Indians in Wyoming. Apparently, the horses run free on a part of their reservation.

"The person who faxed me back, wrote that he'd heard there was some interesting history with these horses, but he didn't give any specifics. He did say that this particular mustang could never have been part of an adopt-a-horse program and wondered how we ended up with her. I finally decided to call Mrs. Erickson, the lady who brought her to you."

Shane grinned. "Wow, you've been busy with this."

Jen shrugged her shoulders. "I've always liked a good mystery. Anyway, Mrs. Erickson told me that she was at a horse auction in Trenton, looking for a pleasure horse. While she was there she kept hearing a loud noise in one of the livestock trailers parked outside the ring. When she looked in the rig, she saw the little mare kicking and pawing hysterically. The owner turned out to be a cranky old trader who was at the auction to sell another horse. He told her he thought the one in the trailer was dangerous, and he was taking the rotten, little nag to the killer market on his way home."

"Mrs. Erickson said she couldn't stand the thought of the mare being slaughtered for dog food, so she worked out a deal with the man to buy her, then paid him to haul the horse to her farm."

Jen paused and took a deep breath before explaining, "She had read one of your old magazine articles years ago. She knew you had a training business in the area and figured you'd be the kind of man who could tame the mare. She didn't know what she was going to do with her if you hadn't taken her. Her two sons loaded her on the trailer through some cattle chutes, then she brought her over here, kicking and stomping the whole way."

Shane sat down on the corner of Jen's desk. "I didn't have much time to talk to the lady. I was just about to get started with a new client when she drove in. The woman told me she felt sorry for the horse. She offered to pay for two months training, then asked if I'd find her a home after I started her. She didn't want any of her money back. She just wanted to give the mare a chance for a good home somewhere. In all honesty, because of how busy we are, I probably wouldn't have considered letting the lady dump the mare on me if a decent check hadn't come along with the horse. I took a quick look at her in the trailer before I agreed. She's put together pretty well, even though she looked scared. I didn't pick up on anything that seemed mean about her. So, I told Terry to let the lady follow him back to the quarantine paddock and unload her. I wish now I had taken the time to find out what I was getting myself into."

Jen asked, "Did you mess with the mare today?"

"No, I didn't have time, but I plan on working with her some this weekend."

"What will you do if you can't tame her?"

He shrugged his shoulders and gave her a lopsided smile. "I don't know, I'm pretty sure she'll come through for me. She's probably never been around someone who knew how to get on her good side."

Chapter 2

Shane made his way to the small bar in their living room, and mixed himself a stiff drink before heading for the shower. The kids were staying at friends' houses tonight, so he and Jen were planning to have dinner somewhere nice. "Let's get cleaned up," he said as he started up the stairs of the two-story farmhouse. "I'm really looking forward to a night out."

Considering the amount of steam that had built up through the large bathroom, he must have lost track of time while standing under the soothing water. He'd barely stepped out to dry off when Jen appeared through the steamy mist. That's when he slid his gaze down her slim, fit body, and noticed the pink lace lingerie she'd changed into for him only moments ago.

"Surprise," she whispered in his ear before she wrapped her arms around his neck then softly pressed her warm inviting lips against his.

Shane looked deep into Jen's emerald green eyes as he brushed back the few strands of her natural blonde hair that had fallen against the side of her face. Then he slowly picked her up and carried her into their bedroom.

After twelve years of marriage they knew well how to satisfy each other's desires, and both of them enjoyed taking their time before reaching the always passionate end. He knew he wasn't the most attentive guy in the world for her to live with, and he truly appreciated the effort she made to keep their romance strong. Beside the physical attraction they had for one another, and beyond even their love and family ties, they were best friends.

After lying in each other's arms and enjoying this rare evening alone without the kids in the house, Shane spoke up jokingly, "Now that I've fulfilled my husbandly duties, can we go eat? I'm really starving."

"So am I," Jen replied with a laugh. They reluctantly got out of their soft, comfortable bed, dressed, and headed out.

On the weekends, the farm had a separate staff that came in to take care of the horses, and Shane was looking forward to sleeping past his usual 5:30 a.m. wake up. Days like this were considered family time, and he truly looked forward to spending them with Jen and the kids.

In his younger days, he was considered pretty wild. He had partied a lot, chased a few ladies, and had a reputation for being able to hold his own in a bar fight if it was necessary. Back in those days, he spent most of his weekends hanging out with friends. He had a lot of good memories from that part of his life, but these days he usually stayed home with his family. Not because this was where he was supposed to be, but because it's where he wanted to be. He still enjoyed going out and having a couple of drinks every now and then, but his priorities were with Jen and their two kids. He knew how quickly the children's younger years would fly by, and he had no intention of missing this time with them.

As they got out of bed late this Saturday morning, Jen could tell Shane was a bit out of sorts. "Is there anything wrong?"

"I'm okay. It's just that I had the weirdest dream last night."

Jen looked at him with an inquisitive squint in her eyes.

"I was high up on a mountain, sitting on the mustang mare. There were all these Indians around me. Some were on horseback, some weren't. I can remember feeling so distraught, so absolutely miserable. I don't know what had me so sad. The Indians were just sitting there with consoling looks on their faces. They weren't saying a word, but I could tell they knew how bad I felt. I asked them what was going on. One of them pointed down toward the base of the mountain and said, "Stay on your path, and you will find what was lost to you.""

"What the hell does that mean?" he laughed. "I guess between the couple of whiskeys I drank last night, and all the talk about the mustang coming from a reservation, my mind was in a bizarre dream mode or something."

"I don't know," Jen said, "that's pretty strange. Are you sure you haven't been dipping into that bottle of pain pills in the medicine cabinet?" she joked.

Shane scratched the back of his head. "I don't know what brought that one on, but I haven't been able to shake it off."

Jen raised her eyebrows and shrugged her shoulders as she headed downstairs to fix breakfast.

It was late morning before Jacob and Tina got home from sleeping at their friends. As soon as they walked in the door they asked, "Hey, Dad, can we saddle up Tory and go for a ride?"

Sometimes it was hard to work up any excitement about going out to the barn on his days off, especially after he'd been there all week working his tail off. But he knew how much the kids enjoyed it. "Eat your lunch, then we'll go for a ride."

The two immediately started bickering over who was going first. Finally, Jen stepped in, "If you both don't knock it off, neither one of you will be riding." Shane chuckled, and shook his head as he walked out the door to go check on the mustang while the kids ate.

When he arrived at the paddock, the mare was enthusiastically munching on her hay, but she was still jumpy and acting worried about everything around her. Shane could only get within about ten feet of her while she was eating. So he relaxed, leaned on the fence, and talked to her in a calming voice. "You're a long way from home, aren't you, girl? You'll figure out soon enough that this isn't such a bad place."

After a few minutes he slowly moved away, leaving the mare to finish her meal. She was by herself in the paddock, and he felt that her herd instinct would soon have her looking for a friend to hook up with. He knew he could use the fact that she was all alone to his advantage while he was gaining her trust. For now he was happy she'd let him get this close.

When Shane got to the barn, the kids and Jen were brushing off Tory. "We'll ride him in the arena. Terry dragged it yesterday so the footing should be good."

Shane patted Jacob on his shoulders, "Why don't you grab the saddle out of the tack room, bud? The girls will finish brushing him."

Jacob and Tina were expected to be a part of the whole process from grooming to tacking up. Even though this particular gelding wouldn't hurt a fly, Shane and Jen made sure the kids knew how to handle a horse safely.

When they were done riding, Jacob asked if he could watch Shane while he worked with the mustang. Jacob loved being with his dad, and Shane appreciated that the boy wanted to be around him. He realized this would all probably change once his son reached his teen years. "Jacob, I want you to remember, you're going to have to stay quiet and sit still when I'm working with her, okay?"

"Yes sir."

As the two headed toward the golf cart, Jacob ran up ahead to claim the driver's seat, and as usual, Shane let him drive.

When they arrived at the paddock, Shane looked over at Jacob, "You know we've got to come up with a name for this horse. You got any ideas?"

"How about naming her Sloppy?"

"Why in the world would you want to call her Sloppy?" Shane laughed.

"It was Tina's idea. She said that the mustang was the dirtiest horse she'd ever seen, and then she started calling her Sloppy Girl."

"Well, the name does kind of fit. Sloppy it is, at least until we think of something better."

Shane realized how important it was to try to keep all distractions out of the way during this first session. He was glad it was quiet here and he knew Jacob would sit and watch calmly on the golf cart as he had been told.

Shane slowly opened the gate to ease his way toward the middle of the field. He knelt down in the grass and watched as the mustang nervously moved from one side of the paddock to the other while turning her hindquarters to him at each stop. At this point, she would let out a quiet snort, settle only for a second, then continue her worried walking from corner to corner. He was very careful not to look her directly in the eye. He had a small amount of grain in his closed hand, but he made sure not to show it to her. This food was not a bribe to get her to come to him, but he would use it as a reward if and when she did make up her mind to come in close. Like any creature with hooves, a horse is an animal that is preyed upon in the wild. Their basic instincts for survival are similar to that of a deer, which would naturally flee from any potential carnivore. Shane knew that once the wild-bred mustang realized he wasn't after her for his evening meal, she would change her fearful attitude. This would take some understanding on his part to change how she perceived him.

Shane noticed right off that the louder his voice was the more bothered she became, so he began using it to his advantage. Whenever the mare was moving away from him he would consistently raise his voice, saying things like, "Hey, where are you going? You're gonna hurt my feelings if you keep walking away."

As soon as she looked in his direction, he would soften and lower his voice. "You know you want to be friends. You just have to trust me first, don't you?"

She quickly learned that when she faced him, the bothersome loud talking would stop and immediately soften into a much more tolerable, pleasant sound. Timing and consistency were imperative in order to make this work. For now the sound of Shane's voice was all the pressure she could handle, and he was using it to draw her attention and mind into him. In no time at all, the mare made her decision to stop trying to ignore him. Instead she began standing calmly and watching Shane with curious interest.

"Atta Girl, see I'm not so bad, am I?" Shane continued softening his tone, still kneeling down on one knee as he rested his arms on top of the other. Finally, the response he was looking for happened. The young horse lowered her head, let out a soft snort, and took a timid step toward him. To someone without Shane's experience this wouldn't seem like a big deal, but Shane knew it was a nice breakthrough. He smiled as he figured, *This is probably the first time she's ever thought about approaching a human.*

Most people would now stand and move toward the horse, maybe even try to touch her. But he knew this would only scare her. Instead, as the mare stepped in his direction. he maintained his low profile slowly moving back away from her. This really got her attention, causing her ears to perk up with curiosity as she moved toward him a few more hesitant steps. Now he was drawing in her body as well as her mind. Every time he moved back a little, the mare would take a couple of steps closer. Soon she was close enough for him to open his hand and let her take the small amount of grain that he'd been holding for just such a moment. "There you go, that's what I was hoping for."

This was the perfect time to end this session on a good note. Still staying low to the ground, he smoothly moved about twenty feet away from her. He then stood slowly, careful not to startle her, and walked to the gate. Shane smiled again as he turned to see the lonely little mare still standing calmly in the field where he had left her, as if she didn't want him to leave. This was a nice change in her behavior, and he felt confident he would have no problem building on this. The session went well, and Jacob had watched his dad intensely with all the wonder of an eight-year-old boy with a bad case of hero worship.

Before Shane turned away from the mustang, he said quietly in her direction, "You sure are lucky you showed up when you did." He and Jen had been looking for a horse he could start training for the kids. Although she wasn't exactly what he had pictured, he felt good about at least considering the mare. Gray in color, she was pretty if you looked beyond her filthy, unkempt coat. Standing at 14.3 hands, she was small enough for the kids, but still large enough for Shane to ride when he put in the many hours of training she would need over the next year. The horse had no real monetary value, but Shane and Jen liked the idea of saving her, and figured they could afford to give her a chance.

Shane sat in the golf cart, then Jacob started driving toward the house. "So, what do you think, Dad, will she be a good horse for Tina and me?"

"I don't know, son. All I can do is put in a lot of time with her and hope for the best. Even if she doesn't make a good horse for you two, I'll still keep my word to Mrs. Erickson to find her a good home. At least she won't end up as meat in a can of dog food."

"I think she'll make a fine horse," Jacob said confidently.

Chapter 3

The farm and family thrived over the next year. Terry was a dad now, and had adjusted well to the job of changing diapers.

Shane and Jen bought him a joke gift at a novelty store — A fake gas mask that read across the forehead, NEW DAD'S SURVIVAL KIT. Terry laughed when he unwrapped the thing, and claimed he really did use it while changing the baby. He said he enjoyed seeing the disgusted expressions on his wife, Beth Ann's, face.

Jacob and Tina had really grown, and the mustang mare was accepting training well. She seemed to look forward to her work, and had become very relaxed around the kids. The name Sloppy had stuck to her, so now she responded to it affectionately. By this time, Shane was starting to put Jacob and Tina on her, and she carried them around with confidence.

It was a warm Saturday morning when Shane took Jacob on a long trail ride through the plush, green hills and woods surrounding the farm. He was on a client's horse while Jacob rode the mustang.

"Hey, Dad, I know Sloppy's doing real good with her training, but have you noticed how she stands in her paddock with her head down sometimes?"

"Yeah, I've noticed," Shane replied. He was impressed that the now nine-year-old Jacob had picked up on this aspect of the mare's behavior. "What do you make of that?" he asked the boy.

"I think that even though she really likes us she still misses her old herd."

"I've got a feeling you're right about that. She was born and raised a wild horse and nothing can take that out of her. She's very trainable and getting real broke for you guys, but I can tell she still thinks about running free."

Jacob was silent for a while. After they rode a little farther along the trail, he asked, "You think one day we could take her back and set her free with her wild herd? I sure would miss her, but I know she would be happier there."

Shane felt a sense of pride as he looked at his little boy who wanted to see his horse content, even if it meant losing her. "Maybe when you kids outgrow her in a few years, we'll plan a trip and see if we can find this herd. Then we could put her back where she really belongs."

Jacob became quiet, and Shane could tell his young son was trying hard not to give into his emotions as he thought about the idea of not having the mare around.

"You know, buddy, it will be a long time before you two outgrow Sloppy. If we do take her back out west someday, I know it will make all of us feel real good. So let's just enjoy having her at the farm for the time being and not worry about setting her free right now."

Jacob remained deep in thought as they rode along at a slow walk. A few minutes later he looked down at Sloppy and patted her affectionately on the neck. That's when he promised, "Sloppy, some day we're going to take you back to your old herd. I bet that will make you real happy, won't it, girl?" Shane smiled as the two of them moved their horses into a trot and headed home.

When they came within sight of the barn, they could see Tina was waiting for her turn on the mare. Before they rode too close, Shane spoke, "Let's not say anything to Tina about our conversation. I think she's a little too young to understand about Sloppy still wanting to be a wild horse."

"No problem, Dad. I won't say anything." Jacob hardly had time to get off Sloppy before Tina was trying to climb on her. The mustang stood patiently while the girl settled herself in the saddle. Tina rode her off at a trot for a short trip around the field.

"You sure are riding like an old pro!" Shane hollered. Tina smiled from ear to ear at the compliment.

*   *   *

Late spring had now given way to the heat of mid-summer. By now the hot days were taking their toll on everyone at the farm. Shane and Terry always lost a little weight and looked a bit more worn during this time every year. The horses in training were also starting to show the strain. The two men had to be careful not to overwork them in the high temperatures.

The heat and humidity of summer eventually turned into the drier, cooler air of fall, which was a change both horses and trainers were glad had finally arrived.

One afternoon while the two men were taking a much needed breather, Shane spoke to Terry about something that had been on his mind. "You know, Terry, you've turned out to be a damn good trainer. I've taught you about all I feel I can. I think you're ready to start your own business."

"Whoa, boss, you trying to run me off?" Terry joked.

Shane grinned, "I'd be glad to send you some of my overflow, so you'll have money coming in while you build up your own client list."

Terry shook Shane's hand in gratitude. "I appreciate the opportunity but, for the time being, I'd be more content to stay here with you and learn. Just knowing I'll have your support when that day does come means a lot."

Shane responded sincerely, "Well, you know I'll do all I can for you."

With the nice fall weather, Jacob and Tina continued riding almost every day. Jacob was now ten years old, and Tina would be eight in a couple of months. Sloppy looked forward to the time she spent with the kids. It seemed they had become kind of a surrogate herd for her because she always perked up when they were around.

Soon it was the start of December 1998, which also meant Christmas was sneaking up on Shane and Jen fast. This was always a favorite time of the year for their family, especially since the kids had gotten old enough to really get pumped up about it. Shane had been an only child, and both of his parents had passed away. However, Jen's mother, Helen, from Florida, and her younger sister, Abby, who lived only about forty miles away, spent Christmas with them every year.

December twenty-third came on a Friday this year, and Terry seemed to be in a holiday mood while he saddled up the last horse of the day. Shane took the horse's reins from Terry, smiling as he handed him an envelope. "Here you go, my friend." The hefty Christmas bonus was expected, but in no way taken for granted.

"Thanks, boss, this check always pays for our trip to my folks for the week."

"Glad to do it, Terry, you deserve every penny. You and Beth Ann enjoy your time away with the baby." A minute later Shane looked over at him from the horse as he tightened up the saddle's cinch for his ride. "Why don't you go ahead and take off? I know you've got a long drive ahead of you. I'll finish up around here."

He could still hear Terry's pickup pulling out of the driveway when Jacob and Tina came bounding in the barn full of excitement. The young horse he was holding spooked and jumped backwards. "Hey, easy guys, you know better than to run in the barn like that!" Shane scolded.

The two had just returned home from the last day of school before a fourteen-day recess, so they were bursting at the seams with excitement.

Jacob cringed, "Sorry, Dad, we thought you were done riding when we saw Mr. Terry leave. Can Tina and I ride Tory and Sloppy while you finish up?"

"Sure, go ahead and get 'em saddled. Maybe a good long ride will help you two burn off some of that wild attitude you got going on." They both laughed, and ran out of the barn to fetch their horses.

By the time Shane and the kids made it back to the house, Jen's mom, Helen, and her sister, Abby, had arrived and were helping Jen put dinner on the table. As usual, the two would be staying all week, until New Year's Day.

"My babies," Helen screeched as the two kids ran over to her with open arms. She hadn't seen them in over six months, which made the reunion very enthusiastic. After they were through with Grandma they ran to Aunt Abby, whom they often saw because she lived so close.

"Merry Christmas, ladies," Shane said as he waited his turn, and then welcomed them both with a warm hug.

The house was always decked out to the hilt both inside and out. Each year, it would consume the best part of a week to take down all the decorations.

This season a light snow came on Christmas Eve, which put everybody in good spirits. Later that night, Tina jumped out of her bed and scampered into the living room. She was shaking as she shouted, "Mommy, Daddy, I heard a noise on top of the house. I think its Santa's sleigh landing on the roof." After that, getting her to sleep was damn near impossible.

Shane looked at Jen, and rolled his eyes when Tina got out of bed for the third time. He leaned over and whispered, "I know all this seemed cute earlier, but it's already ten thirty, and I still have two bikes to put together!"

"Come on, baby girl," Jen said as she took her by the hand and walked her back to her bedroom. "You know Santa can't put presents under the tree until you're asleep."

"I'm trying Mommy, but I'm just too excited! Will you lay with me for a while?" Jen lay down alongside her and rubbed her back until she finally went out.

Jacob had exhausted himself with the exhilaration of the day and was already asleep.

At ten years of age, he was kind of on the fence about the whole Santa thing. Even so, he was easily convinced by Jen that the older kids at school were wrong.

"Santa Claus is as real as the nose on your face," she swore to him. They both wanted to give him one more year of believing in the fat man in the red suit before their little boy grew out of this short, but memorable time of his life.

Christmas morning the kids were up by six, and by seven the

house was a total wreck with torn wrapping paper and open presents strewn everywhere.

Shane always took a break between Christmas and New Year's Day. Every year it blew him away at how fast it went by. This year was no different, and soon it was time to get back in the saddle and resume earning a living for his family.

The next four weeks flew by and the kids had all but worn out their Christmas bikes.

It was Wednesday, hump day on the farm, and it was unusually warm weather for the beginning of February. Shane had just finished with his fourth horse of the morning, and glanced at his watch as he climbed out of the saddle. Terry hustled out of the barn to meet him. "Which one do you want next?"

"It's only eleven, so I should have time for one more long ride before lunch," Shane replied. "Why don't you bring me that big sorrel filly? She only has about sixty days on her, but she's calm and easy going. I think she's ready for her first ride out on the trails surrounding the farm. If I'm not back within an hour, come looking for me."

"No problem, I'll keep checking my watch till I see you ride back in." Terry assured.

A person can never tell how a young horse will react to this kind of exposure for the first time. Even with a nice one like this, he would have to be very careful to stay out of trouble. The ride was going extremely well, and soon he made his way far in to the hilly countryside west of his farm. Suddenly a covey of quail flew up in front of them. The filly spooked with a sideways jump. Shane quickly grabbed the saddle horn and hung on as he skillfully got her back under control.

"Easy girl, those birds scared me too." As he calmed her down, he was pleased to see how quickly she began to relax and walk on as if nothing happened. During the ride back home, he patted her neck often and told her how good she was doing.

As the two made their way down the last hill into the big grassy field next to the barn, Shane looked up to see Terry waving frantically at him. This also caught the filly's attention. "You're okay," he told the worried horse. "I don't know why he's acting crazy like that." Shane had to keep rubbing her neck to try and ease her bother. He was really starting to get upset with Terry's behavior. "He knows better than to carry on like that when I'm on a green horse," he said quietly to the filly.

As he rode in closer he realized that what he first thought was excitement with Terry's body language and expressions now looked more like sheer panic. His breathing was shallow and rapid, and he was having trouble speaking.

"Chill out, man," Shane told him sternly, as he stepped out of the saddle. "Just calm down and tell me what's wrong."

Chapter 4

"It's Jen and the kids, boss. They've been in a car wreck! The sheriff was out here about twenty minutes ago, and said you need to get to the hospital right now!"

"A wreck! When?" Shane's forehead wrinkled as his heart began to pound with fear. "Is everybody all right? What exactly did the sheriff say?"

"He didn't really say much. All he would tell me was that the accident was a bad one." Shane, now trying to control his panic, handed the horse over to Terry and ran to his truck.

He drove like a mad man all the way to the hospital, praying that they were all okay. He crashed through the ER door and found Jen's sister waiting for him in the lobby.

It was a teacher's work day. This meant school was out for the kids, so Jacob and Tina were with Jen for the morning. Jen's sister, Abby, had met them to go shopping and was following the three in her own car to a restaurant for lunch. The accident happened right in front of her and she had followed the ambulance to the hospital.

Abby was sitting on a couch sobbing hysterically, leaning over with her face in her hands. A young nurse was sitting next to her trying to console her. Abby looked up and saw Shane. She immediately jumped up, ran over, and threw her arms around him still crying uncontrollably. "The man that crashed into them ran a red light. It wasn't Jen's fault!" she balled.

Shane was really scared now, and pushed Abby away to arm's length. He looked into her swollen red eyes and loudly asked, "How bad is it?"

She tried hard to answer but had trouble catching her breath. She finally sputtered out the words that stabbed Shane like a knife in his gut. "Jen and Jacob are gone," she said with tears streaming down her face, "Tina's in intensive care."

"What!" Shane whispered. "No. No way. You've got to be mistaken. What do you mean, gone?"

"I'm sorry," Abby said as she fell down to her knees crying.

Shane ran to the counter, and yelled at the lady working there. "I want to see my family. I want to see them, now!"

The lady realized that Shane was on the verge of losing control. He was loudly demanding to see his wife and kids over and over while threatening to tear the waiting room apart if she didn't comply. She wasn't sure how to handle him, and was now in tears herself. She finally picked up the phone to call for help. Almost immediately, two very large male orderlies came rushing through the door. They calmly told Shane that a doctor was on the way to talk to him and asked him to follow them to a small room beside the waiting area. After a couple of minutes, which seemed like hours, a doctor came into the room and gave the orderlies the okay to leave. He took a deep breath and asked Shane to please sit. He really hated this part of his job.

"Mr. Carson, I'm sorry to tell you this, but both your wife and son were killed on impact in the accident."

Shane stared at him in disbelief and confusion. "There has to be some kind of mistake, doc!" The doctor looked down at the floor and shook his head, "Your little girl has extensive head injuries, and she has a ruptured spleen. She's in surgery right now having her spleen removed, and we are trying to assess the extent of her head injuries. I'm sorry sir, but she's in pretty bad shape, and I can't say what her chances of survival are. We'll have to assess her condition through the night, and I'm hopeful her vital signs will improve."

The doctor could tell that this was all too much for Shane. "When you're ready, the nurse will let you know where to go so you can see your wife and son. I'm so sorry for your loss," he said as he quietly stepped out of the room. The doctor nodded to the nurse on his way out, asking her to keep an eye on Shane and to call him if necessary.

Shane barely made it over to a sink before getting sick. As he finished, he slowly reached for a paper towel to wipe his mouth. There he stayed for sometime with his head down and eyes closed, struggling just to stand.

Still in denial, he balled up his fist and clinched his jaw, then begging, prayed, "God, please let me wake up to find that this is all just some kind of terrible nightmare! This can't be happening, dammit!"

When he finally looked up at his reflection in the mirror, a strange numbness overwhelmed him. Keeping one hand on the wall for support, he eased his way over to a seat in the corner of the room. Crumbling down into the chair, he sat motionless, staring into space, soon drifting uncontrollably into a total shutdown of emotions. The next thing he remembered hearing was much later when a nurse came in. "Mr. Carson — sir — Tina is in recovery, you can go see her now."

He stiffly stood and followed the nurse down the hall. He walked into the room to see his little Tina lying in the bed with her head completely wrapped and tubes protruding from her mouth. His eyes drifted to a machine that was beeping and pumping. His baby girl was on life support. The room started spinning as the beeping sound became an intense ringing in his ears. He collapsed before he made it to her side. He awoke on the floor with a woman leaning over him.

The seasoned ICU nurse, an older lady, had seen more than her share of tragedy, "Come on, Mr. Carson, I know this is terribly difficult," she said softly, "but you need to try to pull yourself together for Tina's sake. Okay?" As he struggled to focus on her face he finally came to his senses. He nodded and slowly stood with some assistance.

He couldn't believe how cold Tina's small hand felt — how lifeless. He gently squeezed, trying desperately to make her squeeze back. "Tina, Tina, its Daddy. Wake up for me, baby. Okay?" It was then that his emotions finally came to a head, and the tears rained down his face like a blinding summer storm.

*   *   *

The next few days slowly crept by and Shane never left her bedside. Tina was tough and held on longer than the doctors thought she would. But she never regained consciousness, and at 3:25 on the afternoon of the third day she passed away with Shane at her side, tightly holding her hand. He leaned over, his face wet with tears, gently kissed her on the forehead and whispered in her ear, "Tina, it's okay, you can go now. Mommy and Jacob are waiting for you. I love you. Tell Mom and Jacob I love them, too."

Soon after his last words to Tina, he withdrew into another emotional shutdown. The doctor explained to a worried Abby that the mind was well known to protect a person from more than he can handle in times like these. This mental escape was Shane's subconscious way of shielding himself from a pain he was too exhausted to endure.

Hours later he was still at her side when he felt a gentle arm across his back. Then he heard some familiar voices. It was Helen and Abby. Terry and Beth Ann were also there standing quietly in the corner. No one knew what to say. They were all feeling the loss of little Tina, but their immediate concern was for Shane. It was Helen's quavering voice that finally broke the silence. "Come on, Shane, we have to go. She's gone, there's nothing more you can do here. The doctor's going to give you something to help." He barely noticed the needle piercing through the flesh of his right shoulder or the burning of the sedative as it slowly entered his muscle. It was still some time before he stood and left the room with everyone huddled around.

It took all the strength Shane had to make it through the triple funeral. If it hadn't been for Jen's mom, he probably couldn't have done it. Helen was a strong woman. Shane had seen that by watching her through the death of her own husband years earlier. She and Abby had made all the burial arrangements, and their constant support was the only thing keeping Shane from going completely off the deep end. He felt so alone, sad, and angry all at the same time. What had he or they ever done to deserve this? He cursed at God, screamed at himself, and then turned to the bottle to deaden the pain.

Helen made the decision to stay on for a while. She cooked and cleaned, and, in the midst of dealing with her own grief, she tried her best to console him.

The next couple of weeks were the worst of Shane's life. He was not eating much and he couldn't sleep. He'd taken all of the meds that the doctors had prescribed, and when they were gone, he depended on whiskey to help him escape his hell.

Helen was on the front porch when Terry walked up from the barn and sat next to her. It was 2:30 in the afternoon, and only eighteen days after the accident. "I wish there was more I could do for him," he mumbled.

"You've done plenty, Terry; the way you and Beth Ann have taken over running the farm proves what good friends you are."

"Well, it's easy to see he's in no shape to come back to work yet. You tell him not to worry about the business. All of his clients understand. I'll keep their horses worked until he is ready to ride."

Helen took a deep breath. "I'm very worried about him, Terry. He hasn't been out of the house in days."

"Yes, ma'am, I know what you mean. While you were at the grocery store yesterday, I came over to check on him. I pounded and pounded on the door before he finally opened it. It was only one o'clock, he stunk of whiskey and seemed really depressed. Don't get me wrong, if I lost Beth Ann and the baby I'd probably be in the same condition. But the truth is I'm scared he's close to a breaking point."

Helen closed her eyes, "He's too proud to admit he needs help. I think we'd better keep a close eye on him."

"Yes, ma'am, I agree."

It was late on a Monday, and still only four weeks since the accident. A stormy dusk began closing in on the farm. Abby had come over earlier and was just heading out the door to go home. Shane walked her out to her car to tell her good-bye, when she noticed his speech was a little slurred from the three drinks he'd consumed since 4:00. Even so, both she and Helen were glad to see him out. Helen was standing at the door and waved as Abby drove away.

"Hey, Helen," Shane shouted, "looks like Terry is working late. I'm going to the barn to help him finish up so he can get home for dinner."

Helen was elated at this. "You go ahead, we'll eat when you're done."

The evening was warm. A low growl of thunder rumbled over-head as the slight smell of rain lingered in the air. Because of the im-pending weather, Helen didn't question the long Aussie coat Shane put on before he left the house.

An hour later, the meal Helen prepared was still sitting on the table getting cold. She picked up the phone and dialed Terry's cell to see what the holdup was at the stable. Terry was on his way home when he answered, "No, ma'am, he didn't make it to the barn. I left there ten minutes ago, and I never saw hide nor hair of him."

Helen got a sick, worried feeling in her stomach. "Terry, I think you better get back here!"

"Oh shit! I'm on my way!"

It was growing darker by the minute, and the rain was just be-ginning to fall when Terry slid his truck to a screeching halt in front of the house. Helen flew out of the door to meet him as he got out. "Come on," he yelled. "I think I know where he is. There is a place I've seen him go to think things over. It's through the woods about a hundred yards behind the house. There's a big hill with an old oak on it. He told me just yesterday that he and the kids had planned to build a tree house there this summer." Terry grabbed a flashlight from his truck and the two walked briskly through the dark, dampened forest toward the hill.

Shane had been sitting there drinking out of a bottle for the hour he'd been missing. A bright flash of lightning and a loud clap of thunder was quickly followed by a drenching downpour as he reached into his coat pocket and pulled out the nickel-plated revolver. He gritted his teeth and wiped the cold rain off his face with his sleeve. "I'm sorry about this everyone," he said under his breath as he pointed the .38-caliber pistol to his right temple. His trembling wet thumb clumsily slipped off the hammer when he attempted to cock it, with every intention to end his misery. Just then, he felt a punishing hard thud on his back. The gun went flying out of his hand while he and someone else were now plummeting down the side of the storm soaked, grassy hill. He was too drunk to notice when Terry and Helen came up behind him through the woods. As soon as Terry realized what was going on, he charged in hard and they both ended up at the bottom of the muddy slope.

As he knelt there huffing, Terry faced up to the fact that Shane was in much worse shape than anyone realized. It was then that Helen stomped down the hill and began to yell.

"Damn it, Shane," she cried, "enough is enough! You're going to see the grief counselor the doctor told you about — and there will be no more drinking!"

Helen and Terry looked across at each other, as their emotions came to a head causing quiet tears to mix with the rain on their wet faces. With their hearts still pounding and their hands still shaking, they sat beside Shane to catch their breath. They all stayed there in the storm for a while, not speaking. Suddenly Shane stood up, and with his head bowed, sluggishly walked toward the house in silence. There he found some relief by passing out for the rest of the night on the living room couch.

The next day Terry and Helen came down hard on him. "There's been enough death around here." Helen said. "I stayed to help and I've been glad to do it, but I will not stand by and watch another nightmare. You're not going to cause more pain to the people who care about you."

With tears streaming down her face, she grabbed his shoulders and made him look at her. "Do you think that's what Jen, Jacob, and Tina would want? I know my daughter and grandchildren are in heaven looking down on us, and I know that someday I'll join them there." She took a deep breath and plunged on. "Shane, if you kill yourself, I believe you'll never see them again. Think about that!"

Shane's eyes opened wide; this was a sobering thought. "I've never been an overly religious man, but I do believe in God and that there is a heaven. I'll be honest with you, Helen. I can't understand how God let this happen to my wife, who was such a good person, and to those two beautiful, innocent children." He shuddered with a deep breath, "But maybe believing we could all be together some-day is the one thing that might help me pull myself together."

Gaining control over her emotions, Helen gently put her hand on the side of his face, "Oh, Shane," she whispered. "I know it's true. I just know it."

He shifted his eyes to the right, and then lowered his head in shame, "I'm sorry about last night, I know I really scared you."

Over the next couple of weeks he started seeing the grief counselor, which helped some. Though he was still drinking he was able to keep it more under control.

One afternoon a box showed up on his front porch. One of the kid's teachers had left it next to the door. Their teachers had packed up some of Tina's and Jacob's papers and projects. He sighed as he read the note, "God Bless, we thought you might like to keep these for some good memories." Shane picked up the box on the way in-side. He tried to open it but couldn't bring himself to lift the lid. "I can't deal with this now," he said quietly to himself. He finally car-ried the box over to the hall closet, and put it on the shelf in the back corner where it would be out of sight.

He continued sticking to his promise about controlling his drink-ing and seeing the counselor. Three more weeks crawled by and Helen began to feel that Shane was no longer a threat to himself. "It's good to see the light coming back in your eyes. It's time for me to pack up and go back home. I've been so busy worrying about you that I haven't taken time to deal with my own grief, and I sorely need to."

"I understand," Shane said with mixed emotions. The thought of being alone was still frightening. "I can't thank you enough for helping me get through these last several weeks."

Before she left, Helen made Terry promise to keep a close watch on him, then she gave Shane a final hug and drove away.

Chapter 5

The weeks gradually rolled into months, Shane finally decided it was time to wean himself off the antidepressants. He was now finding some solace with occasional work, but Terry was still doing most of the riding. Shane couldn't bring himself to do much of anything with Sloppy. Although he could tell that the horse was missing the attention, she was simply a source of too many memories.

Terry was glad to finally see his friend becoming more involved at the barn. "I think anything you do around horses is good therapy," he said with a reassuring smile.

Shane responded by forcing a grin and nodding. Most of the time he would just check out Terry's work by riding the horses a few times a week. From this, Shane began developing a sense of pride in the quality of training his good friend had achieved. However, his state of mind was still operating on a simple day-to-day existence, and the concept of time passing by was of little concern. After all, it had only been a few months since the tragedy and every day he was forced to deal with the realization that the house was way too quiet and his bed too cold and empty. Sometimes he swore he could still smell the scent of Jen's shampoo on her pillow. The occasional good night's sleep he did get was usually filled with dreams of his family, followed by a short, but well-fought battle with an all too familiar anxiety as he woke to his reality. He had become somewhat of a recluse, never reaching out for companionship or returning calls of concerned friends. Although he began working more, he still had trouble putting in a full day.

The money from Jen's life insurance was enough to pay off the farm, which set him up financially for at least the near future. This allowed him to give Terry a nice raise for the overload he had taken on, while Shane's name and reputation kept the horses coming in for training.

The seasons steadily rolled by and Shane eventually realized that his work had become his only real salvation. Over time he'd gone from barely riding at all to putting in an exhausting seventy-hour work week.

One day as he and Terry sat in the barn taking a breather, Terry looked from under the brim of his hat and said, "Hey boss, I've never seen you ride so many horses. I can't believe you took on three more this month."

"Yeah, I know," Shane answered with a halfhearted smile. "The truth is, it's hard for me to just sit around. I've found its best if I stay busy."

"It's good to see you back at it again, that's for sure."

"Thanks, man, I appreciate everything you've done."

"No problem, boss, I know you would've been there for me if the shoe was on the other foot." Terry looked down and scratched the back of his neck.

Shane noticed his friend's reluctance to continue. "You got something on your mind?"

"Yeah, I guess I do."

Shane sat quietly and waited for his friend to continue.

"Even though you're doing better now, I can't help but notice you still seem kind of aimless and hollow."

"I'm okay, Terry. I don't want you worrying about me. I'm fine."

Terry hesitated again, "With all due respect, I don't think that working all the time is much of a life. Abby and I were discussing something the other day when she came over. We drew straws to see which one of us would talk to you about it."

"About what?"

"Boss, everyone just wants to see you happy again. We'd like to see you do more than just get through each day like you've been doing. You know, get some fun back into your life again. We think you should take a trip. Go on a cruise or something. Maybe getting away would help give you a new start."

"I know you guys mean well, but I'm okay."

"Would you at least consider it?"

Shane stood and gave Terry a friendly slap on the shoulder. "I'll think about it. Let's get to work."

By six thirty all the horses were fed and the hired help had gone home. Shane grew restless after a shower and some dinner. Maybe a walk around the farm will help me relax, he thought. It was the beginning of spring and good weather had set in so it was a nice evening for a stroll.

Ambling by the paddock where the kids' little mustang was turned out, he couldn't help but stop to watch her munching on her evening hay. As he propped his arms on top of the four-board fence surrounding her small pasture, she quit eating and came over.

"How you doing, Sloppy?" he softly rubbed her neck. The mare quietly nickered, then affectionately nuzzled his shoulder in response. "Sorry I haven't paid much attention to you lately." Shane inhaled a deep, refreshing breath of the crisp, cool evening air as the horse moved sideways over to the fence where he stood. He remembered the mare doing this for the kids when she wanted her back scratched.

"You miss 'em too, don't you, girl? I'm not sure what I'm going to do with you," he said, reaching over to rub her back. "It's been damn near a year and a half now, maybe I can find a nice family with young kids to give you to."

The thought of getting rid of the mare started to bother him as soon as it popped into his head. Even though it was in the horse's best interest, he just couldn't face the idea of parting with his kids' horse. So he promptly put it out of his mind, gave her one last rub, then finished his evening walk.

Over the next month Shane continued working harder than ever, driving himself to the point of exhaustion. Concerned for his friend, Terry confronted him about his worn-out condition.

"Boss, in all the years I've worked here, I've never seen you get sick. But you look like hell. If you don't take some time off soon, you're gonna end up going down."

"I know, Terry, I'm not sleeping real well, and I'm starting to feel it. The truth is that your suggestion of a trip is finally starting to sink in. I'll take some time this evening to look for some old travel brochures Jen had collected to plan a family vacation. Maybe one of the brochures will give me an idea of where I could go."

"Good, now I won't have to badger you about it anymore!" Terry looked relieved as he left the barn to go and fetch another horse.

Later that evening Shane decided to start rummaging through the hall closet, hoping to find the pamphlets there. As he pulled open the door, the first thing he noticed put a lump in his throat and made his chest tighten. "Oh man, I'd forgotten all about that." It was the box the kids' teachers had dropped off almost a year and a half ago. Shane's heart began to race as he picked it up and carried it into the living room. He put it on the coffee table in front of the couch and sat down.

Almost thirty minutes passed before he could bring himself to open it and look inside. There, neatly separated, he found two bundles. The first was from Tina's third-grade teacher. It contained her last spelling test, which had 100 percent written across the top in bright red ink. Underneath that was a math test with a 90 percent grade on it, and a note from the teacher to keep up the good work. There were also some other pieces of graded homework, one of which Shane remembered helping her with the week before the accident.

The other bundle was from Jacob's teacher. It, too, had some tests with good scores and some graded homework. As he flipped through the papers with a heavy heart, he consoled himself with a deep sense of pride that his kids had been doing so well in school.

At the bottom of the stack he noticed a picture from Jacob's art class. It was a drawing of the mustang mare. Shane filled his lungs and slowly let the air out again as he recalled his son talking about the assignment the teacher had given the class. The kids were supposed to draw a picture of something important to their whole family and then do a one page essay about what they had drawn. It seemed like just yesterday when Jacob told him that he decided to do this project about his horse.

It was just what you would expect the art work of an eleven-year-old to look like. The horse's head was too big, her legs were too short, and her neck was too skinny. Shane could tell it was Sloppy by her light gray color and darker mane and tail. However, the real give-away was the broken arrow brand Jacob had drawn on her hip. In the picture she was standing in the foreground with a goofy smile on her face. Behind her were five other horses drawn in the same dispro-portionate manner, all wearing the same brand on their hips. They were grazing in a meadow with a stream running through it. The sun was shining from the top right-hand corner of the page and he'd drawn some clouds in a blue-colored sky. The picture was surpris-ingly titled "Sloppy goes home." Shane had no idea the boy's theme was centered on taking her back to Wyoming. A sad smile spread across his face as he remembered the talk he and Jacob had about someday returning the mare to her wild herd. The essay was attached to the artwork and Shane read it several times before once again staring at Jacob's drawing.

Suddenly, he realized what he had to do. "I'm gonna do some traveling after all," he muttered. "A trip to Wyoming to set the mus-tang free with her herd, just like I promised Jacob we would do some day!" He remembered how proud he was of his son that afternoon for being so unselfish. The boy had wanted to see the horse happy even if it meant losing her.

For the first time in a long while, Shane felt like he had a purpose. He actually became excited as he planned out the trip. He'd take ole Tory along to keep Sloppy company in the trailer on the long drive. When they got there, he'd use the old gelding to lead the mustang into the back country where the herd most certainly lived. He scratched his head and cringed as he thought about the lack of conditioning both horses were in. "I better start taking some time now to get the horses legged up so they can handle the rough terrain and the long ride." He figured if he left soon, he could get there in time to set the mare free well before fall arrived. The warmer weather would definitely make it easier on her while she readjusted to her old life.

Terry and the others at the farm where thrilled to see Shane with a sparkle in his eyes. They could tell he was keyed up about the trip, and all of them eagerly agreed to keep the farm running until he got back. Shane felt that keeping his promise to Jacob was the most important thing he could do, and he hoped it would give him a real sense of closure that he knew had been eluding him.

It took some effort to pull it all together, but the day finally came for him to load up the horses and head out. Terry and Beth Ann were there to see him off. He shook Terry's hand, "I should be home in about three weeks."

"Don't worry, boss, I can handle the farm."

Shane rolled down his truck window as he slid into the driver's seat, then winked. "I know you can, buddy. I'll call you when I get there."

The man at the BLM had told Jen that the reservation Sloppy had come from was thirty miles from a medium-sized town called Reddick in northwest Wyoming. Shane knew he had a long drive ahead of him, about 1,400 miles. He figured with good weather it would take him three days to get there. Luckily, the many years he had spent traveling and putting on clinics around the country had made him an old pro at hauling horses long distances. He planned to have the horses stay on the trailer at night during the drive out, then find a place to board them as soon as he arrived.

He drove a good ten hours the first day, stopping a couple of times along the way to give the horses a break. Tory was not a young horse anymore, so the last thing he wanted was to have the old gelding feeling sore when he reached his destination.

On the third night he decided to stop at a campground about fifty miles short of Reddick. He planned to get back on the road early the next morning. This would give him plenty of daylight to find a place to keep the horses for a few days while he asked around town about the herd's location.

It was 8:30 a.m. on the fourth day when Shane, blurry eyed and road foundered, saw a sign that read REDDICK, 15 MILES. As he drove through the country, admiring the peaceful rolling green foothills, he noticed an older man walking from his farmhouse toward his mailbox. He slowed to a stop, leaned out the window of his truck and spoke, "Excuse me, mister. Do you know anywhere I can board two horses for a couple of days?"

The old man introduced himself as Paul Jensen and offered Shane the use of a small pasture next to his house for a reasonable price. "The pasture has good grass, a water trough, and a small shelter," Mr. Jensen said. "I used to keep my own two horses there, but they both recently died of old age." It seemed perfect for Tory and the mare, so Shane quickly accepted.

Mr. Jensen brought his wife out to meet Shane while he unloaded the horses. Shane felt comfortable leaving them with these people. "Would you like some breakfast?" Mrs. Jensen offered.

"No ma'am. I appreciate you asking, but I need to get into town as soon as possible." The truth was he really didn't want to be around people right now. He hadn't slept a wink at the KOA last night. He just wanted to get to town, find something to eat, take a long hot shower, then, hopefully, get some sleep.

Tomorrow, Shane planned to ask around town for information about where the herd might be located on the reservation. For now, he was happy to see his two horses in a safe place. As he drove off, they were already settling down and starting to graze. Shane got the Jensen's phone number, and told them he would check on the horses after he rested. Sleep had not come easy for him in a long time. Maybe it was the excitement of the trip, but the last several nights had been especially bad. In fact he was now bordering on serious exhaustion, and he needed to crash.

His feeling that this trip was a good thing was now giving way to a slight sense of uncertainty and anxiety. Luckily the Jensen's had let him leave his horse trailer at their farm, which would make driving and parking in town a lot easier. When he arrived in Reddick, he immediately got the impression that this was a nice friendly place. The sign at the city limit told him it had a population of 3,700. As he drove down Main Street, he could see they had all the necessities, including a small hospital, several large restaurants, and a movie theater that probably drew people in from all over the immediate countryside. He checked into the first motel he saw then headed across the street to a diner for a hot meal. After a long, steaming shower, he cracked open a fresh bottle of whiskey, poured himself a double shot, and watched TV until he finally fell asleep.

Shane actually slept soundly until late the next morning and was having trouble shaking off the slumber. *"Maybe a shower will help clear the cobwebs out,"* he told himself.

Chapter 6

Shane barely had time to dry off and dress when he heard a knock on his door. As he opened it, he found himself staring at an older man, but for the life of him, Shane couldn't immediately place him. The man saw the blank look on Shane's face, shook his head, and said, "Son, you look like hell, are you okay?"

The sound of the man's voice helped Shane realize who it was. He let out a sigh, "Yes, Mr. Jensen, I'm fine. Are the horses all right?"

"They are now, but I've been trying to get ahold of you since yesterday. You told me you would call, but we haven't heard a word. So I finally came looking for you. I saw your truck in front of the motel. My friend, Bob, who runs this place, told me what room you were in."

Shane dropped his head shamefully, "I'm sorry I didn't call. I've been a little under the weather. What did you mean when you said they're all right now? Did something happen?"

"Well, the older horse started to colic soon after you left the farm."

"Oh shit!" Shane blurted out. "How bad did he get?"

"Pretty bad," he answered. "I couldn't keep him on his feet. I finally called the vet out. Dr. Baxter gave him a shot of banamine; then he tubed him full of mineral oil and water. He had to come back out a second time to treat him, but that old gelding's tough. He pulled through and seems right as rain now."

Shane's relief was visible, but he was also extremely embarrassed. He sure wouldn't blame Mr. Jensen if he had a bad impression of him.

"I can't believe I slept that long. I'm real sorry I didn't check on them. Thank you so much for taking care of my old horse. I was worried the long trip might be hard on him."

"Well, I could tell by the way you rubbed him on his head yesterday morning before you left that he meant something to you."

"They both do."

"I figured you'd want me to do whatever was necessary to take care of him, but there was a hefty bill involved. I had to pay doc out of my own pocket."

"Just tell me what I owe you," Shane said as he grabbed his wallet from the nightstand. The two men settled up, and he gave Mr. Jensen some extra money for his trouble. "Sir, if you haven't eaten yet, I'd like to buy you breakfast."

The old man laughed. "Son, I ate hours ago, but I'll sit and have a cup of coffee." Shane grabbed his keys, and they walked across the street to the diner.

Mr. Jensen waited until Shane finished his meal then said, "You know, I'm getting older so my memory isn't what it used to be, but my wife remembers everything, especially faces and names. After you two met yesterday she kept telling me that you looked familiar. Later that afternoon it came to her why she recognized you."

Shane sheepishly looked up from his empty plate, "Where'd that be from?"

"She used to be quite a horse woman in her younger days. We raised some quarter horses that she showed in reining and western pleasure. She enjoyed entering the big shows, like the Quarter Horse Congress, every year. She won her fair share of ribbons too. She used to soak up all she could about training horses and she read everything she'd get her hands on." Mr. Jensen smiled as he talked about his wife.

"She remembered driving all the way to Kansas with a friend of hers to see you put on a clinic years ago. At least, she's pretty sure it was you. I remember when she took that trip; I couldn't believe she would drive that far for something like that." Mr. Jensen squinted at Shane and asked, "Was it you she saw?"

"Yes sir, it probably was. I put on a few clinics in that area. It was a long time ago, though."

"What brings you out here now?"

Shane sat quietly for a moment. He was going to have to tell someone about his hunt for the herd, and he thought Mr. Jensen might be a good place to start. "I came out here to see through a promise."

"What kind of promise?"

"It concerns the little mustang I left at your farm." Shane wasn't willing to open up to this man or anyone else about what had happened to his family. All people needed to know was that he made a promise to set the mare free with her wild herd, and he was bound and determined to see it through.

Mr. Jensen sipped his coffee, then sat back. "I think there's something you should know about that horse. I recognize the brand on her hip. Do you realize what you've got?"

"Not really, I know she comes from a herd that runs wild on the reservation."

The old man smiled as he stood. "I'll tell you what, son, you look like you could use a home-cooked meal. You come out to the house tonight and see your horses. I'll tell you what I can about that mare over dinner." He took one more sip of coffee, then leaned over and said, "Let me give you some advice. If I were you, I wouldn't mention that brand around town. You might stir up more interest than you want."

Shane nodded to indicate that he heard his warning, then the old man headed for the door. He thought Mr. Jensen was being a little dramatic with his advice, but figured he would wait until he heard what the Jensen's had to say before he went nosing around town about the mustangs.

After breakfast, Shane went back to his room. He'd slept for over seventeen hours and felt rested for the first time in a while. He quickly grew restless watching TV, so he decided to drive around and have a look at the countryside. Soon he might be packing into the foothills and valleys surrounding the area, and he wanted to see what he was in for.

Shane also knew if he sat idle for very long, his mind would begin to drift to the memories that continually haunted him.

Sometimes he felt guilty pushing the thoughts of the three out of his head, but for the present it was the only way he could survive. So he left the little room and drove northwest toward the mountains in hopes that seeing this country would be a good distraction.

He didn't have to drive far before realizing how special this place really was. The scenery was spectacular, and he couldn't help but be in awe. Soon he found himself on an elevated road, where he stopped his truck to gaze down into a valley. Scanning across this amazing site from his high perspective, it almost appeared as if the countless tree-topped hills below had collided, sometime in years gone by. Each one was shoved up against the other, as if once they had been in motion and then long ago had come to this sudden eternal halt. They seemed to roll on forever, until they finally ran into the base of the distant snow-capped mountains that rose high into the clear blue horizon. It seemed in every direction he looked there were streams and lakes, which meant this wilderness would surely be alive with an abundance of wildlife. Sloppy's herd would be hard to find out here. There was plenty of cover, and Shane began thinking he would probably need a guide to help him locate them.

He sat there for a long time and soon began to wonder how a God who could make country as beautiful as this could be the same God who let his family die in that horrible accident. As the familiar anger built inside him, he quickly stood, took a long, deep breath to clear his mind, and climbed back into his truck. By now it was late afternoon and time to start heading to the Jensen's for dinner.

During the drive, Shane found himself becoming more and more curious about what Mr. Jensen could tell him concerning the mustang's brand. Hopefully he might even know where the herd was, or if not, where he could find a competent guide.

Shane pulled into the driveway, and both of the horses trotted up to the fence. Even at his first quick glance, he noticed that Sloppy had a different look in her eyes. She seemed more alive and animated. "You know you're back in your own country, don't you?" he teased. He affectionately patted the two on their necks and checked them over from head to hoof.

A shallow stream ran through the field where the horses were staying and Shane could see by the mud on their legs that they'd been playing in it. After visiting with them for a few more minutes, he went and knocked on the Jensen's door.

The old brick, ranch-style house was in good shape. The yard was well kept with the surrounding landscape a sight to behold. The small farm sat in the middle of the foothills with a variety of large aspen, sycamore, and maple trees, all in full foliage, randomly scattered about.

Mr. Jensen opened the door, "Hi Shane, come in and take a load off." They sat in the den near the fireplace, which was in full flame. "I don't usually light a fire this time of year, but for some reason I was in the mood for one," he said as he offered Shane a glass with a shot of good sipping whiskey.

"I want to thank you again for taking care of Tory's colic."

"No problem," the old man answered as he poured himself two fingers.

"I hope you like fried chicken," Mrs. Jensen remarked as she walked into the room.

"Yes, ma'am, that sounds good."

The three of them sat next to the fire, and talked. "I can't tell you how much I enjoyed the clinic I saw you put on in Kansas," Mrs. Jensen said. "You know, I must have gone to half a dozen clinics that year. My friend and I decided that we would travel together. We had a lot of fun driving all around to horse shows and clinics. We wore out a set of tires on my horse trailer," she laughed. "You were the one clinician that really stood out for us. Your clinic was full of practical information on how a horse thinks and reacts. We were simply bowled over seeing what you could do with one. Why, you had every one of those animals in the palm of your hands. I even ordered some of your videotapes. I think I still have them. I kept looking for more of your clinic dates, but you just seemed to vanish. I finally assumed you gave it up for some reason."

"Yes, ma'am, I haven't done that for almost fifteen years now." Fearing she might question him concerning the reason he stopped putting on his clinics, which was, of course, his family life, Shane decided to quickly change the subject.

"Dinner sure smells good."

Mrs. Jensen smiled and replied, "Why don't we continue visiting while we eat?" She then led them to the table.

After the meal, they moved back by the fire. It wasn't long before he felt the conversation was once again drifting toward the reason he left his life on the road. These were nice people and he wasn't trying to hide anything from them, but the last thing he wanted was have them feel pity for him. Besides, he was here to find out about the herd.

"I don't mean to shift gears on you, but I'm very interested in getting any information I can on the mustang. You see I promised somebody close to me, and close to the horse, that I would bring her out here and set her free with her old herd. I aim to see that through."

"I think that's admirable," Mrs. Jensen stated.

Mr. Jensen eagerly spoke up. "I've heard a lot about the wild bunch you're looking for. The locals from town call them the broken-arrow horses because of the brand the Indians put on them. The Indians call them the spirit horses. I really don't know why. The Shoshone claim rightful ownership of the herd. They say their tribe has raised them for generations and their ancestors even used the same bloodlines for their hunting and war horses. That's why they put their brand on them. I've heard the horses sometimes wander off the reservation and end up grazing on some of the bordering property leased by a local cattle rancher named Vince Nethers. As I understand it, he doesn't want his cows to share their grass with the mustangs. Nethers's son, Bo, and some of the hired hands who work on the ranch claim the horses are fair game if they wander off the reservation. Unlike most mustangs, this herd has had selective breeding and management through hundreds of years by the

Shoshone tribe. This is well known in the area, so the horses are considered to have some special value around here."

Shane leaned back in his chair as he listened intently.

"The herd is smart and hard to find. Some of the young men around town consider it something to brag on if they can find and catch even a few. They act like it's some kind of sport. This small group of young jerks thinks it's fun to try to piss off and provoke the Shoshone by stealing their horses. Most of the time the tribe tolerates the loss of a few animals to keep from starting trouble, but I hear there's a lot of tension over it all right now."

"Why is that?" Shane wondered out loud.

"Apparently," Mr. Jensen replied, "the Shoshone found out a few of the horses were caught, then hauled straight to the killer market for quick cash. The Indians caught wind of this, and made it clear they won't put up with it anymore. They say the horses are part of their heritage, so they have a right to protect what is theirs."

"Why doesn't the tribe put up a fence to keep them in?" Shane asked.

Mr. Jensen laughed, "The border between Nethers's land and the reservation covers about forty miles of rough country. It would be damn near impossible to fence it. I went up there a few years ago just to see if I could find the herd. I stayed in that country almost a week on horseback, but never did get a look at them. All I ever saw were tracks and droppings. That's a smart bunch of horses. Like I said, the boys from town consider it a real challenge to catch them."

Shane smiled and encouraged Mr. Jensen to tell him more. "How do the Indians keep up with the herd?"

The old man continued, "They say the Shoshone keep watch over the herd most of the time. They're supposed to have a special relationship with the horses. The Indians would be your best bet to find the herd, but I doubt they would tell a white man where they are — especially now. I found out there's been a couple of fistfights in town between some of the Shoshone braves and Nethers's son and friends. The scuttlebutt is that Bo Nethers and some of his cronies are the ones that took the three mustangs to the killer market a few weeks ago. The Indians don't come to town much, so I don't know if they came looking for trouble or just ran into it by accident. If I were you, I'd be careful about going out to that reservation right now. If you ask me," he added, "I think those horses should be left alone. There's plenty of grass up there in the spring and summer for both cattle and horses."

Shane took a sip of his coffee. "Looks like I'm stepping into a real hornet's nest! This may not be the best time, but I still plan to turn that mare loose. I guess I'm a little worried now that she might get caught again, and wind up at the killers. I wish I knew how she ended up all the way down in Tennessee at an auction."

"No telling how that happened," Mr. Jensen shifted in his seat, "she might have been hard to break, and one of the ranches sold her to a trader. She's lucky to have made it to you and not the slaughter house, that's for sure."

"She was kind of hard to start, but once I got her trust she proved to be real trainable."

"Maybe you ought to just take her back home," suggested Mrs. Jensen.

"No, ma'am. This is something I need to do, even if I have to keep a check on her for a while to make sure she stays free."

"Well, if you end up extending your trip, you're welcome to use our spare bedroom," she insisted.

"Thanks for the offer, but I'm fine at the motel."

"Suit yourself, you know you're always welcome."

"Thanks again," Shane said as he headed out the door. The information he obtained tonight was interesting as well as valuable. At this point, he was leaning toward a trip to the reservation in hopes of finding someone who might help. The fact that the Shoshone were on guard about the brewing situation concerning the herd was a complication he wasn't sure how to get around. On top of all this, he needed to be certain the mare would be safe from the trappers, once he did set her free. For tonight he hoped he could get some sleep. He knew tomorrow might be a long one, and he wanted to be rested and ready for anything.

*   *   *

Shane woke to find it raining with a slight chill in the air. Although he slept well, he was now battling that empty feeling with which he usually started his days.

"Shake it off, Carson," he mumbled. "Get your ass up, put on a smile, and see if you can figure out how to find those mustangs."

He really wasn't sure what his next move should be. Trying to hire a guide was still an option. He just didn't know whom he could trust.

So, he got out of bed this wet Wednesday, cleaned up, and went to the diner. About halfway through his eggs and hash browns, he overheard some young men talking at the next table.

"The trap gate is open, and we'll have nine riders trying to push the horses into the canyon."

"This time we should have enough people to get a bunch of them," another claimed.

"I'm taking all six of my catch dogs," a third guy added. "If any Shoshone are out there, the dogs will keep them busy. If that doesn't work, we'll scare 'em off with our rifles."

As the men threw down their money on the table, the group made arrangements to meet at the canyon Saturday afternoon. Shane couldn't believe what he'd just heard. These assholes were planning on stealing some of the Indians' wild horses this weekend! He wasn't sure what to do. Maybe he should ease over to the sheriff's office and tell him about this after he finished eating.

As Shane filled the deputy in, he soon realized this man didn't care about the situation.

"I have no jurisdiction on the reservation; the Indians have their own police for stuff like this."

Shane felt a surge of frustration and snapped, "So call them and tell them about it!"

"I'll try and do that later," the deputy said as he leaned back in his chair.

Shane looked at him in disbelief. "That's it! That's all you're gonna do?"

"Look mister, if the mustangs are off reservation land, then it's legal for those boys to take them as far as I'm concerned. Besides, those horses are hard to catch. They'll probably avoid the trap anyway."

"I just told you the plan was to go on reservation land and drive them down to a trap on the Shoshone's land! That can't be legal!"

The deputy stood up and leaned into Shane's face. "Sir, I told you I don't have any jurisdiction out there. I'll consider contacting the tribal authorities later to tell them what you overheard — while you were eavesdropping."

Shane gave the officer a "go to hell" look. "If someone gets hurt this weekend it's on you!" With that he got up, pushed his chair out of the way, and left.

The deputy stood and followed Shane out to his truck. "Look, mister," he said, "there's nothing I can do. I don't know what your interest is in all of this, but if I were you, I'd put some serious thought into keeping my nose out of it!"

Shane looked straight ahead, nodded slightly, and drove away.

"Damn," he thought out loud. "It looks like these mustangs are the center of a lot of controversy around here."

Chapter 7

He went back to his room and flipped on the TV as he tried to figure out his next move. For now all he could do was hope the herd could avoid the trap on Saturday. It didn't take long for him to get bored, so he walked back over to the diner for a cup of coffee. As he sat at the counter, he kept stewing over his conversation with the deputy. He didn't hold out much hope that the guy was actually going to call the reservation police and contemplated calling them himself.

He was a little surprised to see the rowdy boys walking back into the diner. Shane figured they probably didn't have anything else to do. They were reliving their partying from the night before while laughing about how two of them had been with the same girl. They were really trashing her in a loud way, and it was easy to tell that everyone else in the place was taking offense at the conversation. It was only about eleven in the morning so Shane frowned and shook his head as he noticed them take out a flask to start passing it among them. That's when the owner of the diner slapped his hand hard on the scuffed-up old counter and yelled, "It's time to move it outside. There's no drinking allowed here."

The boys chuckled and hollered back, "Don't worry old man, we'll leave. We're through here anyway."

"Just get out the hell out of here, you boys are bad for business!" the man snapped.

Laughing and shoving chairs out of their way, the obnoxious gang went out and leaned up against the front wall of the diner where they passed the flask among them. One of the boys had pushed a chair against Shane's stool on the way out. Shane gave him a hard look, but decided to let it go.

"Who are those guys?" he asked the man behind the counter.

"The leader of the bunch is Bo Nethers. He's a spoiled, rich troublemaker, whose daddy leases a lot of government property around here to raise cattle. The rest of the group are boys who grew up in the area. They'll hire on as ranch hands from time to time, but none of the crew is worth a damn. They're always causing problems and looking for easy money. I'd avoid 'em if I was you. They love to start fights and gang up on people." The man continued wiping down the counter, and getting set up for the lunch crowd.

"Doesn't the law around here handle them when they get out of line?" Shane asked.

"They've got no worries. Whenever they get into trouble, Mr. Vince Nethers will show up and bail them out. He inherited a ton of money some years back and controls of a lot of the businesses here. Hell, he owns this building along with the bank and the motel you're staying in. He's not that bad of a guy, but in his mind his asshole son, Bo, can do no wrong. Uh-oh!" he said as he looked past Shane through the café window.

"What's up?" Shane asked as he turned to see.

"I don't know for sure, but those guys just saw something that caught their attention. All six of them just trotted across the road. Knowing that mob they're going to mess with some poor soul." The young men moved up the street and out of view.

"You know," said the man, "those guys are all in their midtwenties. You'd think they might have grown out of acting like idiots. Some of those boys aren't half bad on their own, but whenever they get together with Bo Nethers, they act like damn fools."

Shane quickly stood, and paid for his coffee. He wanted to get out where he could see what the boys were up to. Once outside the door, he spotted them catty-corner across the street, as they leaned against an old pickup truck. They were still smoking and passing around the flask. Whoever owned the truck must have been inside one of the stores nearby. Shane sat down on a park-style bench in front of the diner and watched.

About ten minutes went by, and there was still no sign of the truck's owner. The bunch was now passing around a second flask and seemed to have nothing better to do than to wait around for the driver. Shane was beginning to guess it was some guy they knew, and when he came out they would get together and have a good ole time. That's when he noticed a young woman walking out of the drugstore just down the street. She was carrying a small box and was moving toward the truck.

Surely this isn't who the boys are waiting to harass! As the girl moved out of the shadows, it all began to make sense. She was an attractive young Indian woman. He watched as she shook her head slightly and rolled her eyes when she realized what was going on at her truck. Showing no fear, she walked up to the motley group. The girl looked one of the boys straight in the eye as she approached the passenger-side door and sternly requested, "Please get out of my way."

The fella stepped aside, then bent down into an exaggerated bow while she opened the door to put her box inside.

She took a deep breath and rolled her eyes once more before angrily walking around to the driver's side, but the boy standing there wouldn't move so she could get in. Instead, he swept a disrespectful gaze up and down her body as he menacingly said, "You're a damn fine looking squaw. If you'd come and party with us, we'll give you a day you'll never forget!"

If the young woman was scared, she didn't show it. Shane smiled after hearing her sharp response, "In your dreams, you creep, now get out of my way!"

The boys laughed then quickly surrounded her. The Nethers boy, who seemed to be the leader of the fiasco, grabbed her arms and pushed his body up against hers, pinning the girl to the driver's side door. "I'll tell you what, you little bitch, you give me a nice, long kiss, then maybe I'll let you go on your way."

The woman, still showing no fear, spit in the boy's face as she struggled to turn her head away and get free. Nethers quickly retaliated to her justifiable defense by reaching up with his right hand and grabbing her by the throat.

"Let me go!" she hollered while still fighting to break his hold.

This was about as much as Shane could take. He had to do something before the girl got hurt. He stood as he mentally prepared himself for the worst, and then headed across the street.

"All right, guys, you've had your fun, now, why don't you let her go!" One of the men from the unruly bunch stepped in front of Shane, cutting him off from getting any closer to the truck.

"I don't know who the hell you are, mister," the man leaned into Shane's face. "This is none of your freakin' business, and I'm only going to tell you once to stay out of it."

Shane looked him square in the eye. "I'm not going anywhere until you let her go."

The cocky young man wasted no time in throwing the first punch. Shane was expecting it and easily avoided the clumsy inaccurate swing.

Although the punch had missed its mark, Shane knew the talking was over and countered with a pounding right blow to the man's temple. The guy, being half drunk, lost his balance, fell to his knees, and crumbled to the ground.

As he watched the man fall, Shane felt a hard, unexpected punch below his left ear. He turned to defend himself only to realize he was now dealing with two men, both throwing punches at him at the same time. These two were a bit smaller than the first. Shane threw a quick, but well-aimed, uppercut that knocked one of them out cold. The one still standing was a better fighter, but his punches had no real power and did little damage. Shane saw an opportunity and took advantage by kicking the remaining attacker in the groin as hard as he could. The man doubled over groaning in pain and held up his hand. He'd had enough.

Shane thought he had everything under control, but suddenly felt a stinging crack to the back of his head. Someone had taken a rake handle out of the truck's bed and broken it across his skull. This time it was Shane dropping to his knees. His bell had been rung good, but somehow he was able to keep himself from blacking out.

While he was struggling to maintain consciousness, he heard the girl's truck engine start. With the guys focused on the fight, the girl had been able to slip into her driver's seat.

Shane looked up to see the men scatter as she drove her truck right through the middle of the drunken mob blowing her horn. With tires squealing, she raced up beside Shane who was still on his knees. The old truck came to a sliding halt as the passenger-side door swung open.

"Come on, get in — NOW!" she begged. Shane staggered up and crawled into the truck cab as the woman floored the gas pedal. In the rearview mirror, she could see the men were shaking their fists, giving them the finger, and throwing rocks at her accelerating truck, but she was already out of range.

Though badly outnumbered Shane had held his own, but he was sure glad the girl had gotten him out of there when she did.

"Are you okay?" she asked, as she sped out of town.

"Yeah, I'll live."

The woman then shook her head. "Mister, you should have stayed out of it. They weren't going to hurt me. I'm not afraid of those idiots."

"Yeah, well maybe you should be," Shane said, as he wiped the blood from the back of his head and grimaced.

She handed him a handkerchief and said again, "You shouldn't have gotten involved. I could have handled it."

"Ma'am," Shane replied angrily, "I watched the whole thing from a distance before I came over, and I didn't throw the first punch either! Those guys were pretty drunk. There's no telling what they might have done to you. You know, where I come from, people tend to say thank you when someone helps them."

The woman remained quiet for a few moments. "I have to get home so tell me where to drop you off."

Shane thought for a minute. "My truck is at the motel in town, but I don't think we want to go there now. Can you take me to a friend's house a few miles east of town?" He felt sure Mr. Jensen would take him to get his truck later on.

"Okay, but I have to get home. My grandfather needs the prescription I just picked up." The girl knew the area well and took a shortcut. Soon they were pulling into the Jensen's driveway.

Shane slowly got out of the truck, dealing with one hell of a headache. As soon as his feet hit the ground, the dizziness overwhelmed him. The woman quickly jumped out of the truck and ran around to help.

"Hang on and I'll get you to the house."

Shane slowly, with the pain pounding in his head, gave a slight nod. The paddock fence where Tory and Sloppy were staying was only about thirty feet away. As the woman helped Shane get his bearings, the two trotted over.

"Those horses seem to know you," she said as she helped him find his balance.

"Yes ma'am, they're mine. I'm boarding them here for a few days. Hey lady," Shane said, as the horses followed them up the fence, "what kind of Indian are you?"

She shook her head and gave him a hard look.

"You obviously aren't from around here."

"No, ma'am," he replied a bit defensively. "You sure have a chip on your shoulder, don't you?"

The girl looked at Shane out of the corner of her eyes. "Sorry, I guess I still have my guard up. You know most of the folks in town are good people, but that bunch of guys we just dealt with seem to enjoy causing trouble for anyone who is Shoshone."

Shane stopped and pointed at the Mustang. "Do you know that brand on her hip?" He could sense the girl's anger, as she looked over.

"That's a stolen horse," she blurted out. "Where did you get her?"

"I've had her for a few years. I got her in Tennessee. That's where I'm from, and I'm not a horse thief."

"Well that horse is a Shoshone mustang and belongs on our reservation!" the girl exclaimed angrily as she helped Shane onto the porch and watched him sit in a rocking chair.

"Ma'am, my name is Shane Carson, what's yours?"

"I'm Tara. Look, I don't have time to ask any more questions about the horse right now. I need to get that medicine to my grandfather. I'll come back tomorrow around noon with my brothers to talk to you about the mare?"

"I'll be here," he replied.

Tara stepped down off the porch, turned back, and quietly said, "Thanks for your help, Shane Carson. I won't forget it, but I still think you should have stayed out of it."

Shane forced a grin and slowly shook his aching head as he reached up and felt a growing lump from the rake handle.

This was the first time he'd really taken a good look at her. He had noticed right off the bat that she was tough and independent, but she also possessed some class. She appeared to be in her late twenties, and, listening to her command of English, Shane couldn't help but think she must be well educated. All of this was a bit overshadowed by the hard shell she hid behind.

In spite of his aching head, Shane found himself drawn to her natural beauty. It was not the flashy kind that jumps out at you from a distance, but the kind that slowly overcomes a man, the closer he gets to such a woman. Her coal black hair was just short of waist length, and had come somewhat unraveled from her ponytail. She wore no makeup. The truth be told, she didn't need it. Her natural high cheek bones and smooth, caramel skin were obviously Indian traits, but her sky blue eyes made Shane doubt that she was a full-blooded Shoshone. The only jewelry she had on was a beaded necklace, with a light blue turquoise stone. She stood about five eight with a body any woman would envy. Even with all this, she appeared unpretentious and seemingly unaware of her appeal. Shane figured she must have a man in her life. He wondered if there would be any retaliation on her behalf over what happened in town.

As Tara drove off, Mrs. Jensen came out to the porch. She was startled by all the blood on Shane's hand and the back of his head.

"Oh my goodness, what happened? You need to get in the house right now and let me tend to that mess!"

"I'm okay, ma'am, I just bumped my head."

"Bullshit," the old man said, as he followed his wife out. "You've got a black eye coming up along with that big bloody knot on your noggin. It looks to me like you came out on the short end of a fight!"

"It's a long story," Shane answered. "I'll tell you about it later, but for now, could I take you up on that offer to stay here for a few nights?"

"You know you're welcome," Mrs. Jensen said.

"I could also use a ride to the motel, so I can get my clothes and truck."

"No problem," answered Mr. Jensen. "You let me know when you're ready. Right now, you need to let the wife do a little cleanup and repair."

"Thanks, I owe you folks."

After Shane was doctored and had showered, Mr. Jensen took him to town. To say the least, it had been an eventful day. In spite of this, during the drive Shane's thoughts began to drift to his family. The early evening was the hardest for him. It was this time each day that he always looked forward to being with them. That's when he had the time to play and laugh with his kids and visit with Jen while she was fixing dinner.

The ride to town was quiet. Mr. Jensen could tell Shane didn't feel like talking, so he left him alone with his thoughts. He wasn't the kind of man who would pry.

He dropped Shane off at the motel. Then he parked in the next block waiting to make sure Shane got his stuff safely into his truck before he headed home.

By the time Shane arrived at the farm, Mrs. Jensen had dinner waiting. After eating, she showed him to their small guest room where he unpacked and turned in early.

Shane woke after a restless night, with the lump on the back of his head still aching, but decided to ride the horses anyway. They needed to stay legged up for what could be a long, hard trip into some rough country during his upcoming search for the wild herd.

After exercising both horses, Shane took them for a trail ride to cool them down. He rode Tory and ponied Sloppy alongside. Shane felt driven to locate the mustangs as soon as possible, accomplish his objective, and go home with Tory. He was anxious to meet with Tara and her brothers at noon, hoping they would give him information that could help him find the wild horses. Perhaps he could hire one of Tara's brothers as a guide. He had high hopes this meeting would be helpful.

As he rode, he was again overwhelmed by the sheer beauty of this magnificent country, especially viewing it from horseback. Returning to the Jensen's, he noticed the Indians had arrived early. Tara sat on the paddock fence while two men leaned against the bed of the same old pickup she was driving yesterday. "I wonder why they brought a horse trailer," he mumbled to the horses. "I hope they don't think they're taking you," he remarked under his breath glancing over at Sloppy. Cautious of the situation, he rode toward them at a slow walk while leading the mustang beside him. Tara smiled and nodded hello, Shane did the same.

He couldn't help but notice that the two guys with her were good sized, tough-looking characters. Neither of them greeted him. Their lack of response bothered Shane, but he felt it was probably just their way. One of the men walked up to Sloppy and inspected the brand. Then he looked at his brother and frowned, "She's one of ours, all right!"

The other reached up to grab Sloppy's lead from Shane's hand. Shane immediately reined Tory back. The two well-trained horses responded accordingly and moved out of the man's range.

"Mister, we've come to get our horse. She has the broken arrow brand on her. That's proof enough she was stolen from our herd."

Shane didn't know what to say. In that instant the man once more reached for the mare's lead. Shane was beginning to get irritated with the guy now and swiftly sent Tory forward, pushing the horse into the Indian, knocking him against the fence. "What the hell do you think you're doing?" Shane shouted.

"Mister, we came to get our horse. We'll take her by force if we have to!"

Shane quickly bumped Tory into a canter and loped the two horses into the small pen next to the barn. He jumped out of his saddle, slipped the bridle off the gelding, and moved to close the gate. The two men were now standing near the truck, looking like they were serious about the by-force threat.

"You shouldn't be doing this!" Tara hollered at her brothers as she jumped off the fence with a bewildered expression.

Shane picked up a short two-by-four that was leaning against the barn, and headed toward the truck. He was still hurting from the events of yesterday, but if a fight is what they wanted, he was pissed and ready. He wasn't about to allow these strangers to take off with Sloppy.

Outnumbered once again, he angrily marched toward them, with the board in hand. Yesterday had been bad enough, but with the two-by-four, he felt better prepared to take care of himself.

As he approached them, one of the brothers grabbed a crowbar out of the pickup's bed. "Bring it on!" he hollered, as he aggressively started toward Shane to meet him halfway.

Tara quickly moved in front of him. "We came here just to talk to him. Damn it! You should have never brought that trailer." She stood between her brothers and Shane with her arms stretched out, yelling. "Don't do this. This isn't why we came."

Just then, a shotgun blast rang out from the porch. Mr. Jensen was standing there, with his gun in hand. He shouted, "I got no problem with you Indians, and I don't want any. Now you just slide into your truck and get off my land."

Tara was nearly in tears. "I'm sorry, I didn't mean for this to happen." She jumped into the driver's seat and called sternly for her brothers. Shane was glad they listened to her. He stood there holding the board watching as they drove away.

Mr. Jensen stepped off his porch and looked at him with a concerned frown, "Son, trouble seems to follow you around like a shadow."

Shane paused a second, then clearly said, "Sir, before I came to

Wyoming, I hadn't been in a fight in over twenty years, but I can't seem to stay out of one around here." He knew he owed Mr. Jensen an explanation. So he told him what happened yesterday and why the Indians came to see him.

"So, that's why you couldn't stay in town?"

"Yes, sir," Shane replied. "I thought I'd stay out of trouble if I moved out here." Both men laughed as Mr. Jensen shook his head.

He rubbed his brow and looked at Shane. "What do you plan to do now?"

"I don't know, but if I have to, I'll pack into that backcountry on my own. I won't let those Indians or anyone else get in the way of what I came here to do."

"Why is setting that mare free so important for you?"

Shane looked down at the ground. "Mr. Jensen, maybe one day I'll explain it to you. But right now, you'll just have to accept that I have my reasons." Mr. Jensen nodded his head, then walked back toward the house.

Shane unsaddled Tory, then sat down in the barn to think things over. He'd been sitting there for quite some time when Mr. Jensen came back out.

"You figured your next move?"

"No, sir, I was sure hoping the Shoshones would help me, but I don't see that happening now."

"Well, at least it doesn't look as though the girl hates your guts. If you explained to her what you are trying to do, she might introduce you to a guide you can hire."

"I've considered that and, although it seems like the best option, my intuition tells me going out to the reservation might be hazardous to my health." Both men smiled.

"You sure have been making enemies around here. I told you that mustang would stir up trouble for you."

"Yes, sir, you sure did." Shane hesitated before continuing, "Well, looking at my lack of options, I really don't have a choice. I guess I'll have to chance it and go out there tomorrow to see if I can find Tara.

It might be a good idea to lock your gate after I leave, just in case her two brothers come back after the mare." Shane sighed, "I'm really sorry for all the trouble."

"Trouble, hell, I'm not scared of those guys! Besides, this is the most excitement we've had around here in years." He gave Shane a friendly pat on the shoulder as they walked toward the house for supper.

Chapter 8

After a cup of coffee and taking care of the morning feeding, Shane struck out for the reservation.

The Indians lived deep inside the reservation borders a good distance from its entrance. Mrs. Jensen had mentioned that a town called Fort Washakie was the site for the Shoshone Affairs Office. Since the population was only three to four thousand, hopefully someone there would know Tara and how to contact her.

The office was easy to find. He parked, took a deep breath, then headed for the door. As he opened it, he quickly realized he was the only white person in the large room. This made him feel a little as if he had stepped through a magical threshold and had been transported to an exotic, foreign country. *That's kind of an ironic idea*, he mused to himself. *After all, these are true Native Americans who have lived on this continent longer than any white people.* There were at least ten Shoshone working in the office, and most of them were busy shuffling papers at their desks. Almost everyone had a friendly look on their face, but for a second he became the center of attention with all eyes glancing in his direction. A young Indian woman, sitting at the counter, smiled and asked if she could help.

"I'm looking for a girl named Tara."

"Tara who?" she asked.

"I don't know her last name, but she is tall, slim built, has blue eyes, and is probably in her late twenties."

"Mister, even if I know who you are talking about, I wouldn't give you any information until I spoke to her."

Thinking fast, he said, "I owe her family some money, but I don't know how to contact them. Can you call her and let me speak to her?"

She left the room and came out a few minutes later. She told Shane to pick up the phone and push the button for line one.

"Hello, Tara."

"Who is this," she asked curtly.

"It's Shane Carson."

"What do you want?"

"I came out to ask you for some help. Can you meet me somewhere to talk?"

"I don't think so. I don't want any more trouble!"

He answered quickly, "No, ma'am, no trouble. I promise. I'm looking for information about my mustang. We could meet some place public, if that'll make you feel more comfortable. Please, I drove all the way out here, hoping you would help me, and besides, you kinda owe me a favor."

Tara was quiet for a minute. "Meet me across the street from the Affairs Office. There's a little restaurant called The Long Horn. I'll be there as soon as I can."

"Thanks. I'll be waiting."

The small restaurant was busy, and the aroma of food cooking made him realize how hungry he was. It was close to noon, so he sat in a corner booth and ordered lunch. The waitress was well-spoken and friendly.

"How are you today? The special is meat loaf. Everyone sure seems to like it."

"That sounds good," Shane replied with a smile.

Just as he finished eating, Tara walked in. Everyone appeared to know her, however, they seemed a bit surprised when she walked over and sat across from Shane.

"Thanks for coming. Can I buy you lunch?"

Tara shook her head, no. "I'm pretty busy today. What can I do for you?"

"Like I told you on the phone, it's about my mare."

Tara raised her hand, stopping Shane before he could continue.

"First, I want to apologize for what happened yesterday. My brothers never would have treated you the way they did, if they'd known how you helped me in town. I didn't tell them what happened. I was afraid they would go after those guys and get into a fight. When we left the farm, I told them what you did for me and how you got the mare in Tennessee. After they heard the story, they promised they would leave you and the horse alone. So, if that's why you came out here, you don't need to worry anymore."

Shane started to reply, but Tara had more on her mind, so he respectively kept quiet and let her continue.

"I also want you to understand that the Shoshone are good, honest people, and we are proud of our heritage. I know there are plenty of nice folks in the town of Reddick, but there are also some who don't like us because we're Native Americans. My brothers, along with the rest of us, have lived with this all of our lives and tend not to trust others until we get to know them, as friends. When they saw the brand on the mustang, they naturally thought you were one of the gang who steal our horses."

"That wild herd is very special to your tribe, isn't it?" Shane remarked.

"They are an important part of our heritage. That small group of idiots from town knows this, yet they still try to take the mustangs. They force us to keep a close watch on the herd. Usually we're successful in stopping their attempts to steal them, but now and then they do catch some. That's probably how you ended up with your mare."

"I saved her from the killer market three years ago. I can assure you, the horse has been treated well. I've come a long way to put her back with her wild herd. She's the only reason I'm here."

Tara looked puzzled, "Why would you come halfway across the country to set her free?"

Shane was guarded in his answer. "I made a promise to someone very close to me and to the horse, that I would do this."

Tara remarked, "You must really care for this person to go to all this trouble."

He responded with a slight nod.

"What do you want from me?" she asked.

"I had two reasons for coming here today. The first was to let you know I overheard those men we tangled with in town planning to steal more of the horses Saturday afternoon. They talked about a trap they built in a canyon, and they were bragging about taking their dogs and guns."

Tara smiled, "My brothers have already found the trap and destroyed it. The head stallion of the herd is smart. Between the stallion and our herd watchers, those men won't have much of a chance to catch any horses this weekend. But, thank you for the information."

Shane looked relieved. "Do you know anyone I can hire as a guide to help me find the Mustangs, so I can set my mare free with them?"

Tara shook her head. "I'm sorry. It just doesn't work like that. No one in our tribe will help you without my grandfather's permission. He is one of the leaders of my people, and the tribal member in charge of our wild horses. The decision would have to be his."

Continuing to think quickly, Shane asked, "Then, would you take me to your grandfather? Maybe if he understood why I'm here, he would help me put the mare back where she belongs." Shane realized how much easier this would be with the Shoshone's permission. He could also read the immediate doubt in the girl's face.

Tara looked down toward the table and took a slow breath as she mulled over his unexpected request. "I wouldn't get your hopes up, but I'll take you to meet him."

He followed her old pickup on a winding road, heading northwest out of Fort Washakie. After several miles, they drove through a run-down neighborhood of shacks and trailers. Out of the corner of his eye he watched children playing on a rusty old car, men passing around a bottle of wine, and people sitting on porches seemingly doing nothing. He thought about these sad conditions and wondered how many of the three thousand Shoshone on the reservation lived this way.

Soon after passing through this impoverished neighborhood, the scenery began to improve. Only a few miles up the road, Shane noticed several huge, rolling fields. Here, a vast number of quality Angus cattle were grazing serenely on the lush, early summer grass. Just beyond one of these fields, Tara slowed, turned left, and went through a freshly painted entrance. Shane realized as they pulled into the ten-acre compound, that this was the headquarters for the large cattle operation he'd been driving through.

Scattered along the edges within this gated area, were twelve small, smartly painted houses. Each one was complemented with its own recently mowed yard, leaving the aroma of fresh-cut grass lingering heavy in the air. He was a bit bowled over by the contrast from this place and what he had driven through only a short time ago. At the far side of the compound was a large well-kept stable with at least a dozen stalls. Adjacent to the stable was a separate barn where he saw a handful of men unloading a flatbed trailer full of alfalfa hay. He surmised that this hay had probably come from the recently baled field, which they had passed about a mile before.

Located in the middle of the compound he noticed a stoutly built square corral, with a strong looking snubbing post standing in its center. This old-style-type pen was used for breaking young horses — the hard way. He figured these pens were probably a common sight in this part of the country. Built on two sides of the corral were a couple of nice flat one-acre riding areas. These would be perfect to put some initial training on the young horses, once they were started under saddle. Except for the old-school breaking corral, he was impressed. These folks had a nice training center.

He wasn't surprised to see the facilities here. He remembered Mr. Jensen telling him the Shoshone were born horsemen and that they bred and trained working horses to sell. The horses in these paddocks were not mustangs. He could tell they were domestic horses and guessed they were registered stock. It was easy to conclude that these animals provided a good supplemental income for the Indians' cattle business. He wondered if the ranch was owned by an individual or the whole tribe.

Tara stopped in front of one of the small houses, and Shane

parked alongside. As they got out of their trucks, she motioned for him to stay on the porch. "I'll tell my grandfather you're here and wish to speak with him."

Shane sat down on the porch swing to wait. He looked again at the snubbing post in the center of the corral and found it hard to believe that experienced horsemen, such as these, would still be breaking horses this old-fashioned way.

A snubbing post is a large pole set firmly in the ground. An unbroken horse is tied to it and forced to stand relatively still while being saddled for the first time. This procedure provides a way to keep an untrained horse under control while introducing these new scary things.

Shane, from experience, knew this made horses feel even more scared and trapped. It ended up leaving a bad impression on the frightened animal — a feeling that could last for months or in some cases for the rest of their lives. He grinned as he remembered using this method himself a long time ago. The truth be told, if the right person hadn't come along and taught him a much better way, he'd probably still be doing it.

After a short wait, Tara came to the door, "You can come in."

The house was small but well furnished; clean with a comfortable lived-in atmosphere. He could see several modern appliances in the kitchen plus a large TV in the living room. In the small den/office, a beautiful Indian headdress grabbed his attention. It hung almost five feet high on a tall rack and still came within a couple of inches of touching the floor. The entire length of the headdress was adorned with large, bright feathers, skillfully laced together with leather and strings of colorful beads.

There were many other Native American artifacts neatly situated throughout the house. Shane's eyes drifted to one wall in particular, on which hung several impressive knives and hatchets with bone and deer horn handles. On the same wall hung a very old looking bow mounted next to a quiver full of arrows. "This is an interesting blend of past and present," he remarked quietly to Tara.

Before they entered the living room where the old Indian was sitting, she whispered, "My grandfather is very shy with strangers and he prefers to speak our Shoshone language. I may have to do some interpreting for you, but be assured he understands and speaks English."

The three of them sat facing each other while Tara explained, "My grandfather is the shaman, or medicine man, of our tribe. It is one of his responsibilities to teach the younger generation all about our ancient traditions."

The old man sat quietly as Tara spoke. She told Shane again how the Shoshone considered the mustang herd an important part of their heritage. "It is also one of my grandfather's responsibilities to ensure that our herd be properly managed as well as to keep them wild and free, as they have been for hundreds of years."

Shane got a feeling, just from looking at him, that this was a man of status. He looked to be in his late seventies or early eighties, and was in good physical condition for his age. Even though he was dressed in jeans and a T-shirt, there was an air of nobility about him. Wearing the fancy headdress in the other room, this old guy would fit right in with his warrior ancestors who once ruled this country on horseback.

The elderly man pointed his finger at Shane and said only one word, *Tahotay*. Shane smiled and glanced at Tara for a translation. She looked at her grandfather and shook her head, and then turning to Shane said, "It's nothing important."

Shane asked him, "How is this herd so connected to your tribe's past?"

The shaman spoke in his native language for quite a while. When he finally stopped, he indicated to Tara with a wave of his hand, to translate. She appeared reluctant but did as her grandfather asked.

"He wants you to know that these horses are direct descendants of the hunting and war horses that the Shoshone depended on for centuries. Many generations of warriors and chiefs have ridden these particular bloodlines during famous battles, battles that were important in both the white man and Shoshone's history."

Shane sat attentively. Her voice had taken on a storyteller's quality as she translated the exotic sounds of the Shoshone language into English for him.

"According to our ancient tribal beliefs, these horses are spiritual in nature, and some still believe that when a Shoshone dies these horses will carry their soul to the threshold where those who have passed before will be waiting to greet them. My grandfather and others of his generation believe our ancestors still run with the herd when the "great spirit" allows them." Tara stopped, then smiled at Shane and said, "I know this sounds farfetched to you, but my grandfather wants you to understand why these horses mean so much to us."

Shane shook his head from side to side, "No ma'am, I'm not here to make any judgments about your tribes' beliefs or traditions. I just appreciate his time. Please let him know that I'm respectful of what he's telling me, and that I consider this very interesting."

"My grandfather's name is Tigee, and you may speak to him as you wish. I have told him about your mare and how you have taken good care of her, but that is all I've told him."

The shaman then looked at Shane and repeated, *Tahotay*. Tara looked embarrassed and shook her head, "No," at her grandfather again.

Tigee asked Shane in his broken English, "What do you want from me?"

Shane breathed deeply and said, "I want to set the mare free with her herd. I drove a long way from home to do this and hope that you will help me."

Tigee spoke again in Shoshone. When he finished, Tara translated. "He thinks the mare has been away too long and wonders if the herd will accept her."

Shane said, "I plan to stay out there to make sure they don't reject her. If they do, I'll take her back to Tennessee."

The old Indian said, "No," and began talking again in his own language to Tara. When he finished, she looked at Shane. "My grandfather does not think this is a good idea."

Disappointed, Shane became quiet in thought for a moment, "Could I please speak with your grandfather alone?"

Tara looked questionably at Tigee, he nodded his head, yes, and indicated for her to wait outside.

He hoped if Tigee knew the real reason this was so important to him, perhaps he would reconsider. Strong emotions became evident on Shane's face as he told the old Indian about his family.

"We acquired the mare from a nice lady who saved her from the slaughterhouse. I had no idea how much a part of our family she would become. Once she was trained, my two kids rode her almost every day, and believe me, the mare looked forward to every minute she spent with Jacob and Tina."

Shane stopped for a second to control the lump that was building in his throat along with the burning in his eyes. "It was my young son, Jacob, who noticed at times she seemed sad. Even though my son loved that horse with all his heart, it was his idea that one day we should bring her back to her herd. I promised him I would do that, and now I'm here to fulfill that promise."

Tigee was obviously moved by the story, "I must think about this. Please wait outside while I talk to my granddaughter." As Shane started to leave he turned back, "I'd like you to please keep the information about the loss of my family between the two of us." The old man nodded. "I understand."

Shane sat on the porch for about ten minutes before Tara came outside. "I don't know what you said to my grandfather, but he changed his mind. He says you can take the mustang to the herd." Shane breathed a sigh of relief, then sat quietly in bewilderment as Tara continued, "My grandfather believes the mare has lost her wild edge and will not be cautious of humans anymore. He is concerned that she may lead some of the other mustangs into danger. He doesn't think it would be safe for her or the rest of the herd to reintroduce her right now.

"He wants you to stay on the reservation until we find a way to stop the problems with the young men from town. Only then will he allow your mare to rejoin the herd."

Shane was not expecting this, and he didn't know how to respond. "Could I come back in a couple a days and let your grandfather know my decision?" She nodded her head yes.

Shane thanked Tara and climbed into his truck. The drive back seemed to take forever, and he was still pondering on what to do when he arrived back at the Jensen's. Mr. Jensen was sitting in a rocking chair on the porch. Shane greeted him and walked up the steps and sat next to him.

The old man smiled. "Well, you don't seem to have any new bumps or black eyes, so I guess it didn't go too badly."

Shane grinned. "Yes, sir, I guess it was kind of a boring day."

"What exactly did happen?"

Shane got a more serious look on his face and explained the situation. "I definitely hadn't planned on an extended stay, but there's no way I can just leave the mare with the Shoshones in the hopes that they would turn her loose some day. If I go home without knowing for sure what happens to her, this trip would all be for nothing."

Mr. Jensen leaned back in his rocker. "You know, that old shaman's right. As long as those boys from town are trying to catch the mustangs, Sloppy's trust of humans could compromise her own safety as well as the herd."

"Yes, sir, I know."

"So, what do you plan to do?"

Shane took a deep breath, "If I stay on the reservation, I'd have a place to live as well as a place for my horses. It would also put me in a better position to monitor the situation with the mustangs. On the other hand, I'm worried about the Shoshone people accepting me. I didn't come out here looking to make friends, but I don't want any more trouble, either."

"I can understand why you would feel that way. But, I believe when they realize that you want to see the mustangs safe just as much as they do, you'll get along fine."

Shane hesitated in thought, "I guess my next step is to call Terry in Tennessee. I need to make sure everything's okay at the farm and find out if he's willing to carry on alone for a while."

Mr. Jensen, realizing Shane needed some time alone to think, stood and went inside. Shane hardly noticed the old man leaving as he contemplated. If he stayed, perhaps he could help find a way to prevent any further stealing of the horses. He knew it was a long shot, but stopping these thieves might be the only way to keep Sloppy from being captured again and possibly ending up at the killers. He decided to call Terry tonight, then sleep on it.

Even with all of this weighing heavy on his mind, Shane still wondered why Tigee kept pointing at him and saying the Shoshone word *Tahotay*, and he was curious about its meaning."

Mrs. Jensen stuck her head out the front door to call, "Dinner's ready."

As they sat down to eat Mrs. Jensen commented, "I couldn't help but overhear some of your conversation earlier on the porch with Paul. You know you're welcome to stay here as long as you need to."

"I sure appreciate that, ma'am, but I think being on the reservation will give me the best chance of accomplishing what I came here to do."

Later that evening, he called home. Terry encouraged him to stay in Wyoming. "Don't worry, boss, everything is running smoothly. Our clients know I learned from the best."

"You're a good friend, and I won't forget this," Shane vowed.

Then Terry told him some good news, "Beth Ann and I are having another baby!" Shane was happy for him and congratulated him before they said their good-byes. The thought of children running and playing on his farm again made him feel good, but it also unavoidably steered him toward memories of Jacob and Tina. With an all too familiar heavy heart, he went outside to be alone.

The next morning, a slight breeze was blowing down from the Owl Creek Mountains. The fresh mountain air and comfortable temperature made for a perfect day to take the horses on a long ride. This time he rode the mustang and ponied Tory alongside. He rode far into the foothills and again marveled at the vast open country. A man could ride through these rolling hills for days and never find an end to them he thought. A smile crossed his face as he saw a pair of cottontails, out for their morning graze, under a stand of sycamore trees. A large hawk suddenly left his perch above them. Shane and the horses must have scared the big bird away from the rabbits he was eyeing for his morning hunt. Shane looked ahead and caught site of the tail end of a mule deer just as it disappeared over the next rise. There was wildlife everywhere he looked, and being out in this venue was good for his soul.

During the ride he made his decision to stay for the summer. He was financially solvent, and Terry seemed to have everything under control. He saw no compelling reason to leave.

Back at the farm, he gave the horses a good rubdown, then went into the house to find Mrs. Jensen sitting at her computer.

"Mornin', ma'am"

"Good morning, Shane. How was your ride?"

"It was fine. This sure is some beautiful country."

"Yes, it is."

"Since you already have your computer cranked up do you think there's any way to find out on the Internet what the Shoshone word *Tahotay* means?"

"I can sure try. Why do you want to know?"

"It's a word the old shaman spoke a couple of times. I guess my curiosity is getting the best of me."

She wasn't having much luck with the search, and just as she was about to give up Mr. Jensen walked in. They explained to him what they were doing, and he said he knew a part-Shoshone man who lived nearby. "His name is Bobby, and I know he speaks some of their old language. Maybe he can help."

Shane and Mr. Jensen drove to the farm where Bobby worked and found him repairing fences. "What word are you trying to translate?" he asked.

"It sounded like *Tahotay*," Shane answered.

"My Shoshone is a bit rusty, but I don't think this word has a definition. As I remember, it refers to the name of a legendary character that was part man and part horse. Many of the old tribal stories included mystical creatures who possessed souls of both a human and an animal."

Mr. Jensen grinned, "I wonder if the shaman thinks you're the front or the back end of that horse!" The three men laughed.

Shane thanked Bobby. He couldn't make any sense out of Tigee calling him this, and he hoped he hadn't been the butt of Tigee's joke. For now he decided to put it out of his mind. He had bigger things to worry about.

After a decent night's sleep, he loaded his belongings and horses onto the trailer, then thanked the Jensens for everything they had done.

Mrs. Jesnsen gave him a hug good-bye before saying, "In all the years I've lived here, I've never been out to that reservation, and I've always wanted to see it. Maybe we'll come out there to visit."

Shane smiled. "I'd like that very much."

During the drive, he began to wonder what he was getting himself into, but he decided to look at it both as an adventure and a diversion.

He didn't know how to contact Tigee to tell him he was coming, so he hoped it would be okay to just show up. As Shane pulled into the ranch headquarters, he saw a couple of men working with a stout-looking, red roan horse in the corral. Tigee was standing on his porch motioning for Shane to drive his truck and trailer over to a small cabin. He told him in his tribal accent in which stalls to put the horses and that he could move his stuff into the cabin anytime. "Come over to my house after you get settled in so we can talk."

The old cabin was in good condition. There was a sleeping area with a heater and a small TV at the foot of the bed. The small bathroom was the only separate room with a door on it. A gas stove, sink, and a refrigerator made up the kitchen area. "Home sweet home," Shane said, grinning. It wasn't much, but it was all he needed.

He unpacked before he headed over to Tigee's house. When he entered, two other men were standing in the living room with the old Indian. Neither of them seemed particularly happy to meet Shane. The old man introduced them, and then began talking to the two in their Shoshone language. He turned to Shane and spoke in his broken English, which seemed to be improving. Maybe he just needed a little practice or maybe Shane was getting better at understanding him. Either way, both of them seemed pleased that they were communicating better.

"We are very thankful for the information you gave us about the plans to trap our mustangs on Saturday. My braves were waiting for the men when a small incident happened. There were some shots fired. My men did not shoot back. They did, however, kill three of the dogs that were sent to attack them."

Shane asked, "Were any horses caught?"

"The trap had been destroyed, so none were taken, but the men yelled that they would get revenge for their dogs."

One of the younger Indians spoke up, "This is no longer just a dispute over rights to the horses. It's about how they think they're better than us. We have every right to protect what's ours, and we'll do whatever is necessary to keep them from stealing our mustangs! Tigee wants us to take you with us when we check on the herd this weekend. We are doing this only because he asked."

Shane looked at him in a friendly manner, "Hey, man, I'm not one of the bad guys here. I want to stop these horse thieves too."

The young Indian didn't look convinced, "If you want to go, have a saddle horse ready to load by nine Saturday morning. We'll trailer in as far as we can, then we'll need to ride the rest of the way into the backcountry."

Shane assured them he'd be ready.

As the two men left, Shane turned to Tigee. "What do you expect of me for my keep over the next couple of months?"

"Make yourself useful if you want, but you are my guest and owe me no money. You provide your own food and take care of your horses. That is all I ask." Shane nodded then stood to leave.

As he did, Tara came in, smiled, and said hello as she walked by. She was wearing faded jeans with a tight fit, a sleeveless white shirt, and no makeup. Even so, Shane couldn't help but notice how naturally good looking she was. Though he couldn't deny his lighthearted attraction for her, his family's memory was still too strong to allow for any thought of pursuing female companionship. So, it was an innocent request when he asked, "Would you have time to answer some questions and show me around the reservation?"

"I'll be getting off work early tomorrow. You can come over after lunch, I'll give you the ten-cent tour," she offered.

"Thanks, I'll be here."

Shane spent the remainder of the day settling in and stocking his little house. The place was in fairly good shape, but some minor repairs were needed on the front porch railing. After eating a sandwich for dinner, he borrowed a hammer out of the barn and fixed it.

Later that night, while lying in bed, he hoped he would be able to stay busy enough around the ranch. He was all too aware that an idle mind was his worst enemy.

After an early breakfast, he sat on the porch with a cup of coffee. The house was only about fifty yards from the north side of the corral, which was in the middle of the compound. In the corral were the same two men with the horse he had seen there yesterday. They had the big, red roan tied up tight to the snubbing post and were trying to get a saddle on him. The horse was terrified and pulling against the post with all his strength. Shane really wanted to show the men a gentler way to do this, but he knew better than to disrespect them by butting in. *Mind your own business, Carson.* He thought, *You're not out here to put on a clinic for these people.*

Shane finished his coffee and went out to the barn to tend to Tory and the mustang. Since the two horses seemed to be eager to get out of their stalls, he decided this would be a good time to explore the country surrounding the compound.

He waited until they finished eating their morning grain, then he put Sloppy in one of the turnout paddocks and saddled up Tory for the ride. As he led his old horse out of the barn and mounted up, it was hard for him not to notice what was going on in the corral just a few yards away.

The two men had been joined by a young Indian boy, who

looked to be about thirteen. They'd finally put a saddle on the freaked-out young horse, but he was still tied tight to the post. Riding Tory closer to the corral, he saw one of the men slide a blindfold under the halter to cover the frightened horse's eyes. During all of this the roan never quit fighting and pulling against the snubbing post. Shane could hardly believe what he saw next as the men motioned to the young boy to get on the horse.

With the colt already blindfolded, one of the men twisted and held on tightly to one of its ears. This method, earing down, would not hurt the gelding, but would help keep it from moving around or starting to buck before the rider could get in the saddle. Shane squinted his eyes and bit his bottom lip as the boy climbed on. At this point one of the men pulled the blindfold from under the halter and let go of the roan's ear. Simultaneously, the other man turned the horse free from the post.

The boy was on his own now, and the big red roan wasted no time exploding underneath him. The horse bucked hard and honest as the boy held on for dear life. Shane kept waiting for the kid to fall and was impressed by how well he could ride. This rodeo continued for a full thirty seconds, with the horse still showing no sign of weakening. Shane wondered how long the boy could take this punishment, but the kid showed a lot of heart and hung on.

Suddenly, the roan stumbled, falling to his knees. When he jumped back up, he had lost his bearings and crashed through the boards of the corral where he fell to his knees again. Amazingly, the kid was still hanging on as the horse scrambled to get back on his feet.

"Oh shit," Shane whispered under his breath. The bronc and the rider were no longer in the safer confines of the corral. The crazed horse was loose in the compound, bucking wildly with the boy still mounted. Shane grabbed his rope and rode Tory straight into the fury. Tory was a seasoned pony horse so Shane knew he could count on him to remain under his control while he tried to help the boy. He quickly got his rope over the gelding's head and snubbed it up close to his saddle horn. With this maneuver, Shane now had Tory running alongside the bucking horse. He hollered at the boy to let go of the bronc and slide behind him on Tory. The kid grabbed on to Shane and transferred over behind Shane's saddle. Then with an impressive athletic ease, the boy safely slid off Tory and onto the ground.

Shane continued riding alongside the big, tough roan until it quit bucking. Then, he ponied the horse over to a nearby turnout paddock and led him in. One of the older Indians stood at the gate of the paddock and motioned for Shane to ride out. Shane shook his head, no. Instead he politely requested, "Would you please step out and shut the gate?" The man looked puzzled, but did as Shane asked.

The two men and the boy watched from outside the pen as Shane picked up the lead rope on the frightened gelding's halter and began to work with it.

A good pony horse is an extension of a rider's own legs; therefore Shane had total control over where he wanted Tory to be. "Atta boy," he told his horse. "You're an old pro at this stuff, aren't you, bud?"

They were now standing side by side facing opposite directions as he put Tory's nose at the bronc's hip. Shane slowly kept pushing Tory's shoulder into the gelding's flank. When done correctly, this exercise would eventually convince the bronc to let go of his defensive frame of mind and move over, allowing him to be released from his brace and his tension. It wasn't long before the big roan began to relax, and Shane was able to pet him softly on his neck and head. Shane worked on the gelding a while longer, then motioned to the boy to come into the pen and over to him.

As he waited for the kid, he noticed that he had drawn quite a crowd. Tigee was watching from his porch and about a dozen other Indians were standing at the paddock fence. Shane realized it would have been hard for them to ignore the commotion that had been happening in the middle of the compound only a few minutes earlier. The boy showed courage and walked right out to the horses, then looked at Shane for instructions.

"Climb up behind my saddle," Shane said as he reached down. The boy grabbed ahold, swung himself up onto Tory from the other side, and waited for Shane to tell him what to do next.

Still side by side, but now facing the same way, he moved Tory forward a couple of steps while letting the bronc continue to stan still. This now had the boy even with the saddle on the scared young horse. Shane winked his eye, smiled, then motioned to the kid to gently slide over and onto the roan gelding's saddle. "Stay calm and relaxed," he instructed, "and keep on petting him. I want you to make this horse think he is your best friend, so keep rubbing and talking to him."

The boy quietly answered, "Yes, sir," and then did exactly as he had been told. Shane gently pulled on the horse's lead, urging the gelding to step forward with Tory beside him.

He kept the gelding tied in close to his saddle horn in case he blew up again. The first couple of steps, the unsure horse tensed, but Shane and the boy kept talking him out of any more trouble. Soon, they were walking around nice and free. Now the roan was accepting the boy on his back. Shane stopped the horses and motioned the kid back over onto Tory, then down to the ground.

He glanced toward the paddock fence and noticed that the people watching were smiling as they discussed what they had witnessed.

Shane rode Tory, leading the gelding over to one of the men he had seen in the corral. Before Shane handed the man the lead rope, he explained, "The horse will need more work tomorrow or he'll just come unglued again. I'll be glad to work with the horse and the boy in the morning if you want me to." The man thought a minute, looking as if he wasn't sure how to answer. Then, he slowly nodded his head, accepting Shane's offer. Shane gave the man the roan's lead rope, then rode Tory off for the ride he had started on earlier.

As he passed by the young boy he reached to shake his hand. The kid shyly looked at Shane and spoke softly, "Thanks, mister."

"What's your name, son?"

"Tommy."

"Mine is Shane Carson. That was some good riding, Tommy. I'm looking forward to working with you tomorrow." Tommy responded with another quiet, "Thank you." Shane turned Tory toward the compound gate, and rode away at a slow trot.

Chapter 9

Shane's focus since he'd arrived in Wyoming had been centered on finding Sloppy's herd. As he rode out of the ranch entrance, he realized how very little he knew about this reservation she was born on.

He found himself looking forward to meeting with Tara tomorrow, appreciating her willingness to show him around. *I'll try not to drive her crazy with too many questions*, he thought with a grin.

Shane was even more pumped about his first chance to finally see the wild mustangs this weekend. He was a little concerned about getting along with the two guys who were guiding him. However, he felt pretty certain the two Shoshone men would show him respect because they were taking him at Tigee's request.

Tory was already tired from the unexpected workout at the ranch. Even though the horse was still tough at sixteen years old, Shane knew he needed to be careful about overriding him.

They headed down a trail just off the main road across from the ranch entrance. Shane had only ridden about a mile when he spotted a nice place to stop and rest his horse. He dismounted and sat down on the top of a high hill where he could see for a long distance. This country was still just as raw and untouched as God had made it eons ago. Here there were no buildings, roads, or power lines to ruin the view. He was sorry he couldn't show his kids this land and began to feel regretful that he hadn't done much traveling with them. He and Jen had always planned to, but it never happened.

Tory exhaled a relaxing snort before lowering his head to graze lazily on the rich summer grass that carpeted the surrounding area.

Shane twisted the cup off a thermos he'd brought along, then poured it full to the rim with strong, black coffee as he began to think about what his life had become over the last couple of years. Being in this tranquil place made him yearn to try harder to finally make his peace with God, and, somehow, accept His will for what had happened.

He took a sip of the steaming brew and spoke to his family as he often did when he was alone. "Damn, I miss you guys. No matter what, you'll always be a big part of who I am." He filled his lungs with fresh mountain air and gazed out across the wild, open land-scape then continued. "I wish with all my soul that it was me in that car instead of the three of you." He paused for another second and swallowed hard before he finished what he had to say. "I have to believe that we'll all be together again someday. Sometimes, it's the only thing that really keeps me going."

Shane had made a decision before he left for Wyoming that he would only allow himself a short time each day to dwell on his fam-ily. He hoped this would help him maintain some peace of mind. So, after a few minutes, he dumped out what was left in his cup and began the ride back to the ranch.

As he rode into the complex, Sloppy, who was grazing in one of the turnout pens, raised her head and greeted them with a soft whinny. Shane unsaddled Tory and put him out with the mare to graze.

It was now approaching noon, which meant he had about an hour to get cleaned up before he was supposed to meet Tara so she could show him around the reservation.

As he walked back toward his temporary quarters, he looked across the yards and noticed Tigee sitting on his front porch steps. The old Indian was holding out some meat, trying to get two young dogs to eat out of his hand. The dogs were being very cautious, and even though they wanted the food, they kept their distance. As Shane walked closer, the dogs trotted away with their tails between their legs.

Tigee smiled at Shane and waved him on over.

"Sorry, I didn't mean to scare them off."

Tigee explained, "I leave food out for the two pups every morning, but they still won't let me touch them."

Shane had grown accustomed to Tigee's heavy native accent, and he appreciated that the reserved old guy was now talking to him more.

"Are they wild dogs?"

"They have grown up at the ranch. Their mother is one of our cow dogs. She was lost during a roundup last year. About three months later, they found her with a couple of half-wolf pups at her tit. Now the two get a lot of their meals by hunting as a team in the woods around the ranch." Tigee grabbed hold of the railing so he could stand up from his seat on the porch steps, then continued. "The two are good watch dogs so we don't mind them staying here. I've been trying to get them to come up to me for the last several weeks, but so far with no luck."

Shane visited a moment longer and then ambled toward his cabin. During his short walk, he noticed the two half-wolves were shadowing him from a distance. This bothered Shane somewhat, but before he reached his porch steps, he lost sight of the two and promptly put them out of his mind.

After showering, he still had some time to kill before meeting Tara so he walked around the compound to introduce himself to several of the Indians working there. They were neither friendly nor unfriendly toward him; they seemed courteous, but in a cold sort of way. Shane figured they would loosen up after they realized they could trust him.

He estimated that there were about one thousand brood cows on the ranch and about twenty to twenty-five Indians working here. There were several families living on the ranch, so he assumed that the rest of the crew must have places nearby. Shane had noticed about eight kids who lived on the compound with their folks. He thought them to be between five and thirteen years old. The oldest was Tommy, whom Shane had helped with the bronc earlier. All of the children seemed well mannered and playful.

Later that day, as promised, Tara came by the cabin for the afternoon they had planned. He was beginning to feel a connection with the Shoshone woman and hoped they could become friends.

"I've been looking forward to seeing the rest of the reservation this afternoon. Thanks for your time."

She raised her eyebrows as she smiled and looked at him, "Since it's over two point two million acres. I doubt we'll have time to see it all today."

Shane shrugged his shoulders, "Ma'am, I really don't have a clue about this reservation. I have heard that there is a lot of history wrapped up in this land, your people, and the mustangs.

Tara nodded her head. "The Wind River Reservation is home to both the Shoshone and the Arapaho tribes, although the two tribes live separately for the most part.

"I think the best place for us to start is at our Shoshone cultural center in the town of Fort Washakie. This community has been in existence since the mid-eighteen hundreds. There are some of the original buildings from the old fort still standing. The whole area is set up to educate people about Shoshone history, which goes back long before the white man came to America."

"Do you have a lot of tourists?"

"We do have some. My people have tried to promote and build tourism on the reservation to some extent. Without the advertising dollars to put behind it, there just doesn't seem to be much interest. Since our land is not far from Yellowstone and Grand Teton National parks, we have even tried to bus tourists from those parks to visit here. We have our powwows, museums, white water rafting, and our incredible scenery in our ads and brochures."

"I suppose it's hard to compete with the famous national parks nearby."

"Yes, it is, but the truth is, as much as we would like to build tourism, it conflicts with one of our most important responsibilities, that of keeping our land wild and untrampled. We feel strongly about preserving this land just as it was when we first arrived hundreds of years ago. I wish we knew how to bring in the tourist money without jeopardizing our ancestral land. I guess you can't have the best of both worlds, can you?"

"No, ma'am, I reckon not. Too much of America has been sacrificed in the name of progress and profit." Shane took a deep breath as a serious look came over his face. "There used to be so much open land around my farm in Tennessee. Now most of it is being developed for housing and strip malls. Soon, it seems, there won't be any wilderness left unless people like yours, who have control over large tracts of land, care enough to stop it."

"You don't think much like a white man," Tara stated laughingly.

"There are a lot of people who think like I do. Unfortunately, big money seems to speak louder than we do in our society. A few years ago, I turned down a pretty good offer from a builder for my farm. I refused his offer because of my love for the land. I felt good about what I had done, but the truth of the matter is, I was just putting off the inevitable. I envy you and your people having all this open territory to live on."

A short drive later, the two arrived at the old fort. As they stepped out of the truck Shane immediately grasped a sense of the history which surrounded them.

Tara gestured for him to follow. "This place was originally built in eighteen seventy-one, and at that time was the only fort established to protect, rather than to fight, the Indians."

Shane was surprised to see there were no walls surrounding the compound. "This actually looks more like a small town than a fort."

"It was more like a military outpost," Tara replied. "See, over there are the old officer quarters and the soldiers' barracks." They took time to walk through the remaining one-hundred-thirty-year-old structures, many of which were still in good condition. Tara pointed to the middle of the parade yard. There, standing guard, were a couple of old cavalry-style cannons still mounted on their original wooden wagon wheels. Shane paused to get a closer look at these relics before they made their way across the street to the museum. He politely opened the door, then followed her inside.

"Here, you will be able to see for yourself how my tribe's history is so connected to our mustangs."

As he stepped through the entrance, he felt as though he'd walked straight into the Shoshone's past. He slowly scanned the large room and marveled at the many well-produced exhibits showing everything from a miniature ancient village to a life-sized wax figure of Chief Washakie. The door gradually closed itself behind him, shutting out the afternoon's bright glare. He knew the dark, tinted glass was necessary to shield the interior of the building from any harmful ultraviolet rays, which could accelerate the deterioration of the abundance of ancient artifacts and photographs within its confines.

Tara continued, "Unlike other reservations in the United States, the Wind River Reservation was chosen by the Shoshone themselves. In fact, long before the whites came to the area, this valley had served as my tribe's winter home and ancestral hunting grounds."

The room suddenly filled with sunlight again as the door was held wide open by a young, smiling woman. She sternly reminded a group of elementary-age children as they filed excitedly through the museum's foyer, "Okay, kids! You know the rules. Let's all stay together and keep your voices down."

The last person inside looked to be a middle-aged Indian man with a long gray pony tail. He was dressed in a pair of neatly pressed jeans and a bright western-style shirt. Tara moved close to Shane's ear and whispered, "The man in back is James Bearclaw. He's the curator of the museum, so he often gives tours to schools from neighboring towns."

James winked at Tara as he motioned for her and Shane to join his group. "Come on, we'll follow them through an exhibit or two," she whispered.

The kids were all well behaved and eagerly listened to Mr. Bearclaw. "As I already told you, my tribe has lived here since way before it was part of the United States of America. This valley is very unique for many reasons. It's location between two mountain ranges allows it to have mild winters and comfortable summers. It has plenty of water with an abundance of wildlife, which many years ago we hunted for our food. Because of all this the other tribes would sometimes try to take our valley from us."

A little boy piped up from the middle of the group. "Did your tribe ever have to fight to keep your land?"

"Yes, we did," James answered. Then he led the group over to an exhibit that displayed many of the old weapons including spears, knifes, and tomahawks that the Shoshone used to defend their valley.

"Wow!" another boy blurted out. "Can I hold that bow and arrow?"

Mr. Bearclaw smiled, "No, I'm sorry, all of these weapons are very old and priceless to my people. No one is allowed to handle them." Then he pointed to a specific spear and shield that hung nearby. "I'll tell you a story about these," he said.

"A long time ago the very fierce Crow tribe decided to try to defeat my people and take our homeland for their own. A violent battle raged for several days, with each side losing many warriors. In order to stop any more braves from being killed, it was finally decided that Chief Washakie of the Shoshones and the chief of the Crows would fight each other to determine the winner."

Shane leaned over and said quietly to Tara, "The leaders of our countries today would never have the guts to do this."

Tara smiled as the curator continued, "These two brave warriors met to fight each other, knowing that the future of their tribes depended on the outcome of this contest to the death. Each of the chiefs showed up mounted on his favorite horse carrying a sharp lance and a shield." He pointed to the exhibit on the wall, "These are the actual weapons Chief Washakie carried in that battle. When the bloody fight was over Chief Washakie had won, meaning the Shoshone were able to retain the home of our ancestors."

Tara spoke softly to Shane as they listened, "The horses ridden by the two chiefs during this battle became some of the bloodlines that are now part of our wild herd."

Tara and Shane quietly slipped away from the kids and walked over to the next exhibit. This one sparked a childhood memory for Shane. "I remember learning about this in junior high school. A Shoshone woman named Sacagawea had been the main guide for the Lewis and Clark Expedition, on their trip to reach the Pacific in the early 1800s."

"Yes, every kid who has ever taken an American history class has heard of her. I think it will interest you to know how this event in history is so connected to our mustangs."

Shane turned to face her, cocking his head a little to one side in curiosity as he listened.

"Lewis and Clark had struck up a relationship with the tribe, and ended up obtaining the horses used in their expedition from the Shoshone. When the explorers returned from their travels, they gave back all the surviving horses. Those also became part of the herd's bloodlines. Sacagawea's name means bird woman. Her importance in American history was recently honored last year when the U.S. Treasury put her image on the front of the silver dollar in the year two thousand."

"Wow, I had no idea your herd was linked to anything famous like this."

Tara held her hand up, "I'm not finished yet, there's a lot more American history wrapped up in our mustangs." She led him over to another exhibit. This one told of how the Arapaho tribe, long-time enemies of the Shoshone, were forced onto the Wind River Reservation after their conquest of General Custer at the battle of the Little Big Horn.

Tara gave him a few minutes to observe the display of the famous battle scene before talking. "When the Arapahos arrived in Wyoming, they were still riding the war horses they had ridden to defeat Custer. Over time, the Shoshone took some of these horses during skirmishes between the tribes. The best of those captured horses were added to the herd and have also become a part of their lineage. Our tribes, of course, have learned in more recent years to get along."

Shane raised his eyebrows in amazement, "Is there more?"

Tara laughed slightly, "Those were only some of the more recent bloodlines added to the herd. The first Shoshone war and hunting ponies were all from Spanish descent and originally obtained by my tribe from the Comanche. These horses quickly became a very important part of the tribe's early survival and identity. Today we can actually trace the lines of our mustangs to specific events and battles important to the tribe's history, dating back to at least the early seventeen seventies. All of the selected animals for our special herd were considered gifts to our ancestors' spirits and are allowed to run free as an offering."

Tara gestured for Shane to follow her over to a small room that was closed off to the public. She pulled out a key and unlocked the door. "Come in here, and I'll show you something the general public never gets to see." Inside, on a large shelf, were stacks of neatly stored file boxes. "This is where we keep the records of our spirit herd. The oldest breeding records were kept in great detail verbally by our elders. They were handed down from generation to generation until the mid-eighteen hundreds, when everything was written on paper and translated into English. My brothers, from a very young age, have always been involved in guarding our herd and recognized your gray mare when they saw her. She disappeared along with another two-year-old filly in the spring of nineteen ninety-six. We weren't sure if they'd been stolen or if something else happened to them."

Shane remarked, "I guess that's why they were so adamant about taking her from me that day at the Jensen's farm."

Tara nodded, "Once the young horses in the herd have survived their first six months, we brand them in the early fall, then they are added to these records." Tara dug through some of the files and pulled out the 1994 branding records. "See, here are your mare's papers. She was the last foal born to her mother who died of old age recently. There are only a few grays in our herd, and most of them can be traced back to a specific line that came from the horse Sacagawea herself rode during the Lewis and Clark Expedition. Your mare is out of this special line."

"I'll be damned!" Shane whistled as he studied the papers.

Tara continued, "We have only been branding our horses for the last seventy-five years. But, believe me, the older records are just as accurate. The broken arrow brand represents all the battles that were fought to keep our valley, and it is also a symbol of honor for all the braves who have lost their lives during these battles."

Shane handed Sloppy's papers back to her. "I can't help but be impressed with all of this. Now I'm even more excited about seeing the herd for the first time this weekend."

They left the little room and walked back out to the main hall of the museum where there was a large map of the reservation on the wall. He could hardly believe the size of the place with it's variety of terrains, including meadows, foothills, forests, and mountains.

Tara's pride and enthusiasm were evident with her next bit of information, "The Shoshone Indians are the only tribe in history who were able to keep their ancestral home. It's so unique and special that we have been able to retain this land where all our history was actually lived. This is the only reason my tribe has been able to maintain our unique herd here for so many generations."

Shane followed her over to a wall that was full of old pictures with captions. They were all portraits of different chiefs and other tribal leaders dating back to the 1800s. Tara pointed out a very old picture of a middle-aged white woman dressed in Indian clothing. The title read 1868 — BARBARA STEPHEN LIGHTFEATHER, MARRIED TO A SHOSHONE WARRIOR AND MOTHER OF THREE SHOSHONE CHILDREN. "This was my great-great-great grandmother on my mother's side. She had lived among the tribe most of her adult life and acted as an interpreter between Chief Washakie and the United States during the negotiation that made the Wind River Basin officially the Shoshone's reservation."

"How did she end up living with the Shoshone?"

Tara explained, "She had been a schoolteacher in the white world and was kidnapped by the Crows during a raid on a settlement in Utah. The Crows tortured her, beat her, and used her as a slave for almost two years. When she was in her mid-twenties she was saved along with some Shoshone prisoners during a rescue mission by my tribe. Our people considered it a great victory when our warriors attacked and defeated the enemy, and brought her to the village along with the Shoshone prisoners they brought home to their families."

"She must have been a strong woman to have survived all that." Tara agreed with a nod, "Barbara Stephen was in pretty bad shape. The women of the tribe nursed her back to health, and she later decided to stay and make a life for herself. She was the first white teacher to join our tribe. She worked hard all her life to teach our children how to read, write, and speak English."

Shane commented, "Now I know where your blue eyes came from, and why your skin is a bit lighter than most of your tribe."

"I am proud of my white and Native heritages," she said, "but most of all, I am Shoshone."

The afternoon had flown by. The information Shane learned about these people and their mustangs answered many questions. Now he understood why the tribe was so protective of the mustangs. Although he respected this, he couldn't help but recognize how these unique horses might attract an immense public interest. "There must be an award-winning documentary somewhere in all of this," he muttered under his breath.

On the way home, he carefully kept their friendly chatter away from anything personal. This was his standard way of keeping new acquaintances from asking about his past. His intent wasn't to keep his family a secret. It's just he knew from experience that sympathy was unavoidable once people learned about the tragedy.

Tara politely acted as though she didn't pick up on his reluctance to talk about his life, and he appreciated her regard for his obvious reserve.

Chapter 10

It was quiet at the ranch as they pulled up to Tara's house. Shane turned toward her with a lighthearted grin before they went their separate ways, "Thanks for your time. You were such a great tour guide, I feel like I should tip you."

Tara laughed, "That's okay, you can keep your money. I'm already independently wealthy anyway." As they arrived at their own separate porches they glanced at each other across the three small yards between them and waved good-bye.

Because he'd kept their conversation casual, he still knew very little about her, except that she seemed to spend a lot of her time at her job, whatever that was. *Maybe, in the future I'll make an effort to show some interest in her personal life*, he thought. Unfortunately, he realized this was a two-way street, so for now Shane felt more comfortable keeping a friendly distance.

Shane rose on Friday morning as he normally did around six a.m. He was usually awake before the alarm went off, but this morning, after a good night's sleep, it was that annoying buzzer that woke him. "Son of a bitch," he mumbled as he hit the off button. His heart was pounding and his breathing shallow as he sat on the side of his bed, gradually regaining consciousness. Slowly, he stood and staggered into the shower.

As he started a pot of coffee, he heard a knock on the door. "Who the hell would be here at six fifteen in the morning?" Irritated, he cracked the door open, but quickly chilled when he saw who was there.

"Good morning, mister. I saw your light. So I figured you were up." It was Tommy, the kid he'd helped yesterday with the roan geld-ing. The boy had a plate loaded with eggs and bacon. I hope you're hungry."

"Is that for me?"

"Yes, sir!"

Shane looked a bit confused.

"You offered to help me with the horse again today, but I got no money to pay you. So, I made breakfast and thought you might have some work I can do to trade for your time."

Now the food made sense, and he couldn't help but admire the kid's attitude.

"We'll figure something out that's fair. Why don't you come in while I eat, then we can get started with your colt."

"I'll just wait on the porch."

"Suit yourself, son. I'll be out in a minute."

When they walked into the barn, the gelding was acting very bothered in his stall. He was kicking the wall with a back foot while anxiously pawing a hole in the ground with a front one. As Shane attempted to open the stall, the horse immediately charged him, with his ears pinned back in an aggressive posture. Shane quickly backed away and shut the gate. He looked at Tommy, "Does he act like this every morning?"

"Yes, sir. I don't know how to break him of it."

Shane shook his head with a grin, grabbed an empty feed sack, walked back over to the stall and went inside. The boy watched as the beligerent gelding, once again, charged aggressively. Shane harshly rattled the feed sack at him, sending the horse back to the far corner of his stall. Shane then walked out of the stall, waited a minute, and repeated this several times. Soon, he no longer needed to do anything but walk up to the stall, and the gelding would respectfully move back.

"Now that he's not trying to attack me anymore, I need to get him to come to me with a nice attitude so I can put his halter on."

Tommy watched intensely as Shane walked into the stall with

the big roan now standing with his head in the back corner. Staying near the door, Shane began to rattle the feed sack softly. Finally, the gelding turned around and faced him. As soon as the horse responded in this way, he released the pressure by keeping the bag still and quiet. Timing was imperative to make this work. After several repeats of this process, the horse made the decision to walk over in a friendly manner, so Shane rewarded him with a gentle rub between his eyes.

With the gelding now acting calm, Shane put his halter on and led him out of the stall.

Tommy looked amazed at how easily Shane fixed this problem. "Mister, can you teach me how to do that?"

Shane laughed, and said, "All I did was make the right thing easy and the wrong thing difficult for him. In the process, I made my idea of how he should act into his own idea. I think this horse has a good mind, he's just a little pissed off at the way you've been trying to break him." Tommy seemed puzzled. Shane winked, "Don't worry, son, you'll catch on soon. Now, grab my saddle and tack up ole Tory, while I take the colt outside to the corral and begin with some groundwork."

His first goal was to teach the big roan to accept a saddle without a fight. The horse had already learned to hate this, so Shane knew he had his work cut out for him. As he worked with the roan, he noticed the same two men, who had been with Tommy the day before, come over to the fence. Shane walked over and shook their hands. "I hope you don't mind that I'm helping Tommy." The last thing Shane wanted to do was to inadvertently show these two guys up and cause any hard feelings.

Only one of the Indians answered, "It's okay, we have no problem with it." Shane nodded and went back to work. It took some effort, but soon the big roan was saddled and standing quietly. He gently sent the young gelding out to walk around him inside the corral.

Since this corral was an old-style square breaking pen, Shane used a lunge line, hooked to the horse's halter, to keep it moving in a circle around him.

The roan walked off okay, but Shane could tell by the gelding's expressions he was still thinking about blowing up. Shane looked over at Tommy, who was sitting on Tory, "When I ask this horse to trot, he's gonna come unraveled and start bucking, so you pick up Tory's reins and hold on in case the old horse reacts to it." Sure enough, as soon as Shane tipped the horse into a trot, he blew sky high. It only took a couple of minutes before the gelding started to settle. Before long Shane had the animal long lining around him without any more trouble.

At this point, Shane asked Tommy to get off Tory so he could get on him. He began working with the bronc from Tory's back, just as he had done yesterday. Soon he helped Tommy ease onto the roan and he led them around with Tory. Today, Shane was careful to keep the unsure, young gelding snubbed up tightly to his saddle horn.

This was about all the horse could handle in one session, so Shane told the boy to dismount. "You spend a lot of time petting him. You need to let him know how good he did for us today before you turn him out."

"Yes, sir," the kid said excitedly. He thanked Shane and led the horse away.

The big roan had done well, and Tommy did a great job. Shane was impressed with Tommy's courage and natural feel for a horse. He was having fun working with both of them.

Later that evening, Shane noticed Tara sitting on her porch. He walked over, and after they said their hellos, he asked her about Tommy.

"He's a good kid," she said with an affectionate sparkle in her eyes. "His father left his mother before Tommy was born. His mom is very poor, so she reluctantly lets him live on the ranch. She loves him very much and comes to see him often, but she knows he's better off here. He lives in the bunkhouse across the compound, and all of us make sure he's taken care of. He'll start school again when the fall semester begins. I always help him with his homework in the evenings. Until then, he'll earn money working around the ranch. One of the good things about being Shoshone is that we always look out for each other. I heard you've been helping him with a tough horse. I want to thank you for that. Tommy would spend all of his time with the horses if we'd let him."

"He sure has a lot of ability," Shane said.

Tara paused for a few seconds, "Do you train horses professionally? Everyone here thinks you're pretty good."

"I started about the time I was Tommy's age and never considered doing anything else for a living." Before Tara could ask him any more questions about his previous life, Shane wished her good night, and turned to leave.

As he walked down the steps of the porch, he glanced back and caught her watching him with those piercing, deep blue eyes. It was as if she were trying to figure him out. This casual look between them only lasted a second before they both became a little uncomfortable and shifted their eyes away.

Tomorrow was the big day. He was finally going out to see the wild horses. He had a couple of good stiff drinks before he hit the sack, hoping it would help him sleep. Shane tried hard, every night, to keep himself in a positive state of mind and not dwell on his family. Tonight for some reason he was having a difficult time. He finally fell asleep watching the old black-and-white TV at the foot of his bed. When he woke at six a.m., the TV was still on with an irritating, loud static and a snowy, gray screen.

When the two Indians showed up with the horse trailer, Tory was already saddled and prepared to load. The men didn't have much to say as Shane hopped into the back seat of the old crew cab pickup.

About five miles into the trip, Shane broke the silence by reintroducing himself. The Indian on the passenger side shook his hand, "I'm Timothy Hawk. Most people just call me Hawk." He was about five eleven and 180 pounds, looked to be about thirty years old, and in pretty fair shape, except for a slight beer gut. Hawk pointed to the driver, "This is Johnny Badger, we call him JB for short." JB gave Shane a halfhearted glance with a nod and quickly looked back toward the dirt road he was driving down. "JB doesn't talk much, so don't take it personal," Hawk said as he poked at JB and laughed.

Shane estimated JB to also be about thirty. He was a little taller than Hawk and in better condition. This Johnny Badger character sure seemed to have a chip on his shoulder, and Shane thought this was not someone he wanted to tangle with.

JB turned down a narrow grade that would be easy to miss if you didn't know exactly where it was. The woods were thick here. The narrow road wound around for several more miles until the landscape finally started to open into a series of small ravines. There were few trees in this area but the rough terrain was not drivable, so the rest of the trip would be on horseback.

The two Indians stepped out of the truck without saying a word and walked around to the back of the trailer. Shane followed them around, but the men just stood there and made no attempt to open the trailer door. Shane sensed that they had something to say, "What's on your minds, guys? If you have something to tell me, go ahead and spit it out!"

The two men looked at each other and then back at Shane before Hawk began to speak. "You are only out here with us because Tigee said to bring you. As far as we know, no white man has ever come into the valley this way. Those assholes who try to steal our horses come in from the far north side. If they ever find out about this easier route, it would make it harder for our tribe to protect the horses." After saying this, the two Indians continued staring Shane down.

Shane stared back unsure of what to say, "Don't worry, guys, you have my word, I have no intentions of saying anything to anyone about how we got here."

JB clinched his jaw, "Mister, I haven't met too many white men who thought it was important to keep their word to an Indian." Then he turned to unload the horses.

Tory had been the last horse loaded, so now was the first one out. Shane took him aside to tighten his cinch. He was now feeling a little awkward, but he wasn't going to let JB or Hawk's bad attitudes get in the way of his enjoying this unique opportunity.

Shane mounted Tory then waited for Hawk and JB. Both of their horses were nice quality animals, but what caught Shane's attention was their saddles. They had no fenders or stirrups, and were scarcely more than a small pillow of soft leather stuffed with padding. The horses wore old Spanish-style bridles and bits, and both carried a long braided cord around their necks about the diameter of a man's large finger. The two Indians used this cord to lead their horses around.

Hawk noticed Shane looking at the equipment. "These were the type of saddles our ancestors rode. It's tradition to ride as our fore-fathers did when we come out to check the mustangs. I guess this seems ridiculous to you," Hawk snapped.

"No, not at all," Shane answered. "Actually, I think it is pretty cool." The two showed no reaction to this as they mounted their traditional Shoshone saddles and rode north with Shane and Tory following.

The only modern things the Indians had with them were their two-way radios, binoculars, and rifles equipped with long-range scopes mounted in scabbards on the side of the small saddles. Watching these two on horseback, Shane could picture in his mind what it must have looked like to see Shoshone warriors riding across this same land two hundred years ago.

They worked their way around the numerous deep ravines. These formations were a series of tiny canyons that all seemed to run together. "This looks like it would be a great place for the herd to hide out," Shane commented.

Hawk responded without a look, "We never see them here."

Farther ahead, the three came to a ridge. It did not appear to be very high on the side they were riding in on, but when they reached the top and looked down the other side it took Shane's breath away. It was a four-hundred-foot drop, and Shane could see for miles. There, running from east to west through the center of the valley below was the Big Wind River. Surrounding the river were plenty of trees and brush as well as scattered open meadows carpeted with thick green grass. *This is a paradise for wild horses*, thought Shane. To the southwest were the majestic Wind River Mountains. Beyond the basin they were now looking across and just to their north, one could see the snow-capped peaks of the Owl Creek Mountains. Shane knew about the geological layout of the area from the map at the museum. But actually being here and seeing it for himself was damn impressive. Between the ridge, where they stood, and these mountains were seemingly endless miles of untouched wilderness.

"How in the world do you know where to find them?"

Hawk answered in his usual short manner, "We'll start looking for signs at the river's bank and then track them from there." It took an hour to slowly work their way down to the river. When they finally got there, the two Indians told Shane to wait under a big tree by the water's edge. Shane nodded, climbed off Tory, and sat on a large rock. The two men rode off at a fast trot, one headed up river and the other down. After forty-five minutes, Shane began to wonder if the two had played a cruel joke by leaving him out here in the middle of nowhere. Soon after this thought, he heard a rider coming in fast. It was JB. He stopped for only a second, "Come on, white boy, Hawk found some tracks up river." Shane didn't appreciate the "boy" part, but he let it go as he mounted up and followed at a hurried gallop. After a mile of hard riding along the river's bank, JB held his hand high, signaling Shane to slow down. The tracks weren't hard to see, and it was obvious Hawk had gone ahead to find the herd.

JB turned and looked him in the eye with a scowl. "All right, slick, stay close and be quiet." Shane gave him a shit-eating grin and followed the Indian up a steep hill. When they reached the peak, Hawk was crouched there, pointing to a low area on the other side. Looking down in the meadow, Shane got his first glimpse of the horses. Immediately, he could feel his heartbeat quicken.

"Damn, Jacob, looks like I finally found them!" He must have unknowingly voiced it as JB looked at him.

"What did you say?"

"Nothing, man, I was just thinking out loud."

It was a large herd, bigger than Shane had imagined. There were at least seventy-five mustangs grazing in the grassy field of about thirty acres. The horses looked up from their feeding and began to get restless.

JB looked over at Hawk. "They can smell the white boy." Hawk quickly gave him a hard look. JB grinned as he corrected himself, "I mean they smell the white man."

Shane snarled, "What the hell's that supposed to mean?"

Hawk spoke in a firm voice before the two men had time to increase the tension building between them. "No offense, but JB's right, the herd knows you're not one of us. Every time they smell white men they're getting chased. Just sit still and be quiet. They'll get used to you and settle." Shane knew how keen and sensitive horses were, so it didn't surprise him that they were aware of the human presence even though the three men were out of sight.

He had seen a couple of wild herds before in his travels, but nothing like this one. These were healthy, vibrant, and much bigger than the other mustangs he'd encountered. About half of them were larger than Sloppy, and she was a nice stout horse. He noticed several mares with newborns by their sides. These mothers with their babies were in their own group, separated from the rest. He spotted a few yearlings playing in a shallow creek that ran through the middle of the low-lying pasture. The remainder of the horses were scattered over the large meadow, heads down, munching on the early summer grass.

Hawk tapped Shane on the shoulder and handed him a pair of binoculars. He pointed to a ridge across the pasture. Overlooking the herd was a magnificent stallion. He was an impressive blood bay with a black mane and tail and four white stockings. This charismatic horse was the epitome of great conformation, muscle, and class.

"That's Naatea-Poha," Hawk said. "He's thirteen years old and has been the lead stallion for the last ten years. He's the daddy to about two-thirds of those younger ones. We geld most of the colts at our yearly branding. But we always make sure there are at least three quality stallions in the herd. This keeps inbreeding from being a problem. That's one of the reasons, along with a good natural food source and warm winters here in the valley, they get so big and stay so healthy."

"He's one hell of a horse!" Shane commented as he studied the stallion through the binoculars. "What did you call him?"

Hawk smiled and politely repeated the Shoshone words, *Naatea-Poha.*

The last thing Shane wanted to do was irritate Hawk or JB with too many questions, but he reluctantly asked, "What does it mean?"

After a short pause, surprisingly it was JB who spoke. "Many years ago one of the foundation sires of our herd was called *Poha.* This word means 'power.' The old stories tell of *Poha* as a great horse that looked much like this one, who is his direct descendant. We usually just call this stallion by the first part of his name, *Naatea.* This word roughly translates to mean a blood relative."

Shane thought for a second. "So, his full name means that he is of the same bloodlines as *Poha* the powerful."

Hawk nodded with a smirk. "The Shoshone language can be tricky to translate into English, but basically, yes, that is what Naatea's full name means." He then told Shane to stay put while he and JB went down to get a good count.

Shane sat there and watched the herd in awe. They were incredible, and knowing about their history made them even more impressive. He felt privileged to be here witnessing these unique, free ranging horses, still existing as they had for centuries. It gave him a sense of inspiration he hadn't expected.

Suddenly, something spooked the herd. In an amazing example of unity, they banded together and moved at full speed toward the lead stallion, Naatea, before disappearing with him over the next hill.

When the two Shoshone returned, Shane asked, "What scared them?"

"Who knows," Hawk answered. "It could have been a bear they caught wind of. The truth is, they've been chased almost every week lately by those jerks from town, so it doesn't take much to set them off right now. We'll spend the afternoon looking for any traps they may have set."

Shane wondered aloud, "Why do these guys spend so much time out here trying to catch the horses?"

JB answered. "They used to only come up here a couple of times a year. It's always been a game for them to try to steal the mustangs. The sons of bitches think it is funny to piss us off this way. They know how important the horses are to our tribe."

"Do you have any idea why they're coming after the herd so often now?"

"We don't know," Hawk said. "But lately they've been a lot more aggressive. We already told you they shot over our heads with rifles last week. We had to ride up a steep slope to get away. That's when they sent their dogs to attack us. We had no choice, but to shoot a couple of the mongrels."

Shane was beginning to wish he'd brought his rifle. He'd left it at the cabin, figuring he wouldn't need it. Next time he would know better. "Where are we going now?"

Hawk replied, "We're riding to the north side of the valley, where the horse thieves always come in. If we see fresh tracks, we'll follow them to their trap. They usually set up stock panels in a place where they can use rock walls to funnel the horses into their traps. With *Naatea* at the lead, the mustangs are hard to trick. Still, if they get enough men on horseback, they could potentially catch a lot of them. That's why it's important for us to come up here every week."

Shane commented, "It still doesn't make any sense that these guys are spending so much time and money coming out here so often. Do you think there could be some other reason they want to get rid of the herd?"

"We can't figure it out," said Hawk. "Whether it is for fun, spite, or money, they sure are hell-bent on trying to catch our horses. We're worried that if they keep up this kind of pressure on the herd, the horses may leave this area in search of safer ground. The fact is they could not survive the winters if they didn't live in this protected valley."

The three men finally arrived at the north entrance. There were no fresh signs of the men from town today so the Mustangs were safe, at least for the time being. The trio rode back to the truck and trailer, satisfied the day was a success.

During the long, bumpy ride to the ranch, Shane, again, broke the silence. "With Naatea being as smart as he is, how do you catch the horses every year to brand the weanlings?"

Hawk hesitated to answer. After a brief pause, in a reluctant voice, he said, "We pen the herd early in the winter, before the roads become deep with snow. This is the only way in here that time of year. The north accesses that the white men use are impassable then. On this side of the canyon, there is a place that only we know about. It's the lowest area in the valley and is well hidden, even from an airplane. This protected area keeps its grass and other foliage longer than anywhere else in the valley. It is unlikely that the white men could find this place on their own, and Naatea is too clever to lead them to it.

"When it's branding time, everyone on the ranch comes out to help. JB and I will go out weeks earlier and set up feeders with grain and hay, so that the herd will get comfortable coming in. When we organize the branding, we do it Shoshone-style. Unlike the white men who would try to chase the mustangs into a trap, we are very patient. Sometimes it takes us two or three days to quietly move them into the meadow. When the horses do get into our secret valley, they are calm and settled.

"Once we have the pass closed off, we will go in quietly and set up sorting pens with portable stock panels. Only a few of us will do the actual branding. We take our time, so we don't upset the mustangs any more than we have to. When we are finished we take down the pens and leave the herd in the meadow with the pass still closed. We keep them there, so they can feed and put on weight to help get them through the winter.

"After a couple of weeks, we reopen the pass. We don't feed them any more after this. If we did, it might make them soft and spoil them, and they could lose their wild state. Then they'd be an easy catch for the wrong people."

When they got back to the ranch, Shane offered a handshake to each of them, but only Hawk reached out for Shane's hand. JB just turned to open the trailer. As soon as Tory was out, Shane started toward the barn.

He was almost there when he heard JB call, "Hey, white man!" Shane looked back and saw Tigee standing at the trailer with the other two. JB yelled out, "He wants you to go back out with us next week." Shane could tell the two Indians weren't happy about this, but they would do as the old man wanted.

Shane hollered back, "Just let me know when."

It had been a long day, and Shane was ready to eat a good meal and get some rest. As he started walking to his cabin from the barn, he looked at the mountains in the distance. He paused at the sight, and took in a long, deep breath. A heartfelt sense of satisfaction slowly overcame him. He had finally located the herd. This was a big step toward finally fulfilling Jacob's wish.

As he walked to his porch, he was startled to hear a voice, "Hello, mister." Tommy had watched him unload and was patiently sitting on the porch, waiting.

"Hey, bud, I didn't see you sitting there."

The young boy smiled, "You know how Indians are, if you don't watch out, we'll sneak right up on you."

Shane laughed at the joke and invited him inside. "What can I do for you?" he asked while he scrounged around the kitchen looking for his coffee cup.

Tommy wasted no time answering. "Mister, I was wondering if I could do some work for you. I asked you before about trading for more help with some horses I'm breaking. You make it look so easy. I'd really like to learn how you do it. Like I told you, I don't have any money, but I can clean, feed your horses, or do whatever you want."

Shane appreciated the kid's willingness to earn his way. "You meet me at the barn at seven sharp. I'll show you how to do the morning feedings. After that, I have some tack that needs cleaning. When you're done, we'll play with your horses."

"Yes, sir, I'll be there." With that said, the boy bounded out the door.

That night, Shane fell asleep early. He slept soundly until two a.m. when he was awakened by a dream. He guessed it was the crisp mountain air coming in through the open window that had him dreaming so vividly. He often dreamed about his family. The dreams were usually about familiar things that had actually happened in the past. Things like playing with the kids or reliving a conversation with Jen. He'd learned over time not to let them bother him. However, this one was different.

This time the images surrounding him were shockingly more three-dimensional. Jen stood in front of him, just as if in real life, pointing up to a high cliff. On the top of this cliff were at least twenty Indians mounted on horses. They were all wearing long head-dresses and their horses were painted with bright war paint. One of the warriors galloped his horse to the edge of the drop off, sliding to a stop at the last possible moment. He held a spear high over his head and shook it while he yelled out some native-sounding words. Then Shane looked back over at Jen and heard her say very clearly, "They're asking for your help." Never before, in his many dreams of Jennifer had her presence seemed so real, so absolutely physical. Shane inhaled deeply as her familiar, appealing scent filled the air around him. He slowly lifted his hand to touch her face, but she was standing just out of reach. Before he could ask her what the Indians wanted him to do, he abruptly woke up. Shane laid there in an almost panicked state of confusion for quite some time.

The dream jogged a long-forgotten memory of a similar one he had a few years ago, when his family was alive. He recalled the despair he'd felt during the dream, along with the odd message an Indian had spoken. "Stay on your path, and you'll find what you have lost."

Looking back now, he wondered if he'd had some kind of premonition of the terrible tragedy that changed his life.

If another person told him they were having these strange dreams and interpreting them this way, he would probably think they were off their rocker. But, this wasn't someone else, and he could not shake the feeling that there was some kind of an eerie connection between the two dreams. It took him a while to put this all out of his mind and finally fall back asleep.

Chapter 11

The next morning, Tommy was in the barn waiting. He already had one of Shane's saddles sitting on a rail and was cleaning it as Shane walked in. "Mornin' bud, follow me and I'll show you what else I want you to do." After Shane gave Tommy his instructions, he told the boy he'd be back in a couple of hours to help him with his horses.

Just as Shane started to leave, the boy pointed to something lurking near the barn. It was still dark outside, and all Shane could see was some movement in the early morning mist. "What are you pointing at, Tommy?"

"They were following you over to your porch last night, too."

"What the hell is it?" Shane asked quizzically.

Tommy laughed, "I think they may want to eat you. I guess they never tasted a white man."

Then Shane saw in the dim morning light what was stalking him. It was the two wolf pups he had seen Tigee trying to hand-feed.

Shane turned back to Tommy, "They wouldn't really attack me, would they?"

Tommy grinned, "No sir. They're not like that, but they sure are curious about you."

Shane hadn't noticed the animals following him. He decided he would keep an eye out for these two from now on.

While walking home he saw Tigee putting food out for the dogs, but, as usual, they kept their distance. Shane watched as Tara's grandfather sat down on his porch steps in hopes the animals would come close. The pups continued to maintain their cautious space and waited patiently until he went inside before they approached the bowls and scarfed down the scraps.

Shane sat down on his own steps to watch the dogs. They kept looking over in his direction while holding their noses high and sniffing the air. Shane gazed down at the ground so he would not be looking directly at them. Soon he could feel the wolf-dogs moving closer. The two carefully edged their way toward him until they were only five yards away.

Tigee came back outside and watched from his porch. The two then laid down a few feet in front of him, still sniffing the air. Shane slowly raised his head and looked into their yellow wolf eyes. This made them nervous enough to quickly stand and trot away. The old Indian clapped his hands, gave Shane a thumbs-up, and yelled, "You got them close, hey!" Shane smiled and waved back, then he went inside.

After a quick cup of coffee, he jumped into his truck and drove to the nearby reservation town of Crowheart. He had seen a pay phone there the other day, and since his cell phone didn't have any signal out here, this would be his main line of communication with the outside world. There was a phone at Tara's and her grandfather's house, but Shane felt awkward asking to use it. Besides, the smallness of their house created a privacy problem.

He had two calls to make this morning. The first was to Terry. He had not checked in for some time now and wanted to make sure everything was okay at the farm.

"Things are going well," Terry assured him, "The business is doing fine, and I have everything under control." The old friends chatted for a few minutes, and Shane thanked him again for all he was doing.

His next call was to Mr. Jensen. "How are you, Shane? Are you staying out of trouble out there?"

Shane replied with a laugh, "Yes, sir, so far I am, but it's still pretty early in the day." The two kidded around a minute more before the sound of Shane's voice changed into a more serious tone. "I'm telling you sir, there has to be more going on in the valley than just some white men chasing mustangs to tick off the Shoshone. I'm beginning to wonder if someone could be trying to get rid of the herd for some other purpose. I may be grasping at straws, but someone sure as hell wants these horses gone, and they're going to an awful lot of trouble to make it happen."

"It sounds like living on the reservation is making you a little paranoid."

"You might be right, but I want to make sure my mare is going to be okay when I set her free. From what I've seen so far, I'm not too sure she will. I know you have a lot of friends in the area, and I'd really appreciate it if you could, discreetly, check around town and see what you can find out."

Mr. Jensen remained quiet for a moment and then replied, "I'll start by talking to my cousin who works at City Hall. If there is anything happening concerning that land out there, he'll know about it. I'll get back in touch with you if I come up with anything."

Shane then gave him Tigee's phone number. "He'll let me know if you call. I'll get back to you as soon as I can." When Shane returned to the ranch, Tommy was just finishing up his chores. The two spent the rest of the morning working with the three young horses that Tommy was training. One of the horses was, of course, the big roan gelding. He was doing well. By the end of the session, Tommy was able to ride him around the corral without Shane's help.

The second horse was also a gelding. This one had a naturally good mind and was a good, safe horse for the boy.

The third horse was an Appaloosa mare. She would be more of a challenge. She was very sensitive, and, if you even blinked your eye wrong, it seemed to scare her. This one would need a ton of preparation before she could be saddled for the first time.

Tommy watched intensely as Shane skillfully worked with the mare in the corral. In about an hour Shane took the filly out of the pen and gave her to Tommy. "That's about all she can take for the day," he told the boy. "I want you to turn her out, then come to the barn."

When Tommy returned, Shane was sitting on Sloppy and

holding Tory, who was also saddled up. He handed him Tory's reins, "Mount up."

The kid's eyes opened wide. "I can ride him?"

"Yep, go ahead and climb on. The best way for you to learn how to put a good foundation on a horse is to ride a well-finished one. Then you will be able to see and feel what it is you're after."

The boy already knew how to properly sit on a horse and displayed some pretty good hands and rein control. One of the things Tommy still needed to learn was how to position a horse for what he was asking it to do.

Shane started with some instruction that would help Tommy get a better feel for what Tory's feet were doing underneath him. Then, from atop Sloppy, Shane demonstrated how he could separately control the horse's hips, ribs, shoulders, and head.

"In the beginning, we teach our horses how to control all of their different parts individually. Once a horse can do this, we're able, step-by-step, to break down our maneuvers, much like a dancer learns step-by-step how to put together a complete routine."

Tommy couldn't believe how much control he had on Tory. Soon, Shane had him maneuvering the horse sideways, backing him in circles, and moving into position to open and close gates, all with ease. Shane was extremely impressed with how he absorbed all this in only one lesson. "Okay, bud, I think we better stop now before I overload you with too much information." Tommy was a natural and, even though Tory had never left a walk, the boy was bubbling over with excitement at what he had learned. Tommy's enthusiasm brought a smile to Shane's face. "I've shown you some pretty cool stuff today, haven't I?"

"Yes sir!"

"Well, now it's your turn to show me something pretty cool."

"What do you mean?"

"I want you to show me a place you think is very special on this reservation. Take me somewhere with incredible scenery — a place where you wouldn't normally take a visitor from Tennessee."

Tommy thought for a second, then suddenly his face lit up. "I know just the spot."

They rode for quite a while and talked about horses, school, and how much the boy liked living on the ranch.

Tommy asked, "Did you notice, they're following you again?"

"Who's following me?"

"The wolves," Tommy said as he pointed to an opening that ran parallel to the trail. They were now four miles from the ranch and Shane was surprised to see the dogs here.

"Do they usually follow you away from the ranch?"

"No sir. They aren't following me, they're following you! Maybe they think you're their ma," he said with a grin.

The two rode for at least another hour before arriving at the location Tommy had picked out. What a scene! It was a large, clear pool situated in line with one of the many Alpine streams that flowed through the area. It had a waterfall on the far side of it steadily splashing into the pool, as well as the creek that ran in one end of it and out the other. There were large shade trees scattered about and you could see the majestic mountains in the background.

"Is this good enough for you?"

"You did okay, bud."

They tethered the horses and decided to go down to the water for a quick cooling swim, before making the long ride back. They stripped down to their skivvies and plunged into the clear, refreshing pond. They'd only been in the water a few minutes when Shane noticed the horses snorting loudly as they pulled back on the reins that were loosely tied to some small trees close by.

At that moment, Tommy spoke in a high-pitched voice, "Mister Shane, look!" He pointed at a large rock about fifty yards behind the horses. There, crouched down in a stalking position, was a full-grown mountain lion. Just then, the two horses broke away from the saplings and took off in a panic.

"Oh, shit," Shane hollered, as the cat jumped off his perch in hot pursuit. Shane had brought a rifle, but it was in his scabbard on Tory, who was now running for his life. Tommy and Shane began to yell and splash, trying to break the cougar's charge at the horses. A helpless feeling came over Shane as he watched his two horses inadvertently corner themselves against a rock wall near the pond. The cougar had slowed his approach and was moving in for a kill.

All of a sudden, out of nowhere, the two wolves came leaping down off the six-foot-high rock wall. They positioned themselves between the horses and the big cat, snarling and baring their fangs. Shane watched in disbelief as the two dogs attacked the cougar, who wasn't about to give up his dinner easily. It was a vicious battle, but the dogs had the cat outnumbered and worked well as a team. The three moved around fighting for several minutes. Finally the cougar decided he'd had enough and ran off in defeat. The brother wolves were victorious, but both had cuts and were bloody from head to toe. As Shane and Tommy jumped out of the pond to catch the terrified horses, the tired dogs sorely eased down to the pool for a drink.

Shane gave the horses to Tommy and gestured to him to let them get a drink also. The boy watched, in amazement, as Shane walked right up to the wolves that were lying down, catching their breath next to the creek. He leaned down between the two, with each of them only a couple feet away. "I owe you guys one," he told them, as he looked closer and saw their injuries weren't too severe. "When we get home, you're each getting a big steak." Then he stood up, still in only his undershorts, and walked back to get dressed for the ride home.

"That cougar must have been awfully hungry," Tommy exclaimed, as they were mounting up.

"Well, I think the dogs taught it a lesson. I doubt it'll try that again," Shane replied.

The wolves stayed closer to Shane and Tommy on the way home. "We need to come up with some names for 'em," Shane said, as they rode.

"Yes sir, no one around the ranch has given them names, but I think they deserve them now. And since they think you're their ma, you should be the one to do it."

"Very funny," Shane said, as they approached the entrance to the ranch.

Before Shane ate his dinner, he did as he had promised. He thawed out two sirloins for the wolves. When he walked out onto the porch, he was surprised to see the two lying there. He set down the steaks with a bowl of water and then relaxed in the old rocker next to his front door. The dogs wasted no time in gobbling up the meat. After finishing their meal, they lay down only a few feet from Shane's chair, keeping just out of reach.

"What am I going to call you guys?" Both of the pups perked up their ears. "You two are always sneaking around like a couple of outlaws, so I think I'll call you," while he pointed to the black and brown one first, "Butch. That's short for Butch Cassidy. And you," he pointed to the gray one, "I'll call you, Jessie. That's short for Jessie James. Those were two famous outlaws from the Old West," he told them. The two wolf dogs cocked their heads and looked at him like he was crazy. But Shane took it as though they were pleased with their new names. He laughed at the curious look they had given him and then went inside.

The next couple of mornings Shane and Tommy worked hard with Tommy's three young horses. The two geldings were doing well under saddle. Tommy was doing most of the riding, but when it appeared that he might be getting in over his head, Shane would climb on the horses and demonstrate for him what he needed to do.

Although both of the geldings were coming along nicely, the Appaloosa mare was much more complicated. She was smart, but her mistrust of humans made it difficult to get her confidence. Without confidence, her insecurities made her dangerous. She was quick and athletic, which are great things to have in a horse when they're working for you, but bad if she used them against you. One nice thing about her was that she wasn't aggressive. She was dangerous only because of what she was capable of doing to a person if she felt threatened. Shane knew from experience, once they got her trust, she would make a nice horse. He also knew she would need someone with his skills and experience to get her going in the right direction. He would have to do the foundation work with this one before Tommy could deal with her.

Every day, after they finished with the three young horses, Shane would put Tommy on Tory or Sloppy for riding lessons. The boy was learning every day how many buttons and how much control a rider can have with a well-trained horse. Tommy was taking to all this like a fish to water, and Shane enjoyed watching his progress, as much as Tommy enjoyed the instruction.

Most of the Indians at the ranch tried to be inconspicuous as they watched the sessions progress. They still didn't talk to him much. However, some of them began waving as they walked past him on his porch in the evenings.

The two dogs were now spending every night on Shane's porch. He would sit in his chair and talk to them at the end of the day. Butch would now let Shane gently scratch him on top of his head, but that was all. Jessie would only stretch out his neck to take food from Shane's hand without any contact. Shane was careful not to force the issue, and the dogs seemed to be slowly gaining confidence in him. Soon Tommy had all the Indians joking about Shane being the pup's ma. Tigee seemed to get a kick out of how the dogs had taken to Shane.

One day he remarked. "I was right about you." When Shane asked him what he meant, Tigee just smiled and said, "I knew you were different," as he turned and walked away.

The week had flown by, and Shane was looking forward to his trip back out to the river to check on the herd. He was supposed to meet Hawk and Johnny Badger on Sunday morning.

It was Friday, and Tommy had plans with his mom today, so the two geldings and the Appaloosa mare were getting the day off from their training. Shane decided to pack a lunch and take Sloppy out for a long ride to check out the countryside. He knew it was important to keep the mustang in good condition, so she could keep up with the herd when he set her free.

It was a pleasant morning for a long ride, and since he was able to get an early start, he decided to head northwest toward the stream with the large pool that Tommy had shown him. The two wolf-dogs weren't anywhere to be seen this morning. *Hopefully, they'll pick up my trail and catch up with me later on,* he figured. Their company would be a welcome comfort. He made sure his rifle was loaded before he packed it on his saddle.

The first part of the six-mile ride took him through some open country in the foothills. He noticed a herd of elk grazing in a low area and spooked a couple of mule deer farther up the trail. Sloppy perked up her ears and began getting anxious as they approached some large pines near the edge of a forest. Shane moved her to a high area and pulled out his binoculars to see if he could spot what was worrying her. He scanned the edge of the woods and quickly caught sight of a large grizzly and her two cubs moving east along the tree line.

"Easy girl," he told her, "you're okay. They're moving away from us."

Shane smiled. It felt good to see nature untamed like this. He once again found himself wishing he could have shown this country to Jacob and Tina, but he quickly put the thought out of his mind. The bears stayed on the other side of the hill, and the mare finally relaxed as Shane rode her into the woods.

There were large spruce and fir trees scattered everywhere. The rolling hills added to the beauty, and the woods became thicker as he rode on. The air was fresh and crisp, while the popping in his ears told him he was gradually riding toward a higher elevation. Soon, he could hear the sound of running water, and it wasn't long before he saw the creek's edge. He knew from here the pool was only about a half mile up the narrow stream.

Two more mule deer having their morning drink jumped into the brush, disappearing in a flash. He looked up and saw a bald eagle circling high above him. It was a large male with his distinct white head and tail feathers making him easy to identify. The eagle was probably looking for a trout in the pool just ahead. Shane had to

ride away from the stream's edge to get around a thick area of brush
and young saplings that bordered the creek. He knew when he made
it around this thick patch, he would be able to see his destination.

He was about halfway down a small hill when he rounded the
thicket and caught sight of the waterfall. The relaxing sound of rushing water made this picture even more serene. He stopped his mare
and took a deep breath of the clean mountain air while he stared at
this amazing place and soaked it all in.

It was then that he noticed the outline of a horse tied to a small
tree next to the stream. Shane looked through his binoculars and, to
his surprise, saw a woman move from behind the waterfall and dive
into the pool. As she climbed out of the water, Shane realized she
was an Indian who was wearing very little. He slowly dropped his
binoculars, feeling a little embarrassed for looking so long. He knew
he should leave and also knew he shouldn't have another glance,
but the truth was he found himself totally entranced by this young
native woman in her element.

Her skin was light bronze, and her hair was long and jet black.
Her figure was sleek and athletic. She wore only a dark halter top
with black panties, which were pulled up high on her waist. This
only complemented the curves of her trim, shapely body. Shane
again made an effort to put the glasses away, but he was captivated.
He felt like a guy he'd seen in a comedy, who had a devil sitting on
one shoulder telling him to look, while an angel sat on the other,
shaking her finger at him. For now, the devil was winning, so he
hastily raised the binocs for one last glimpse before he left. The
young woman dove into the pool and then walked up a narrow rock
slope by the edge. Her legs were lean and muscular and flexed in
good condition when she walked out of the glistening water. The
girl was now standing with her back to Shane as she reached behind
and squeezed the dripping wet out of her long black hair. Shane
breathed deeply and swallowed the lump in his throat while the guilt
started to get to him again.

He was about to stop looking, when the woman turned and for
the first time her face came into view. She couldn't see him, but

Shane realized immediately it was Tara. Her beautiful native features only helped to accentuate her alluring physique, and Shane felt ashamed and infatuated all at the same time. Seeing her like this, stirred up feelings that had been shut down in him since the loss of his wife almost two years ago. Shane thought this part of him was lost and gone forever and wasn't sure how to feel about it. However, out of respect for Tara, he decided he should leave now.

He quietly got up on his horse, slowly backed her into the shadows, and then turned the mare around and rode toward home.

Chapter 12

On the ride back, he could not get the image of Tara out of his mind. She was like a song that was stuck in his head. Shane smiled and thought to himself, "It's good to feel like a man again."

He was less than halfway home when he looked back and noticed Butch and Jessie trotting behind. "I swear, you two are like ghosts the way you sneak around!" There's no telling how long they'd been following, but he was glad for their company.

The comfortable morning temperature had slipped away and now the heat of the afternoon was beginning to wear on Sloppy. Noticing the white lather beginning to appear on her neck, Shane decided to stop and rest the horse. They were halfway home at this point and had already traveled a good ten miles since he left the ranch. He had stopped before he left the creek's edge so Sloppy could have a drink, but he didn't stay there long. To be honest, he was worried about Tara riding up on him after her swim and he was still feeling awkward about watching her.

The two wolves were also in need of a break and quickly found the shade of an old cedar tree to lie under. Shane noticed a bowl-shaped rock near where they had settled and poured them some water from his canteen. He felt privileged they had accepted him, and figured, someday, he would try to return to check on them and the mare. "It's a nice thought anyway," he mumbled.

Suddenly, a loud snort from Sloppy, who was merely clearing her nostrils, moved Shane's attention over to her. The sight of the little mare standing in the shade triggered a memory of a forgotten afternoon with his kids. He'd been giving Jacob and Tina a riding lesson on Sloppy and recalled how proud he felt watching them ride. After directing them to take the mare into the barn to unsaddle her, he worked another young horse nearby.

Tina climbed on a bucket so she could reach the mare's back with her brush, but slipped and hit her head on the floor.

Jacob ran outside and yelled, "Dad, Tina fell and she's hurt!" He remembered running to the barn to find Sloppy gently sniffing her as she lay, crying.

"Come here, baby girl," Shane crooned, as he picked her up. Tina quickly latched onto her daddy, throwing her arms around his neck and her legs around his waist. "Shhhh, you're okay. With that hard head of yours, I'm a little worried about my barn floor, though." Tina cracked a grin as Shane gently pulled her off and looked into her eyes, "I've told you a hundred times, you have to be tough to be a horsewoman."

Tina, now with a tearful laugh, playfully slapped his chest, "Quit it, Daddy!" During all of this, Sloppy never stopped nuzzling her.

Shane sat quietly in the shade next to the dogs, and wiped away some moisture that had sneaked out of his eyes. Looking over at Sloppy, it began to sink in how much he would really miss the little mare when he finally did set her free. But, before he could even consider letting her go, he'd have to figure out some way to help sort out the problems concerning the herd's safety. Whatever those idiots from town were up to must be wrong, and Shane was determined to get to the bottom of it so he could stop them.

As he rode onto the ranch, he noticed a familiar truck parked in front of Tigee's, and he saw Mr. and Mrs. Jensen sitting on the front porch.

"Hey, stranger," Mr. Jensen said as Shane rode up to the house and greeted them. Both of the dogs had stolen out of sight. Shane stepped down off his saddle just as Mrs. Jensen came out to greet him with a hug. Mr. Jensen followed with a strong, friendly handshake.

It was Mrs. Jensen who spoke first, "Your friend, Mr. Tigee, says you've been pretty busy out here helping with some young horses. I told him you were definitely the right man for the job. I hope you don't mind that I told him a little bit about your credentials." Shane shrugged his shoulders.

"I told her to keep quiet," said Mr. Jensen, "but she enjoyed bragging about your clinics to Tigee."

"That's okay," Shane said, "I wasn't trying to hide anything. It just never came up."

"Well, I think they should know how lucky they are to have you here helping with their horses," she said.

"All right woman, that's enough," Mr. Jensen scolded. "Why don't you sit and talk with Mr. Tigee, while Shane and I unsaddle the mustang?" The old Indian motioned for her to sit next to him on the porch.

Mr. Jensen walked to the barn with Shane and looked around to make sure they were alone. "I drove out here because I wanted to tell you in person what I've found out."

"Thanks for coming. I was going to call you Monday if I hadn't heard from you."

"Well, son, I talked to my cousin and learned something that might interest you. He told me that there was a permit pulled to do some preliminary testing on some private land adjacent to the Indian's Wind River Valley."

Shane, puzzled, asked, "Testing for what?"

"Oil," Mr. Jensen answered. "Vince Nethers owns a lot of land that borders the reservation and has a long-term lease on a bunch more property beyond what he owns. I told you about him before. Vince is the largest cattleman in the area and for years has used all that land to graze his cows. I always figured he had his eye on a bigger prize in those hills. I heard he'd spent a fortune a couple of years ago testing around that whole area."

"Did he find anything?"

"They did find some oil, but apparently it wasn't a big enough reserve to pay for pumping it out. My cousin said there was a rumor going around the office back then that the geologists believed there could be a real mother lode a bit farther to the southeast. That would put a lot of oil in the area of the valley where those mustangs live. Nethers tried to put an end to these rumors two years ago. He claimed the tests had been a big waste of money. He whined all over town about how it almost bankrupted him."

"It sounds like you don't believe him," Shane replied.

Mr. Jensen shrugged his shoulders. "I know I'm just guessing here, but what if he's been buying time, you know, waiting till the rumors die down while he tries to confirm the bigger deposit. Then all he has to do is figure out how to hoodwink the Indians into some kind of a deal to give him control over that particular part of their land. If he could get a lease done before the Indians figure out what's going on, he could make millions."

Shane rubbed the back of his neck, thought for a few moments before he asked, "If Nethers is trying to keep this possible mother lode a secret, why is he bothering to get a permit to look for it?"

"Well, there's no way he could bring the specialized equipment along with that many people into this area without it being noticed. He would also need fuel, supplies, and lodging for the crew. Besides, I don't think the oil companies would come in and do this kind of thing if they didn't believe it was legal."

Mr. Jensen paused to clear his throat, "Maybe he can't hide what he is doing, but he can sure mislead everyone about where he's testing. What if the testing on his land is just a smoke screen so he can sneak the equipment over his property line onto the reservation? If he can prove the oil is where he thinks it is, he'll probably wait a while longer, until the rumors die down again, and then try to con the Indians into a lease. This is all speculation now, but I know ole Vince. He is pretty smart. I think he may have a long drawn-out plan to make all this happen. If I am guessing right, he is just trying to make sure the oil is really there, and then he'll start to put his scheme into motion."

Shane listened intently as Mr. Jensen went on, "Vince is a very influential man with a lot of money and political connections. If my theory is correct, he is the one man in the area who could pull this off. If he can't trick or force the Indians to sign a lease, he'll probably try to buy his way into it. One way or another, this guy will stop at nothing to get to that oil if it's there."

Shane thought for a minute, "Okay, if this guy is as smart as you say he is, he must realize how important the herd and their grazing land is to the Shoshone. He would know the first thing he has to do is to get rid of those mustangs. Once they're out of the way, he probably figures the Indians would be more willing to lease him the valley." Mr. Jensen winked and nodded in agreement.

Shane took a deep breath and rolled his eyes. "If you're right, I've really stepped into a hornet's nest."

Both men stood quietly, looking down at the ground, contemplating the situation. A minute later Shane looked up. "We're really assuming an awful lot, so it would probably be best if we sit on this information for now and not say anything until we have a chance to look into it further. What we need is some proof."

"I agree." Mr. Jensen complied. "If it's true, with the kind of money that's involved, it might be hard to know who you can trust. I've seen Vince Nethers operate before, and he would have no qualms about stepping hard on a few toes to get what he wants." Shane bit his lip and nodded his head in agreement.

"Sir, thank you for all the information, but I think I'd feel better if you didn't go nosing around anymore. The last thing I want to do is cause you and your wife any trouble."

"Well, I won't pry into it unless you ask for my help. But I want you to understand, I'm not scared of that SOB Nethers. If I see anything unusual going on around town, I'll let you know." Shane smiled at the old man's candor as they left the barn and walked over to Tigee's.

The two men were almost there when they noticed Tara riding through the compound gate returning from her swim. She saw her grandfather and Mrs. Jensen sitting on the porch and waved to them as she rode by. Then, she gave Shane and Mr. Jensen a smile and rode toward the barn.

The old man slapped Shane on the back, "That is one pretty

lady, right there. If I was about a hundred years younger, she'd be in trouble." Both of them laughed as they got to the porch steps.

"I hope my wife hasn't bent your ear too much," he motioned to Tigee.

"No, we had a nice talk."

Mr. Jensen then suggested they should start for home. The two said their good-byes and left. Shane smiled and nodded at Tigee, as he turned to leave. He was still feeling a little embarrassed about what happened at the pool and wanted to go before Tara walked up.

"Wait, Shane!" the old Indian called. "I want to invite you to a party my friends are having for me at Fort Washakie tomorrow night. It's my eighty-sixth birthday. I'd like you to come."

Shane really didn't want to go, but he felt obligated to accept. He figured he'd make a quick appearance and then come back to the ranch as soon as he could slip away.

"Good, then you can go along with Tara and me. We'll head out around six."

Again, Shane was on the spot, so he reluctantly agreed. As he turned to leave, he realized Tara was standing only a couple feet away. "Hi, Shane, nice day for a ride, wasn't it?"

"Yes, ma'am, it sure was."

Then she looked at him with her deep blue eyes and said, "Did you see anything interesting out there?"

His face turned a light shade of red, "I always see interesting things when I ride through this country." Tara grinned, patted him on his shoulder, and went inside. Shane closed his eyes and thought, *I sure hope she didn't see me at that pool.* The idea made him blush again, so he quickly walked home before anyone noticed. He went inside and cleaned up then ambled out to sit on his porch. Jessie and Butch were resting comfortably next to his chair.

Most of the Indians who worked on the ranch were participating in a roundup in a large field next to the compound. They were separating calves from their mothers for weaning. Once they were separated, they'd move them up the road to another field.

It was a nice afternoon, and Shane began to doze. The last thing he heard was the distant bellow of cows, calling each other as the Indians moved the calves away from their mothers. The sounds lulled him into a deep sleep. When he woke an hour later, he slowly peeked out from under the baseball cap he'd tilted over his face and noticed eight sets of little eyes peering at him through the rail. Next he heard a giggle followed by a whispered, "Shut up!" The dogs must have left the porch when the children arrived. Since Butch and Jessie were familiar with the kids, they didn't bother to alert Shane before slipping away.

Shane sat there a little longer, still feigning sleep, then he said in a deep low voice, "I've been known to eat little people when I'm really hungry." The eight stood up tall and froze, their eyes wide open. He could see they were thinking about running away, so he opened his eyes and smiled. The group included six boys and two girls between the ages of about five to nine years, with the two little girls appearing to be the youngest. Shane looked them over and seeing the worry in their eyes, spoke to them. "Does anybody here like chocolate chip cookies? I've got a whole bag inside." All but one of the little girls nodded their heads, yes, and grinned from ear to ear. "Well, come up on the porch. I'll go get the cookies."

When he came out, they were all eagerly waiting with their hands out, except for the youngest girl who was still standing in the yard. Shane looked down from the porch and offered her one of the treats. She avoided eye contact and didn't respond. "She's real shy," one of the older boys said.

"Here take this to her." She smiled as the boy handed her a cookie and in no time she ate it, as had the others.

"You know, we have enough people here to play a game of touch football if you guys want. All nodded yes, except the shy little girl. When he left home, he decided to bring one thing from each of his family members. This included Jacob's football, Tina's favorite doll, and one of Jen's old pillows, which he used to sleep on every night. Playing with these kids would make good use of Jacob's football.

For the next hour Shane played hard with the kids, he even got the shy little girl to join in. With the others pretending to miss her, she made a touchdown while laughing all the way to the makeshift end zone. The last play of the game, Shane was the quarterback. He halfheartedly attempted an escape as all the kids, even the ones on his own team, ended up tackling him in a roar of screams and laughter. As he got up and brushed himself off, he noticed Tara and her grandfather standing on their porch laughing and cheering the kids on. He gave the two a grin and then high-fived all the children before he picked up Jacob's football and walked back to his house.

Chapter 13

It was Saturday, the day of the big party. Although Shane wasn't into crowds these days, he didn't want to let Tigee down. After taking it easy that afternoon, he was ready at six. As they climbed into the truck, Tara remarked, "Since my grandfather is a tribal leader, most of the tribe will be at Fort Washakie for the event. My two brothers are already in town setting up for the party. There will be plenty of food, drink, and even a live band. Most of the tribe pitched in money for it." She looked at Shane with a mischievous glint in her eye. "There will even be a few other white people from town, so you won't stand out too much."

Shane grinned back at her, "Where have your brothers been? I haven't seen them."

"My grandfather sent them on a two-week hunting trip. He told them to go because they got into a fight with those same guys you and I had trouble with. He decided the best way to cool things down would be to send them away. You'll be seeing them at the ranch now. They both have houses in the compound. My oldest brother is married, and two of the kids you were playing ball with yesterday are his."

As they drove, Tara spoke again, "I hope you don't mind, but my grandfather wants to go to a place we call Red Moon Ridge. It's a tradition for him on his birthday."

Tigee explained, "My father was also the shaman of our tribe. He would take me to this place often, and always on the day of my first day. I have some good memories of those times I spent with him watching the sun go down." Shane felt a little awkward being part of this family tradition, but the old man seemed to want him along.

Tara drove down a dirt road Shane had never seen before. When they arrived, it was easy to see why this spot was so revered by Tigee. It was another slice of paradise. The cliff sat high above the valley. Below you could see for miles. The ridge faced northwest and on the horizon were the now familiar Owl Creek Mountains. "Wow," was all Shane could say, as he approached the edge and looked at the view.

"The sun will be setting soon," Tigee said. "You and my grand-daughter will stay here." Then he turned and walked down a narrow trail heading toward a specific place only he knew.

Tara leaned back against a tree and began to speak. "As a younger man he came up here often. Now it is very important to him that either I or one of my brothers bring him here on his birthday. He prays and says he seeks advice from our ancestors. He must think a lot of you to want to show you this."

Shane took a deep breath and looked across the valley below.

"This is the kind of view most people only get to see in pictures or movies, myself included, until I came on this trip." The two sat quietly and enjoyed the brilliant colors of the sunset, then Shane looked at her inquisitively. "I've noticed you spend a lot of time at work."

"Yeah, I guess I do."

"What is it that consumes so much of your life?"

"I'm a teacher and administrator for our schools."

"You must really like it."

"Yes, it's my purpose. Educating our kids is the only way our people can better themselves. The Shoshone nation has many bright capable people, but for so long they have been held back because the lack of resources has not allowed them to get a quality education. The funding that most schools in this area get seems to dwindle down to almost nothing before it makes it out here. Because of this, the opportunities for our children to make it to college are not very good."

"You seem to have earned a degree."

"I was fortunate enough to have a mother who had gone to college to become a nurse. She came back to help our people in the old

clinic that's still on the reservation. She had been awarded a government scholarship given out to the Indians in the 1960s. Most of
the Indians given the opportunity to go to college do not have the
foundation of learning skills it takes to succeed at a university.

"I have goals to upgrade our schools at the elementary and high-
school levels so our children are more prepared for college. In return,
they will be able to send their own children to a good university."

Shane was impressed with the depth of Tara's commitment and
purpose in her life. He was gaining a new respect for her and her
people's struggle. Unfortunately, many of the Indians still lived here
in poverty, but with the efforts of tribal members like Tara, things
were bound to improve. In fact he felt a little guilty about how self-
serving his own life had become lately.

Right now, he was focused on seeing through his promise to his
son. But maybe, when all this was over, he would take some time in
his life and get involved with a worthwhile cause of some kind. The
more he found out about Tara, the more intriguing she became, and
the more he realized she was an intelligent, strong, selfless woman
with much to offer.

Shane's growing admiration for her left him feeling a bit uneasy.
Adding to his concern was the notion that she also seemed to be
showing more interest in him. Tara still didn't know about his family, or much else about him for that matter. The last thing he wanted
from her or any of the Shoshone was for them to feel sorry for him.
But most of all he did not want to lead Tara on. Even while Jen was
still alive, he often looked at and appreciated other women, just like
any man does. But, in their many years of marriage, he never seri-
ously considered crossing that vital line of trust and commitment. He
figured it was normal for a person who had survived a long-time
spouse to struggle with moving past this kind of strong devotion to
them. In one sense, taking this enormous step some day would mean
having to let go of his old life and the powerful loyalties he still carried deep inside. He hoped in the future he would be able to move
beyond all this. For now, it just seemed too difficult and complicated
to even consider.

After all, his plan was only to be out here until he could set his mare free, then he and Tory would be heading back to Tennessee. He knew Tara's life was very busy and full of purpose, so he reasoned that their attraction toward each other was probably no more than an innocent flirtation that he was making more of than he should. "Hell, all this is probably just in my own head anyway," he said quietly to himself.

Tara was well aware that the men here on the reservation had all but given up on pursuing her. Many of the young men in the tribe wondered if she thought she was too good for them. On the contrary, she was committed to them in a way they could not comprehend, and because of this, her personal life had been pushed aside.

It was not a carefree thing for Tara to finally admit to herself that she did have an attraction to Shane. It embarrassed her as she realized he was the first man in a long time that could inadvertently bring out the mild flirtatious side of her personality. She could not ignore the fact that her mood seemed to be uplifted when she was around him. But she would listen more to her practical side, which told her that this was someone who would never fit into her world. Even so, she couldn't help but admire him as the brave man who had stood up for her that day in town. Although she wondered about his guarded past, she believed he was a man of honor and integrity. She also held him in high regard for his strong commitment to keep a promise he had made to someone involving setting his mustang free.

It still seemed a little strange that he had sacrificed so much time and energy to accomplish this. Perhaps, someday, they'd become close enough friends for him to tell her his secret, along with why, at times, he seems so lost and faraway in his thoughts. For now, she would respect his privacy and not ask any personal questions.

The ridge she and her grandfather brought him to see would be inspiring any time of day. But sitting here watching the sun set gave Shane an almost spiritual feeling. The two sat quietly mesmerized,

watching the bright orange sky in the west as the day faded away
into dusk.

After the sun finally disappeared behind the mountains, Shane
interrupted the silence again by asking Tara a question that had been
on his mind since the first day he met Tigee. "Why does your grandfather call me, *Tahotay*? He has called me this several times, and I
can't help but wonder what it means."

Tara took a deep breath and looked down for a moment. Then
she gave him a quick glance and again shifted her eyes away. Shane
patiently waited for her to reply. Tara inhaled one more hesitant
breath before answering, "Tahotay is a mythical creature that according to our legend has appeared at different points in our tribe's
history to help our people during times of crisis. The older generation describes this creature as part human and part horse. Since the
early 1700s, our tribe has been considered a horse culture. It has always been believed that horses were sent here to help us survive,
and it is our responsibility to care for these animals. Knowing this,
you can understand why such a creature appears in the old stories."

"Why does your grandfather call me this thing? He called me
this the first time he saw me, before he even knew I was good with
horses."

Again, Tara shifted her eyes away, and hesitated before looking
at him, "This is where it may get a little weird to you. For a few years
now, my grandfather has had a reoccurring dream. He calls it a vision.
In his vision, a *Tahotay*, in human form, comes to save our wild herd
of horses, and in the process also helps our people find a better life.

"I know this all sounds pretty far-fetched to you, but my grandfather is worried about both the future of our people and the survival
of our horses. He believes, as I do, that these horses are a strong link
to our past, and he passionately feels that if we lose our past we lose
who we are as a people. In essence, we lose our very soul as a tribe.
If our past is lost to us, then so is the bond that holds us together. My
grandfather is an old man, and his whole life has been dedicated to
preserving these things. Our herd is a big part of all this. He wants
nothing more than to know they are safe before he dies. For gener-

ations, my family has been responsible for the herd, and now the horses' future is in question."

Shane asked, again, "So what does this *Tohotay* have to do with me?"

Tara looked into Shane's eyes, "He sees you as the *Tahotay* in his dreams and believes the mustang mare from our herd has brought you here to fulfill his vision."

Shane shook his head. "Tara . . . I can't even help myself right now . . . so if the future of your tribe or your horses depends on me, you're in big trouble."

She gave him an understanding look before continuing, "Sometimes I can see the sorrow in your eyes, and I can tell you are trying to deal with your own demons. I believe we all have a destiny to fulfill. I have no way of knowing what yours is, but there must be a reason for you being here now. There have been times when I have doubted my grandfather and his old native beliefs, but I have learned from experience that he is usually right."

"Well, ma'am, once I set that mare free, I plan on going home to Tennessee, so, if I were you, I wouldn't count on me for any more than that."

Tara smiled, "I knew telling you about his dreams would make you feel uncomfortable, that's why I kept it from you. He's just an old Indian with old Indian beliefs. Once you go home, he will realize he was wrong about you."

Shane looked at her with his eyes wide open and nodded his head in agreement. Then, in an attempt to get off the subject, he turned to gaze at the sensational view.

It was a clear evening and a full moon was slowly beginning to rise from behind the mountains on the horizon. Its yellow glow was already shining bright enough to cast hazy shadows from the tall trees that were all around. "Grandfather should be back soon," Tara said.

Shane seemed to be deep in thought when he asked, "As an educated, modern woman, do you hold any stock in your grandfather's tribal beliefs?"

"Some I do. It seems the older I get, the less I doubt him. I think the more you get to know him, the more you will see that he is a very wise and sensible man. I don't expect you to accept his ancient beliefs, but I can tell you, if you keep your mind open to him, you could learn a lot."

"When I first met your grandfather, you told me he believed that when one of your tribe dies, the wild horses will carry their spirits on to the next life. Do you believe this?"

Tara smiled. "This traditional ideology suggests that our mustangs are able to carry our souls to the threshold, where the ones who have gone on before will be waiting to greet us. Whenever I consider this, it always gives me peace of mind. This makes me want to think it is true. So, I guess, in a way, I do believe."

Shane nodded. "Well, it sure is a nice idea anyway."

Just then, Tigee walked up through the moonlit shadows. Shane didn't hear or see the old man until he was standing by his side.

Tigee grinned at the startled look on Shane's face. "I'm ready to go now."

When they arrived at Fort Washakie, the party was well under way. It was centered in a large courtyard in front of the cultural center and museum. There were at least a thousand people meandering around and a live band played loudly in the middle of the festivities. Several cooks were working over large spits cooking beef, venison, and chicken along with a variety of side dishes. Tara said, "These are the same facilities we use to put on powwows and gatherings for the tourists, but tonight it will just be the locals.

Shane made his way up to one of the several kegs of beer and drew himself a cold brew, then sat at a table, alone.

Many of the people were coming up to Tigee to wish him happy birthday. Tara walked over to a group of four Indian women about her age.

A girl named Lisa asked, "Who's the white guy you brought along? Is he with you?"

"He's with my grandfather and me."

"Oh, so it's not like you finally got a date or anything," another girl joked.

Tara laughed, "No, he's just a guy who's staying at the ranch for a while."

Lisa boldly pronounced, "Well, then I think I'll go over and introduce myself." With that said, she and two of the others walked toward Shane's table.

Tara and her other friend rolled their eyes and ambled over to the band.

The three girls were in their late twenties and were all reasonably attractive. Shane was a little taken back when the women sat next to him. They had all been at the party a while, and after a few beers were in a friendly mood.

"Hey, mister, we saw you come in with Tara, so we decided to introduce ourselves. I'm Lisa, this is Terri, she's Faith."

"My name is Shane. Nice to meet you ladies."

"You don't mind if we sit, do you?" Lisa asked.

"No, not at all, make yourselves comfortable." The girls were all good company, and he enjoyed talking with them. Before he knew it, they were on their third round of beers, and they began telling bad jokes and laughing loudly. Hawk came by to sit for a while but soon moved on.

It was about eight o'clock when the dinner bell rang, and everyone made their way up to the three chow lines.

Tara caught up with Shane in line. "My grandfather asked if you would join him to eat."

"Sure, I'd like that."

Then Tara laughed and said, "That is if you can tear yourself away from that group of women you're hanging out with. You might want to watch out for Lisa, she can be pretty aggressive if she likes a man."

"Oh no, I was just making conversation. I'm not looking for anything beyond that."

Tara kidded Shane, "You do like girls, don't you?"

"Yeah, it's just a bad time for me right now." Tara could tell the conversation was changing from joking around by the more serious tone in Shane's voice, so she left it alone and changed the subject.

"Are you hungry?" she asked.

"Yes, I'm starving." The two loaded their plates, then went over to join Tigee.

After dinner, Lisa kept coming over and asking Shane to dance. He finally gave in. She was pretty drunk by now and started to hang all over him. As soon as he had the chance, he asked Tara to save him by dancing the next dance with him. Tara laughingly agreed, then endured a sneering look from Lisa.

The next song the band played just happened to be a slow one, so Shane was glad he had Tara running interference. The dance started off in good humor, but as they moved close enough to feel each other's heartbeat this all began to change. The subtle attraction they had been experiencing up to now was suddenly becoming stronger and more difficult to ignore. "It's a nice evening, isn't it?" Shane said in an attempt to keep things low-key. Both of them felt the building passion, but neither was willing to acknowledge it. Each had his own reasons for this, and they were good ones at that. As the song began to wind down, Shane breathed in the aroma of her perfume one last time, then they slowly separated.

Still face-to-face, a momentary glance into Tara's sky blue eyes was unavoidable. This look between them only lasted a second, but it haunted Shane for the rest of the night. He did not ask her to dance again.

On the ride back to the ranch, everyone was feeling the effects of the alcohol they had consumed and were tired and quiet.

When they arrived home, Shane thanked them for a nice evening, wished Tigee a happy birthday, and headed to his cabin. He would need to get up early tomorrow to prepare for his trip to check on the herd with Hawk and JB.

Tara stood just inside her screen door watching him walk home. *There're a hundred reasons why this could never work*, she mused. With a sigh, she headed off to bed thinking this man from Tennessee, with all his secrets, would soon be leaving anyway. Then he would be out of her life and her head forever.

Chapter 14

Sunday, Tara woke to the sound of a truck and trailer pulling out of the ranch. It was Hawk, JB, and Shane going to the valley. She was fixing breakfast for herself and Tigee when he walked out of his room and set a package on the table.

"What is this?" she asked in Shoshone as she scraped some eggs out of the frying pan onto their plates.

"Something for you to read," he answered.

Tara sat down and started to eat as she opened the large envelope. Inside were three magazines and two videotapes. The magazines were well-known horse publications. Tigee took a sip of coffee and told her, "Look at the cover of the magazine on top." Her eyes opened wide in surprise as she saw Shane, sitting on a horse in a round pen while working with another horse in front of a large crowd. The title read "Starting Horses the Modern Way with a True Pioneer, Shane Carson." She looked at her grandfather, then back at the magazine. Tara ate a forkful of eggs and started reading the article. On the first page of the story, there was another picture of Shane standing with a young horse in the middle of a round pen. He looked a little younger, and he had on a headset and microphone. The crowd sitting in the grandstands was paying close attention to him. The article began with the author, Megan Tillie, telling how she first heard about this popular new clinician.

I had heard about this man, Shane Carson, from Tennessee, who was doing some incredible work with horses. He was using interesting new techniques he learned from a well-known master trainer from California named Tom Dorrance. Tom had taken on this young man as a student because of his natural talent.

I was looking for some good material for an article and had been struggling with writer's block for some time. It took almost a week to talk my editor into letting me make the trip to Stevenville, Texas, where Mr. Carson was putting on a clinic.

I had taken a similar trip six months earlier to see another clinician, who was also popular on the circuit tour. This man had been a disappointment, and my article was never published. So, my editor and I were very skeptical about this trip.

The *National Horseman's* magazine is one of the largest and most respected in the industry. Because of this, we are only interested in writing about the best of the best, and I really wasn't sure if this man would fit into that category. So I went incognito.

The clinic was held at the Stevenville county fair. It was obvious that Shane Carson was a big draw. This was the largest crowd I'd ever seen at any horsemanship clinic.

I sat in the grandstands and watched him at work with a very difficult young stallion that had never been saddled or ridden. His ability to read the young horse gave him a tremendous advantage in dealing with its problems. The timing and skills he used while applying his techniques were simply amazing. This young man was, by far, the most effective and talented clinician I had ever seen.

Mr. Carson had brought his own horse that he used to demonstrate many things to us. He also used his horse to pony the younger ones at the clinic. This gelding was trained to the hilt and was nothing less than an extension of Mr. Carson's own legs. Although he did not have the most entertaining of personalities, his occasional wit, along

with his incredible horsemanship, was more than enough
to put on a terrific show.

The article went on to tell about how well his style of horsemanship seemed to work with every horse he dealt with. The author
then posted his upcoming clinic dates and locations.

The second article, written by a different author, had been published six months later, and was just as complimentary. The third
magazine, with more facts about Shane, was another story by Megan
Tillie written eight years later. It was about the longest lasting clinician still on the road at that time — an in-depth story of Shane's life
and career.

Tara was fascinated as she read on. She was finding out some very
interesting things about this man who would not talk about his past.
She soon began to feel a little nosy reading all this behind Shane's
back. The third article continued on about how the author had become good friends with Shane Carson over the years and how he
had trained horses for her personally. The next part of the story told
about the mixed feelings she had after finding out that Shane would
soon be giving up the "on the road clinics" to start a full-time training business in Tennessee. She stated she would miss seeing and writing about this man and his clinics, which were now the most popular
of their kind in the United States. On the other hand, she was
thrilled to know he was now engaged to Jennifer Barlow, a girl she
had introduced Shane to. Megan finished by allowing Shane to express his appreciation to all the people who had come to his clinics.
He wanted them to know that he would be available at his new
facility in Tennessee by the end of the year.

From the dates on the magazines and the information in the articles, Tara gathered Shane had spent at least a decade on the road
doing these clinics. From the date of the last article till now, it had
been another dozen years, although Shane didn't look much older
than he did in the magazine's pictures.

Tara wondered if he had married Jennifer and if she was part of the reason he came out to Wyoming. Perhaps she left him and broke his heart. Maybe setting the mare free was some kind of closure for him. This could explain why he didn't talk about his past and why he seemed to be emotionally shutdown at times. Tara still had a lot of questions about Shane. What she did know, was that she was spending a lot of time thinking about him lately.

She finished reading the articles and took another sip of her now cold coffee. Then she glanced down on the table where she had laid the two commercially produced instructional videos on training horses. The boxes for these tapes had pictures of Shane on the covers.

"Where did you get all this?" she asked her grandfather.

"That Mrs. Jensen brought them out and loaned them to me. I've seen the way you look at him when you think no one is watching. I also know that he does not talk about his past. Because of this, I assume you must have a lot of questions about him. So I thought you might be interested in seeing all of this."

Tara took a deep breath, then looked into her grandfather's eyes. "I don't know what to think about him. I feel he is a good man, but I wonder what he's hiding. I remember he talked to you alone the day you met. Did he tell you anything I should know?"

"He confided in me, in hopes that I would change my mind and allow him to return his mare to our herd. I promised him I wouldn't betray his confidence — I am bound to honor that. I can tell you, he is a good man, but I don't know if he could ever give his heart completely to anyone again. I think that one day he may tell you his story. Only then will you really get to know him."

When Tara finished watching the videos, she put the tapes and magazines back into the envelope and out of sight.

The drive out to the Wind River Valley was a slow and bumpy one. Traveling down the many miles of old dirt roads that led to the south pass was always a treacherous trip. At the last minute, Tara's two brothers decided to come along. They both shook Shane's hand and said there were no hard feelings from their meeting at the Jensen's farm. "When we saw the brand on the mare, we figured you had taken her from our herd." They apologized for having jumped to the wrong conclusion. Their names were Ivan and Willie Two Feathers. Many of the Indians had Anglo first names and Indian last names.

The information Shane received from Mr. Jensen had been valuable in surmising a theory about the escalating attempts on the mustangs. But it was only a theory, with no evidence. Recognizing tensions were already close to a boiling point, he felt for now it was important just to keep his mouth shut. All he could do at this point was hope Mr. Jensen was wrong about the oil, and that the men from town had decided to leave the herd alone. The truth was he had serious doubts that the trouble in the valley was anywhere close to being over.

JB still wasn't happy about Shane coming along, but Hawk and Tara's brothers didn't seem to mind.

It was a warm, overcast day and the smell of rain was in the air. The five men tacked up their horses with a rifle packed on the sides of each of their saddles and slickers tied on the back in case of bad weather. The Indians were eager to get down to the river so they could pick up the herd's trail before the coming rain washed away any fresh tracks. Shane and the others rode down the long gorge and through a tall forest to get to the banks of the Big Wind River.

Shane felt a sense of privilege to be part of this scene. Here he was, riding with four natives of this land, down the same trail their ancestors had used hundreds of years ago. Before they rode out, Hawk reminded him that he was probably the only white man who had ever been down these particular trails.

The Indians picked up the herd's tracks about five miles downriver. Ivan told Shane, "The horses are smart, they rarely return to the same place on the river's bank to drink. This behavior keeps patterns from emerging that predators could use." The Indians seemed concerned because the horses were treading toward the north.

"The white men only try to catch the horses on the north side of the valley," Hawk said. "The area has easy access for them, and they like to stay close to the end of the old logging road where they park their trucks and trailers. Unfortunately, this same territory also has some of the best grazing."

According to the tracks, the horses had been moving along at a nice walk and then suddenly were spooked into a frantic run. What really bothered the Shoshone was that the herd had divided up into two groups—each going at high speed in a different direction. Shane sat on Tory and listened.

"What could have caused this?" JB asked.

"I've never seen them do this," Hawk said. "We'd better split up."

Shane, Ivan, and Willie rode toward the northwest, while Hawk and JB followed the smaller bunch of tracks that separated to the northeast. Shane and Tara's brothers had been riding hard and fast for about fifteen minutes when they heard the sharp echoes from a high-powered rifle.

Soon after, they heard Hawk's voice shouting over the radio. "You guys need to get over here now! We're at the base of the northeast trail, just before you get to White Tail Creek." Shane could hear, in the background over the radio, JB screaming out, what sounded to him, like some kind of angry war cry.

Willie hollered, "I know a shortcut. Come on!"

The three rode fast, down the winding, wooded trail. Shane was a little concerned about Tory, but the old horse easily kept up. He knew they were getting close when both of the Indians reached down and pulled their rifles from their scabbards while their mounts were still at a full gallop. Suddenly, they reined back their horses to a quick stop. Shane also pulled his rifle out as he swung his leg over to dismount. They could see JB on a cliff to the north, shooting in the air and hollering a bloodcurdling yell.

Chapter 15

As the three men rode into a clearing at the end of a trail, they cringed at the sight. There were five dead horses on the ground, including three mares, two with their weanling foals lying beside them. Shane noticed a third foal nearby. This weanling was still alive but had a gapping gunshot wound at the base of his neck. The colt was suffering terribly, and Hawk, who was able to move in close enough to assess its injuries, quickly made up his mind. He wasted no time in raising his rifle. With careful aim, he shot the young horse between the eyes, immediately putting it out of misery.

JB, still up on the ridge, fired off some furious rounds in the direction the shooters had fled, then rode down toward Shane and the others.

"Those sons of bitches!" JB yelled, as he rode in at a fast trot. The expressions on JB and Hawk's faces were of pure rage. Ivan and Willie sat in helpless disgust as they stared at the senseless slaughter.

The shooters were long gone by now and had probably made it back to their trucks. It was a good thing they had already left the area, because JB and Hawk were mad enough to kill.

They soon discovered the tracks of three men and their horses, who had been waiting on a small cliff overhanging the trail's end. Once the mares and foals made it into the clearing, the shooters had them clearly in their sights. This was a sad, inhumane scene and all five men stood there in quiet disbelief for some time.

Hawk suggested they backtrack this doomed part of the herd to try to find out how they'd been separated and forced into this ambush. The five rode back to where the herd had split and started scouring the woods for clues. If they could find out how the shooters set up the hunt, it would be easier to prevent this from happening again.

All four Shoshone got off their horses and began looking for signs. What they found suggested there were six other men on horseback chasing the mares and foals into the clearing. They used at least ten dogs to move the whole herd in the direction they wanted. Obviously, the men did not plan on Naatea leading the main group of the mustangs off to the northwest. Further down the trail, Hawk found a dog violently stomped to death.

Shane was amazed at the tracking skills these Shoshones naturally possessed. Before long the four confidently determined what had occurred. The whole group of nine men used the dogs to track and to find the horses. They patiently kept their distance after locating the herd, in order to give themselves time to set up the ambush. Once they had sent the three snipers ahead to open ground, the other six men and dogs pushed the horses toward them. During the frenzy the smaller group was cut off by the dogs from the rest of the horses that narrowly escaped to the northwest.

"Those mares with their foals would have been in the back of the herd while they were being chased," Ivan told Shane.

JB explained, "According to these tracks, Naatea turned back to try to save the three mares and their foals. He made it a couple hundred yards in their direction before he was attacked by at least three dogs. Naatea put up a good fight and killed one before he was forced to abandon the mares and foals and return to lead the larger group to safety."

Willie was furious. "This was definitely an organized attempt to eliminate as many horses as possible. If Naatea hadn't outsmarted the hunters, the whole herd could be dead."

For Shane, this senseless slaughter only strengthened Mr. Jensen's theory about the oil. He was almost sure these bastards would be back to finish the job. Now, more than ever, Shane needed to figure out how to prove if he and Mr. Jensen were right. Until then, he still felt there was no choice except to keep his mouth shut.

It was a long, quiet ride back to the trailer. When they finally arrived, JB spoke, "We should post a twenty-four hour guard. We know their methods, so it shouldn't be hard to get in the way of these sons of bitches. You can bet they'll be back." Everyone could see the rage building on JB's face, "I can make those assholes wish they had never come out here!" As he stood next to his horse he pulled his thirty-thirty rifle out of its scabbard and fired an angry round into the air. Tory and the rest of the horses reacted with a startled look.

Everyone agreed the mustangs needed full-time guards. Hawk suggested that Ivan and Willie stay out to watch the herd, while Shane, JB, and he went back to the ranch and talked to Tigee.

It was obvious that Hawk did not want JB to stay, fearing what he might do to the shooters if there was an encounter. Hawk knew it was important to keep his friend away from any potential trouble until he had a chance to cool down.

Tara's brothers agreed to take the first watch. Hawk would come back later, with supplies. They planned to set up a base camp on a well-hidden high perch close to the area where the horses were killed. From this high spot, they could hear any trucks coming down the old logging road that led to the north entrance. This would also put them in a good position to head off another disaster.

On today's trip, Shane had seen these Indians were very much at home in the wilderness. He was impressed with how silently and efficiently they could move through the woods on foot, as well as on horseback.

When they finally got back to the ranch, Shane unloaded the horses so the two Shoshone could talk to Tigee privately.

The old shaman answered the loud banging on his front door. By the distraught look on their faces he immediately knew something bad had happened. "What's wrong?" The two went inside and Hawk broke the news to him.

"One of the foals was the colt you hoped would replace Naatea someday," JB told him.

"He was shot up real bad. We had to put him down," Hawk added.

The old Indian just sat there, staring at them. Then, as his eyes misted and his hands began to shake, he slowly stood up and left the room to regain his composure.

When he returned, he sat in thought for a long time. Finally he spoke, "We have to call the sheriff from town and our reservation police."

JB stood up with his bad temper boiling over, "You know they won't do anything. The sheriff will say it is not his jurisdiction, and the reservation police will say they don't have the manpower to guard the herd. They'll end up asking us to help them anyway and then try to control how we handle the problem. There are only two Shoshone on the police force, the rest are Arapaho. To them the herd is just a bunch of wild horses. To us they are an important living symbol of our pride and our heritage. In the end it will be up to us to stop the killing. We don't need the so-called authorities getting in our way!"

Tigee listened to everything the men said, then he spoke in their Shoshone language, "I know how badly you want these people to pay for what they have done, and so do I, but we must report this to the reservation police and the sheriff. I want all of them to go out to the valley to see what has occurred. If we try to get the authorities to handle it, and they don't do anything, then no one can blame us for doing what we must to protect what is ours."

JB and Hawk had tremendous respect for the old Indian and reluctantly agreed. "Ivan and Willie have stayed in the valley to keep an eye on the herd," Hawk said. "We planned to meet them at the drop-off point in a couple of hours with supplies."

Tigee thought for a moment. "I want all four of you to stay out of sight. I don't want anyone to know we have people guarding the herd. The element of surprise will make it safer for you as well as help us to spoil any more attempts. I will take Shane and Tara with me. We will bring the sheriff and police in from the north logging road. You must get there before we do to tell my grandsons that we are coming, so they don't think we are the herd hunters when they hear our trucks."

Tigee walked over to the phone to call the authorities. It took some convincing, but the sheriff agreed to meet the reservation police and the old Indian at the north logging road in three hours. This would give JB and Hawk time to gather supplies for Ivan and Willie and to let them know Tigee wanted them out of sight.

"Where is Shane?" Tigee asked.

"He's in the barn, tending to the horses," Hawk replied.

"Go and ask him to come see me."

Hawk headed out the door to get Shane. As he arrived at the barn, Tara was stepping down off her horse from a morning ride. She wondered why he walked by her so abruptly.

He found Shane inside finishing up. "Tigee wants to talk with you. He'll fill you in on his plans."

Shane nodded and started walking toward the barn door. Tara could tell something was up and stopped him, "What's going on? Is my grandfather okay?"

"Yes, ma'am, he is fine."

"Well, something's wrong!"

"Someone shot some of the mustangs. We found them this morning."

Tara's face went blank, "Why would someone do that?"

"I don't know. Let me help you with your horse, so we can go talk to your grandfather together."

"Does he know about it?"

"JB and Hawk just told him."

Shane and Tara made short work of unsaddling her horse.

When they walked into the house, the old Indian was just hanging up the phone from talking with the reservation police.

"I want you both to come with me. Tara, I want you to make sure you have some film in your camera. Shane, I hope the sheriff will be more willing to help us if you're there."

Shane scratched his head. "You know I'll do all I can to help, but the sheriff and I have already had a run-in when I was in town. I don't think he likes me very much."

Tigee smiled. "You didn't make many friends in town during your brief stay, did you?"

"No, sir, I guess not."

"Well, I'd appreciate it if you would come anyway. You're a part of this now. We'll meet the authorities at the north entrance in three hours. They should see what has happened! I want the sheriff and police to know how serious we are about stopping this."

"I'll be ready."

Tara followed Shane out to the front porch and sat down while he leaned against the rail. Shane could see she was stunned and still trying to absorb the shocking news. "It's a damn shame," he said.

Tara shook her head. "I just don't know why anyone would want to shoot them. I'm worried about the horses, but my biggest concern is for the violence all this could cause. Our young men won't stand for this. They'll fight back, no matter what the consequences."

Shane tried to be the voice of reason. "Let's not jump to conclusions. Hopefully, this was just an isolated incident and it will all die down soon."

"Hopefully," Tara said, "but I don't think so. Trouble has been brewing for a long time, and tensions were already running high. I am afraid to think what could come of this."

Tara stood up and moved over to lean on the rail next to Shane. She hesitated for a minute as she glanced down at the wood floor of the porch, then looked back up at him. "I don't know what those jerks are capable of, but I do know they think they're above the law around here. You watch out for yourself and please keep an eye on my brothers. If there is a fight, I know they'll be in the middle of it.

"With everything that has happened today we can't guarantee your mare's safety, and it may be a long time before we can. My grandfather said you're a part of this now. I feel I should remind you, it's not necessary for you to go with us today. You aren't obligated to get involved, and no one would blame you if you loaded up your horses and went back to Tennessee."

She was leaning on the rail close to him and gently bumped her shoulder into his. "You know if you do leave, there would definitely be some people around here who would miss you."

Shane didn't know how to respond, so he just stood quietly for a moment, then said, "I don't plan on turning that mare loose until its safe, but I also don't plan on leaving until I see through what I came out here to do. I know it's hard for you to understand why it's such a big deal for me to set her free. Along with my personal reasons, I've come to understand and appreciate how special these mustangs really are. This land and these horses are at a crossroad. If a stand isn't taken, these links to the past could be lost forever. I guess I need a worthwhile cause in my life right now, so I think I'll stick around to see how it turns out."

Shane paused before adding, "Besides, if I were to leave there might be a couple of people around here I'd miss, too."

Tara, still leaning against the railing next to him, looked back down at the deck with a bashful smile that would melt any man's heart. A few quiet, awkward seconds passed before she shifted her blue eyes toward his. Once again they found themselves caught up in an intense gaze. He wanted to reach out for her. Maybe even just move his hand on top of hers, now only a few inches away from his on the rail. He was almost sure she wanted him to do something. Instead, he politely made his exit. "I'll be back in an hour," he said as he ambled away. Shane had become an expert at shutting off strong emotions, so by the time he made it down the steps, his mind had conveniently slipped back to the day's events and what lay ahead.

It had already been a long afternoon, and it wasn't over yet. The two dogs were lying on his porch waiting for him. Both of them perked up their ears when they saw him walking up the steps. Jessie still wouldn't allow Shane to touch him, but Butch came over for a light rub on his head. Then Shane went inside to clean up. He found himself looking in the small mirror above the bathroom sink while he waited for the shower water to warm. Staring aimlessly at his reflection, he could not help but ponder on the spark that seemed to be growing between him and Tara. He stood there thinking how good it felt to just be near her and wondered if she really did feel the same way. Then he slowly wiped a handful of water on his face and mumbled, "I don't think I'm ready for this."

After showering, he went out to the barn. The day had flown by, and Tommy was preparing hay for the afternoon feeding. Both Tory and Sloppy were nickering at him. "They're talking to you," Shane said, as he walked up.

"Yes, sir, they do every time I feed them. Are we working horses tomorrow?"

"You bet, son, I'll be here, bright and early. You have the roan saddled up and ready to go by eight." Tommy grinned from ear to ear at the idea of Shane helping him.

Just then he heard the horn blowing from Tara's truck, signaling they were ready to leave.

The drive out to the valley was solemn, neither Tara nor her grandfather wanted to look at the scene that awaited them. When they arrived at the north logging road, the reservation police were already there. They waited another half hour before Sheriff Benson finally showed up. The sheriff's attitude was as expected. "Let's get this over with. It'll be dark soon, and I've got dinner waiting at home."

From this point on, the trees were too thick to drive through, so they all started the fifteen-minute walk to the Deer Creek clearing, where it happened. No one talked during the walk except for the sheriff asking if anyone brought any bug spray.

When they got to the clearing, it was an emotional scene for Tara and Tigee. Rigor mortis had set into the carcasses and there were large puddles of blood around each of the slain animals. The flies were thick, and the buzzards were beginning to circle low overhead.

"You have to do something about this!" Tigee sputtered.

"Sir, this is an awful thing someone did," the sheriff said, "but there's nothing I can do. This was probably just some poachers that happened upon the horses."

"No!" Tara insisted. "My brothers backtracked the horses and can prove that this was an organized effort to kill the whole herd. It was definitely not a chance encounter."

"You can't prove that, miss," the sheriff said. "How about you boys?" He pointed to the reservation police. "Do you see anything that makes you think it was more than a random incident?"

"No, sir," one of the Indian officers answered, "These were probably just some kill-happy hunters who would have shot at anything."

Shane had heard enough. "I've seen the tracks of the shod horses and dogs that were chasing the herd. I'm telling you, if you go down this trail and look beyond your own noses, you'll see this was a large group of men who obviously came out here for one reason. They were well prepared and knew what they were after. If it hadn't been for some bad luck, when the main part of the herd split off, they would have killed a lot more horses."

"Mr. Carson," the sheriff said, giving Shane a pissed-off look, "the last thing I need is for you to be causing trouble by putting bad ideas into these people's heads. Just what the hell are you doing out here anyway?"

"No one is putting ideas into our heads. We are perfectly capable of thinking for ourselves!" Tigee responded angrily. "He is here because I asked him to come. I figured you wouldn't listen to us, but I hoped Shane could convince you to help."

"I'm going to tell you one more time," the sheriff said. "It doesn't make any sense for someone to have an organized hunt for these mustangs. If they were going to go to all that trouble, they would have taken the meat to the killer market. This was just some punk kids who happened to come across these mares. Now, if you have any more trouble out here, you let me know, and I'll help your reservation police try to catch these guys. Until then I can't waste valuable time chasing phantoms for a crime that doesn't have a motive. Now these dead horses are beginning to smell real bad, so I'm going home!"

Tara, looked over at the two native policemen and sneered sarcastically, "You guys sure were a lot of help!"

"I don't see any reason to think differently than the sheriff," one of them said. "I really think this is just a one-time thing. We'll come out next week on horseback and look around, but I really don't think you'll see these hunters again." After saying this, the two officers started hiking to their truck.

Listening to all this talk about no motive made Shane want to speak up about the oil, but this was still an unproven theory, which would only fan the flames of potential trouble. Shane noticed a figure moving up beside him. He was startled by Hawk, who appeared out of nowhere and was now standing next to him. Then just as quietly, Tara's brothers and JB emerged.

"We can't expect any help from the law," Tigee said.

"We know, we heard," replied Hawk.

"You knew those assholes were useless," JB added.

The old shaman then took charge. "I want at least two of you out here at all times. We'll figure out a schedule later. Ivan and Willie, you stay here the first couple of days. Use your long-range radios to stay in touch with me at the ranch. You men need to keep your horses quiet and stay out of sight. Watch your tracks, stay off the main trails, and no fires except late at night. We need to keep the herd safe until we figure out a way to handle this. If the shooters show up, try to spoil their attempt without them even knowing you're here. This way we can avoid any unnecessary violence. If you find yourselves in a situation where you need to protect yourself, you do whatever you have to do."

The four Indians nodded and slipped back into the trees, blending in and soon disappearing into the foliage and shadows.

Shane knew that if Nethers had pulled permits for oil exploration in the area, sooner or later, the test crews would show up. Once he knew they were here, he would have to catch them testing on reservation land. The more he thought about it, the more he realized he would need the Shoshone's help. The area bordering the Indians' valley and Nethers's land was vast and rough. It would take the Shoshone's intricate knowledge of this terrain, along with their amazing tracking skills, to come up with the proof Shane was after.

Hopefully, when the time came, Tigee would be able to give him a trustworthy guide who would not stir up trouble. Shane understood the tensions the Indians were feeling. They were ready to fight for their sacred horses that were such a valued part of their heritage. If his suspicions fell into the wrong hands, someone could get hurt or even killed, and Shane didn't want that on his conscience. His intuition told him the shooters would lie low for a few days. After all, it would be stupid to try this again too soon. They would more likely let things cool down before putting together another large-scale hunt. Hopefully, this would give Shane time to figure out what to do next.

Shane overslept the next morning and had to rush to get to the barn at eight. Tommy had already fed and turned the horses out of their stalls for the day. It was a cloudy, windy morning and all the horses were a little frisky because of the threatening storms. By now Tommy was doing most of the hands-on training with the roan gelding, so Shane usually just gave the boy instructions while he sat on the fence. With Shane's help, the roan was trying harder every day to please the kid.

Shane told Tommy, "We've got the basic steering and buttons on him now, so you should have enough control to stay out of trouble on the trails. I'll ride along this morning to make sure you're okay with him." Shane quickly saddled Sloppy. She hadn't been ridden for a few days so the exercise would be good for her.

An hour later the two were back at the ranch, and Shane was pleased with the session.

"Don't expect too much too soon. It'll take a lot of time and miles to really get him broke. Now, let's get out your mare and see how she's feeling today." Shane's mind was not entirely on working with the horses. As soon as he finished with Tommy, he planned to get in touch with Mr. Jensen and try to come up with a plan to investigate their theory.

Shane spent an hour working with the mare. She was coming along slow but sure. The more he worked with this one, the more he realized how potentially dangerous she could be. So, he advised Tommy, "I'll do all the work with this mare until we get her further along. I want you to promise me that you won't try to work with her on your own."

"Yes, sir, I promise."

"Now, go put her away, and saddle up the last horse. I'll get you going with him, and then I have to leave."

Tommy was already complaining about beginning school in a few weeks. Once it started, Shane would have to help him with the horses in the afternoon. He told Tommy he needed to try his best in school, and he would only help him if he kept his grades up. This reminded him of his son, Jacob, who would much rather stay home and help him at the barn than be in class. "Horse training is a business," he would tell Jacob. "To succeed in any business, you must be educated. The people who make it in this world, whether working with rockets or horses, are the ones who tried their hardest in school." Shane felt a little melancholy as he told Tommy the same thing.

After getting Tommy started with his last horse, Shane headed straight for his truck. The two wolves were lying on the porch after their morning's hunt. They both perked up and watched as Shane drove out of the compound gate. His original plan was to go to the pay phone and call Mr. Jensen, but then he decided to drive over to the farm so he could talk to him in person. His growing concerns about the mustangs had him hoping they were wrong about the oil. One way or another, he needed to find out for sure.

When he pulled into the farm, Mr. Jensen's truck was not there. Mrs. Jensen was excited to see Shane. She invited him in and, as usual, offered to fix him something to eat.

"No thank you, ma'am. Do you know when your husband will be home?"

"He should be back anytime. I don't know what you guys are up to, but he sure wanted to talk to you. When I asked him what was going on, he said he would tell me about it later, so I left it alone. He'll be glad you're here though. He mentioned he might drive out to the reservation this afternoon to see you. This will save him the trip."

Mrs. Jensen was in a talkative mood, so Shane sat and listened. "That Indian friend of yours is an interesting character. He told me his family had lived on that land for hundreds of years."

"Yes, ma'am, I've never seen people who were so connected to the land and their heritage. I think if they had a choice, they would turn back the hands of time and live off the land the way their ancestors did."

She smiled and nodded her head. "It is refreshing to see people whose priorities aren't so wrapped up around progress and the almighty dollar. You have to admire that."

"Yes, I do," Shane answered. "Before I came out here, I didn't know the Wind River Basin existed. I have to admit, the awesome beauty of this country and its history have affected me in a big way. I just hope they can continue to hold on to all that wilderness and keep it from ever changing."

Mrs. Jensen agreed and switched the subject. "That Tara sure is a pretty girl. Where did she get those blue eyes?"

"She told me her great-great-great-grandmother was white. One of her brothers has the same blue eyes, but believe me, everything else about their family is definitely Shoshone."

"You know, Shane, I think she may have an eye for you."

Shane became a little embarrassed at hearing this. "I think your imagination is getting the best of you, ma'am. I don't know what she would see in me."

"Oh, I don't know about that. I remember a lot of ladies at your clinics being pretty smitten!"

Shane was trying to figure a way out of this conversation without being disrespectful to the nice old lady. Just then Mr. Jensen walked in remarking, "Woman, why do you always try to play the matchmaker? Shane's a grown man. He doesn't need you meddling in his personal affairs." Mrs. Jensen just laughed and walked into the kitchen.

Chapter 16

Mr. Jensen hung his hat on the coatrack, "It started out stormy this morning, but it seems to be clearing. I'm glad you're here, I was planning on coming to see you today."

"That's what your wife said. Before you go on, let me tell you what's happened in the valley." Shane told him about the shooting of the horses and the tension building with the Indians. "I've kept quiet about our suspicions. Telling them now about our theory, would be like pouring fuel on a hot fire."

"Well, son, I haven't seen any strangers around town. No oil company trucks or crews, either. I was beginning to think we were wrong, then I decided to drive out to the old mountainside motel just outside of town. There's a little coffee shop there, so I went in and sat down. This was about seven o'clock Saturday morning. The restaurant was pretty busy with their breakfast crowd so it was easy for me to blend in. From where I sat, I had a good view of the motel, and I was surprised to see Vince Nethers drive into the parking lot, then go up to one of the rooms. He had his son with him. A few minutes later, I saw two Indians show up and go to the same room. They knocked on the door and went inside."

"Indians? Were they Shoshone?"

"I don't think so. They were driving a pickup with one of those magnets on the side that people use for advertising. The sign read Hunter Guide Services, Arapaho, Wyoming. That town is located on the southeast part of the reservation. From what I hear, those two tribes get along fine these days, but they still live within their own communities. I don't think there are many Shoshones living there.

"The group stayed in the room for quite some time. When they did finally come out, there were three more white men with them. I guess these guys were already there waiting for Nethers and the rest to arrive.

"Those three men came out last. I watched as they walked behind the building and disappeared for a minute. Then I saw them drive back around in a pickup truck. The truck had a sign that read IN-CORE OIL CORP.

"Now, it sure looks to me like Vince Nethers is going out of his way to keep a low profile — especially if all he's trying to do is look for oil on his own land. And an even bigger question is why is he talking to an Arapaho Guide Service?"

"I don't know," Shane said. "It's looking more like we might be right. But, we still need some proof before I stir up a whole lot of trouble by telling the Shoshone. If I could see them actually testing on reservation land, then we could be sure."

"Well," Mr. Jensen said, "you've got the best guides in the world living around you. Are there any Shoshone you can count on to keep this under their hat until you have your proof?"

Shane thought for a moment as Mrs. Jensen walked into the room with a glass of tea for her husband. "I know Tara and her grandfather are worried about someone getting hurt over all this, but the young men are just brewing for a fight. I'll probably have to talk to Tigee. Maybe he can set me up with a guide and get me back in where I can watch the oil people." Shane said his good-byes, and drove back to the reservation, reflecting on what he'd just learned.

Vince Nethers was a very wealthy person with strong political connections, just as Mr. Jensen had told Shane. Money and power were his driving force in life. The man built an empire through real estate and cattle deals, and had no regrets about the people he ruined along the way. If Mr. Jensen's theory was right about oil, then this could mean there's a lot more trouble to come.

*   *   *

Three days later a Cessna plane touched down at Vince Nethers's private airstrip on his ranch about twenty miles north of the reservation. The Cessna taxied up the grass runway to the three-plane hangar. The doors opened, then two casually dressed men with briefcases in hand stepped down out of the plane. Both of them had the smell of hard liquor on their breath.

One of the men was Barry Russell, the CEO of a small, struggling corporation called In-Core Oil. They specialized in exploration and drilling of oil deposits all over the Midwest. The company was looking for the one great deal that could put them on the map. This was a very competitive business, and Vince knew they would be willing to push the limits of the law.

The other man was John Rasolli, a mob-connected business man from Chicago with unlimited resources. Vince needed this guy's money to get things started. John had been very successful and currently had his hand in a number of legitimate businesses, most of which had been acquired through illegal practices. He would force a buyout of small, high potential companies at less than market value and then sell them for a large profit. If needed, he would know how to put the squeeze on the Shoshone financially and otherwise.

Vince's son, Bo, was waiting at the hangar in his Jeep to pick up the two men. Bo greeted them with a handshake. "Mr. Russell, Mr. Rasolli, my father is waiting at the house. He is looking forward to meeting with you." Both men nodded and climbed into the Jeep for the mile ride to the mansion.

When they arrived, a pretty young maid, wearing a short black dress, greeted them at the front door and directed them into the study. Vince was finishing up a call and he motioned for the men to have a seat. He then gestured for Bo to leave the room. Although this irritated Bo, he did as his father indicated.

"Hello, Barry, John, I have lunch waiting by the pool. I figured we'd have something to eat before we get down to business."

"That sounds good," Barry answered.

"Me too," John said, "I'm starving!"

The men sat by the pool making small talk while the servants, who were all attractive young women, brought them their meal. After lunch, the conversation became serious.

"Since you asked us to fly all the way out here, I suppose you found what you were looking for," John commented.

"It looks pretty damn good!" Vince exclaimed. "As far as the geologist and everyone else involved knows, the testing I've had them doing has been done on my land. I hired a couple of Indian guides to take Barry's men and their sonic testing equipment into the area on the reservation that we thought would be productive. The crew didn't have a clue that they weren't on my property; only my two Indian guides knew. These Arapaho guides have been paid well, and know they stand to make a lot more money if they keep their mouths shut. But just in case, to keep them honest, I've threatened them with their lives if they say anything. The first round of test results has shown a high percentage of likelihood there is an ocean of crude under that valley."

Vince handed Barry the results of the tests and watched his eyes light up.

"Holy shit!" Barry said. "Look at the bright spot on this readout. It's been a long time since I've seen paperwork this promising."

Barry went on to explain, "Most of the oil in this part of the country is not concentrated in large enough reservoirs to make it feasible to reach. These results are showing a big pool of viscous crude that is contained within very porous and permeable rock. This will make it fairly easy to pump out, at least in the first stages."

"So, what's our next move?" Rasolli asked.

"Let me take some time to explain the situation in that valley," Nethers said. "There are two tribes that control the Wind River Valley." Vince motioned to one of the young maids to bring out an easel with a large map of the area's terrain. "We'll need representatives of both tribes to sign a lease. The Arapahos have no significant ties to the area. They were moved here by the U.S. government in the late 1800s, against their will. I don't see any real problems persuading them to sign.

Now the Shoshone are a different situation altogether. They

have a deep-seated connection to this land that goes back hundreds of years. This particular area, where we want to drill, is especially important to them. It's actually in the middle of their ancestral hunting grounds. To them this land is sacred. The Shoshone also have a large herd of horses that live and run free in the valley."

John Rasolli looked puzzled and asked, "What the hell do wild horses have to do with this?"

"This is the only part of the reservation where the horses can survive year around."

Vince explained to the group how long the Shoshone had watched over the mustangs and how important the herd is to the tribe. "As long as these horses are in the valley, there's no way we could con these Indians into signing a lease. They just won't do it."

"So what are our options?" Barry asked.

Vince poured himself another cognac and continued. "First, we need to keep them from finding out about the crude. Next, we need to get the horses out of the picture. Then, in time, as long as the Arapahos help to push it through, we should be able to buy into a lease. I'll tell them it is to run cattle on or to use as a hunting preserve. In the fine print of the lease, we will give ourselves enough leeway to do whatever we want out there."

"Sounds like a lot of things are going to have to happen, for this to work," said John. "If plan A doesn't work, what is plan B?"

Vince slowly took a sip of his drink and said, "First, we will try to reason with them by offering more money, but if that doesn't work, things could start to get real ugly. The Shoshone's largest source of income is their cattle. Since I am the biggest cattleman in the area, I can put quite a financial squeeze on them. I can use my connections in the cattle industry to discreetly blackball their sales. With my political connections, I can get some of their government funding held up for a while. Between the loss of cattle money and the delay of their government funds, they would be hurting pretty bad. Now if it did come down to a worst case scenario, it would probably require John to get real creative with some strong-arm persuasion."

"What if they find out about the oil?" Barry asked.

John Rasolli stood up and leaned across the table. "Hey, I've 'persuaded' many an unwilling company to become partners with me — once they found out it was in their own best interest to do so."

Vince raised his glass to John and said loudly, "John, my man, that's why you're here. One way or another we're going to get a big piece of this fortune, and personally, I don't give a damn what we have to do to make it happen!"

Barry, looking a little confused, asked one more question. "Why don't we just go to the Shoshone and try to work something out with them? I mean, without the financial resources that you and John can provide, along with my equipment and expertise, that crude might as well be on the moon as far as those Indians are concerned."

Vince smiled sarcastically, "For one thing, there are plenty of other investors they could get interested in something like this. And like I told you before, this land is sacred to them. Even if we could work out a deal, they would definitely want to take control of the drilling. That would mean operating in a way that wouldn't harm the land or bother those damn horses, and that could severely limit our profits. I estimate, with the right money and people in control, we could set up at least twenty times the number of drilling rigs than they would allow. If the Shoshone were in control, they would never put that kind of impact on the land. I look at it like this: it's a matter of making some decent money over time, or getting an unlimited amount of money and power almost overnight."

John Rasolli, after thinking for a minute about what he was hearing, looked up. "So, I guess the first thing to do is to get rid of the horses. How are you planning to do that without causing any suspicions from the Shoshone?"

Vince grinned. "It just so happens there has been an ongoing feud. It's been a kind of a game with the young men from town, to try to steal as many mustangs as they can. The boys usually sell them to the ranches around the area or to the slaughterhouse for quick cash. But, the real fun has always been just pissing off the Indians and, of course, the challenge of catching the wild things.

"There's been a lot of trouble between some of the braves and the boys from town recently. There have been some fist fights and mean threats made by both sides. This all makes for a perfect time to eliminate these horses from the equation. It will come across as just a cruel act to get even. I pretty much have the local law in my hip pocket around here. I don't think killing the mustangs is going to open any eyes in terms of what we are really after. As a matter of fact, we've already shot some of their horses.

"Actually, I thought it was rather ingenious of me to use the hunt as the diversion when we slipped across the property line onto the reservation and did the first round of our seismic testing. We have more to do in some other areas, but the initial phase went like clockwork. The Shoshone were so wrapped up in those dead mustangs, they never knew what was going on, and we were just a few miles away with the equipment. The Arapaho guides stayed behind to cover up any tracks or signs the oil crew left. We had a good rain later that night that also helped cover things up. So far, everything seems to be working just as I hoped. As soon as we're sure they aren't watching for us, my boys will go back in and kill the rest of the mustangs. This time, I'm sending the two Arapaho guides to help with the job. These Indians are expert hunters and trackers and know the country like the back of their hands. With them involved, we'll make short work of eliminating the herd. Once the horses are out of the way, we'll wait a while and then make our offer on the lease. If that doesn't work, we'll move full force ahead with plan B."

John Rasolli spoke up, "I think we should do whatever we can, now, to screw up this tribe's income. If you have a way to hurt them with their cattle business, let's start the process. The hungrier they are when we're ready to make our move, the more likely they will be to deal with us. In the meantime, I'll look into whatever else I can be doing to mess up their income as well as any investments they may have. By the time we make them an offer on that land, they'll be in the palm of our hands."

"That sounds good to me," Vince said. "I'll want Barry to begin setting wells up in there, as soon as we get the papers signed."

"Yes, sir," Barry answered, "I'll be ready to start moving the minute you give me the word. It won't take me long to have oil rigs out there as far as the eye can see. If these test results are accurate, we can set up as many as two pumps per acre on every bit of level ground we can get onto. Within a year's time, we could be pumping up to five thousand barrels of crude a day out of that valley."

Vince poured all three a fresh drink, then made a toast, "To our future wealth and power, let nothing stand in our way!"

Chapter 17

Shane had run out of ideas on how to gather evidence. It was time to talk to Tigee and see if he could get a guide to take him into this remote part of the reservation with the hope of catching these crooked guys searching on Shoshone land. There were an awful lot of unknowns in this little adventure. What he knew for sure was the young Shoshone men would fight to the death to protect their land and horses. He guessed that Nethers and his bunch weren't the type to back down from a scrap either. Since Nethers had the law in his pocket, Shane had no idea what to do with any evidence that he did come up with. He felt confident, though, that Tigee was a peaceful man and would want to keep a lid on the violence while they carefully thought through their next move.

It was three in the afternoon when Shane returned to the ranch. Most of the Indians were out baling hay so the compound was almost vacant. Tigee was sitting on his porch. Shane had never seen him look so somber. The situation in the valley was taking its toll on the old man. Shane parked his truck in front of his small ranch house, then took a deep breath and headed over.

"How are you today, sir?"

Tigee forced a smile.

"I need to talk to you about the situation down at the river."

The old Indian questioned, "What's on your mind? Why don't you sit so we can talk?"

"Sir, before I start, I need you to know that what I'm telling you is only a theory. I need you to promise me you'll keep this between us until we're sure I'm right. I want you to know how much I appreciated your confidentiality concerning the loss of my family. I know, because of this, I can count on your word. Once we have some proof, you can do what you want with the information. Until then, I'm afraid, it would only stir up more tension and trouble."

"I'll keep quiet," the old man assured.

"I think these guys are after a lot more than your horses in the valley. What's the one thing that drives most of the world, outside this reservation?"

Tigee looked confused, "I don't understand."

Shane answered his own question. "Greed."

"How can anyone profit from killing our horses?" Tigee asked.

"I think the herd is just in the way of what they're really after. I'm talking about your valley and what is underneath it."

Tigee, squinted his eyes and asked, "What's under our valley?"

"Sir, I think there may be oil there."

"Oil!" the Indian said. "What makes you think that?"

"I know for a fact that a man named Nethers has been testing just north of the valley."

Tigee nodded his head. "Yes, I knew they were looking out there last year. I also know the tests showed there was not a high enough concentration to make it worth drilling."

"Yes, sir," Shane said, "but I do think they've found there is a strong possibility of a much larger reserve, south of where they were looking. This would put the oil right smack-dab in the middle of your valley."

The old man looked Shane in the eye. "What has led you to believe this?"

Shane told him everything he knew.

Tigee sat quietly, pondering on what he had just heard. "How can we find out for sure?"

"Vince Nethers has equipment and crews out on his land right now. If we can catch them sneaking over and testing on the reservation, then we'll know I'm right."

Tigee hesitated. "There is a big difference between thinking the oil is there and actually finding it. Why would they feel the need to get rid of our mustangs, if they don't know for sure?"

Shane shrugged his shoulders. "I think ole Vince is pretty certain it's down there. I also suspect he needs to pull in some investors. If that's the case he'll need to be one hundred percent sure. That's probably why he's brought in more testing equipment under the cover story that he is looking on his own land."

The old man again took his time before he replied, "There is another reason why we should keep quiet about this. Not only could we aggravate an already tense situation that could get some of our young men hurt or in trouble, but I also have to consider there are members of my tribe who would sell out our horses and our land. After all, we're talking about a lot of money. If there really is oil in the valley, I fear our ancestral territory is in grave danger of being desecrated. If we can prove they've been testing on the reservation, then I would need to think long and hard about how I should handle this."

"Yes, sir, I agree. Do you know of someone who can keep their emotions in check, and their mouth shut, who could help me find the oil company's base? They have to be set up somewhere near the reservation's north property line. Once I find out where they're camped, I could keep an eye on them and see what they're up to." Shane sat patiently as he waited for Tigee to consider his proposal. He knew the wise old shaman wouldn't jump into any plan of action until he'd thoroughly thought it through. After some time Tigee began to speak,

"We would need someone who can take you around the guards I've posted to watch the herd. They check in with me regularly on their radios. I can send them south for a while. This would clear your way, allowing you to slip by them and get close to Nethers's property line unseen. Once you're in place, there should be three or four miles between you and my braves. I'll give you a radio with a different frequency, so we can keep in contact. I'll take you, your guide, and your horses to a drop-off point well north of where our other men have been unloading. Hopefully, we can keep all this quiet. I do know someone we can trust who will understand how fragile this situation is. If this person agrees to guide you, we could take you in as soon as tomorrow. I can set you up with the food and supplies you will need, along with a pack horse. You'll need to take warm clothes, a rain suit, your gun, and binoculars. Make sure your horse has a fresh set of shoes."

"Yes sir. I'll be ready in the morning."

It was now late afternoon, and he knew he would find Tommy at the barn feeding up. "I'll be leaving for a few days, so I won't be here to help you. I'll be taking Tory with me, but I'd like you to ride Sloppy everyday to keep her legged up."

"Yes sir, I'll work her every morning."

Shane continued, "I'll help you with the young mare in the morning. After tomorrow I want you to leave her alone until I'm back. You can work with the two geldings on your own. Just be careful, and I'll check your progress with them as soon as I return. I'll be out here first thing tomorrow to start with the filly."

"Yes, sir, Mr. Shane."

Shane tossed and turned all night in anticipation of his trip. He woke up early to prepare for a possible extended stay in the wilderness before going to the barn.

The dependable Tommy had already fed the horses and was saddling up the filly when Shane arrived. "How does she seem this morning?"

"She's seems calmer than I've ever seen her," Tommy bragged.

"Good," Shane replied. "Maybe all our hard work is finally paying off."

Shane led her into the corral, and for the first time she began the session on a good note. Tommy was learning more every day by watching Shane work with this tough horse, and Shane was enjoying the challenge as well as the satisfaction of spending time with the kid. The boy truly had a natural-born feel for these animals, along with an uncanny ability to communicate with them and bring out their try. Shane was really beginning to feel like Tommy could be a top pro someday.

When Shane was finished with the young mare, he handed her to Tommy. "We'll work with her again as soon as I get back, okay?"

"Yes sir, I promise to wait. Where are you going with Tory?"

"Oh, just a little camping trip."

"Mr. Shane, have a good time, and don't worry, I'll take good care of Sloppy. Whatever made you start calling her Sloppy anyway?"

Shane wasn't sure how to answer this since it was his little girl who named her. He paused for a second, then said, "It's a long story, I'll tell you about it another time." Tommy nodded, told Shane goodbye and took the filly to the barn.

Shane finished packing, then saddled up Tory. He tied him up to the trailer that was hooked up to Tigee's old truck. There was a pack horse already loaded up in the first stall of the four-horse rig. The weather was good this morning, and he hoped it would hold for the rest of the week. Even though the circumstances surrounding this trip were of a serious nature, Shane felt a sense of exhilaration about going out to the valley again. He knew there were plenty of people from his world who would pay a small fortune for a trip like this. He made sure to pack his camera this time so he could take pictures of the dazzling landscape, as well as any evidence they found.

Shane's curiosity was beginning to get the best of him, wondering who his guide was going to be. As he walked up the porch steps, he could see Tigee through the screen door, motioning him to come in. The old Indian was on the phone, so he sat down and waited.

"There was a small problem with your guide, but I've worked it all out and she'll be here soon."

Shane looked puzzled, "She?"

"Yes," the old man answered, "When she found out it was a strange white man she was packing in, she became uncomfortable about going with you on her own. So, now you'll have two guides."

Shane didn't know what to say, so he just sat quietly while the old man continued.

"The woman's name is Tashawa. Her family has been among the best of our hunting and fishing guides for generations. I've seen her spot signs of elk that were a week old and follow them until she found the animals. Tashawa has spent a large part of her life in the outdoors and knows how to live off the land.

"Her grandfather, who is no longer with us, was my good friend. We use to spend a lot of time together in that backcountry camping and hunting. We would often take Tashawa, Tara, and my grandsons with us. We made sure from a young age they were all capable of sur-viving in the wilderness."

Chapter 18

Shane heard a truck drive up. It was Tara. She got out of her truck, then immediately headed for the barn.

Tigee looked at Shane. "I am telling anyone who asks that you have hired Tashawa as a guide for a fishing trip. This is a common thing for her family's guide service to do. So, no one would second-guess this is a cover story."

A few minutes later, Tara came in. She smiled at Shane as she walked by him and said, "I'll be ready to go as soon as I pack some clothes."

Shane looked at Tigee, surprised. "What does she mean by that?"

He replied, "I was getting ready to tell you, your guide, Tashawa, asked Tara to go along. I had to find someone who I could count on to keep quiet. So, when Tashawa asked for Tara, I thought it would be a good idea."

Shane was at a loss for words. It wasn't that he had any objections to going with the two women. It was just that he naturally was expecting a man. Shane questioned Tigee, "Sir, what if we run into the shooters?"

"You are to avoid any trouble. You three are only out there to gather information. If you see any shooters coming after the herd, you are to stay out of sight and call me on the radio. I'll send over my men who are posted out there. You'll be staying in an old hunting shack located near the northeast border. It's next to a place called Shadow Creek, so you'll have plenty of water and there's a corral next to it for the horses. This is one of the places Tashawa's grandfather and I used during our hunting trips. You would have to be a Shoshone to know where this place is, so you'll be safe there."

Tara was still in her room packing when Shane heard another vehicle pull up. A young woman about Tara's age walked to the front door and knocked. The old man hollered to her in their tribal tongue. Apparently he told her to come in, because she did just that. Tigee introduced them, which prompted a quick nod from her in Shane's direction, but no eye contact.

Shane said, "Hello," and left it at that. He figured that trying to converse with her right now was out of the question. Just then Tara came into the room, and the girl immediately lit up. The two were obviously close friends.

Tashawa was definitely all Shoshone. She had the typical high cheekbones and dark skin of most of this tribe. She was small in stature, about five foot five and slightly built. Her jeans and T-shirt were clean, but worn — unlike the dirty old Aussie-style hat she wore on her head. While they were in the house, she only spoke to Tara, and then all she said to her was, "It has been too long."

Tara replied, "We've missed you, too. I see you've met Shane." The girl looked at him for the first time, with a slight grin. Tara commented, "Tashawa doesn't talk much, so don't take it personally."

"No problem, I'm just glad she is here to help out. Now, is everyone ready to go?"

Tigee stood up. "Yes, let's head out." The horses were loaded on Tigee's trailer in no time, and the last of the provisions were being put in the pickup when Shane noticed the two wolf dogs, sitting next to the trailer. Tigee remarked, "Looks like they want to go. I think those two could be helpful. They seem to have a quiet way of letting you know when there are strangers around, and they're also good at staying out of sight."

"Yes, sir, now that I think about it, I'd like to take them. I'll grab some dog food."

The old Indian laughed. "You don't need dog food, they're half wolf. They can hunt for their meals. You've got them spoiled."

"Well, sir, maybe that's why they like me so much." Shane knew the dogs would hunt, but he hoped the dry food would help keep them close to camp, if for no other reason than to keep the horses safe from any large predators that might be sneaking around at night.

Both dogs were apprehensive about getting into the bed of the old pickup. Since it was their first ride in a truck, Shane decided to sit back there with them, to make sure they wouldn't jump out and hurt themselves.

The spot where they finally stopped to unload was a heavily wooded area. Tigee told Shane they would have about a two-mile ride to a steep drop-off that would lead down to the valley. From there, it was another three miles to the river, and then a few more miles downriver to the cabin they would call home for the next week.

"Some of the ride will be slow going," Tara said, "but we should be there before dark."

Tashawa said something to Tara in Shoshone and then shook her head.

Tigee translated, "She couldn't believe you rode in the back of the truck with the two dogs. She has heard the joke that they believe you're their mother. Now she knows why people say this."

Tashawa tried to reach out and pet Jessie who quickly pinned his ears and slipped away. Shane laughed, "They're kind of shy, like you, Tashawa."

She had no response to Shane's comment as she continued getting the packhorse ready for the long ride. Tashawa was not happy about the packhorse having to carry the ten-pound bag of dog food Shane had brought along. Tigee told her it was okay, so she reluctantly tied it on. The three were finally mounted and ready to go.

Tigee gave Shane the radio, along with extra batteries. "You check in with me at eight a.m. and eight p.m., every day, to let me know you're okay."

Tashawa started riding toward the thick woods with Tara behind her, followed by Shane riding Tory and leading the packhorse. Tara told Shane, "The first part of the trip will be the slowest, because there are no trails through this forest."

"Do you know the way to Shadow Creek?" he asked.

"Kind of," Tara answered. "I could get there on my own, but it would take me a lot longer than Tashawa. She knows every deer trail and hilltop out here by heart. With her in the lead, we'll get there much quicker and a lot easier."

It took a couple of hours to wind their way through the thick, green trees, before finally getting to the drop-off that led down into the valley. They stopped to rest the horses before continuing down the steep trail, which would be the most strenuous part of the trip for the animals. Shane tied Tory to a small tree, then climbed up on a high rock to have a long look at the view. It was a bright, clear day, so he could see a great distance from this vantage point. Tara climbed up and stood next to him. She took a deep breath. "I've seen this so many times, but every time I look out there it takes my breath away!"

Shane pulled his camera out of the case hanging on his shoulder and took some pictures of the view. He couldn't help but snap one of Tara as she sat on the edge of the rock looking across the valley at the mountains. She looked so much like she belonged to this country! For a moment, Shane found himself intrigued watching this young Indian woman as he thought how much her natural, native beauty blended in with the remarkable scenery around her. Out of the corner of her eye, Tara caught a glimpse of him looking at her. Like a kid with his hand caught in the cookie jar, his face turned a light shade of red. He promptly turned away and gazed back down toward the valley below. Tara merely shifted her eyes out toward the mountains, then smiled at the idea of him looking at her that way.

A few minutes later, Tashawa, without saying a word, mounted her horse and started riding toward the steep slope that would be their next challenge on this trip.

"I guess that's our cue," Shane said, as he and Tara scrambled down the rock. They quickly mounted their own horses and soon caught up with her. The ride down this part of the ridge was much more difficult than the area where he had ridden in with Hawk and JB. Had it not been for Tashawa, knowing exactly where to go and how to zigzag her way from point to point, they would have found themselves in a precarious situation. Now Shane understood why she was so concerned about the packhorse having to carry the extra ten pounds of dog food.

The dogs had made their way to the top of the ridge on their own while staying out of sight. Shane knew from past experience that they liked to follow him in the shadows. He figured it was only natural for them to lurk hidden on the outskirts of the trail because they were half wolf. The two dogs did not know Tashawa at all or Tara very well. This made them even more cautious. For some reason, during this part of the trip, which involved some very narrow steep trails, the dogs decided to show themselves and stick close to Shane and the packhorse. He was glad he had brought them along. Shane understood that he was in their world now. Knowing he could count on them gave him some added peace of mind.

About three-quarters of the way down the ridge, the ride became less dangerous and the trail began to level out. Shane looked down to check on Butch and Jessie, only to realize the two had once again vanished. Tashawa had also noticed the dogs, sneaking in and out of sight, so suddenly she turned back toward Tara. "You tell your boyfriend to keep those two away from me! Leave it up to a *Tahotay* to make friends with those strange creatures!" Tashawa, calling him this, took Shane by surprise.

Tara chuckled at this comment. "He's not my boyfriend, and he can hear you just fine."

When they finally reached the valley, Tashawa climbed off her horse and sat next to a large oak. Shane appreciated the woman's consideration for the horses. It had been a slow, strenuous ride down the ridge, and it was still a three-mile ride from here to the river. Shane knew the horses and dogs would be ready for a drink when they got there. For now, they were resting at the edge of a forest near one of the many grassy meadows that were scattered all over this part of the valley.

The thought of a place like this being congested with oil wells made Shane cringe. For reasons he could not explain, he was feeling a growing need to try to keep this from happening. He knew if there was oil in the valley, the Shoshone should be the ones to gain from it. He felt certain they would not rape the land and the scenery to get to it. Shane could only hope there would be a way for this wilderness to coexist with any profit that could be made here. The one thing he was sure of is the control must be left in the hands of the people who would see the greater value in this land as it was now.

Shane had called home before leaving on this trip, and had received the news from Terry that much of the property around his farm in Tennessee had been sold to a developer. The hills and fields he'd spent many years riding his young horses through would soon be disappearing for all time. Maybe finding this out had something to do with his growing desire to try to help keep this place from changing. Perhaps it was also the need to feel responsible for something more than just himself. After all, it wasn't long ago when he was consumed with a sense of duty to the other people in his life. He decided it was probably a combination of things that had him focusing so much on this new purpose. Whatever the reasons, this intention now went beyond his promise to his son to set Sloppy free.

He and the women sat on the edge of the grassy field not speaking a word. It was easy to see how content these two natives were out here in their ancient homeland.

The Shoshone, who had lived and died here since before Columbus, were a vital part of this unique country. Without them still here, this valley would certainly be like a puzzle without all its pieces.

Shane noticed some motion a short way up the tree line. It was Butch and Jessie, crouched down, stalking a rabbit. Using their instinctive, coordinated hunting skills, they made short work of killing and devouring it. Watching the two dogs eat, Shane was reminded that as beautiful as this country was, it was also a harsh, survival-of-the-fittest environment. He knew and accepted this as the way things are supposed to be. Without this balance of nature, life would cease to exist in this wilderness.

Finally, Tashawa stood up and stretched her back like she usually did before mounting her horse. Shane and Tara followed, and the three rode on with the packhorse in tow. When they arrived at the river's edge, Tashawa made it a point to direct everyone over to a particular spot where they could let the horses drink. "Why is she so worried about where the horses get their water?" Shane asked Tara.

"My grandfather doesn't want us to leave any tracks around the river. This place has hard rocky ground so we won't leave any obvious signs. The herd sometimes comes over to this area. As you know, Tigee doesn't want anyone who may be tracking them, including our own tribe members, to know we're out here. The herd rarely goes as far as Shadow Creek where we will be staying. So, we won't have to worry about leaving tracks there."

As they rode along the wooded tree line toward the cabin, the river remained in plain view. Tara pointed ahead to a moose that was swimming across the river.

"I'll be damned!" Shane exclaimed as he stopped to take a picture. During the remainder of the ride they saw some mule deer, antelope, and even a small herd of mountain goats.

It was five p.m. when they finally reached the Shadow Creek cabin. It had been a long, tiresome ride.

Shane didn't get his first glimpse of the camp until they were only several yards away. It was well concealed behind a thick patch of trees, between a couple of high rock ledges, which made a natural corral on two sides. The rest of the corral was made of log fences that appeared to be in fairly good shape.

The dwelling was small with only two rooms and a fireplace. The rooms were barely separated by a five-foot-high wall, open at the top, to let the heat from the fireplace circulate freely through the building. There were two old fold-up cots in each room. *Someone had sure gone to a lot of trouble to pack this bedding so far back into this isolated country*, he thought.

Tara looked around, with a reminiscing glimmer in her eye. "Tashawa and I have a lot of good memories of times spent here with my brothers and our grandfathers."

Shane could see that they had made the place homey and surprisingly comfortable.

After a quick inspection and some minor repairs on the corral log fences, Shane and the women fetched some water for the horses and fed them. The canned stew they ate for dinner was a welcome meal after the long day on horseback. The two dogs showed up when they smelled the stew cooking on the fire, so Shane gave them a good helping of the dry food he'd brought.

Tara and Tashawa told Shane about a clear pool around a bend only seventy-five yards downstream. The two women grabbed some clean towels and a bar of soap and Tashawa took her rifle. "When we get back, you can go clean up," Tara remarked. "No offense, but you look kind of cruddy."

"You ladies look a little dusty, yourselves. You sure you don't want some help?"

Tara smiled at his joke, but Tashawa gave him a dirty look and commanded, "You stay here!"

"Yes, ma'am," he chuckled.

When the two women returned, Shane walked down to the pool with the dogs following at a distance. He cleaned up and then lay there, letting the cool water soak on his tired body. After a few minutes, he told Butch and Jessie it was time to head back to the cabin.

Tomorrow they would ride over to the north border to try to spot the oil crew's base camp. Hopefully, Tashawa would be able to find it early in the day. Then, it would just be a matter of watching their activity to see what they were up to.

At eight p.m., Shane made a radio call to Tigee to let him know they were at the cabin.

"Did you have a good ride in?" he asked.

"Yes sir," Shane answered. "The weather was perfect and the scenery incredible. We are all pretty beat, and ready to turn in. I'll check in with you at eight a.m., over. Oh, sir — "

"Go ahead," the old man replied.

"Tommy's going to be riding the two colts out on the trail this week by himself. I would appreciate it if you'd check to see that he makes it home in one piece every day, over."

The old man's voice came back over the radio, "Yes, Tommy has already told me. I'll be waiting for your morning call."

Before collapsing on his cot for the night Shane cracked his window open and the sound of the nearby creek soon lulled him to sleep.

He woke in the morning to the sounds of the bubbling stream, and the smell of fresh, clean mountain air. He walked down to the creek, splashed some water on his face, and sat to watch the sunrise. As he relaxed while admiring the peaceful surroundings, his mind slowly drifted to a recollection of Jen.

It was an old memory from before the kids were born and just the two of them had gone on a camping trip up in the mountains, not too far from their home in Tennessee. It was this same time of the summer, but some twelve years ago. He remembered they'd had their first real argument the afternoon before. Shane couldn't even remember what it was about. They had gone to bed still upset with each other.

Shane remembered waking early the next morning, going down to the lake, and sitting in an old camp chair. He felt badly about the fight and knew he'd overreacted. Now, he recalled the warm feeling that came over him when he felt Jen's hand on his shoulder while whispering in his ear, "I love you so much, and I never want to argue like that again." Then she moved around, sat in his lap, and the two stayed there a while, with their arms around each other, not saying a word.

Interrupting his memories, he heard a voice behind him, "Good morning. Did you sleep well?"

He looked up to see Tara standing near. "Yeah, I did."

As she sat next to him, Shane couldn't help but notice how fresh and beautiful she looked.

"What were you thinking about?" she asked. Shane just shrugged his shoulders. They sat for a minute longer not talking, then Tara continued, "I've seen you before in this place you drift away to. You seem to be caught up in a strange combination of happy and sad. Mostly, you seem sad. I can't help but wonder why those old memories haunt you the way they do."

"You have no idea," Shane replied, as he forced a smile and stood.

Tara also stood and looked at him with her deep blue eyes, cocked her head to one side, and told him in a quiet voice, "I would never ask you what it is that bothers you so much, but if you ever want to talk, I'm a pretty good listener." Shane glanced down at the creek for a moment before slowly lifting his head to face her. He reached in his pocket, pulled out his wallet, and handed her a picture. In the photo, Shane was holding Tina in his left arm with his right arm around Jen while Jacob stood in front of them. The picture had been taken in front of a Christmas tree, with all of them smiling from ear to ear.

Tara didn't know what to say at first, then after a few seconds, asked, "You have a family?"

Shane looked down at the water again before he took a deep breath to help him keep his composure. During this awkward moment of silence, he assumed she was thinking he had broken up with his wife and was having trouble dealing with it.

"They're beautiful kids," she said. "Where are they now?"

Shane took another breath and swallowed the lump in his throat. "It was a car accident. One moment, we were a close, happy family on top of the world; the next minute, they were gone." He pointed at each of them, in the picture. "That's my little girl, Tina; my son, Jacob; and my wife, Jen. I lost them a couple years ago. I'm okay now, and I've learned to accept it, but sometimes I still miss them real bad."

Tara's hand began to tremble, so she quickly gave him back the irreplaceable photo for fear she might drop it in the creek. Then, she raised both her hands up to her quivering mouth as her eyes swelled with a surge of emotions. "I didn't have any idea, Shane. I'm sorry, I shouldn't have pried."

"No, Tara, there is nothing to be sorry for. I appreciate the concern you've shown for me, and we've become close enough friends for you to know. I just didn't know how to tell you. The last thing I want from anyone right now is sympathy, especially yours."

As Tara moved around in front of Shane, it was obvious that she wanted to console him for the terrible truth that her curiosity had inadvertently drawn out. Now face-to-face, she placed her open hands on his chest, and for the first time since she had met him, she was able to look beyond his features into his soul.

Shane's pulse began to race as he slowly and unsurely slid his hands around her waist. For a moment he found himself lost and confused between past and present feelings. But one glance into her still tearful blue eyes, and he became rapt in her gaze.

Tara spoke her next words softly, "You have a big heart, Shane Carson. Do you think there's some room in there for me?"

Shane lifted his right hand, then gently brushed the hair from her cheek, "The truth is I haven't been able to stop thinking about you since we met. And even though I wasn't looking for this, I think you're already in it." No one made the first move, it just happened. The kiss was soft and gentle, but so revealing.

Neither of them could shy away from their attraction anymore. As they slowly separated, they each could sense the fear and apprehension that still lingered. For a while they stood there stunned, looking into each other's eyes, but soon the feelings that had been growing between them overcame their doubt. Shane now knew in his heart that enough time had passed, and this was okay. He felt his family would want him to take this step, to find a way out of the prison of loneliness where he'd been trapped for so long.

He'd become comfortable in his odd and lonesome existence. This really was the last thing he was seeking out in his life. It must be this particular woman and this special place that was the catalyst for this to be happening. Tara was definitely a woman whom any man would desire, but he also saw her as a person with a good heart, a person that he could trust and believe in. She was beautiful down to her core.

With a smile that could melt any man's heart, she looked deep into his eyes and asked, "Are you all right with this, I mean, I'll understand if you're not ready." Shane just pulled her in close to let her know he was willing.

Suddenly, the door of the cabin slammed shut as Tashawa barreled outside toward the corral to get the horses ready.

"I guess I should go up and throw some sort of breakfast together, before we leave."

Shane nodded. "I'll be up in a minute."

Tara only took a few steps before turning to give him another heart-stopping look, then slowly walked away.

Shane took a deep breath and knelt down at the creek's edge to splash some water on his face. "I don't know if I'm ready for this." He smiled at how good it felt to have this attractive young woman show an interest in him. Jokingly, he let his male ego surface, mumbling, "Looks like this ole man still has it." He grinned at the thought as he looked down at his reflection in the now settling water. Knowing there was a busy day ahead, he shifted his mind back to the job at hand and hustled up to the camp to help Tashawa tack up the horses.

After joining Tara inside for a quick breakfast of instant oatmeal and coffee, they went back outside. Tashawa reached into her saddled bags and handed Shane a silencer that she said would work on his rifle. He noted both women already had one mounted on their guns.

Tara explained, "You can hear a gunshot out here for miles, so Tigee asked us to use these. We don't want the whole valley to know we're here when we're shooting for food or protection. If we get separated, we have the radios that are set on our own channel."

"You ladies are old pros at this, aren't you?"

"You just wait and see her tracking skills," Tara remarked as they mounted their horses and headed out.

Tashawa had them riding at a fairly fast pace. She hoped to arrive at the northern border in a little over an hour. Shane noticed the two dogs slipping into the woods when they left the camp. He knew they were in the vicinity and would be following.

Tashawa led the group to an area she thought would be the most likely place for the oilmen's camp. Unfortunately, this was a low-lying area and the morning's fog had settled in, which made for poor visibility. Even though they could hardly see their hands in front of their faces, Tashawa could sense there was no one else around. She suggested they ride further east.

She guided them to a place on higher ground. By now the fog had lifted, so from the top of this canyon wall they could see for quite a distance along the property line in both directions. Shane pulled out his binoculars and began to scan the area while still sitting on his horse. The two women stepped off their mounts and propped their rifles on low tree limbs, while looking through their scopes. It was Tara who spotted the camp. "There they are," she said, "look northeast from here, at about one o'clock."

The camp was about two miles away. It was set up near an old logging road that ran across Vince Nethers's land.

"You sit up here and keep an eye on them," Tashawa told Shane. "Tara and I will go down and see if we can find signs of them coming onto the reservation with that equipment."

Just then, the three heard the rumbling sound of thunder off to the west. The dark sky indicated that a bad storm could be heading their way. Tashawa, thinking out loud, suggested, "We better get down there quick and have a look around before the rain washes away any tracks. The storm is still pretty far away; if we're lucky it will go around us. Down below, there is an overhung cliff about a hundred yards east. If the storm comes, we'll meet you there. It'll be a good place to stay dry until the weather clears."

With that said, the two women rode out at a fast trot. Shane sat on the high ridge watching the oilmen. All the trucks seemed to be staying put, and the men were just lounging around. Tory was resting calmly; the two dogs had shown up and were lying contentedly nearby. Watching the storm move in his direction was quite a sight from this high perspective. It was still several miles away, but the whole western sky was dark and angry. Lightning was bursting through the black clouds, and every now and then, he could see one of the bright jagged streaks make it to the ground. The storm was growing in strength, minute by minute.

Chapter 19

He waited impatiently as the hour passed, and finally decided it was time to make his way to cover. Feeling the first drops, he hastily rode down the slope, barely making it under the ledge as the dark sky opened to a drenching downpour. He was surprised and concerned to see that the women weren't there. All he could do was hope they found shelter. He, Tory, and the dogs sat and waited out the storm for the next forty minutes. Shane attempted three times to contact the women on the radio with no luck. He figured the storm was interfering with the reception and finally gave up trying. When it ended, he tried to contact them again, still with no answer.

Tigee picked up his call at the ranch. "What's going on, Shane? Over."

"We were separated by a storm. I'm still waiting to hear back from them. I thought something might be wrong with my radio. Over."

"I can hear you fine. If we can't reach them soon, you'd better go look for them. I'll stay in touch. Over."

"Roger. I'll give them a few more minutes, then head north to see if I can locate them."

A short time later, Shane rode out in the same direction as the women. He'd seen them ride off from the high ridge, and since the heavy rain had now washed away their tracks, his memory of watching them leave was the only way he could follow. That's when he noticed the dogs had picked up their scent. With their noses to the ground, they were now moving at a fast pace. He cued Tory into a slow canter and followed for about twenty minutes.

Suddenly, the wolves slowed down and started acting very anxious. Butch and Jessie both trotted over to Shane, then looked ahead
toward a thick group of trees before starting a low, deliberate growl.
Obviously, the dogs were trying to tell him something was wrong.
Shane slowed his horse through the heavy foliage. The last thing he
wanted to do was to ride in on a feeding bear.

During the storm, the women had made it into a large cave. It was
well hidden behind the thick patch of trees through which Shane was
now riding. Tashawa had used this cavern many times before for cover.
When they first arrived, Tara tried to contact Shane via radio to let
him know they couldn't make it back to him before the storm hit. Just
like Shane, they couldn't get through on the radio due to the weather.

When the bad weather passed, Tara decided to try again. As she
took the radio from her saddle, someone grabbed her from behind
and snatched it away. The two women looked back toward the cave
opening to see three very wet male figures standing there. Tashawa,
who was sitting on a rock, made a quick dash for her rifle that was
in its scabbard on her horse. Just as she got to her gun, one of the
men tackled her and wrestled it away.

"What the hell do you think you're gonna do with that, you little
bitch?" he shouted. Two of the men were Indian, whom Tashawa
knew as hunting guides from the Arapaho tribe. She also knew these
guys were bad news and had been in and out of trouble with the law
their whole lives.

The Arapaho tribe were a proud and honest people, but these
two men were different. They'd been bad seeds since the day they
were born and had shown no respect for the Shoshone, or anyone
else for that matter. Tashawa had heard a couple of months ago about
their latest stint with the authorities. They were the only suspects of
a convenience store robbery in a nearby town where the clerk had
been violently beaten. The prosecutor handling the case couldn't
put together enough physical evidence to convict them. Their
names were Jack and Thomas. The third man with them was Vince's
son, Bo.

The two Arapahos were familiar with this shelter, and had headed over to escape the storm. As they arrived, they could tell someone was already there. They tethered their horses out of sight and sneaked in on the unsuspecting women.

"Let her up," Tara yelled as she tried to jerk her own arm away from Bo, who had a tight grip on her. "What do you guys want?"

"Oh, we're just out on a little hunting trip," Bo said. "We didn't expect to find you two sweet things way out here. What do you say we have us a little party." Bo pulled out a flask of whiskey and shoved it in Tara's face. She struggled to get free, knocking the flask out of his hand and spilling it. He laughed maliciously, "Don't worry blue eyes! I've got more in my saddlebags." As he leaned over to pick up the flask, Tara kneed him in his throat as hard as she could. Bo dropped to the ground letting her go while he grabbed his neck, struggling to inhale. Tara ran for her rifle but was cut off by Jack. With Thomas holding on to Tashawa, and Jack gripping Tara, both men began laughing uncontrollably at Bo, still on his hands and knees, gasping for air.

Bo crawled over to a rock he could lean against while he tried to catch his breath, cussing and gesturing obscenely at the two men.

Jack took a close look at Tara and sneered, "Look at you, you're a fine little bitch. You and me are going to have some fun!"

Thomas, who was still holding Tashawa, looked down at her and said, "When I'm done with this one, I want a turn with the pretty one."

Jack, a big, strong guy, picked Tara up, kicking and screaming, and carried her outside. He threw her down on a wet grassy spot, tore off her shirt, and slapped her hard across the face. "Stop fighting me you little whore. You know you want it."

At the same moment, Shane happened to be cautiously slipping through the trees to see what had bothered the dogs.

In spite of Jack's hard slap to her face, Tara continued to hit, kick, and fight back with everything she had. It only took Shane a second to realize what he'd ridden up on. He spurred Tory to a full gallop through the rest of the woods and into the clearing where

Jack had Tara pinned down. The Indian saw the horse charging him and scrambled to get to his feet. Tara, adrenalin pumping, got herself off the ground and made a quick getaway. As Jack stood up, he reached for a long knife from a sheath attached to his right boot. He wasn't entirely upright, so the knife had barely cleared the sheath when Shane smashed into him with his horse. This sent the knife flying out of his hand and the Indian tumbling across the ground. Jack stared at his knife that was now lying on the grass a few feet away. By this time, Shane was out of his saddle, and had reached Jack just as he was stretching for his blade. With one swift, accurate kick, Shane used his spur to slice the Indian's face open from his mouth to his ear. Jack grabbed his cheek and hollered in pain as the deep wound began to gush blood. Enraged, the Indian reached down and pulled a second knife out from his left boot. He let out a screaming war cry and then charged Shane with every intention to kill him.

With no time to get to his rifle, Shane picked up a rock and readied himself for the unfair advantage Jack had with the large knife. Jack, still screaming and charging, nearly made it to Shane when out of nowhere, came a vicious, coordinated attack from Butch and Jessie. The two wolves were on top of Jack with all the speed and precision they had acquired while hunting together since they were pups. One bit down hard on Jack's knife hand while the other went for the back of his neck.

Tara, her shirt ripped, and her face bruised, had already grabbed Shane's rifle off of Tory and hers from her horse. She tossed Shane his gun and yelled, "There are two more men in the cave, and they have Tashawa!"

Thomas had since moved off the feisty Tashawa and was running out to see what all the hollering was about. Shane met him at the cave entrance with a crashing blow to the forehead from the butt of his 30-30 rifle. Thomas barely got a look at Shane before the blow dropped him hard to the ground.

Tara was right behind Shane and soon inside holding her gun within an inch of Bo's face as he was still leaning on the rock, recovering from her previous kick to his throat. Bo stood up, pointed at Shane with hate in his eyes, and yelled, "You tell this squaw bitch to get that gun out of my face so I can finish you off, man-to-man, like I should have done in town that day." In the meantime Tashawa stumbled over and begun hysterically kicking Thomas in the back as he lay unconscious at the cave's opening.

Shane looked at Tara, who was pointing her gun at Bo, and told her, "If he moves or even twitches, shoot him in a knee." Then he went over to get Tashawa away from Thomas as she continued relentlessly kicking the still unconscious Arapaho. "All right, girl! That's enough," he said, as he put his arms around her from behind and pulled her back. "He can't hurt you any more. Just get your rifle and keep a close watch over him."

He then hurried outside to check the dogs. They had Jack on the ground propped against a tree, and he was pretty mauled up. He was also still bleeding profusely from the cut Shane gave him with his spur. Shane called the dogs off, walked up to Jack, leaned over, face-to-face, and said, "Man that's got to hurt." Then, with a look that could kill, he told him, "I'm going to let you go get some help now before you bleed to death. Seeing as how we're out here in the middle of nowhere, I don't have much of a choice. But just keep in mind, the next time I see you, I won't give you a chance to pull a knife on me. You'll be dead before you can get it out of the sheath." Shane grabbed the injured Jack by the collar, dragged him over to his horse, and pushed him up into the saddle.

Jack was hurt badly. With blood pouring from his face, he could hardly speak, but somehow he managed to look down at Shane and muttered painfully, "Fuck you, white boy, this isn't over yet."

Shane looked him square in the eye, "Not by a long shot, asshole." Then he slapped Jack's horse on the hip, and sent him galloping into the thick woods.

Shane quickly made his way back to the cave. Thomas was now beginning to regain consciousness. Tashawa still had her rifle stuck in his face, and he saw the dogs were now helping her keep him pinned to the ground. Shane was confident that Thomas was under control and wasn't going anywhere. Then he walked over to Tara, put his hand on her shoulder, and told her to stop pointing her gun at Bo. "All right, dipshit, I'm going to give you that opportunity you asked for. Man-to-man, you can show me what you've got."

Bo, with a cocky smirk, stood up. Trying to seize the advantage, he suddenly threw a sucker punch at Shane before they had a chance to square off at each other. Shane was expecting a cowardly move like this and adeptly blocked the sorry punch. Quickly reacting, he hit Bo with a crushing blow to his face, breaking his nose and knocking him to the dirt. Bo furiously struggled back up onto his feet and took another swing at Shane, hitting nothing but air. Shane countered his punch once again, this time connecting with Bo's left eye. Bo dropped to the cave floor, out cold.

As Shane stepped back, he noticed Butch was still helping Tashawa with Thomas, while Jessie had come over and positioned himself to pounce on Bo, in case things had gone the other way with their fight. He looked down at the wolf and said, "What's wrong, Jessie, didn't you think I could take him?" The dog looked back up at Shane and wagged his tail.

At that moment, Tara walked over to Shane and sighed emotionally as she put her arms around his neck.

He pulled her in close and whispered in her ear, "It's all over now."

"I sure am glad you came looking for us," she said, as she took a deep breath and recovered her composure.

Shane whistled for Tory, and the horse immediately came inside the cave and over to him. He untied a jacket from his saddle and wrapped it around Tara's torn shirt.

"What are we going to do with these jerks?" Tashawa asked.

The two men were now beginning to regain consciousness. "We don't have much choice," Shane answered. "We're too far out to do anything but let 'em go. We'll talk to the law about them when we get back." Tashawa was not happy with this. She would have killed them if Shane had not been there to stop her. Reluctantly, they let the two injured men leave.

Tashawa led the trio down to a stream, where they rode a while in the water. This would make it difficult for the Indians and Bo to track them to the camp if they had a mind to. All three men were hurt badly enough to need to go home and lick their wounds. However, Tashawa figured it was better to be safe than sorry.

On the way back, Tigee's voice came over the radio.

"Shane, come in."

"This is Shane. Over."

"Did you find the girls?"

"Yes, sir, we ran in to a little trouble. Over."

"What do you mean, trouble?"

"We're traveling pretty fast right now. We want to get back to the cabin before dark. I'll talk to you later, but everyone's okay."

The old man hesitated and then said, "All right, over and out."

The women were pretty shook up and hadn't spoken much since they left the cave. It was Tara, who finally broke the silence. "With all the commotion, we forgot to tell you what we found. Tashawa spotted some covered up tire tracks. The storm hit before we had a chance to follow them very far, but someone had definitely gone to a lot of trouble to hide them."

Tashawa finally spoke, "That's probably what those pigs were out there doing before the storm drove them to the cave."

"Do you think you can follow the tracks after the hard rain today?" Shane asked.

"Yes, I believe so," she answered.

"We'll go out in the morning and have a look-see then," he said. "I don't think those three will be coming out to the valley tomorrow. They were all pretty banged up."

Suddenly Tashawa held up her hand, stopped her horse, and pointed down. She noticed some fresh mountain goat tracks in front of them. She told Shane and Tara to stay put, slipped off her horse, and quietly walked into the woods. It wasn't long before they heard the faint shot of a rifle, with a silencer. Soon, Tashawa was back with a goat slung over her shoulder.

"Fresh meat tonight," she said as she threw the animal up in front of her saddle.

The shack was a welcome sight. Shane suggested the women go to the pool and clean up, while he fed the horses and put them away. As an afterthought, he sent the dogs down to keep an eye on the ladies. By the time they returned, the goat was skinned, cleaned, and ready to cook.

Tara walked past him holding her head down as she went by. Shane wasn't sure what was wrong, but it was obvious to him that she wanted some privacy. So he headed on down to the pool to wash up. While relaxing in the cool, refreshing water, he had a chance to reflect on what happened that day, along with the connection he and Tara had made. His thoughts then shifted to how enraged he'd become when he saw her pinned down to the ground by Jack. He was glad he'd kept his cool, though, and had not done something he would have regretted. He recalled what that son of a bitch told him as he rode off, "This isn't over yet."

Shane knew in his gut that it wasn't the last time he would see Jack. He tried to put it out of his mind as he soaked in the pool a while longer.

Approaching the cabin, he could smell dinner cooking. As he walked within sight of the porch, he noticed Tashawa putting some of the fresh meat down for Butch and Jesse. He jokingly said, "You aren't feeding those dogs our food, are you?"

All she said back to him was, "They did good today." Then she turned and went inside.

"Looks like you boys finally won her over," Shane mumbled to the wolves as he followed Tashawa into the cabin. The two women were busy preparing dinner. Along with the fresh meat, they had canned vegetables, potatoes, biscuits, and gravy. "Wow!" Shane exclaimed in surprise when he saw everything they were cooking. "You ladies went all out tonight."

Tara still kept her back to him and didn't say a word, but Tashawa looked at him and said, "This is because you did good today." The meal was Tashawa's way of showing her thanks without actually having to say the words. Tara continued to work with her back to Shane, and he was beginning to wonder if he'd done or said something to upset her.

He decided to go outside and sit with the dogs until dinner was ready. It was a nice, warm evening, and the afternoon storm had helped to settle the dust, leaving the air fresh. A few minutes later, Tashawa came out to tell him it was time to eat. As he stood, she gestured to him to follow her away from the front door.

"You seem to be a good man, Shane Carson, but I have something I need to say to you privately. Tara would be very angry at me if she knew I was talking to you about this."

Shane looked confused. "About what?"

"I have known her since she was a little girl, but I've never seen her look at a man the way she looks at you. Even with what you did for me today, I'm telling you now, if you hurt her, you will have to deal with a lot of pissed-off Shoshones — including me."

Shane wasn't sure what to say. He thought carefully for a moment before he replied. "I don't know what the future will bring for us, but I do care about her, and I'll never lie to her or lead her on."

Tashawa looked at him sternly. "I guess that's all I can ask of you." Then, she turned to walk back inside.

"Hey, wait a minute, why is Tara upset with me?"

Tashawa smiled out of one side of her mouth and answered, "She's not mad at you. She doesn't want you to see the way she looks. Her eye is turning black and her cheek is swollen. She's pretty tough though, she'll be okay."

After they ate and cleaned up, Tashawa grabbed a couple of blankets to sit on and told Shane and Tara to follow. Tara was still shyly trying to keep the left side of her face away from him. The long day had given way to night, and a bright full moon lit the way as Tashawa led them up the steep trail that began near the back of the cabin. The narrow path wound its way up to the top of the ridge that served as one side of the corral where the horses were being kept.

"Our grandfathers call this place *Gewaga-Mukua*. In English it translates to *next to the spirits*." Tashawa knew all the constellations of the stars and the Indian folklore for each. Shane had never seen her so talkative and was pleased to see she was opening up around him. Then, all of a sudden, she stood and said casually, "I'm going to bed now. You two should stay up here and enjoy the evening."

Shane moved over to sit next to Tara on the handmade Indian blanket. She shyly looked at the ground, still trying to conceal the left side of her face. "If you hadn't come to the cave looking for us when you did, who knows what they might have done to us. I want to thank you, again." Tara was usually in control of her emotions, but the thought of what could have been had induced a single tear to run out of her injured eye. Without thinking, she reached up to wipe it off and grimaced at the pain when she touched her swollen cheek. "I look as though I've been hit with a baseball bat," she said, with a quiet, angry tone. Then she looked away again.

Shane, sitting next to her, had picked up a stick and was scratching around in the sand in front of them. He slowly glanced over at her and said, "I've never been very good at coming up with the right words to say at times like this. One thing I do know is that sitting here next to you in this moonlight, I've never seen any woman look more beautiful than you do tonight."

She slowly raised her head and met his eyes with her own. "Well, you're either better than you think you are at saying how you feel, or you're a smooth talker from way back. Whichever one it is, it's working real well for you. So if I were you, I'd go ahead and make your move."

The two then came together for a long kiss that both had yearned for all evening. Tara gently fell back on the blanket as the embrace turned into a passion that neither one of them wanted to control. It had been years since either of them had chosen to be with anyone, but tonight, under the moonlight and bright stars, they each knew this was right. They were meant to be here, together, in this place, at this time.

They lay there, tangled in each others arms under the clear star-lit sky, totally at peace with the idea of being together. The closeness and comfort they felt with each other had allowed them to reach a level of passion they both realized could only be for one another.

They were completely satisfied, although too tired and still too afraid to proclaim out loud their true feelings.

When they went back to the cabin, they crawled together into one of the soft cots. They fell asleep knowing that no matter what happened for them in the future, this would be a night they would both remember.

Shane woke just before sunrise. Even in her sleep, Tara seemed to still be trying to hide her injuries as she lay with that side of her face on the pillow. They had fallen asleep in each others arms, she with her head on his chest. Now, as she lay next to him, he found himself unable to take his eyes off her delicate light brown features. He again wondered if she had any idea how stunning she really was. He carefully slid out of the cot so as not to waken her. Tashawa was still asleep in the next room as he quietly tiptoed out of the door to go tend to the animals.

Late yesterday afternoon when they returned to the shack, he had called Tigee on the radio as promised. He told him about the trouble they had run into at the cave. He also told him about the truck tracks Tashawa had found. The old man was worried about them remaining out there, and he tried to discourage their going back out to investigate further. Shane promised they would get in and out of the area as quickly as they could. Hopefully, the equipment tracks would lead them to the evidence they came out here to find.

Either way, he and Tigee agreed they needed to get the women back safely to the ranch as soon as possible. If there was any more trouble, Tigee would send over JB and Hawk, who were already in the area watching the herd. They still didn't know that Shane and the women were out there, and Tigee wanted to keep it that way if possible. Especially since the potential for a dangerous fight seemed to be growing everyday.

Bo Nethers, Jack, and Thomas had made it back to town the previous night. Jack was in the worst shape, but they all needed to go to the emergency room. The doctors fixed Bo's broken nose, stitched up

Jack's face, and then treated Thomas for a concussion, as well as the two cracked ribs he received from Tashawa's furious kicks.

"Who was that son of a bitch?" Thomas asked as he slowly sat up in the bed grabbing his side in pain.

Bo answered, "I don't know, but my friends and I already kicked his ass in town about a month ago. He ran off with that hot little Shoshone bitch, holding his tail between his legs. That's the last I've seen of him, until today."

"Well, whoever he is, he's a dead man walking," Jack said angrily.

Bo had called his father to tell him about the trouble, and Vince Nethers was at the hospital waiting for them when they came out of the emergency room.

"You're telling me that one man did all this?"

"He got the jump on us, Dad. We were caught off guard."

"What was this white man doing that far out in the valley, anyway?"

"I don't know, I guess he was on a hunting trip."

"Well, he must have had a guide to get him that far out. Did you see anyone else?"

"No sir, he was alone," Bo said, as he gave a keep your mouth shut look to Jack and Thomas. Bo didn't want to have his father find out what had really started the trouble.

Vince Nethers was a devious man when it came to business, but there was no way he would have put up with his men trying to rape the women. After all, they were supposed to be keeping a low profile in the valley.

"I want to find out who this guy is, and what he is doing around here. I don't want this prick getting in my way."

"I'm sure he was just hunting," Bo lied. "I don't think he'll be any more trouble. We worked him over pretty good."

Thomas and Jack kept their mouths shut. The two had revenge on their minds. As far as they were concerned, their beef was with Shane and had nothing to do with what Nethers had hired them to do.

Vince looked over at them and said, "Did you get everything covered up out there?" He was referring to the equipment tracks at the two new locations where they had done some testing.

"Yes sir, Mr. Nethers," Jack said. "It would take a real pro to find anything out of the ordinary around there."

"Well, at least that's been taken care of, but I'm still going to check into this guy and find out who the hell he is."

"I've seen him talking to old man Jensen," Bo said.

Vince nodded his head. "I'll have a talk with Jensen tomorrow. In the meantime, I want this hunt set up, and I don't want a single horse breathing when it's over."

"Yes, sir," Bo answered. "With Jack and Thomas here, we'll be able to come up with a plan to take the herd out of the picture real soon."

Vince looked at the two Indians. "How many guns will you need to get all the horses at one time?"

Thomas shrugged his shoulders and said, "There are probably sixty to seventy horses all together. If we can get them all into Jasper canyon, I think a dozen good shooters could handle it."

"You guys will have a big bonus coming to you if you pull this off," Vince replied. "You just let us know when you're ready, and Bo will get you all the men you need." Vince turned and walked away.

By the time the women were out of bed, Shane had the horses tacked up and ready to go. He was eager to get back out to the area where Tashawa spotted the equipment tracks. As he turned he was surprised to see Tara standing in front of him. "Damn," he said, "why do you people always sneak around like that?" Tara laughed and with no hesitation she slid her arms around his neck and softly kissed him.

"Did my hideous face scare you out of bed?"

"It was like waking up next to the bride of Frankenstein," he replied.

This caused a frown and a mixed reaction from Tara at first, then she playfully slapped him on his chest. "Very funny," she said as she turned her bruises away from him.

Shane slowly reached his hand out to her chin and gently pulled her face back around to look in her blue eyes. "You know between me and the two dogs, that jerk ended up paying quite a price for hitting you."

"I thought for a minute that you were going to kill him."

"If he ever touches you again, I swear I will."

Tara quickly replied, "I want you to promise me that you won't go looking for trouble with him. He's bad news and capable of almost anything. I don't want something bad to happen to you because of me."

"Okay, relax, we don't have to talk about this now. You know," he said, changing the subject, "that eye will look just fine in a few days. Until then, maybe you could wear a veil."

"Shut up," she answered, as she caught him off guard and pushed him backward into one of the horses.

"Easy," he said, "or I might have to tag that other eye of yours."

"Yeah, right, I'd kick your skinny ass," she replied.

Still joking around, they walked back to the cabin. As they got close to the porch, Tashawa was coming out the front door with some more meat for the dogs. "You keep feeding them like that, they're going to start thinking you're their ma," Shane said.

After breakfast, they went outside and finished packing the horses for the day's ride.

Tara asked Shane, "Do you mind if I try your horse out for a short ride?" The request took Shane by surprise, but he had no objection to it.

"Why do you want to ride him?"

"Tommy went on and on after he rode your horses. He said their training is pretty cool, and if I ever had the chance, I should get on one."

Shane took a few minutes to show Tara some of his horse's control and maneuverability.

"Wow! How did you get him so light and responsive?"

"You like that, do you?"

"Yeah, he feels great."

Working with Tara on his horse, brought back memories of when he put his wife Jennifer on Tory for the first time. The horse was only about four years old then, but her reaction was the same as Tara's had been today. As Tara stepped off Tory, she noticed the change on Shane's face as his mind slipped to the past. It was only a few seconds before he snapped out of it, stuck his foot in the stirrup, and climbed in his saddle.

"It's a good thing that you still keep your family alive with your thoughts of them," Tara said when she got back on her own horse. "I admire how you honor them with your memories."

Shane wasn't sure how to respond to this, so he didn't. He was just glad that she understood that Jen and the kids would always be a part of him. She seemed to accept and appreciate this, and to be secure enough with herself to keep it from getting in the way of her feelings for him.

"Well, now that everyone is on their own horse," Shane said loudly, "let's go finish what we came here to do." The three planned to stay close together today. All of them, including the dogs, were, of course, more on guard after what happened yesterday. Just as he and Tigee had discussed on the radio, Shane was dead set on getting in and out of the area as fast as possible.

As they rode through the wilderness, Shane tried to think of how he might describe this place to the folks back home in Tennessee. He just couldn't think of words that could do it justice. After all, there were plenty of mountains with their wilderness beauty in the great state he came from. But, for some reason, things seemed more invigorating out here. He couldn't quite put his finger on why, they just were. The mountains, forests, and even the sky seemed to have an ambience that was unique to this place. Maybe it was because this land and these people had given him back his life and a reason for living. No matter what the future brought, he would be forever grateful for that. It was hard for him to believe, in this vast valley where there were so many similar fields and forests, that Tashawa could find the exact spot where she'd seen the tire tracks yesterday without any wavering.

It was easy to see that someone had put a lot of effort into concealing the signs. If it wasn't for the unique tracking skills possessed by this Shoshone woman, neither Shane nor Tara would have been able to locate them. They followed the tracks to an open field, where Tashawa climbed off her horse and began to look around. At first she seemed puzzled, then Shane could see the light go on in her head. With a smile, she motioned for Shane and Tara to follow.

"Someone has worked very long and hard to cover these tracks," she said. Then she led them to an area on a side of the field that had a lot of brush and high grass. Hidden in the brush was a strange burrow. The long trench was about fifteen feet wide and not very deep. It ran about half the length of the large field. Now Tashawa seemed very confused. She stepped into the burrow and felt the bottom with her hand. "This ground had not been dug out, it's been packed down. How and why would someone do this?"

Shane reached in his saddlebags and pulled out his camera. "I believe we've found what we're looking for," he said, as he snapped a couple of pictures. "They sure did a good job of hiding it."

"What is it?" asked Tara.

"This is what a sixty-four-thousand-pound thumper truck does,when they use it to look for oil."

"How does it tell them if oil is here?" Tashawa wondered.

"I'm no expert," Shane answered, "but I did some research on the Internet at the library in Fort Washakie. Apparently, these big thumper trucks pound the ground with a huge metal plate causing vibrations deep under the surface, then they take seismic readings to see if it picks up any pockets of oil."

Tashawa climbed out of the burrow and began to look around for more signs. "Look here." She pointed at the ground. "These are tracks of shod horses." The horseshoe tracks had been nearly washed out from the heavy rain the day before, but Tashawa was able to follow them. "There were three men on horseback," she said. "I think it would be a safe bet to say those three at the cave were covering all this up when the storm hit."

Tashawa stepped back up on her horse and gestured for them to follow her again. She left at a slow trot, continuing to look down at the ground as she traveled. They headed north to the other end of the clearing, and then rode through a pass, which opened up into another large field. It didn't take her long to find the hidden burrows here, also. She showed them how the equipment had been carefully guided in and out on hard dry ground. They followed the faint tracks to the edge of the reservation and then out to Vince Nethers's land.

"Looks like you and Mr. Jensen were right," Tara said to Shane.

"Yep, now we know what's going on, but we still don't have any proof of who's behind all of this."

"I wonder if these people found what they were looking for?" Tashawa added.

"I believe they have," Shane answered. "Considering all the money and effort this guy is putting out, he and his people must want this valley real bad. I've got a feeling that things are going to get complicated from here on out."

Chapter 20

It was a relief for Shane to get the women back safely to Shadow Creek. As soon as the horses were put up, he called Tigee to tell him what they discovered.

Tigee hesitated before responding, "Now we know you were right. Over."

Shane answered, "The problem is there's no way to prove that Nethers has any bad intentions. He's bound to deny that he knows of any testing on the reservation. I'm sure he'd just say that the crew running the thumper truck had gotten lost and ended up on reservation land. I'd sure keep a close eye on your mustangs."

Tigee's voice came back on the radio. "Well, Hawk and JB are watching the herd, so the horses should be safe for now. I'll have to think about all this. You and the women try to relax and enjoy the rest of your day. You can pack back out tomorrow. Let me know when you're about an hour from where I dropped you off, and I'll meet you there with the trailer. Over."

"Will do. Over."

It was just past noon, and all three were looking forward to some downtime at the creek.

Once they had finished the last of the fresh meat for lunch, Tashawa had a good reason for another hunt. Shane watched her silently disappear into the foliage.

Tara asked Shane, "Do you like to fish?"

"Sure," he answered. He had noticed some old fly rods on the wall in the cabin.

"There are some really good places for trout just upstream."

The two left the camp on foot with the dogs following and rods in hand. It was about a fifteen minute walk to the bend in the creek where Tara said the trout like to hang out. This part of the stream was perfect for wading and casting. Shane had only been fly-fishing a few times, and struggled getting the hang of proper casting again. Tara, on the other hand, was skilled, and it didn't take her long to catch a nice cutthroat trout.

"These cutthroats are plentiful in most of our Alpine streams this time of the year," she hollered over the sound of the nearby rushing water. Tara smiled sheepishly as she watched Shane make one good cast out of every eight or ten. Finally, she put her rod on the bank and waded over to him. She stood behind him as she slipped her hands onto his. "Loosen up, stop trying to throw so hard; it's all about rhythm and flow." With both their hands on the rod, he relaxed as he let her take him through the motion of the cast, then she let him do it alone.

"See," she said, "it's not so hard once you get the hang of it."

Shane cast out again, with her standing next to him. Just as the fly landed gently on the surface of the stream, an explosion boiled from underneath, and the fight was on.

"All right," she hollered, "that's a nice one. Bring him in slow and easy. They have real soft mouths and can tear out the hook in a blink of an eye." A few minutes later, the two-pound fish was in the net.

"Who taught you how to fly-fish?"

"My father, when I was very young. After that, I used to fly-fish with my grandfather."

"You've never mentioned your parents before, I know your grandfather raised you. Are your parents still around?"

Tara looked a little distraught. "My mother died giving birth to me so I never knew her. She had heart problems all her life. When she became pregnant with me, the doctors tried to talk her into an abortion, but she wouldn't let them do it. My father said it took all her will to survive to full term. She wrote letters to me during her pregnancy. My father gave them to me as soon as he felt I was old enough. She explained in the letters that her bad heart would not have allowed her to survive much longer even if she hadn't become pregnant. She said bringing me into the world gave her a purpose at the end of her life. She wrote in the letters that she would always be there to watch over my brothers and me.

"My grandfather went out to the valley to be near the mustang herd the day he lost his daughter. He said he wanted to be there with her when they carried her spirit away. It was his way of telling her good-bye. My father and grandfather made sure my brothers and I knew all about her through their stories of her. She was a good person and everyone loved and respected her."

Shane kept quiet and let her continue. "My father loved her very much, and tried hard to take care of us. They say he was never the same after her death. He finally drank himself into bad health. He died when I was twelve. So you see, I can understand, to some degree, what it has been like for you to lose your family. Luckily, I have my grandfather who has kept my brothers and me together."

Shane nodded. "I know how proud he is of you."

Tara smiled before she replied. "Okay, that's enough sappy stuff. Let's catch another trout for Tashawa."

It was Shane who got the next bite, but he lost it before he could get it in the net.

Tara laughed when she saw him stomping the shallow water in frustration. It wasn't long before she caught the next one. She had a good time teasing Shane when they got back to the cabin, about catching more fish than he had.

"Yeah, yeah," he said, as they walked in the door of the old shack. "Those trout just felt sorry for you with that big black eye." She rolled her eyes and gave him a hard look. Shane quickly apologized, "Sorry, I guess that was a bad joke."

"Well, then show me how sorry you are," she said as she reached out to run her fingers over his fit shoulders. Shane could feel the warmth of her breath on his neck and the rate of her heart beat increase as he slid his hands around the small of her back and gently pulled her in tight. Now, here in the cabin alone, and this close to one another, things were rapidly evolving into a willing loss of control. Looking into his eyes, she took a step backward, smoothly dropped her clothes to the floor, and then paused before slowly moving to him. As she did, he remembered watching her at the waterfall and thinking then how perfect her body was, and how he couldn't get her out of his mind for the rest of that day.

Now, as she lay on the cot in front of him, he could hardly believe he was here with her. Hypnotized once again by her stare, he slowly moved down to her. Flesh to flesh, she softly whispered in his ear. "Shane Carson, the only reason I'm with you is because you are in my heart, and I feel I am meant for you."

When it was over, they continued to lie face-to-face in each other's arms without saying a word. Neither of them wanted this time to end, but Tashawa would be back soon.

As he sat on the edge of the cot and reached for his clothes, he quietly murmured, "As soon as all this is over, I want just the two of us to go off together."

"I'll hold you to that," she replied as she sat up next to him with a blanket wrapped around her and laid her head on his shoulder.

A short while later, Tashawa walked in with a plump turkey thrown over her shoulder. The bird, along with the trout, would make a great feast for them and the dogs. Tigee was expecting them late in the afternoon. This meant they could sleep in tomorrow morning. Considering everything that had happened on this trip, good and bad, all three were looking forward to relaxing and enjoying the evening at Shadow Creek.

The smell of the turkey roasting on the open spit filled the air, intensifying their hungry anticipation. The large bird would take a while to cook, so the trout became a welcome appetizer while they waited for the main course.

Shane remembered a flask of whiskey he had brought along just in case of a rainy, cold night and thought this would be a good time to pull it out and pour everyone a drink. Neither of the women was used to drinking, so it took very little to lighten up their mood. Soon, all three were sitting around the cooking bird telling dumb jokes that seemed hilarious.

It had been a long day, and once dinner was over, it took all the energy they could muster to just get up and go inside to their cots.

Shane woke up before the women and grabbed his camera. It was another invigorating morning at the creek, so he climbed to the top of the ridge called "Gewaga-Mukua." He reached his high destination just at the right moment to take some amazing shots of the rising sun's yellow-orange glow, edging its way from behind a dark horizon to gradually illuminate the whole eastern sky. Then he pointed his small camera down at the cabin, and next toward Shadow Creek with its rich, green, forested background.

Click. Click. Click. When he felt he had captured all he could on film, he put his camera in its case and enjoyed the time alone while he absorbed the serene wilderness surrounding him. Soon he began to feel regret for having to leave.

By midmorning everything was packed up and ready for the six-hour-plus ride ahead of them. Shane contacted Tigee, via the radio, to let him know they were on the way.

With Tashawa as their guide, they made the trip back to the drop-off point in good time. Tigee was waiting there with his truck and trailer. The old Indian seemed quiet and distant. He greeted Shane with a handshake, then gave each of the girls a hug. However, it was easy to see he was not quite himself. As they drove into the ranch, he asked Tara and Shane to come see him as soon as the horses were put up.

Tommy spotted them when they pulled through the gate, and ran over to help with the horses and gear. "How was your fishing trip, Mr. Shane?"

"It was great, Tommy. How are the geldings doing? Have you been working with them every day?"

"Yes, sir, I'm looking forward to showing you what I've done with 'em."

"I'll be out at the barn at eight a.m."

"Yes, sir, I'll be ready to start as soon as you get there."

Tara and Shane said their good-byes to Tashawa . Before she left, she gave the dogs the leftover turkey she had in her saddlebags. Curious about what Tara's grandfather would have to say, the two of them hurried to his house.

As they walked in the front door, Tigee said, "I know you're both tired, but I needed to speak to you now."

"What's wrong, grandfather?"

"Well, some problems have come up in the last few days with the ranch."

"What kind of problems?"

"Before I tell you what is going on around here, I want to hear about your trouble in the valley, and how you got that bruise on your face, Tara."

She told him about Jack, Thomas, and Bo Nethers, and how Shane came with the dogs and stopped it all before anything really bad happened. "We think they were out there covering up the tracks around the test sites and came to the shelter when the storm hit."

Tigee replied, "Shane and I discussed it briefly on the radio. I'm just not sure how to handle it yet."

"Maybe it's time to call in the law," said Shane. "Especially since those three guys tried to assault the women."

Tigee looked at Shane. "You've seen what the local law is like around here. It would be your word against theirs, and with that Nethers boy involved, they wouldn't get more than a slap on the wrist. Besides, it sounds as though you taught those fellas a lesson they won't soon forget. The last thing I need right now is for any of our Shoshone men to find out about this incident. If they did, there could be some bad trouble over it. There is already a lot of tension building over the killing of the mustangs." It was obvious that Tigee was torn between making the three men pay for hurting Tara and Tashawa and doing what was best to keep the peace.

The three sat quietly in thought for a few minutes, then Tigee spoke again. "Without the law to help us, I'm not sure how to protect the land or the mustangs. I'm afraid I have some news that makes the matter even worse," he added. "The whole tribe is very worried about our finances for the winter."

"What's going on?" Tara asked.

The old man took a deep breath and explained, "Some agricultural inspectors came the day you left for Shadow Creek. They claim that one of the calves we took to auction last week tested positive for anthrax. Then they found a sick cow on one of the other Shoshone ranches. Our people said the sick cow wasn't theirs, and that they don't know how it got in with the herd. Since then, the inspectors have quarantined all the ranches on the reservation indefinitely. This means we can't sell any more cattle this year. The local banks have caught wind of it and won't even loan the ranchers money to get through the winter."

"We've had a really good hay crop this year," Tara said. "I know it won't pay all the bills, but it might help carry the ranch over until we get the cattle problem solved."

Tigee's head dropped as he spoke. "Someone has started rumors all over the territory that we didn't spray our hay properly and that we have a bad infestation of blister beetles in the alfalfa. As you know, if a horse eats even a small part of a blister beetle, it will die. Our hay was excellent this year, and we did spray it, but the rumors will keep the locals and the big shippers we usually sell to from buying any. I don't understand this run of bad luck."

Shane couldn't sit quietly any longer. "It can't be a coincidence that all these things are happening at the same time. I think someone is trying to put a squeeze on your income for the winter. If they did find oil in the valley, then this could all be part of a plan to force you to accept a land deal. These people know that the whole Shoshone tribe would have to be desperate before you would lease any part of the valley. They also know that as long as the horses are there, the majority of your people would resist a land deal. My guess is they will be coming after the herd soon, and probably with a lot of guns."

Tara asked, "What if we just told them that we know what they're trying to do, and we won't sell or lease any land no matter what?"

Shane thought for a minute. "The way I see it, these guys can really make things tough around here until they get what they want. With the local law probably being on Nethers's payroll, they won't be any help. We know that for sure. If we confront them now, they may get even nastier. I think it could work in our favor if they don't realize we are on to their scheme."

Tigee added, "Besides, in the end it will come down to a tribal vote on any property sale or lease. If enough of our people are really in need of money, we won't be able to stop them from giving into a deal. I agree with you, Shane, it would be best if we don't poke at the angry bear until we have a plan. We will eventually have to prove to our people that there is oil out there and that if they're patient, it could one day be a good income for our tribe."

The three sat contemplating for a while until suddenly, Shane's face lit up. "I have an idea," he said "but I'm not sure if you'll like it."

Tigee asked, "What is it?"

"Have you ever seen what a bunch of roaches do when you turn on a light?" Tara and Tigee look puzzled. Shane continued, "They quickly scatter back to where they came from, don't they? What if we put a spotlight on this situation from outside this territory?"

"I don't understand," Tara commented, frowning.

Shane smiled. "Your people have a resource here that can get a lot of national attention if we can get the right exposure for it." Tara and her grandfather still looked confused. Shane continued, "The herd! There are a lot of people that would take an interest in those mustangs because of their rare bloodlines. The fact that you have direct links that lead back to the Lewis and Clark expedition and horses that were part of Custer's defeat at the Little Big Horn is fascinating, not to mention the bloodlines that date back through your tribal history all the way to when the Spanish first brought horses to the continent in the fifteen hundreds. These are all things, which if they are publicized correctly, would have a lot of people wanting to help protect and preserve your herd."

"I don't know if I like this idea," Tigee replied, shaking his head.

Tara walked over and put her hand on her grandfather. "This may be the only way we can keep them safe. With the public eye on our horses, Nethers would have to leave them alone. The last thing he wants is publicity."

Tigee seemed puzzled. "How would we get the public's attention?"

"I've got some friends in the magazine business who are always looking for a good story. I can't guarantee you anything, but I'm pretty sure this is the type of story they'd jump all over. The kind of national exposure they could give you would make a lot of people more than just sympathetic to what's going on out here. This would give you the time you need to convince your people that Nethers and his bunch are trying to take advantage of them. I'd sure like to catch Nethers by surprise with some big-time publicity about what he is trying to do to the horses and your valley."

"We've seen the articles about you in the magazines," Tigee said.

Shane looked surprised. "How did you see any articles about me?"

"Your friend Mrs. Jensen brought them out for us to read."

Shane shook his head with a bashful expression. "I didn't know she did that. But I can tell you this, hundreds of thousands of people read those magazines every month. I also know some animal-rights activists. They would love to get involved with saving the mustangs, and they may be capable of getting those shooters along with whoever is behind them into a lot of trouble. You just give me the okay, and I'll start the ball rolling."

The room grew quiet. Finally Tigee looked at Tara and then turned toward Shane with a single nod. A reluctant yes.

"Normally, I would bring this up in front of the tribal council. But, since there is so much going on here that they are unaware of, and so little time to act, I will take the responsibility."

Shane breathed a sigh of relief. "Good, I'll begin making calls first thing in the morning."

As Shane stood to leave, Tigee said, "Your friend Mr. Jensen called yesterday. He said it was important that you contact him."

"Do you mind if I call from here?"

"Sure, go ahead." Tara and Tigee went out to the porch while Shane picked up the phone.

The two sat on the swing together, as they often did. Her grandfather patted her leg and said, "I can see a difference in the two of you since you returned. You seem closer than before."

"Yes, Grandfather. I think we have some real feelings for each other."

The old Indian smiled and said, "He's a good man, but did he tell you about his past?"

"Yes, he did."

"Did he tell you why it is so important for him to set his mare free with the herd?"

"No, but he told me before that it had something to do with a promise he made."

Tigee nodded and said, "It isn't my place to say. I'm sure he'll tell you about it when he is ready. Just be careful with giving this man your heart, Tara. He's dealing with a lot of grief, and I don't want to see you get hurt."

The two sat quietly for a while, and then Tigee said in a concerned tone, "I had another vision, involving a *Tahotay* that resembled him. In this dream, he showed no fear as he battled the enemy that was in front of him. Unfortunately, he was not aware of the real danger that was sneaking up from behind. I fear for his safety."

This really shook up Tara. "Could this dream be about the trouble we had during the trip? He fought those men bravely. If it had not been for him and the dogs, things could have turned out really bad for Tashawa and me."

"I think my vision was more about the future than the past. Only time will tell. For now, I'm glad to see you happy." Tara smiled and put her arm around him as they quietly sat on the swing.

Shane reached Mr. Jensen and was listening closely. "I was shocked to see Vince Nethers standing at my front door ringing my bell. I've talked to him in town a few times, but he's never been out to my house. I invited him in for coffee, and we had quite an interesting chat. At first it was just small talk, but then he started asking questions about you."

"That doesn't surprise me. I had quite a run in with his son, Bo, and two of his friends. I think I may have broken Bo's nose in the ruckus."

Mr. Jensen laughed. "According to their side of the story, the boys told Vince that they worked you over pretty good."

"No, sir, the only ones they worked over were the two women I was with. Believe me, those sons of bitches paid a price for that."

"What were those boys doing out there, anyway?"

"They were covering up some test drilling sites that were on reservation land. You were right all along. Those people are sniffing around for oil out there. Now, I suspect Nethers is trying to mess up all kinds of income for the Shoshone so that they will be behind with their bills when he makes them an offer on the land."

"How about the mustangs?" Mr. Jensen asked.

"The Shoshone are keeping a close watch on them, but I've got a feeling they're going to be dodging bullets again real soon. I've got a plan I'm working on that might help. But right now, I'd like to know what Nethers was saying about me."

"Well, he wanted to know who you are, where you came from, and what your business is out here. I acted as if I really didn't know. I told him I had boarded your horses for a couple weeks and thought you just came out for some hunting and fishing. I don't think he bought it though. He got real cocky and loud when he said if I saw you again, to tell you to mind your own business or you could get hurt. He said to let you know it would be a good time for you to go back to wherever you came from. I just kept acting like I didn't know anything about you. I told him I doubted that I would see you again, but if I did, I'd pass the message on. You need to be very careful, Shane. Ole Vince is worried about you spoiling his future fortune."

Shane quickly replied, "I'm not too worried about him. Besides if my idea works, that old scoundrel is going to find a major complication in his scheme."

"Shane, you watch your back, and you let me know if I can help."

"Thank you for everything, sir. I'll talk to you later."

He hung up and walked out on the porch.

"Is everything okay with the Jensens?" Tigee asked.

"Yes, sir, they're fine." Shane didn't see any need to worry these two with the fact that Vince Nethers was threatening him, so he didn't mention it.

Tara got up from the swing and went over to lean against the porch rail next to Shane. "My grandfather is going to a neighbor's house for dinner. That leaves me free tonight. If you want, I could come over and cook."

"Why don't we go out to eat? I don't have any food in my cabin anyway. We could run up to Fort Washakie and get a steak."

"Sounds good to me. I'll meet you here as soon as I get cleaned up."

The hot shower felt good on Shane's aching back. Although he was in good shape for a man his age, the many years of making his living in the saddle had taken a toll on this part of his body. With the last of the trail dust washed off, he dressed and went to meet Tara.

A clap of thunder rumbled overhead as a few sprinkles of rain began to fall from the evening sky. It was almost dark when Shane sat down on the porch swing to wait for her. His mind was racing, thinking about the events of the day.

His mind suddenly went blank as he looked up to see Tara coming out the door. Man, she was easy on the eyes! She wasn't dressed fancy, just snug-fitting white denim pants and a light pink sweater. Her medium-high heels and turquoise earrings complemented the outfit, and it was obvious she had taken some time to primp. The dumbfounded look on his face must have shown his approval, as she looked at him teasingly and smiled. Shane stood up and walked toward her. Tara kept her blue eyes gazing into his as he came closer. When he got near enough, she slowly slid her arms around his neck and softly kissed him.

"Damn, you look good," was the most romantic thing he could think of to say.

Tara laughed. "So do you."

The drive to the restaurant in Fort Washakie was a thirty minute trip. It went by quickly as they talked and enjoyed each other's company.

She stayed with Shane in his cabin that night, taking little heed in Tigee's advice of caution for her feelings toward him. She also knew the Indians on the ranch had a live-and-let-live attitude. Gossip was not in their nature.

The next morning they were both up early. She had a lot to do at work since school would be starting in a couple of weeks. Shane had promised he would help Tommy with the horses, and then he planned to try to reach his reporter friend, Megan Tillie. As they headed out the door to go their separate ways for the day, Tara turned to Shane with a serious look on her face.

"What's wrong?"

She hesitated, then said, "I know you'll think that what I'm about to tell you is only Indian superstition, but my grandfather had another vision. In his dream, you were in a great danger. He is worried about you, and so am I."

Shane smiled at the intense look in her eyes. "I'm sure he means well. I'll be fine."

Tara forced a grin and gave him a strong hug. "Just say you'll be careful, okay? I'm telling you, my grandfather has a gift, and his predictions are often right on the money."

"All right, I promise I'll be careful," Shane conceded as he winked and walked away.

Chapter 21

The light rain last night was just enough to settle the dust and firm up the sandy footing in the corral. Tommy was already in the barn with one of the geldings saddled and was leading him over to the corral for a warm up. "How's the gelding doing?"

"Real good, Mr. Shane, I've got Sloppy saddled up in her stall. I thought we'd take them out on the trail together, so I can show you what I've got done with him."

"Well, let's go."

Tommy had accomplished a lot with the horse. Shane was impressed with how eager he was to please his rider.

"You've done a good job, and I think he's broke enough for you to begin putting some real buttons on him. From now on, your rides on both the geldings will involve more technical training. We're going to teach them how to operate just like Sloppy and Tory." Shane could see the excitement in Tommy's eyes.

Shane had worked with a lot of people in his long career, but he'd never seen anyone with as much natural feel and God-given talent as Tommy. Tommy seemed to naturally know why a horse had to be in a certain position to properly perform a maneuver. Shane could only guess this came from the boy watching horses move around in the fields since he was very young.

"I want you to ride Sloppy every day and keep practicing the hip control, the shoulder control, and the lateral movements I've shown you. Now let's get the mare out and see how she is doing."

After Shane finished helping Tommy, he patted the boy on the back and turned to leave.

"Wait a minute," Tommy hollered. Then he ran into the barn and came out with something in his hand. "Mr. Shane, I made you this to thank you for all you've been teaching me." It was a hand-braided rope, like the ones Shane had seen on JB and Hawks's horses. "The Shoshone have used these on their horses for hundreds of years. You don't have to ride with it, but I thought you might like it for a keepsake. It took me all week to braid it. Mr. Tigee helped me make it for you."

Shane was taken aback. "Thank you, bud, this means a lot to me. I'll keep it forever." Then he affectionately squeezed the boy's shoulder before walking away.

He would have liked his son, Jacob, to have been able to know this young Shoshone boy. Tommy was a few years older and would have been a good example for Jacob to look up to.

Shane took the rope and hung it over the fireplace in his cabin. Then he took an address book out of the old saddlebags he used for storing personal items. He hadn't talked to Megan Tillie since he lost his family. They'd been friends a long time, and as she had written in one of her articles, she had actually introduced Shane to his wife, Jennifer. Megan had tried several times to reach him after the accident, but like a lot of other old friends who tried to contact him, he'd never responded to any of her messages. He felt badly about not calling these people, but it would have been too hard to listen to their well-meaning condolences.

When he got to Tigee's cabin, the old Indian was sitting on the porch, as he usually was this time of day. "Good morning, sir."

"Good morning," Tigee replied.

"Well, are you ready to make these horses of yours famous?" Shane asked jokingly. The old man just smiled, shrugged his shoulders, and gestured for Shane to go in and make his phone calls. He had Megan's personal cell number, but all he reached was her voice mail, so he left a short message, asking her to get back in touch as soon as possible. He hung up and was on his way out the front door when the phone rang. He could see on the caller ID that it was Megan. He eagerly answered. "Hello."

"Shane, is that you?" Megan asked excitedly.

"Yes ma'am, how the hell are you?"

"I'm fine. It's so good to hear your voice. Where are you?"

"I'm in Wyoming."

"What in the world are you doing out there? Are you putting on clinics again?"

"Nope, no clinics. I guess you could say I'm out here on vacation."

"Well, what can I do for you?"

"I think I might have an interesting story for you to write about."

"I'm listening," she replied. "But, before you tell me about it, I have to say how sad I was to hear about Jen and the kids. I tried to call you several times."

"I know you called, Megan, I just wasn't in a frame of mind where I could talk to people about it. It's still hard."

"I understand. I just needed you to know I was thinking about you and I was ready and willing to do anything in the world for you. I still am."

"Thanks, Megan, I appreciate that."

"Now, what kind of story do you have for me?"

Shane told her about the mustangs and their unique history and how their survival was in real jeopardy. "We've already found several mares and foals shot down in cold blood."

"Do the Shoshone have any documentation on the history of these horses?" she asked.

"They sure do, there are records dating back over hundreds of years. The tribe has papers in their museum that can tell you when a particular horse was introduced to the herd, why that horse was significant in the tribe's history, and special enough to be set free with their herd. The breeding records are well kept and can trace each of the present-day horses back to these special foundation lines. Believe me, these horses are the real deal. The Shoshone consider these mustangs a sacred part of their heritage. The fact that the herd's lineage also intermingles with a lot of significant American history should really interest your readers. The only reason the

Indians will let you write about them is to expose these bad guys to the public eye before they can destroy the whole herd."

He explained about Vince Nethers and his secret oil explorations on the reservation. "This guy knows as long as the herd lives on the land, the Shoshone would never lease it to him." He also told her about the mysterious sick cows and the rumors of the bad hay, which had shut down the tribes income for the winter. Then he explained how the local authorities were of no help to the Shoshone. "We're out in the middle of nowhere, and the only law around here is in this guy's hip pocket. I'm hoping that a little national attention to this situation will help back these guys off and maybe bring some justice out here."

"Wow, you sure got yourself caught up in a mess. How did you end up in Wyoming anyway?"

Shane told her about Sloppy and the promise he made to his son. This stirred some sad emotions for Megan, and he could tell she was fighting back some tears. Megan had stayed at his home on several occasions and spent a lot time with the kids. Every Christmas there were gifts from her for Jacob and Tina under the tree. Even though she lived far away, she and Jen had stayed close friends and called each other often.

Shane gave her a moment to compose herself and then asked, "So what do you think?"

"It sounds pretty interesting," her voice quavered. "I just need to run it by my editor, and I'll call you back."

"Listen, Megan, time is everything if we are going to save these horses."

"I understand. If my editor gives me the okay — and I'm sure he will — I'll be out there in a couple of days. I know the magazine is still looking for a unique story for next month's issue, so the timing couldn't be better. I'll get back in touch with you before noon to let you know what he says."

"I'll be waiting to hear from you, and Megan — thanks."

Shane was encouraged by his friend's desire to do the story, but he still had one more phone call to make. This one would bring in his real secret weapon. Shane couldn't help but laugh when he thought about the fire he would be lighting under Nethers and his people with this part of his plan. He fumbled through the pages of his old address book, and then a smile lit up his face as he found the number. The woman's name was Kate O'Hanson. Kate was the national director of an organization that was a watchdog for inhumane treatment of horses.

She stood about five feet tall and three foot wide. Whenever she locked onto a worthy cause, her strong Irish backbone made her a force to be reckoned with. She was a wealthy widow with plenty of time and money, plus she had an army of well-meaning people in her organization. Kate was also a loyal client of Shane's. He had started and trained at least half a dozen horses for her over the years. She called her organization the HTH, which was the acronym for Humane Treatment of Horses.

Shane had seen Kate and the HTH get involved with many causes through the years, and he knew her organization could be a real thorn in the side of whomever they went up against. Shane knew from past experience that Megan Tillie and her magazine would not partner with the HTH. These would be two separate entities coming at Nethers from two different directions. Megan and the magazine would be shining a spotlight in his eyes, while Kate and the HTH would put a boot on his ass.

Shane was aware that in the past Kate had been involved in saving wild horses in Montana and Utah. When he told her about the Shoshone's unique herd and what was going on, she agreed to come out as soon as she could get her group together.

Shane sat with Tigee on the porch, waiting for Megan to return his call. "I think this will work." Shane could see the old Indian was still uncertain about bringing outsiders in. The herd and their heritage was always a private thing to the tribe.

"I hope I'm not taking our horses out of one bad situation and putting them in another," Tigee replied.

Shane understood change was difficult for a man like Tigee, who had spent his whole life trying to preserve the past and the old ways. He tried to assure him, "If it allows you to keep your valley, then your tribe will be able to control the amount of access the public will have to the mustangs. In the end, this will be good for your people and the horses."

Tigee reluctantly nodded.

As soon as Megan Tillie hung up the phone, she walked to her senior editor's office at the *Journal of the Horse*. Rick Bivens was reviewing an article as he looked at her over the top of his reading glasses. "Hi Megan, what can I do for you?"

She walked in and sat in a chair at the front of his desk. "I think I may have an interesting story for us. Do you remember Shane Carson?"

"Wasn't he the clinician you did a couple of articles on when you first came to the magazine?"

"Right. I told you that a couple of years ago he lost his family in a car accident."

"Sure, how could I forget that? You had been a friend of his wife for years."

"Yes, actually I introduced them, and I spent a lot of time with the whole family, so you can imagine how shocked I was when I heard about Jen and the kids. I can't even fathom what it was like for Shane."

Rick closed his eyes and shook his head. "How is he doing these days?"

"He just called me, and he sounded good. I tried to contact him after the accident without any luck. I've thought about him often and now, out of the clear blue, he called me just a few moments ago."

Rick put his hand up to stop her from going on. "Look Megan, I feel bad for what the guy has been through. I know he was a special trainer. But the guy hasn't been in the limelight for, what, about ten years or more? He may even be a better horseman than some of the ones who are well known now. I'm sorry, he's just not worth us spending the time and money it would take to do an article on him. If he's looking to do a comeback on the clinic tour, all I can do is offer him a good discount on some advertising."

Megan jumped in to stop Rick. "No, no, Shane's not asking for a story on him. He's run into a real interesting situation in Wyoming that I think will spark the interest of our readers." Megan told Rick all about the mustangs.

"Wow," he said. "The powers that be here at the magazine have been on my case to come up with a good human-interest story. This sounds like just what I've been looking for. Our deadline for the next issue is in ten days. Do you think we can put it together by then?"

"Just give me some plane tickets and a photographer. I'll fly out Monday. I've got a good feeling about this story. I think the idea is good enough to write itself."

Rick smiled at her enthusiasm as he told her to make the arrangements.

Shane and Tigee were sitting quietly on the porch when the phone rang. Tigee looked at Shane and motioned toward the door. Shane was at the phone before the third ring. It was Megan calling, all excited since she had gotten the okay from her boss.

Today was Friday. She would be flying into Riverton early Monday morning along with a photographer. Shane offered to pick them up at the airport, then drive them out to the Wind River Reservation that afternoon. "You can bunk here with me Monday night, but I'd rather you stay in town after that. I need the word to get around town as soon as possible that you're doing a national article about the Shoshone mustangs being killed off. It's a small town, so it should be the buzz around there pretty quick. There's no doubt the news will get back to Nethers, so he'll have to postpone any future hunts and rethink his next move."

"Shane, you know I can't write about anyone's involvement in all this unless I have hard evidence."

"I know. Even if you can't bring any names into the story, we do have pictures of dead horses, as well as pictures of test sites on the reservation. Those photographs show that someone was definitely looking for oil and then covered up their tracks."

Megan thought a moment. "I'll run that angle by our legal staff, but I'm pretty sure we'll be okay as long as we aren't accusing anyone without proof. You know, Shane, the *Journal of the Horse* is a horse-related publication. The article can't stray too far away from facts about the herd and their plight."

"I understand, and I look forward to seeing you Monday."

"Me too. I'll see you then."

Shane walked out onto the porch to join Tigee and leaned on the rail. "Well, everything seems to be in place. My friends will be out the first of the week. These are all good people whom you can trust, and I can assure you they will have your horses' best interest at heart."

Again, the only response he got was a slight nod. As Shane started to walk away, the old Indian spoke to him. "My grandsons have been in the valley keeping an eye on the horses. JB and Hawk will be relieving them tomorrow. If you'd like to go out to the valley and help, they're leaving here at ten. I'm worried that there will be an attempt on the herd soon. I'm sure they could use a third man if there is any trouble."

"I'm working with Tommy in the morning, but I'll be ready to load by ten."

As he started to leave, Tigee called after him so Shane turned. "I just needed to thank you for all you're doing." Shane smiled and left.

Later that day when Tara came home from work, she cooked dinner for her grandfather, then went to see Shane. When she walked into the house, she could tell he was off in his own world again. The sight of her snapped him out of it and immediately put him in a better frame of mind.

"Did your grandfather tell you I have a few friends coming out the first of the week?"

"Yes, he did. He appreciates what you're doing and trusts you, but I know he has mixed emotions about sharing our herd with the world."

"I don't blame him," Shane said. "So far, the only interest out-siders have shown with your horses is to shoot at them. He'll feel better when he sees there are other people beside the Shoshone, who will care about the herd. You're going to like Megan. She will write a great article, one that will make the horses and your people come across to the public in a special way. Who knows, she may even kick up some tourism business in Fort Washakie. I really don't think any-thing bad can come out of this."

Tara shrugged her shoulders with a disheartened look on her face and looked away from Shane. "What's wrong?" he asked.

"When all this is over, and it's safe for your mare in the valley, you'll set her free."

"That's what I came here for."

Tara took a deep breath, looked back in his direction, and said, "I know. And once you set her free, you'll be going back to your farm in Tennessee."

All of a sudden, it hit Shane like a ton of bricks. He hadn't put much thought into life after he accomplished his objective, and he certainly hadn't expected to end up in a relationship with this Shoshone woman. Now everything had become more complicated, and he didn't know quite how to respond to her.

Neither one of them were naive about this situation. The fact that their two worlds were a nation apart was something they had consciously chosen to ignore. But, as a couple, they could overlook this for only so long.

Shane's first response was to walk over to her. He wanted to tell her that everything would be all right, even though he really had no idea if it would be. As he reached down to lift her chin, he saw the heavy look in her eyes, and his heart began to sink.

"Come back with me," he said as he pulled her face around to look at him.

No matter how much she wanted to be with him, Tara knew she would never become comfortable or fit in Shane's Tennessee. The fact that he wanted her to go, told her how much he cared. This alone, meant the world to her. But with a quivering voice, she mumbled, "My place is here."

Shane nodded. "I know. Look, I don't have any idea what the future holds for us, but I do know I never thought I could feel this way about anyone again. I don't want to lose you."

"I don't want to lose you either," she said as she moved her hands onto his chest and looked at him with misting eyes.

He brushed back the hair from her face and tried to think of some words to reassure her. "You know, there's not a lot left for me in Tennessee. Who knows where my life will lead me. I'm still just living one day at a time. I can't even conceive of making plans for the future right now."

"I'm not asking for any promises," she said, "only that you be honest with me. Beyond that, we'll just see where our destinies take us." For now, what they had between them was too good to let go, and neither one had any intentions of walking away from it. They stayed together that evening, and in the morning, she and Tommy helped him load Tory onto Hawk and JB's trailer. Then she kissed him good-bye.

JB wasn't too sure about bringing the dogs along. He had no idea how much help they could be. He and Hawk still didn't know about the trip Shane and the two women had gone on, or what had happened during their stay at Shadow Creek. Tara's bruises were healing, and what was still noticeable, she covered with makeup and sunglasses.

The possibility for trouble was still very much on the horizon. If the young Shoshone men knew what was going on, it would be impossible to keep them from going on the offensive. It was more important now than ever to keep the lid on this potential keg of dynamite until Shane's plan could start working.

After watching Tara say good-bye to Shane the way she did, JB and Hawk could not help but razz him about it as they drove off. "You know, I've seen a lot of guys go after Tara," said Hawk, "but none seem to get past a date or two. What the hell does she want with you?"

"I guess she likes old, skinny white boys," said JB as both the Indians laughed.

"Yeah, yeah, you guys are hilarious," Shane growled, "Or is it you're just a little jealous?"

Hawk laughed again. "Shoot, JB and me are the studs of the Shoshone tribe. We've got women waiting all over the reservation. Besides, Tara thinks she's too good for us. You probably told her you're rich or something."

"That's how I get all my women," Shane answered. "Now why don't you guys cut me some slack?"

JB, who was driving, looked across at Hawk and then at Shane before saying, "All joking aside, Tara means a lot to us. If you hurt her, there will be a lot of pissed-off Shoshone, including me, to deal with."

Shane nodded while looking out the truck window, "Yeah, I've heard that before."

As they pulled into the unloading spot, some dark clouds were beginning to roll in, and it looked like a sure bet they were going to get wet. Jessie and Butch jumped out of the truck's bed as soon as it stopped. They slipped into the woods before the men had a chance to get out of the truck. "Hey, your two pet wolves have run away," Hawk pointed out.

"Nah, they just like to stay out of sight; they'll keep close."

JB stepped up on his horse as he spoke. "Tigee told us to keep a low profile. Those damn dogs better not give up our position to the horse hunters if we get into a situation."

"Don't worry, they have too much wolf in them to bark at anything." Shane knew if they encountered any trouble this weekend, Butch and Jessie might be of some help.

The rain came down hard that afternoon, but luckily, it didn't last too long. All of their gear would have a chance to dry out before the cooler night air was upon them. It took about two hours to get to the high ridge where JB, Hawk, and Tara's brothers had set up camp.

This was the perfect place to keep an eye on things. It had easy

access to and from the lower ground. The best part was that the narrow trail on the far side of the hill next to them formed the north entrance to the valley. This was where hunters would park their trucks
and trailers.

"We have plenty of trees and cover between us and their
unloading area," Hawk said, "but we'll still be able to hear their
vehicles if they come in. We'll know they're here before they even
get out of their trucks."

The camp the Indians had set up was just a lean-to built on the
side of an undercut rock ledge. It didn't look like much but would
serve as a good, dry cover. A light wind was blowing out of the north,
which would allow them to build a fire tonight. Any smoke would
blow in the opposite direction of the poachers' parking area.

"I'm going hunting," said JB. "I saw sheep tracks on our way in.
I'll try to find us one for our dinner." He went alone and on foot but
took his rifle and a compound bow with a quiver full of arrows. "He'll
shoot the sheep with his bow," Hawk said. "It won't make a noise and
give away our position."

Hawk slapped Shane on the shoulder in a friendly manner and
said, "Grab your rifle and binoculars and follow me." He explained
the position of the camp. "From where we are now, we can see a lot
of the west side of the valley. The ridge we're on comes to a point
about a half mile southeast of our base camp. From this side of the
point, we'll have a good view to the south. Once we work our way
around the high rock wall that forms the point, we'll be able to see
the Wind River a long way off to the east. There's plenty of cover
down there," he added, "but we'll still have a good view of most of
the trails and the grazing areas on this whole north end of the valley."

The path they started out on worked its way up and away from
the camp. At one place they climbed an eight-foot-high crevice between two rock ledges. When they got to the top of the crevice, it
was an easy quarter-mile walk through woods on good solid ground.
As they approached the point, the southwestern view of the valley
below slowly began to emerge. Magnificent scenery had become a
common sight for Shane, but no one, not even Hawk, who had

grown up here, could help but stop and take a minute to gaze down into this natural wonder. It seemed like you could see forever and the view of the valley below left Shane in awe. The six-hundred-foot drop to the bottom from this high cliff, called Devil's Point, startled him. Hawk laughed as Shane's natural fear of heights caused him to gasp and step back from the edge.

"Holy shit," he said as Hawk showed him the narrow ledge they'd be moving across to get around the point. It was about thirty feet long on each side of the point, making it a total of sixty feet to safe ground on the other side. The scary part wasn't the length; it was the one-and-a-half-foot width between the drop off and the high rock wall behind it. Scaling this obstacle was the only way to get around to the other side.

"Just stay close to the wall and don't look down," said Hawk. Shane took a deep breath and followed Hawk out onto the narrow ledge. His legs felt weak, and his heart raced as they made their way around the point to the east side. "See, there's nothing to it. Now, look down at the river and this side of the valley, and tell me it wasn't worth risking your life to see this."

Shane took a deep breath as he tried to regain his composure, and then looked to where Hawk was pointing. Down in an open meadow near the Big Wind River, was the herd of mustangs. Hawk looked at Shane and said, "I don't know if Tara or Tigee told you, but the older ones in our tribe call them the spirit horses. The Shoshone words for this are *Mukua dehee'ya nee*. The old ones believe they will carry us to where we will cross over into the next life when we die."

"Yes, I've heard this."

"Take a look at that palomino stallion," Hawk said, as they both raised their binoculars to look down at the herd. He's a three-year-old son of a different stallion than Naatea. Ivan and Willie told me that he's been getting bolder with Naatea over the last week. I think he may challenge the old stud for head of the herd soon."

Just then, the young stallion, who was still about seventy-five yards away from Naatea, started rearing and striking out with his front feet. The young horse was screaming so loud Shane and Hawk could hear it up on the ridge. Then the young palomino started kicking out wildly with his back legs.

"Looks like he's working up nerve to do it right now," Shane remarked.

Hawk smiled and nodded as they watched. The horse settled down only long enough to get his breath before aggressively pawing the ground with his right front foot and then charging toward Naatea. Now both stallions were screaming as Naatea bravely charged back to meet the younger one, head on. The two soon met violently, mingling into a blur of teeth and hooves. This was a desperate fight for control of the herd. A fight that was as old as time itself.

Naatea had been challenged many times before and had the advantage of experience on his side. He also had a heart as big as the valley of which he had been king for many years. The palomino sported youth and flexibility as well as an unwavering desire to win. He felt it was his turn to be top dog. Naatea knew he needed to overpower the young horse quickly in order to retain his status. For every move the palomino tried to make on Naatea, the older stud would have a counter. Finally, Naatea's savvy prevailed. A crushing blow by both his back feet made solid contact with the palomino's left shoulder, which sent him away with a heavy limp. Naatea knew the younger stallion would try again as soon as his wounds had healed. The next time might have a different outcome, but for now the old king reared high in the air. As he stood on his back haunches, he gave his victory call — like he had done so many times before. The sound of this call echoed across the valley and sent chills up Shane's spine.

"He's a hell of a horse," Shane remarked, still looking through his binoculars.

"He's mellowed some in his old age," replied Hawk. "In his younger days, he would have chased down that palomino after the fight and worked him over again. But the coolest thing about old Naatea is, if he needed to, he'd sacrifice his own life to save that same palomino, even after this fight. He learned this from his own father who he defeated years ago for the position. Hopefully, the younger stallion, who will someday take over, will have learned this kind of character from Naatea.

"There's a story my father told me about Naatea's sire. It happened when the old stallion was nearing the end of his reign. During the heat of a battle to retain his position as leader of the herd, a pair of mountain lions attacked a mare and foal nearby. The two stallions both stopped in the middle of their fight to go after the cougars. The younger stallion broke his neck and was killed while they were defending the other horses. I was told Naatea's father stayed next to the dead challenger's body for days without food or water, mourning his death."

Shane watched the stallion a minute longer, then Hawk patted him on the back. "Come on, let's head back around the point."

"All right, let's go," Shane said as he stood and put his binoculars back in the case hanging around his neck. He carefully followed Hawk back around the narrow ledge, breathing a sigh of relief as he made it to the other side. Shane tried his best not to show the intense anxiety he was working through even though he'd made it around to solid ground again. Hawk gestured quietly for Shane's attention and pointed down to some activity that was moving at a fast pace underneath the cover below them. The two watched through their binoculars until they caught a quick glimpse of what it was. JB had gotten his bighorn sheep and was heading toward camp with it slung over his shoulders. Even with the extra hundred plus pounds to burden him, he kept at a fast, smooth stride as he moved skillfully and quietly through the woods.

"Look over there," Hawk said as he raised his glasses to his eyes. Shane lifted his binoculars and pointed them in the same direction as Hawk's. It took him a minute to spot the medium-sized creature that was moving across an open field toward a small creek.

"Is that a wolverine?" Shane asked.

"Yep, we call them badgers around here. Pound for pound that's the toughest and meanest animal in this valley. I'd almost rather tangle with a bear than one of those things. That's the animal that ole

Johnny Badger, or JB, got his name from, and believe me, if you ever see him in a fight, you'll find out he definitely lives up to it."

The time the two spent watching the badger and other wildlife at Devil's Point had allowed JB to make it to camp ahead of them.

From their position at the top of the rock wall, which was half way back, they could see JB below them. Hawk motioned for Shane to stop, sit, and watch JB. The Indian slowly dropped to his knees next to the animal he'd recently killed. He raised his hands to the sky and looked upward as he chanted. The two men watched him slide a knife out of his deerskin sheath. He held the knife in his open hands and lifted it above the sheep while he finished his prayer. Then he cut the animal open and did something very disturbing to Shane. JB, still on his knees, skillfully cut out the heart, held it up to the sky, and cried out with a short, yelping sound. Then he brought the raw heart to his mouth and took a small bite.

"What the hell is he doing that for?" Shane asked.

Hawk smiled and said, "To our people, that is the highest form of respect we can show for the animal's life he has just taken for our meal. I told you JB is hardcore Shoshone. He prefers the old ways, and, just like that badger we saw, he is also a great warrior. One that should be feared." Shane shook his head as he watched JB dressing out the animal with the blood from the heart still on his mouth.

"Well, I have to tell you, he's scaring the hell out of me, just watching him eat that."

Hawk laughed. "Come on, let's head down to camp."

Chapter 22

When they made it back to camp, Hawk and Shane helped prepare the fresh meat. The two dogs caught wind of the sheep and showed their faces for the first time since they'd bailed out of the truck bed.

Butch and Jessie were very cautious around JB and Hawk. Both men had bold personalities, which made the dogs hesitant to come near. But the scent of a fresh kill had overridden their cautious attitudes and brought them out of the shadows.

Shane was surprised when JB offered the dogs some meat. Butch hesitated for a second and then slowly took the food from JB's hand. Jessie only came within a few feet of him, then patiently waited until JB threw a piece in his direction.

As dusk fell over the valley, a cool breeze began to blow at their campsite on the high cliff. The break from the afternoon heat was a welcome change.

While the meat cooked, Hawk pulled out a bottle of good blended whiskey from his saddlebag. He poured them each a stout drink in their tin coffee cups. "You ever eat sheep before?" Hawk asked Shane.

"Nope," he answered.

"Well, you're in for a real treat. As far as the wild game out here goes, a nice young ram is about as good as it gets." After dinner, they sat around the fire, and Hawk generously poured them each a couple more drinks of his whiskey. The liquor helped loosen the mood between Shane and the two Indians.

Shane learned that JB had been a Marine and did a tour of duty in Desert Storm. Hawk boasted about his friend and told Shane that

JB had received a Medal of Honor and a Purple Heart from his actions in combat. "He was a forward scout when he sneaked up on and took out a whole squad of Iraqi's, lying in wait to ambush his company. He saved a lot of Americans that day." JB looked a little put out, and quickly changed the subject. "How about you, what's your story?"

"What do you mean?"

"Well, we've heard you're some kind of famous horse trainer, but, we were wondering why you would come all the way out here to set free one little mustang?"

Shane became quiet. He wasn't sure how to answer. He didn't want their pity, but he also felt at this point they were entitled to know the truth. They could tell he was trying to find the words to answer, and they waited patiently for his reply.

"It was my eleven-year-old son, Jacob, who wanted to see the mustang come back here someday. He was real close to the horse, and he knew she would be happier with her own herd." He hesitated for a moment, looked over at the Indians, and continued, "I lost the boy, along with my wife and daughter, in a car accident a couple years ago."

Hawk and JB were taken by surprise. During this awkward moment, they sat quietly looking at the fire, waiting for Shane to finish.

"It took me quite a while to finally get myself back together, but when I did, I remembered the promise I had made to Jacob, that we would set her free out here where she came from."

It was JB who finally broke the silence while watching Shane stir the fire with a long stick.

"He sounds like a boy to be proud of. You were lucky to have a son like that." Shane nodded his head and forced a smile as he continued to poke the campfire with his stick.

Hawk then lightened up the mood with perfect timing. "You know, they told JB he wasn't allowed to have any kids." Shane and JB waited for him to elaborate. Hawk smiled before he continued, "They told ole JB, nope, you can't have kids. We'll cut off your nuts before we let you pass on that horse face in our tribe." Shane laughed.

JB wasted no time with a comeback. "You asshole, you never had any balls to start with. That's why you don't have any kids."

Shane appreciated the way they jokingly changed the subject and didn't dwell on his story. At least now they understood why the safety of their ancestral herd had become so important to a white man from Tennessee. With the whiskey making them groggy, the three crawled into their bedrolls and were soon asleep.

Shane felt as though he had only shut his eyes for a few minutes when he was awakened by low-sounding growls and whines from both dogs. It was still dark. He pulled his arm out of his bedroll and held his watch up close to his face. He knew it was early morning by the position of the quarter moon, still sitting high in the eastern sky. As he focused on the five a.m. reading on his watch, he wondered what was upsetting the dogs. Shane felt a slight hangover hit him from Hawk's whiskey as he sat up to look around. Just then he heard what sounded like a truck door slamming shut somewhere in the distance. "Hush up," he told the dogs, as he listened intensely. Soon, he heard the sounds of several vehicles pulling up and shutting off their engines. The noise was coming from the other side of the hill just north of their camp.

By now Hawk and JB were awake and listening as well. They both scrambled out of their bedrolls. "Looks like we have company," Hawk said, as he grabbed his rifle and disappeared into the dark toward the top of the hill.

Shane started to follow when JB grabbed his arm. "We'll stay here. There's less chance of being spotted if only one of us goes."

About fifteen minutes later, Hawk came back. Still a little out of breath, he whispered, "There are seven trucks and trailers and at least twenty-five men and horses along with about a dozen dogs. All of them are dressed in camouflage and armed with rifles and scopes. They're after the horses, all right; I could hear them talking. They're sending half the men east over to Jasper Canyon to wait, while the rest of the men take the dogs to move the herd over to them."

Shane asked, "Should we radio for help?"

"We'll call in and let Tigee know what's happening, but he knows if he sends a lot of our men out here now, someone will end up getting hurt. We're supposed to try to stop this without these bastards knowing we're here."

Hawk grabbed the radio and made the call.

"Stay out of sight," Tigee demanded. "You men get to the herd before they do and send the horses west over to the thick forest at Timber Creek. My grandsons and I will be out with the reservation police as soon as we can."

Hawk and JB knew the herd had been grazing most mornings in a clearing a couple miles east of their camp. Unless these bad guys had been watching the herd and also knew this, the three of them should have an advantage in reaching the mustangs first.

What they didn't know, was that Thomas and Jack, the two Arapahos Vince Nethers hired, had already entered the valley from a different entrance. They had come in the night before with Bo Nethers and two other men and were already slowly moving the herd west toward the soon-to-be waiting guns at Jasper Canyon. The two Arapahos and Bo were directing more of the gang, via radio, to meet up with them behind the herd. The hunt had been well set up, and so far everything was working as planned. As soon as the other twelve men hooked up with Bo and the Arapahos behind the mustangs, they would have enough people to contain the herd and force the mustangs into the canyon's deadly trap.

The sun was just rising over the mountains to the east when Hawk, JB, and Shane arrived at the clearing where they expected to find Naatea and the herd. Shane could see the concern on the Indians' faces as they saw the herd's tracks heading toward Jasper Canyon.

It wasn't long before Hawk and JB found the tracks of the five shod horses that were obviously easing the mustangs toward the east. JB said, "They're moving slow and easy so they won't scatter them. I don't know who these guys are, but they know what they're doing."

Hawk noted, "Since they're moving slow it should give us time to work our way around and get in front of the mustangs. There are only four or five guys pushing them right now. If we get Naatea concerned, he'll break away, and they won't have enough men to contain the herd. We'll work our way up to a high point over there and see if we can spot them."

The three rode hard and fast up to cliff with a good view.

"Look, there they are!" yelled Shane.

"Oh, shit!" said Hawk as he pointed behind the mustangs. The three had reached their high vantage point, just in time to see the other twelve men and dogs joining up with Bo and his four. Now there were seventeen men on horses, and they were in perfect position to keep the mustangs bunched up and moving toward the ambush.

"Damn it!" JB hollered. "Come on, we have to get to the mouth of that canyon! That's our only chance to head them off and stop this. I can tell you now, we're going to have to make ourselves known when we get there." They took off again at a full gallop. "You guys be ready for anything when we make it to that canyon," he added as they sent their horses down the steep grade at a dangerously fast pace.

Tory and the other two horses were lathered up and sucking wind hard when they arrived at the canyon's only opening. They were still on the outside of the canyon, so there was little concern about being spotted by the shooters positioned on the ledges inside the canyon walls.

"Here they come!" yelled Hawk. By now Bo and his men had the herd stampeding straight for the opening, and straight at Shane, JB, and Hawk. With the herd only a couple hundred yards in front of them, JB began to scream out with one of his bloodcurdling war cries. All three of them began firing their guns in the air and hollering at the top of their lungs, trying to turn the mustangs away from the doom that awaited them inside the small canyon.

In an instant, panic and confusion filled the air. The herd was moving down the wooded trail toward the three men at an alarming pace. Shane could see the terrified look in the mustang's eyes as Naatea cut to the left and broke through the containment with the main part of the herd. In spite of their efforts, about ten of the mustangs made it by the three men and into the canyon.

With the seventeen bad guys who had been chasing the herd now coming right at them, Shane, Hawk, and JB had no choice but to follow Naatea and the rest of the herd to safety. If they allowed themselves to be pushed back into the canyon, they could easily be cut down by the waiting guns, along with the ten doomed mustangs that had just run by them and through the pass.

The snipers in the canyon opened fire. As the shots rang out, Shane and the two Shoshones stopped their horses and turned to look at the canyon opening. This was just in time to hear the horses screaming in pain from the array of bullets piercing their flesh. In the silence that followed, the three men just sat there staring at the pass with agonizing, hopeless looks. Then suddenly, the expression on JB's face changed. He raised his rifle over his head with his right arm and readied himself to charge toward the pass. Shane, sitting on Tory next to him, reached down just in time to grab the reins on JB's horse. "No man, there's too many of them."

JB's common sense quickly overcame his rage. Shane looked him in the eyes and waited until he was certain that JB had regained his self-control before he let go of the reins. A moment of calm soon ended with the distant sound of growling dogs, followed by a single gunshot. Shane was almost knocked out of the saddle as the bullet creased his left bicep. The unexpected shot startled the three men and their horses. Shane grabbed his arm in pain and then noticed both Butch and Jessie behind the two shooters' horses, snapping at their heels. In the process, Butch took a solid kick from the horse on the right and ran off yelping to the woods with Jessie by his side.

The dogs had arrived just in time to foil the men's first attempt to shoot Shane square in the chest. JB, with his rifle already out of his scabbard, reacted instantly by returning fire and hitting one. The two gunmen on horseback were only about a hundred yards away. As Shane looked in their direction, he immediately recognized them as his two Arapaho rivals, Jack and Thomas. Jack still had his rifle held up to his cheek and it was pointed directly at Shane. Suddenly, realizing that JB's bullet had hit his friend and partner, he dropped his gun, jumped down off his horse, and pulled the wounded Thomas behind a rock for cover.

Shane could clearly see the fresh stitches in Jack's cheek where he had cut him with his spur during their fight over Tara last week at the cave.

"Come on, let's get out of here!" Hawk yelled. The three turned their horses and rode fast toward the west where the two Shoshone knew there were plenty of thick woods and a stream to water their tired horses.

Shane was worried about Tory and hoped he hadn't pushed his aging friend beyond his limits. As soon as they reached the water, he dismounted and was relieved to see the tough, old gelding would be fine after he caught his air, cooled down, and then had a drink.

"Why in hell were they shooting at you?" Hawk asked.

"I had a run-in with them last week," Shane replied. He wasn't sure how to answer beyond that without going against Tigee's wishes, revealing what was really going on in the valley. Although they'd done all they could to avoid violence, blood had now been shed. The three men knew that Thomas was shot, but they had no way of knowing how badly the Arapaho was hurt. Even though Shane realized the bullet that JB fired in return had probably saved his life, his appreciation was overshadowed by his fear of the consequences that would certainly result from it.

Shane knelt next to JB at the creek, then took some cool water to wash the blood off his arm, revealing it was nothing more than a deep scratch. He realized there were two things that saved him today. The first was Butch and Jessie causing Jack's horse to move just before he pulled the trigger. The second was JB's quick reaction that took out Thomas, who also held Shane in the sights of his rifle. He looked at JB and said, "I owe you one, man."

JB took a deep breath and replied, "That son of a bitch had it coming. The lives of all of those pricks aren't worth one of those mustangs they just slaughtered. They just shot them down for no good reason. If you hadn't held my horse back when you did, I would have ridden in and shot a lot more of 'em."

"It's a good thing he stopped you," Hawk said. "You would have been killed, and we would have an even bigger mess than we do now."

Shane had no way of knowing that Nethers would send his crew in so soon to try to eliminate the herd. He had rolled the dice, gambled that Megan Tillie and the activists would be able to throw a monkey wrench in Nethers's plans before he went after the horses. Nethers's success revolved around the idea that no one outside their small community would give a damn about the Indians or their mustangs. All of this might have changed if Shane's people had arrived a day or two earlier. He wondered, perhaps, if this tragedy would have happened if they had confronted Nethers and told him they were onto his plan. But, he and Tigee felt strongly that the potential for more problems would be lessened if Shane's plan to expose Nethers's intentions to the outside world was a surprise.

The situation was complicated. There was also the fear that the rest of the Shoshone leaders would jump at the chance for a big lease deal to bail them out of the financial bind that Nethers was already putting on the tribe.

Shane's friends were due tomorrow. Luckily, he, JB, and Hawk were able to save Naatea and most of the mustangs. As long as the main part of the herd survived, Shane's plans still had a chance to work.

Once Kate O'Hanson and her activists saw pictures of this gruesome scene, she would have an army of her peers all over town protesting to stop this senseless killing. Shane's biggest concern, at the moment, was that a man had been shot. If Thomas was badly hurt and the authorities became involved, it would be his, JB, and Hawk's word, against Jack and Thomas, as to who pulled the trigger first. The last thing Shane wanted was to see JB get into trouble for saving his life. With all this going through his head, Shane was also concerned about the two wolves. Butch had been kicked hard by Thomas's horse during their heroic attempt to, once again, help Shane out of trouble. He could only hope his friend was okay.

As Shane sat next to JB at the creek's edge, a call came over the radio from Tigee. Hawk told the old Indian what had happened to the mustangs, and they agreed to meet back at Jasper Canyon. By now, enough time should have passed and the horse slayers would be gone. At least heading back to the canyon would give Shane a chance to look around for the injured dog.

He followed Hawk and JB's lead as they dismounted their horses and tied them up about a quarter mile before they reached the pass at Jasper Canyon. They planned to slip in quietly and unseen, just in case any of the shooters were still in the area.

When they reached the place where JB had shot Thomas, the three men stopped to look around. There was blood everywhere. The two Shoshones studied the signs and concluded that Thomas had been put on his horse and led off. They guessed the man was not conscious when this happened.

With patience and careful observation, Hawk and JB slowly worked their way through the thick trees and into the canyon pass. Shane followed their every move, trying to emulate the smooth, swift silence the two Shoshones used to slip through the woods.

As they made it into the canyon, Shane felt an eerie stillness in the air. All the men and dogs were gone, and there was nothing moving. The small part of the herd that had run by them and into the canyon had come in hard and stayed close together. As soon as the mustangs heard the first shots, they attempted to scatter. None of them made it very far. There were nine carcasses scattered over about one acre.

"There must have been at least a dozen rifles," Hawk said.

JB added, "At least these guys could shoot. Most of the horses went down quickly and didn't suffer. Only two ran a little way before they fell. Those were the ones we heard screaming. Look over there, one may still be alive!" He pointed at some tracks that showed there was one horse moving out in front of the others at high speed. These tracks continued toward some cover about a hundred yards from where the dead horses lay.

The three men were still on foot and followed the tracks through the small stand of trees where the horse had run to escape the line of fire. Emerging on the other side, Hawk pointed across an open area to the back edge of the canyon. It was the young palomino stallion that Hawk and Shane had watched trying to challenge Naatea. Somehow the colt made it through the shower of bullets and hid under a ledge without sustaining a single scratch.

The young horse was dazed and scared, but his only injury seemed to be the slight limp he still had from yesterdays fight with Naatea. Hawk said, "Let's see if we can slowly move him out of the canyon so he can catch up with the rest of the herd."

The young stallion, still in a survival mode, snorted loudly as they eased up behind him. At first, he seemed to cooperate and moved calmly toward the opening. Things were going well until they were about halfway out. That's when the horse caught the smell of his slain group and bolted off in their direction. The three men stood in the distance and watched the large palomino sniff and paw the ground at each one of the nine dead horses.

Shane was carrying his small digital camera in a pouch on his belt. "I'm going to slip in closer and get some pictures of this," he announced.

"Why would you want pictures of a sad thing like this?" Hawk asked. Of course, Hawk and JB knew nothing of Megan Tillie, so Shane could understand that the two would think this was strange.

"A picture is worth a thousand words, and a good shot of this could help me turn some heads in our direction. If people can see this senseless mess, it may just help save the rest of the mustangs." Shane eased up closer to the gruesome scene, and although they still didn't understand, Hawk and JB trusted Shane enough not to question him further.

Eventually they were able to move the colt out of the canyon so he could find Naatea and the rest of the herd.

Ten minutes later, Tigee, Tara, her two brothers, and the same tribal authorities who were at the first shooting all drove up in a four-wheel-drive police Jeep. They had met at the north entrance and rode out together in the only vehicle that could get into the canyon. Tigee hadn't bothered to call the sheriff from town.

As the three watched the Jeep drive up, Shane looked over at Hawk and JB then said, "Why don't we keep quiet about the little shoot-out we had with those two Arapahos?" They agreed.

The two tribal police were genuinely sympathetic about the killing of the horses, just like the first time. In their defense, there wasn't much they could do about it.

Tigee knew even if he told the authorities the whole story, they wouldn't have enough evidence to arrest Vince Nethers or anyone else involved for that matter. He knew now Shane's plan would be the best way to outsmart this guy.

"How did you get that wound on your arm?" one of the policemen asked Shane.

"I'm pretty sure it was a ricochet," Shane answered. "We got here just in time to turn the main herd before they made it into the pass. There were a lot of bullets flying around those horses. I guess I was just in the wrong place at the wrong time."

The officer didn't question it further.

Tara pulled Shane aside while the rest of the men were talking. She wet a clean cloth with some water from a canteen and wiped the dried blood off his arm. The troubled look on her face revealed how she felt. But she didn't say a word. Tara looked Shane in the eye, laid her open hand on his chest, but still did not speak. She just forced a smile, then walked back to the Jeep. She glanced, only once, at the dead horses and couldn't bring herself to look again.

The tribal police department was adequately managed but sorely understaffed. They promised to send out some patrols to try to head off any further poaching on the mustangs. Since they had no way of knowing the true situation, the authorities felt any presence they could provide in the area might prevent a recurrence. The truth was it was a very big valley, and they didn't have the manpower to keep a constant presence way out here. They suggested that Tigee keep his men in the valley to watch the herd until all this blew over.

"You think?" Hawk questioned sarcastically. Tigee gestured to him to be quiet.

JB told the group about the young stallion that had somehow survived the shooting. This brought some life back into Tigee's grim face. He proclaimed this colt was special and deserved a name. "We will call him *Gabaimi'a Kuna*." Hawk turned to Shane and translated the Shoshone words, "In English, this means *walks through fire*."

As the Jeep drove off down the narrow trail, Shane, JB, and Hawk headed toward their horses. There was nothing that could be done with the carcasses lying in the canyon. Like the others that were shot, these horses would simply become food for the predators while the meat was fresh, and then feed the scavengers, once it began to rot.

They felt it was unlikely that the poachers would be back in the next couple of days. The three men were tired and hungry, as were their horses. They would ride back to the truck and trailer to stay in a real bed tonight. Tara's brothers would come out tomorrow for their shift and keep an eye on things.

They had not ridden far when JB noticed two sets of wolf tracks. The tracks were definitely Butch and Jessie's. JB pointed out that one was dragging a back leg. "They're probably headed for water," Hawk said. "There's a small creek in the direction they're traveling."

It didn't take long to locate the dogs. They were lying near the water, just as Hawk said they would be. Shane stepped off his horse and handed JB the reins. He walked over and could tell right away that Butch was badly hurt. Jessie was lying beside him and sat up as Shane knelt down next to the injured wolf. "Hey, bud," he said, as he gently patted him on the top of his head. "Maybe I can carry you in on Tory and get you some help." Shane tried to carefully rub his hand down the dog's body to see how bad his injuries were. He saw no blood, but with only the light touch of his finger tips on the dog's ribs, Butch yelped in pain and knocked Shane's hand away with his nose.

"There's no way you're going to be able to carry him," Hawk said.

"I guess I'll have to leave him here and hope for the best." Shane had seen the two dogs share their kills before. He figured Jessie would bring his brother food, and there was water nearby. Shane and JB constructed a sturdy lean-to from some nearby downed trees over the injured dog to help protect him from the weather. Since Tara's brothers would be coming out to watch over the herd, he would ask them to check on Butch. It was hard for Shane to leave him. The two dogs had saved his life more than once. There was just nothing more he could do right now.

Meanwhile, back at his ranch, Vince Nethers heard the news from his son, Bo, about the botched attempt to get rid of the mustangs. "Damn it, boy, how many did you kill?"

"Not many, Dad, that guy Shane and two Shoshones made it to the pass just in time to turn 'em away."

"Who the hell is this freaking guy?" Vince yelled. "If my partner knew all the trouble he is causing, he'd be a dead man by tomorrow." Vince was furious, and he could tell by the look on his son's face, that there was more bad news. "Boy, you'd better tell me everything. Now."

"It's Thomas," Bo said, sheepishly.

"What about him?" Vince yelled.

"He was shot! I don't know what happened for sure. I wasn't there when he got hit."

"Son of a bitch," Vince screamed. "That Indian better keep his mouth shut."

Bo took a deep breath, with a worried look on his face, and said, "I don't think he's going to be talking to anyone, Dad. He's dead."

Vince grabbed his son by the collar and pulled him in close. "Where's the body? Damn it."

"I dropped his partner off with it near one of their old hunting camps. I made sure they were off the reservation land and told Jack to stay put until I talked to you."

"Does anyone else know about this?"

"No, Dad, it happened outside of the canyon. None of the hired guns saw it."

"What about the guys who shot him?"

"It was that Shane and two Shoshones. Jack told me the three of them took off on horseback right after the shot. So they don't know he's dead."

Vince grabbed a bottle of bourbon and poured himself a shot over some ice. He drank it quickly. "Was anyone else hurt?"

"I don't think so, but if Jack gets a chance, he says he's going to kill that Shane guy on sight."

"Oh, shit!" Vince growled. "Take me out to where that Indian is. Now!"

Nethers had time to think things over during the ride out to where Bo had dropped off the two Arapahos. His foremost concern was how to keep anyone from finding out about the dead man. He knew no one could connect him to the killing of the horses. None of the hired guns had any idea Vince was involved. Bo had set everything up and told all of the men that the reason for the hunt was because of all the trouble over the last year between the young men in town and the Shoshones. All of the shooters were boys from town whom Bo had grown up with. They had all easily bought into the story because they were aware of the history of bad blood between the two groups. To these rowdy guys, getting paid to piss off the Shoshone was like getting paid to go to a bar on Saturday night. It just sounded like fun.

Vince knew the Shoshones would never lease him the land as long as the horses were on it. He stayed deep in thought all the way out to the Arapahos' hunting camp. He didn't speak a word to Bo during the hour drive. The only people who knew of his scheme were his partners, his son, Bo, and the two Arapahos. The crews from the oil company didn't know they were on reservation land when they were conducting the seismic tests. If his strong-handed business partner, John Rosolli, or his oil company man, Barry Russell, knew there was any trouble going on with this scheme, they would surely back out.

Especially, since at this point, they didn't have any money invested. Because of this, it was crucial that he keep anyone from finding out about the dead Arapaho and, of course, keep his sidekick, Jack, quiet about it. There were millions to be made with this scheme and Vince would do whatever was necessary to keep Jack's mouth shut.

Chapter 23

The light of day was quickly fading away into dusk as they arrived at the place where Bo had dropped off Thomas's body, Jack, and their two horses. From the road, it was about a half-mile walk into the woods to their camp. This was a secluded spot, far away from any ranches or main drags. Vince felt comfortable this was a safe place to deal with the situation. Bo had done at least one thing right today when he dropped the Indians off way out here.

As they walked into the open area of the camp, Vince saw Jack sitting on a chair near the old hunter's shack. His face was blank as he stared off into the woods. He was aware the two men had walked into the camp, but he just kept staring into space. Jack had wrapped his dead friend in a blanket and laid the stiff, lifeless body next to the shack's entrance. The blanket was soaked with blood.

Vince walked over to Jack and pretended to show remorse for Thomas's death. "I'm sorry about your friend." Jack continued to look straight ahead as if Vince wasn't there. Vince commanded, "We need to keep this quiet for now, do you understand? We can't call the authorities.

"Jack slowly changed his line of vision over to Vince and nodded his head. "I don't need any law involved. I'll take care of the bastard that's responsible."

"Not now!" Vince insisted. "Listen to me, there is a lot of money at stake here. I'll pay you well to wait for your revenge. If you don't wait until this land deal goes through, I'll have your neck. Now, do you want to be a rich man or a dead man?"

Jack looked Vince in the eye and answered, "I can wait until you have your lease, but I want some money now!"

Vince anticipated this, and had brought along some cash. He reached in his pocket and handed Jack a bundle of money. "There's ten thousand dollars there. That's just a drop in the bucket to what you'll get if you dispose of the body and keep your mouth shut. Does Thomas have any family or people who will be looking for him?"

"He had no one but me. If anyone asks, I'll tell them he went to Utah. There are a few who know we had a job offer there to guide some elk hunts later this year."

Vince looked Jack in the eye. "Once this is over and you're paid off, that would be a good place for you to go. Do you understand?"

Jack nodded. "I understand. I'll need to disappear, but not before I get that son of a bitch, Shane."

"As long as you wait until I get my lease, I hope you do kill that piece of shit. Until then, you lay low, all right?" Jack nodded. "Now, you make sure no one ever finds your partner's remains." Then he and Bo turned to walk toward the truck. They could hear Jack calling out the Arapaho death chant as they left.

Later that night under a clear sky with a quarter moon, Jack took his lifelong friend deep into the wilderness and sent him off in the old traditional Arapaho way. When this lonely ritual had ended, he buried Thomas in a shallow grave, just as his tribe had always done with their dead. Then, suddenly, in a fit of rage he fired his rifle several times into the dark night sky, vowing angrily under his breath, "You'll pay for this, Shane Carson. I'll make you wish you had never come to the Wind River!"

Shane, JB, and Hawk arrived back at the ranch around five. They unloaded their horses and gear, then went their separate ways in a solemn mood. There was no way anyone could have been through what had happened today and not be affected.

Tommy was just starting to feed up when Shane walked into the barn with Tory. The boy's face lit up when he saw him. "Can you help me with the horses tomorrow?"

A tired Shane replied, "Tommy, I can help you early, but I have to leave by eleven to pick up a friend of mine at the airport."

Shane was looking forward to seeing Megan Tillie. He also knew that seeing her would trigger bittersweet memories of the times she'd spent with him and his family. Nevertheless, he was excited about her visit and her potential for helping to solve the tribe's problems. But, the way things were rapidly evolving, he knew they were running out of time.

"How did your hunting trip go this weekend?" Tommy asked. The boy knew nothing about what was going on in the valley.

Shane smiled, patted him on the back, and answered, "It went fine, bud." Then he quickly changed the subject. "How is Sloppy doing? Did you have a chance to ride her this weekend?"

"Yes, sir, I'm keeping her in good shape for when you turn her loose. When are you going to let her go?"

"Soon — I hope real soon. I'll be here at the barn by seven."

"Yes, sir, I'll have everyone fed up and ready to go." The boy's eagerness to work with the horses every day and learn all he could put a grin on Shane's face and lightened up his fretful mind.

Shane was walking back to his shack when he noticed Tara stepping out onto her front porch. As soon as they saw each other, a slow uncontrollable smile came over each of them.

Tara was standing at the top of the stairs, leaning against the porch upright with her hands in the pockets of her taut-fitting jeans. Shane walked up onto the porch, leaned back against the post on the other side of the threshold, and crossed his arms. For a long moment they stood there with stupid grins plastered on their faces, not saying a word. Finally, Tara spoke.

"Did you think of me at all while you were out in the valley?"

Shane hesitated for a second, shyly looked down, then looking back up at her said, "Only when I wasn't getting shot at."

Tara grinned and shook her head. "I guess no one has ever

accused Shane Carson of being much of a romantic, have they?"

"I guess not."

"I've got a thick cover of trail dust to clean off me," Shane said. "I'll pick you up in about an hour, and we'll go eat."

Tara moved over to kiss him on the cheek, and then whispered, "I missed you," before she turned and went inside. Even though she didn't give him any time to respond, he knew he should have said something. Instead, he just stood there speechless, like a school boy with his first crush.

His wife, Jen, used to call him romantically challenged. "I guess she was right," Shane said aloud, to himself. Then he shook his head, grinned, and walked down the porch stairs.

Dinner with Tara was a good distraction, but he did have a lot to stress about. Could he expose Nethers in time to save what was left of the mustangs? Was the Arapaho whom JB shot hurt badly? He knew he was making friends out here, but he was also making some pretty dangerous enemies, and these were the kind of people who would love to see him out of the picture. He also carried a guilty, helpless feeling when he thought about having to leave the injured wolf in the valley. Maybe he could hire a vet and take him out to Butch in a Jeep. Hopefully, there would be time for him to look into this tomorrow after he picked up Megan at the airport.

On top of all this were his thoughts of Jen, Jacob, and Tina that were always just a breath away. Yes, Tara was a powerful distraction for him, but his feelings for her were also confusing. Especially since neither one could say if they had any kind of future. He knew Jen would want him to go on with his life, but he struggled between pursuing his affections for Tara, and the strong feelings he still carried for his wife and kids. Ever since he lost them, his mere survival had depended on dealing with life on a day-to-day basis. For now, he needed to find solace in this philosophy and let destiny run its unpredictable course. So, tonight he would allow himself to enjoy life in the arms of this remarkable woman, who cared for him probably more than he deserved.

From the moment he picked her up for dinner, the evening was

filled with conversation, laughter, and friendship. While out in public they both held in check their consuming desire for the passion
that already felt so familiar to them. When they made it home to
the privacy of Shane's cabin, it was a different story.

The following morning, Shane arrived at the barn by seven as he
had promised Tommy. He knew, without a doubt, that all the horses
would already be fed and tacked up. The boy had always been dependable. By now he was beginning to feel if Tommy worked hard
enough, he could surpass even his own abilities and skills. After all,
the Shoshone kid had been born into it. Horses were a part of
Tommy's ancient culture.

As much as he wanted to work with the boy this morning, he
couldn't get his mind off his many concerns. Tommy was aware that
he was distracted, but respectfully didn't question Shane about his
mood. When they finished, Shane patted the boy affectionately on
the back and told him, "I'm going to be pretty tied up for the next
couple of days, Tommy, but I'll check out the horses at the end of the
week and see how you're doing. You keep Sloppy legged up for me."

"Thanks, Mr. Shane."

"No problem, son, you have a real knack for this. You promise me
you'll keep after it, okay?"

"Yes, sir, I will."

Megan's flight would be arriving at one. He planned to bring her
and the photographer back to the reservation this afternoon and put
them up for the night. This would give him the evening and all day
tomorrow to get her up to speed on the current events and introduce her to Tigee for an interview. He also planned to take her to
Fort Washakie so she could gather more background information on
the history of the mustangs.

Tomorrow evening they would stay in the town of Reddick at
the local, upscale hotel. In town they could rent a car, and Megan
would be able to work on the article without interruptions. He also
wanted her to interview some of the locals on their views of the
situation. This would get the word circulating around town about

the article, and he knew this would quickly work its way back to Nethers. Getting Megan and her photographer deep into the valley to see the mustangs might prove to be a bit more challenging.

The herd was getting pretty spooked now, and it was getting harder, even for the Shoshones, who were guarding them, to keep up with their position. Even though Shane had plenty of pictures of the mustangs, Megan would want to see the herd for herself. He would just have to cross that bridge when he came to it.

Kate O'Hanson with her group of activists had left a message at Tigee's. She said there would be about a dozen of them driving into town on Tuesday afternoon. Shane figured the large group would draw a lot of attention in such a small town. He wasn't sure what they were planning, but he knew whatever Kate had up her sleeve would be loud and very visible. Good ole Kate would definitely stir up a big pot of publicity over what was happening to the mustangs in the valley. Shane chuckled to himself as he thought about the look on Vince Nethers's face when all this got back to him.

Megan's plane was on time, and she hurried over to Shane as soon as she laid eyes on him, greeting him with a big hug. "It's been way too long," she said as she turned him loose and looked him in the face.

"It certainly has," he said with a big smile.

"This is Brett, my assistant and camera man." After claiming their baggage and equipment, Shane took them to a restaurant and bought them lunch. Brett sat quietly while Megan and Shane talked about old friends and times they shared. Megan was a considerate and classy woman and didn't mention Jen and the kids. There would be a time and place for that.

During the drive to the reservation, the conversation finally turned to business. Megan listened intensely as Shane filled her in on all the latest details, which included the killing of the mustangs on Saturday morning.

"My gosh," Megan exclaimed, "do these guys really feel they have to eliminate the horses to gain control of the land?"

"Yes, they do. Once you talk to the Shoshone and realize the importance of the horses to their heritage, you'll understand.

"Nethers has been smart; he's covered his tracks well. Without any hard evidence against him, there's no way we would be able to get outside authorities to help stop him before it's too late. Because of the financial pressure he's putting on the tribe, along with his aggressive attempts to kill the herd, we're really working against the clock."

"I understand you can't point fingers or name names in your article, but I do need you to know I have pictures that prove someone has been actively testing for oil in the valley. We also have pictures of the horses that were shot down in cold blood."

Megan sat quietly and thought about what she'd just heard. "I can't write about any connection between the illegal oil testing and the dead horses without some kind of evidence or witness to support the theory. Our biggest problem now, is that you and I are working against the clock. You're trying to ward off any more attempts on the herd, and I have a deadline to meet. My editor needs this article done by the end of this week. If he approves it, it will be in our subscribers' mailboxes in about fifteen days."

Shane thought for a second. "If all you can do right now is write about the mustangs, their unique history, and the fact that someone is killing them off, that should get us the exposure we need to save them. Maybe you can sell the idea for a possible follow-up article about the rest of all this to your bosses, once the truth does come out."

"Okay, then we've got our angle for now. But, like I said before, I'll need to go see the surviving herd, as well as the carcasses. We'll need pictures of our own, along with whatever photos you have." Megan noticed the grimace on Shane's face and asked him what was wrong.

"Well, it's pretty rough country out there, and the herd isn't always easy to locate."

"No problem," she answered. "I anticipated this, and I've already got the okay from my boss to rent a helicopter and pilot for a couple of days. The people at the airport said they had a five-seater available. Normally my magazine wouldn't allow me to be quite so frivolous with my budget, but after my preliminary research on the story, we realized just how big the Wind River Reservation is. I convinced my editor a helicopter was the only way we could put this together in the limited time I have. I was hoping one of the Shoshone would be available to guide us on Tuesday. Today I hope to gather as much information as I can from the Indians. Then we can go to the Fort Washakie museum for some research and fact-finding on the herd's background."

As usual, Megan was well organized and in charge. Shane reached over from the driver's seat and patted her on the knee.

"Megan," he said with a grin, "I'm just damn glad you're on our side."

She laughed and replied, "To tell the truth, I'm really excited about writing this story."

Shane planned to take Megan to speak to Tigee as soon as they arrived at the ranch. He wanted her to learn from the old man first hand about the spiritual ties the Shoshone shared with these horses. He also knew Tigee would be concerned that the public might laugh at or mock these ancient beliefs. He would need to convince him that Megan could depict this in a way that would gain the respect and admiration from her readers for the Shoshone and the relationship they had shared for so long with these unique horses.

Earlier in the morning Shane had asked Tara to come home from work in time to drive over to Fort Washakie with them. Her knowledge and connections at the museum would come in handy.

The interview with Tigee went well, and Megan left the house excited. While they were at Tigee's, Shane made arrangements for JB to go with them as a guide tomorrow in the helicopter.

As usual, Tara was on time, and the four of them spent the rest of the afternoon at the museum. Tara was able to get copies of some of the old pictures for Megan to take with her, along with copies of the records showing the herd's bloodlines.

They stopped for dinner on the way back to the ranch. "I have a favor to ask of you, Megan," Shane said.

"What do you need?"

"I need your helicopter pilot to take JB and me into the valley before the trip out with you. It shouldn't take more than a half hour. I can do it first thing in the morning, and I'll pay for the helicopter's time. As soon as we're back, we'll take you in and show you everything you need to see."

"Can you tell me what you're doing?"

Shane told her about the two wolves and how Butch had been injured.

"These dogs have saved my life more than once. While you and Tara were gathering the materials you needed at the museum, I contacted a veterinarian and asked him to meet me at the ranch in the morning. I need to fly him out to check on Butch and, if necessary, transport the wolves back with us. Tara's brothers, who are out guarding the horses, checked on him this morning. They radioed in and said he didn't look too good. I'm worried if I don't get him help soon, he may die. Your helicopter could be his only chance of surviving."

"Sure, you go and get him. I'm supposed to call the pilot at seven a.m. I thought if the people at the ranch didn't mind, I'd have him land and pick us up in that big field just west of the compound."

"Thanks, Megan"

Later that evening, Shane and Megan relaxed on his porch. Megan's photographer, Brett, had already crashed in a sleeping bag inside on the floor.

Megan looked over at Shane with a smile and said, "I couldn't help but notice the way you and that Shoshone girl look at each other."

This was very awkward for Shane. After all, it was Megan who had introduced Shane to Jen. Shane sighed, looking out into the dark night. Megan put her hand on Shane's shoulder and said, "You know how much I cared for Jen and the kids, but I'd be happy for you if you found someone. It's been two years. You need to go on with your life."

Shane nodded and sighed again. "I still miss them so much." This caused a few quiet tears for Megan as she bit her lip. The two sat there for a long time, neither one knowing what to say next.

Finally Megan spoke her mind. "I need you to know that I didn't find out about the accident until the day of the funeral. You realize I would have come, if I'd known."

"I know you would have. I'm sorry I didn't return any of your calls. The whole thing was such a nightmare. Shortly after, I jumped head first into a bottle of whiskey and stayed there for about a year. If I hadn't found the school paper Jacob had written about Sloppy, I'd still be back at the farm, struggling to find a reason to get up every morning."

Megan interrupted, "There's no need for you to apologize. I knew eventually we'd get a chance to talk, and now we have." It felt good for both of them to clear the air.

The next morning JB was nervously waiting at Tigee's when Shane arrived. "I want you to know I'm not happy about this."

"About what?"

"Helicopters. I hated flying in those freakin' things when I was in Desert Storm, and I'm going to hate it today. If I get sick, I'm going to do it on you, damn it!"

Shane laughed and said, "Sorry man, if I had known I would have asked someone else."

"Yeah, yeah," JB answered. "Let's just get it over with. Tara told me we were going out to get the dog first. I'm glad about that, anyway. We need to either help him, or put him out of his misery. He's a good dog."

The veterinarian's name was Dr. Burrows. He owned a mobile vet service in the area. Shane had called several small-animal hospitals in town, and they all recommended Dr. Burrows for the job. He arrived at the ranch at eight, and after Shane described the dog's injury, he quickly grabbed some meds and equipment from his truck. Shane asked him to bring two crates, figuring if Butch did need to be transported, they would also bring Jessie back. He knew Jessie could survive on his own, but he'd feel better if the wolf was at home.

JB directed the pilot to an open area about a hundred yards from the creek where Butch was. They were afraid if they landed the chopper too close, they might spook the dogs. If the two slipped off into the woods, they may never find them. The pilot stayed with the helicopter, while his three passengers carried the crates and equipment to the creek. As they approached, Butch appeared to lay motionless, Jessie sitting at his side.

"Hey, buddy, we're going to get you some help now," he told the wolf as he slipped a muzzle on him, then motioned for Dr. Burrows to come over. Butch yelped in pain at the vet's slightest touch. "What do you think, Doc?"

"I suspect he has multiple broken ribs, but my main concern is a possible diaphragmatic hernia."

"What's that?" Shane asked.

"Basically, it's when there is a tear in the lining of the chest cavity, allowing the intestines to push through. Hopefully, if the hernia is small enough we can repair it, but I'll be honest, I think his chances are slim. I won't know for sure till I get him to the hospital for some X-rays. Hold his head while I sedate him. Let's get him in the crate and start running some fluids during the return flight." Shane looked over in time to see JB coaxing Jessie into the other crate with some raw meat. Soon they were all back at the ranch.

Chapter 24

The flight shook up Jessie, but Butch was heavily sedated and too badly hurt to care. They unloaded the crates and the vet's equipment into Shane's truck and drove the dogs across the field to the compound. As soon as Jessie was let out of his crate, he hightailed it straight to Shane's porch. The dog nervously watched as the vet loaded the crate, with Butch still inside, and drove off to the animal hospital. As he watched the truck leave the ranch, Shane stood there with a helpless feeling, hoping his friend would make it. He turned to check on Jessie and smiled as he noticed JB on the porch, petting him and calming him down.

Megan, Brett, Tara, and Tigee, came walking out of the house and asked, "How is he?"

"I don't know. At least he has a chance now. The vet has your phone number and is supposed to call when he knows more. I've told him I'll pay for whatever they need to do to try to save him." Tigee nodded, gave him a pat on his back, then went into his house.

Tara walked over to Shane and put her hand on his shoulder. "You've done all you can. I have to go to work now. I'll call Dr. Burrows later and see how Butch is doing." She kissed him on the cheek and left.

"All right, let's load up and go," Shane spoke. "We've got a lot to do today." Tigee had given Shane a radio so the chopper could stay in touch with Tara's brothers in the valley.

"This valley is breathtaking," Megan remarked as they flew above the Big Wind River.

Tara's brothers had found the herd just a couple miles south of where the chopper was, and soon the pilot spotted them. The helicopter noise put Naatea and the herd into a wild run, which gave Brett some great action photos of the horses in their element. After that, JB guided the pilot to Jasper Canyon so Megan could see first-hand the carcasses of the slain horses.

Next, they flew out to where the thumper trucks had scarred the ground while searching for oil. Tigee had finally told JB and Hawk about the illegal testing after they returned from their last trip to the valley, and Tashawa let JB know where to find the testing spots. Once Megan had taken all the pictures she needed, Shane asked JB to direct the pilot to a place with a view that would blow these people away. "You choose the spot, JB. I just want Megan to get a real grasp of how special this valley really is."

JB smiled, nodded, and then directed the pilot to the edge of the mountains on the northwest side of the valley. Shane had never been here, either.

"Oh, my gosh!" Megan exclaimed, as she stepped out of the helicopter. The pilot turned off the engine to join them. Brett went crazy taking pictures as the five of them stood there in awe. "This area is called South Fork," JB informed them. "It's the only place around here where two mountain ranges join together. If you look up and behind us to the north you'll see the Carter Mountains. To the east are the Owl Creek Mountains." JB pointed down as everyone looked. "That's Muddy Creek over six thousand feet below us. The creek runs into the Wind River a few miles south of here."

Far beneath them, gracing the majestic landscape was a unique formation. Like a big city sky-scraper, the mesa stood on its own nearly 1,300 feet high but only 40 yards across. Its walls on every side dropped straight down to the valley's floor, making its hard, rocky top totally unattainable to anyone or anything, except maybe a high-soaring bird of prey.

The group stood speechless with the wind at their backs for a while.

"Wow," Megan breathed as she looked across the basin. "I've only been here a couple of days, but I can see how you've gotten caught up in this country. I can't wait to get started on my article."

Shane replied, "This place is really something, isn't it?"

Everyone profusely thanked their Shoshone guide for sharing this sight called South Fork. JB responded to their gratitude with a simple expressionless nod. Shane thought they would never get Brett to stop taking pictures so they could leave.

It was mid-afternoon before the helicopter landed in the field next to the compound. Shane's next move was to take Brett and Megan to their hotel in town, and then meet with Kate and her activist crew, who would have arrived by now.

As soon as they returned to the ranch, Shane checked in with Tigee to see if he'd heard from Dr. Burrows. "Yes, the vet called about two hours ago. He wanted you to know that the dog does have a hernia, but it was small, and he was going to attempt to repair it. He said they would operate today, and if Butch makes it through the night he should be okay. He also said to tell you that the dog would not have survived another two hours in the valley."

Shane remarked with a frown, "We'll just have to hope for the best."

Tigee nodded and asked, "Did your friend, Ms. Megan, get the information she needs for her story?"

"Yes, sir, it went well today. I'm taking her and the photographer to check into the hotel now. Tara will meet them at the museum later for a tour."

Tigee nodded again and walked with him to the door. He grasped Shane's shoulder and squeezed it tightly. "I trust you, Shane, the *Tahotay*."

Shane smiled, patted Tigee on his back, and walked away.

On the way to Reddick with Brett and Megan, Shane called Kate O'Hanson on his cell phone. Once he got close to town, he was able to get enough of a signal to use it. The activist group had arrived and would meet with him in the hotel conference room in a half hour.

Megan said she would write about the fact that this group was in town trying to save the mustangs, but couldn't get involved with their opinions or promote their organization. "I think it's a good idea they're here, but I plan to stay clear of them. Now, all I need to do is interview some of the local town people about their feelings on the situation, then get the article started."

Shane gave her the Jensen's phone number and told her that they would probably be glad to talk to her. "Just make yourself as visible as you can around town while you talk to the locals. We want this Nethers guy to know you're here."

Megan smiled and winked. "No problem."

When Shane reached the conference room, the activist group was there waiting. The room was loud with conversation, and everyone was in a good mood. Kate O'Hanson came over and greeted him enthusiastically. "It's good to see you, Shane."

"Yes, ma'am, it's good to see you, too. Thanks for coming and bringing this mob with you." Kate laughed and turned to the other fourteen in the room.

"Everyone, please be quiet. I know we're all tired from the long drive. First of all, I want to thank you for coming out here for this good cause. For those of you who don't know him, I'd like to introduce you to Shane Carson. He's going to talk to us now about what we've gotten ourselves into out here." She then stepped aside and motioned to Shane to take center stage.

Shane began by handing out informational materials he had picked up at the museum concerning the lineage of the mustangs, and their centuries-old ties with the Shoshone Indians. "There is no other managed group of wild horses in this country that can be traced back through American history the way these horses can."

He continued, "The literature I just gave you will amaze you with the herd's bloodlines going back to important occurrences in our history like the Lewis and Clark Expedition as well as Custer's fall at the Battle of the Little Big Horn. In order for a horse to be set free with this herd, he had to be chosen by the chiefs and had to have been involved in events that made a mark in time." Shane then reached into his folder and held up photos of the slain horses. A shocked sympathetic groan sounded throughout the room. "This is what has been happening to these horses."

An angry voice shouted out from the group, "Why would some-one want to do a terrible thing like this?"

As a reply, Shane handed out copies of the pictures he had taken of the oil test sights. Shane wanted and needed this group to expose the oil as a strong possibility for why someone was trying to destroy the mustangs. The public, finding out about the oil, would shine the spotlight on Nethers's and his partners' scheme.

"Who's behind all this?" someone yelled out.

"We know who it is, but because he's a very smart guy, I don't have enough evidence to accuse him publicly — yet." Shane went on to explain the situation in great detail.

"One of the things we have going for us is that this man and his accomplices don't know that we are on to them. You people are my surprise attack. If we can blindside him by letting the public know about the unauthorized testing for oil, along with your strong save-the-horses protest, he'll have no choice but to abort his plans. I want all of you to realize that it's not just the horses we're trying to save here, but also some of the most incredible country you've ever seen."

Everyone applauded, and a loud chatter filled the room.

Kate stood behind Shane and requested the group's attention once again. "Everyone, please listen. All of you can see what a wor-thy cause we have here. This has been proven to me by what I'm about to tell you. WATV out of Casper Wyoming, which is about fifty miles east of here, has decided to do a feature news story enti-tled, 'Who's Killing the Horses?' " Once again the enthusiastic group began to applaud.

"Wait, wait!" Kate cautioned. "There's more! Once WATV got on the bandwagon, I was able to get three other local TV stations and several newspapers interested in the story. It looks as though the 'Whose Killing the Horses?' story is already becoming a hot news item in this part of the country. Folks, I mean right now — *today!*"

Shane just shook his head and started to laugh. He knew Kate was an expert at stirring things up for her causes, but he never imagined she would be able to do all this so quickly, way out here in the middle of nowhere. The people in the room were now more excited than ever and couldn't wait to get started spreading their SAVE THE MUSTANGS posters around the town tomorrow. Kate looked at Shane and said, "You think you can get more copies of all those pictures?"

"You bet!"

She nodded and then continued, "I've hired a helicopter pilot to go out tomorrow to get some video footage of the herd and the dead horses for the TV stations. Funny thing," she added, "the pilot said he knew you, and knew just where to go."

"Megan Tillie's in town, doing an article about the mustangs for her magazine. He flew us out there this morning for some still shots."

Kate smiled and shook her head. "I know we don't want to disturb the horses any more than we have to. I thought if I hired a chopper for my cameraman and me, it would mean only one more flight out to the valley. I'll give everyone in the media any footage they'll need. This will keep all the TV stations from flying in there for their own film."

"I'll tell the Shoshone you're doing this for them," Shane said. "They'll appreciate it. I do need to hook the pilot up with the men guarding the horses in the valley. They can tell him, via radio, where to find the herd. We'll coordinate all this tomorrow."

Kate walked outside with Shane to his truck, and, in an understatement said, "Looks like we're about to set this little town on its ear."

Shane climbed into his truck and rolled down the window. "Well, Kate, that's exactly why I got you out here." Then he smiled, winked, and drove off.

When Shane returned to the ranch, Tara told him Butch had survived the operation. The wolf would need to stay in the animal hospital for a few days, but then he could come home to finish his recovery.

Shane let Tara and her grandfather know everything that was happening in town. "Hopefully, all this trouble will be over soon."

Chapter 25

The next morning, Shane helped set up the communication between the helicopter pilot and Tara's brothers. The second trip into the valley went as planned. The film that Kate took of Naatea and the herd, along with the carcasses at Jasper Canyon, turned out to be just what the doctor ordered.

Megan told Shane she thought she'd be able to finish up her magazine article, and would be flying home in a couple days. Shane and Tara would take Megan to dinner before she left town. He planned to say his good-byes to her then.

Kate, who enjoyed being the center of attention, was handling all the press and media from the surrounding cities. Shane had set the ball in motion and was now sitting back, letting everything take its course. Both the TV and newspaper reporters, understandably, needed the Shoshone to be part of this human interest story. So Kate contacted Shane to have him set up interviews with Tara and Tigee at Fort Washakie. Tara did a great job answering their questions with her grandfather by her side.

Everything really began to accelerate over the next week. Soon all the major networks picked up the story from the local stations. Now the "Who's Killing the Horses?" story had the nation's attention. Never in his wildest imagination could Shane have foreseen that this story would explode onto the national scene like it did. Even though he tried his best to stay away from the media, Megan's story and some of the newspaper articles did mention his name, and explained that bringing his mustang mare out to set her free was the reason the situation had become public.

All of the news stories and Megan's article ended up mentioning the possibility of greed and oil being the reason for the brutal shootings of the horses. Megan's editors, along with their lawyers, decided that this was an important part of the story. As long as no names were mentioned, they would be clear of any libel. The news media had all taken the same views, and most were using Shane's pictures of the test sites on the reservation as part of their stories.

The initial media frenzy of the mustang's plight was over as quickly as it began. Kate O'Hanson's fifteen minutes of fame had now ended. She and her people had done what they came to do, and were now leaving town. With the public interest still strong, a couple of the investigative reporters lingered around hoping to find out who was behind the death of the mustangs.

Vince Nethers's first reaction to all the news was extreme anger. He had seen Shane's name mentioned in the reports and knew he was behind it. "I lost a fortune because of that son of a bitch — all because he wanted to turn one stupid mustang loose with that herd!" Over the phone, Vince screamed an order to his mafia partner, "I want that prick to pay for this."

John Risolli laughed at his request. "I'm out of it! There's way too much attention directed toward what's happening in that valley right now! Up to this point, there's no tie-in between your oil testing and me, and it better stay that way, or you'll be the one who pays! If I were you, I'd leave this Shane Carson alone and maybe even leave town for a while." A hard click sounded as Risolli hung up on him.

Nethers had also talked earlier to his other partner, Barry Russell, with the oil company. He got the same reaction from him. "If anyone should ask me," Barry said, "I'll tell them my men went where your guides told them to go. I'll claim I didn't know they were on reservation land when they did your testing."

Vince planned on using the same excuse if the reporters or authorities questioned him. He would just tell them that his guides made a mistake and wandered over the property line onto the reservation by accident. Whether or not any ongoing investigation did zero in on Vince and his scheme, his dream of getting richer from any oil in the Wind River Valley was over.

During the couple of weeks the media was in town, Shane had done his best to lay low and hang out at the ranch. He quietly reveled in knowing the valley was now safe, while Nethers squirmed in his boots. His plan had worked. Now with the public interest and the activist eyes on the mustangs, no one would be trying to catch or kill the herd anymore.

The tribe's business interests were beginning to turn around, too. Several oil companies had approached the Shoshone and Arapaho about testing in the valley. With the Indians in control, the drilling could be limited so there'd be minimal impact on the land.

While Shane was keeping a low profile at the ranch, he'd spent a lot of time working with Tommy and his horses. The young boy continued to soak up the knowledge like a sponge, and Shane enjoyed every minute of it.

It was an easy decision for him to stay on the reservation for the remainder of the summer, especially since he and Tara were now spending much of their free time together. They both believed that fate had brought them together and were now determined to figure out some way to build a future with each other. Just the sight of Tara brightened each day, and with her understanding and support, Shane was slowly moving from his getting-by-one-day-at-a-time philosophy to actually feeling good about life again.

With plenty of summer left and the herd now safe from Nethers's gang, Shane was having to face up to doing what he originally came out to do — setting Sloppy free. The decision to stay for the rest of the summer, however, provided an excuse for him to temporarily put off the inevitable, which was becoming more and more difficult for him to face. He knew doing it soon would allow him plenty of time to keep an eye on her during her reentry stage. It was important for him to ensure that she was accepted by the rest of the herd, and to give her time to acclimate back to her wild life before winter set in.

He chose the following Saturday to take her out to the valley.

Tara, Tigee, JB, and Hawk offered to go with him, but he felt strongly that this was something he had to do on his own.

On Friday, the day before he would move the mare out to the herd, he decided he would take her on one last ride. It had been a couple of weeks since Butch came home from the animal hospital, and he was healing on schedule.

The mare seemed anxious during the ride. Maybe she was picking up on Shane's mood, about riding her for the last time. She and Tory were, after all, the last living links to so many fond memories he had of his wife and kids. While he rode, he couldn't help but think of Jacob and Tina.

As he unsaddled the mare and turned her out for the evening, he knew in his heart Sloppy would finally be content when he set her free tomorrow. "You'll do fine out there," he said out loud to her. "After all, you were born and raised in the valley, and that's where you belong."

Her shoes had been pulled several weeks ago so her feet could toughen up, and Tommy had kept her in good shape. She was ready. He just didn't know if he was.

When Shane returned to his cabin, Tara was waiting for him on the front porch. As he reached the top step, she walked over to him, put her arms around his neck, and hugged him tightly. "Are you sure you don't want me to go with you tomorrow?" Shane shook his head no, and gestured for Tara to follow him inside the cabin. He asked her to wait a minute as he ruffled through the old pair of saddlebags he had brought with him from Tennessee. He pulled out the paper Jacob had written in school about Sloppy and handed it to Tara. For the first time ever, he was letting someone else read it. On the top of the paper was the boy's name, Jacob Carson, sixth grade, along with the date and a big B+ written in red ink.

My horse's name is Sloppy. She was named by my little sister, Tina, who said she looked filthy dirty when we first got her. My dad broke and trained her because he thought she would make a good horse for us kids.

He taught us to ride on her and he said she does real well for us. My mom found out from a brand on her that she is a wild mustang from Wyoming.

We love Sloppy very much and she loves us too. Sometimes I think she is sad and misses her own family though. I know if someone took me from my family I would miss them.

I asked my dad if someday we could take her back to her herd and put her with them. He promised me that someday we would do it. I think when we take her home it will make her very happy. I will be happy too but also very sad because she is a good horse and she is my best friend.

Tara smiled as her eyes began to well up. She carefully folded the paper back to its original creases and handed it back to Shane. "Having a son such as Jacob would make any man proud."

Shane nodded slightly while he shifted his eyes toward the floor. "He was a good boy, and I know he would have made a good man."

"She's finally going home tomorrow. This will please your son." It startled Shane a little to hear Tara speak of Jacob in the present time, but he now understood how strong the Shoshone believed in an afterlife. Her words made him feel good. Now that she had read Jacob's letter, she understood why this was a personal thing between him and his son, something he had to do on his own.

With the rising sun, Shane loaded Sloppy and Tory and drove out to the valley. Hawk reported to him that the herd had been seen grazing almost every morning in a meadow on the south side of Owl Creek. Shane knew this place and felt confident he could find it.

After unloading the horses at the valley entrance, he rode Tory and led Sloppy alongside. Shane couldn't have asked for a better day to do this. The temperature was in the low seventies, and there wasn't a cloud in sight. An hour into the ride, Sloppy became anxious. Shane knew this meant he was getting close to the herd.

"Well, Tory, this is as far as you go," he told the old horse as he stepped down out of the saddle and tied him to a tree branch. The last thing he wanted was for the mare to be confused whether she should stay with Tory, who had been her running partner for some-time now, or go to Naatea and the herd. For this reason, he would lead her the last couple hundred yards through the woods on foot.

As they eased through the trees and into the meadow, the herd was already aware of their presence. "All right, girl, there they are," he said as he softly rubbed her muzzle. "It took me a while, but I fi-nally got you home." Sloppy stomped her front foot and whinnied to the herd, and Naatea responded by doing the same.

Shane slipped off her halter to let her go, but Sloppy was unsure if she should leave. She turned and gently pushed him with her nose as if to ask what she should do. "Go on, girl, you're with them now," he said as he pushed her away. She only made it about twenty yards before she turned back to face Shane. "Git," he yelled, as he threw up his arms and choked back the emotions. Sloppy stood there a few moments longer, shook her head, snorted again, then turned and ran off toward the waiting herd.

A few of the lead mares came running toward her, squealing and striking out at her with their front feet. Sloppy held her ground and didn't back up an inch from the group. Just then, Naatea ran in close to check her out. The mares surrounding her all moved back out of his way to see if he would accept her. The stallion charged aggres-sively at first, but Sloppy stood firm and acted as if she had a right to be there. Naatea sniffed her from head to tail while grumbling his studly growl. Then, he stepped back, reared straight up in the air striking out with his front feet, screaming his wild call. Shane had watched him do this before when he defeated the young stallion who had challenged him several weeks ago. He knew this was Naatea's way of letting the whole valley know that Sloppy was now one of his mares, and that no one better mess with her.

Chapter 26

Shane took a deep breath as he checked his emotions. "Well, there you go, Jacob," he whispered under his breath.

It was evident that Sloppy had been accepted when the herd began to settle. Shane quietly slipped into the woods, while the little gray mare turned to watch him leave. He quickly made his way back to ole Tory and rode away at a fast gallop, making sure she wasn't trying to follow.

It was about four in the afternoon when he got back to the ranch. As he drove in the gate, he was surprised to see a huge party going on. There was a band playing and meat cooking on a large open grill. Everyone seemed to have a beer or drink in their hands, and it was obvious they were enjoying themselves.

Shane drove to the barn to unload Tory. He was still there when Tara ran up to him and threw her arms around him.

"What's going on?"

"This is all for you," she answered. Shane could tell she'd had a couple of beers and was in good spirits as she smiled and softly kissed him on the lips.

Shane sighed. "I don't know if I'm in the mood for this right now."

Tara grabbed his hand, urging, "Come with me, I'm going to mix you a strong drink and put you in that chair on your porch, then I'm going to sit on your lap and nibble on your ear. You'll get in a party mood in no time." Shane couldn't help but grin at Tara's lively attitude.

They had not been on the porch long when Mr. and Mrs. Jensen ambled up. It was good to see them, and they sat down to join Shane and Tara. While the four of them watched the festivities from his porch, people wandered up to greet him, the smiles on their faces showing their gratitude.

"I've got some more good news," Tara said.

"What's that?"

"One of the investigative reporters has been in contact with my grandfather over the last couple of weeks. His name is Chad Dunning. He said he had talked to you."

"Yeah, I gave him all the information I had on the situation and told him, off the record, that I suspected Vince Nethers.

"Well," Tara said, "my grandfather gave him the names of all the people who had stopped doing business with us concerning our cattle and hay sales. We heard back from him today. It seems three of the men admitted that Vince had forced them to stop buying from us. Apparently, since the situation here had become so high profile, all of this was enough to spur a federal investigation on Nethers for land fraud and racketeering. I don't know if he'll get convicted, but ole Vince is in some deep muck right now."

Shane tilted his head and nodded. "Now that's the best news I've heard in a while. I do believe I'll have a drink to that."

"I think I'll have one too," said Mr. Jensen.

The party continued until late that night. The Jensens stayed till the end. Mrs. Jensen had to drive home because her husband had partied a little too much, but before the two of them drove off into the night, she made Shane promise to come over to dinner soon.

After everyone went home, Tara lay in Shane's arms, and said the words that neither of them had spoken before. "Shane, I've never experienced such strong feelings for anyone, I want you to know that I've been head over heels in love with you since that night at Shadow Creek." Maybe it was the influence of the alcohol that gave her the courage to say it, but now it had been said.

Shane was taken aback by Tara's confession. At first he wasn't sure how to respond, but his feelings for her had become too strong to push aside any longer. "I never thought I could feel this way about anyone again, but I'm in love with you, too." They lay there for hours tangled up near the fire, wasted in the powerful feelings they'd finally owned up to, until eventually they fell asleep.

The next day, Shane called Terry back at the farm in Tennessee. He received all the latest news from him about his wife, kids, and the farm. Shane informed him he would be staying in Wyoming at least for the rest of the summer.

"It's good to hear your voice, boss," Terry said. "Don't worry about the farm. The training business is as busy as ever, and everything is fine. We saw the story on the evening news about the horses being killed out there."

"You did?"

"Yes, sir. Sounds like you've been involved in quite an adventure. Has it settled down enough for you to set Sloppy free yet?"

"I did it yesterday." The two old friends chatted a while longer before hanging up.

Later, Shane went over to talk to Tigee and Tara about an idea. "I've been trying to think of a way you can keep the horses safe from anything like this happening again. You never know when those kids from town will start playing their games of stealing horses. At this time, the mustangs are very much in the public's eye. Because of this, no one is going to take a chance of messing with them. When all this oil money starts coming in, why don't you use some of it to pump up your tourism business using the herd as an attraction?

"You could build a vacation resort. People could go hunting, fishing, white-water rafting, and you could take them on tours to see the famous spirit horses. With guided tours out to the high ridges, you could keep people from bothering your mustangs down in the valley. I believe you could build a real business around the herd, and keep up the public's fascination in them. This, in return, will help preserve them for many generations to come.

"Believe me, people will come back every year just to see this inspiring country you have out here. I'm not talking about opening your gates to the general public. I'm suggesting controlled numbers of people making reservations at an expensive resort. This way, you could control where they're allowed to go on their own.

"I've already talked to Megan about coming back to do a follow-up story on the herd. The article she wrote has horse enthusiasts all over the U.S. wanting to see this valley and the famous historical mustangs. If she were to mention a future resort in her follow-up article, the place would be booked up before it was even built."

Tigee sat for a minute in deep thought. Maybe, with this kind of attention and admiration for the horses, his dream to ensure their long-term safety before he died could finally come true. "As long as our valley can maintain its original wilderness state, I would consider bringing something like this before the council. Maybe you could help me put together a proposal for them, when the oil money becomes a reality."

The next several days rolled by in a slow, relaxing manner, in stark contrast to the prior weeks.

It had been one week since Shane had set Sloppy free. He could hardly wait to get out to the valley with JB and Hawk tomorrow to see how she was doing.

The yearly branding of the weanlings would take place soon. Shane was hoping to still be out here at that time and was looking forward to a close inspection of the mare to make sure she was holding up okay.

Even though it was Saturday morning, Tara had to leave around eight o'clock to go to work. She needed to tie up a few loose ends, as the first day of school was only two days away. She woke before he did and gently slid her smooth, warm body onto his. With his eyes still shut he smiled as he felt the heat of her breath on his cheek, followed by the pleasing sensation of her lips gliding along the side of his neck. Shane's eyes slowly opened, allowing the early morning's delicate light to reveal all of her appeal. His pulse quickened while he stared at the contours of her beautiful face and the fit shape of her perfect body with her silky, caramel-colored skin. Seconds later came a kiss that felt like it could last forever. This morning was special and they both knew it. It was as if their spirits had somehow intertwined, becoming one. Still out of breath, they held each other tight, then Tara whispered, "I love you, Shane Carson." He gently caressed her face as he looked into her eyes in a way that told her he felt the same. A short time later she glanced at the clock and moaned as she forced herself to get out of bed and leave for work.

For the first time in a long while, Shane was happy and totally relaxed. He and Tara were getting along better than ever. All the trouble in the valley seemed to be over. But, even with all this welcome contentment, his family was still constantly on his mind. Tara knew this and accepted it. Her willingness to share him with his memories was certainly one of the main reasons he had fallen for her so deeply.

Shane got out of bed later than usual and was eating breakfast when he heard a knock on the door. As he opened it, he was surprised to see Tommy standing there with tears in his eyes. He'd never seen the boy cry before. Noticing the bruising on his face, Shane thought that Tommy had been thrown off a horse. But then he saw how shook up he was. Tommy was struggling to regain his composure and having trouble catching his breath in order to speak.

"What the hell happened to you, bud?"

"A m-m-m-man broke into my house this morning. He came in my room and pulled me out of bed," the boy stuttered, still trying to catch his breath.

Shane's blood began to boil as he realized the boy had taken a beating from someone. "Who did this to you?"

"He told me his name was Jack, and he gave me this note to give you." Shane took the note and almost fell down when he read it.

"Son of a bitch," he mumbled under his breath as he crumpled the note into a tight ball and threw it hard against the wall. "Come here, let me look at your face." He leaned over to get a closer look at Tommy's shiner. "Did he hurt you anywhere else?"

"No, sir, I thought he was going to though. He held me up against the wall and yelled at me, real mean. He told me if you didn't do like the note says, he'd be back for me. And next time he'd hurt me bad."

Shane's heart nearly broke in two when he saw the terror in Tommy's eyes. Tommy looked down at the floor, a little ashamed that he was crying in front of this man he admired so much.

"Look at me, son," Shane said in a calming voice to the young boy. Tommy slowly lifted his head. "You did real well today. I'm proud of the way you handled this. Hell, everyone gets scared sometimes. But I can promise you this, that man will never bother you again. Now I've got to go. Are you gonna be okay?"

"Yes sir."

Shane grabbed his hat and lifted his rifle off the gun rack. He peered at Tommy with a rushed look in his eyes and spoke rapidly. "I need you to go fetch Tory for me, saddle him up just as quickly as you can, while I hook up the truck and trailer."

Tommy looked back at Shane with concern and asked, "What are you going to do, Mr. Shane?"

"Just go get my horse for me now. Okay?"

"Yes, sir." Tommy raced out.

Within ten minutes, Shane was loading his gear and his horse. The two dogs tried to jump on the trailer, but Shane wouldn't let them go. "No," he told them in a strong voice. "You stay here!" Butch and Jessie couldn't understand why Shane had hollered, so they trotted back to the porch with their tails between their legs. Tommy was confused, too, and didn't know what to do as he watched Shane drive out of the ranch gate with his tires spinning in the dirt.

Tigee just happened to be looking out of his living room window and noticed Shane loading up and leaving in a big hurry. He walked out on the porch and saw Tommy standing in the road where Shane had left him, a dazed look on his face. He motioned for the boy to come over. As Tommy got closer, Tigee saw the abrasions on his face, and immediately asked what happened.

Tommy, bewildered and shook up, told Tigee what he knew.

"Do you know what the note said?" Tigee asked calmly.

"No, sir, but Mr. Shane got real mad when he read it, then he balled it up and threw it on the floor at his house."

"I want you to run as fast as you can and get that note for me," the old man demanded. Tommy took off like a bullet. Tigee wasted no time calling JB and Hawk. "Load your horses and get here as soon as possible," he urged. His two grandsons were at a horse sale in Casper, too far away to help.

Tara had forgotten some papers she needed for work and was driving back in the gate when she noticed Tommy running as hard as he could from Shane's place to her grandfather's. She instantly got a feeling something was wrong and hurried into the house. She walked in the door just in time to see the stricken reaction on Tigee's face as he finished reading the crumpled up note. Right off the bat, she noticed Tommy's swollen eye and rushed over to him.

"What happened, Tommy?" By this time the boy had regained his composure, but his right eye was nearly swollen shut, and turning a deeper shade of purple.

"I'm okay, Miss Tara," he said with his head held high.

Tigee spoke, "Jack did this and sent the boy to Shane with a message." He handed her the note with one hand while he put his other hand on her shoulder. The words she read were cold and taunting, and quickly revealed the rest of the situation to her.

> I've been reading about you and your mustang mare in the newspaper. It was easy to figure out which one she was, since she still had the holes in her hoof walls from her shoes. The little mare still likes her grain, too, so setting a trap and catching her was easy. She's tied up to a tree just outside Jasper Canyon, in the same spot where my partner Thomas was shot down. I told you it wasn't over between us. You cost me my fortune and my best friend, but not my leave. If you want the mare to live, you have to come and get her. I'll be watching you come into the valley, and if you have anyone with you or you bring the dogs, the mare gets a bullet between her eyes. My word is my honor, and

if you can come out to meet me alone, I'll let the mare live. If you don't come alone, I'll drop her where she stands, and still get to you later. You have till noon today.

Tara's heart was in her throat as she put her hand over her mouth and sank back into a chair. "Where's Shane?" she asked Tommy.

"He left about twenty minutes ago with Tory in his trailer."

Tara jumped out of her seat, and started to run out the door to go after him.

Tigee grabbed her before she got out of the house. "Wait. JB and Hawk are on their way."

"Tommy, go get my horse," she begged. "I'm going with them. Grandfather, don't try to stop me." Tigee knew he couldn't, so he nodded to Tommy to do as she had asked.

By the time JB and Hawk arrived at the house, Tommy was coming out of the barn with Tara's horse saddled up and ready to load in their trailer. Tigee and Tara filled them in on what was happening and let them read the note. "You're not going," JB told Tara. "It's not safe."

"Damn it, JB," she said. "If you don't take me, I'll go on my own, and right now we're just wasting time." No one was going to stop her from getting out to Shane, and she was right, there was no time to argue.

"If you go," JB said, "you stay behind us and do exactly as I say!" With that said, JB and Hawk reluctantly loaded Tara's horse and let her in the truck before they sped away.

JB and Hawk put together a plan during the drive. "Why don't we go in from the southeast pass," Hawk suggested. "It's a rough trail for the first half mile or so, but it's less distance over to Jasper Canyon from there. This Jack guy will be watching Shane come in from the southwest, so this will give us a chance to slip into the area unseen."

"Shane was only about a half hour in front of us when we left the ranch," said JB. "Using the southeast entrance we should be able to get to Jasper Canyon about the same time he does. Maybe we'll get lucky, and that white boy will get lost."

Hawk looked over at JB with concern, "I wouldn't count on that. Shane's gotten pretty damn good at getting around in the valley."

JB and Hawk were correct; Shane was riding in from the southwest. This was the only way he had ever gone to Jasper Canyon. He had to use familiar trails if he was going to make it there in time.

"Sorry, old man," Shane said to Tory. "I've got to push you pretty hard if we're going to get there before the morning is over." An unusual late morning fog was just rising in the area of the canyon as he arrived. Shane could only hope that the low visibility would work in his favor. He rode fast through the thick, moist air until he was close. Once he thought he was within a few hundred yards of the location, he slowed Tory down to a cautious quiet walk. Alert and ready for trouble, Shane pulled his rifle out of its scabbard and rode in the direction that Jack's note specified.

Then, through the rising fog, he heard a familiar whinny. It was Sloppy all right. Shane knew the sound of her call all too well. Although he couldn't see her yet, her frequent yells told him she was only about fifty yards away. Sloppy was screaming to the herd, and they were answering by matching her, whinny for whinny, off in the distance.

Shane eased Tory up closer until he finally came into Sloppy's view. He slipped off his horse and paused, looking and listening for any movement or sound, which might be Jack waiting for him. Realizing he was in a vulnerable position, he kept his finger on the trigger of his rifle as he began his approach. Using the skills he had learned from JB and Hawk, Shane worked his way silently up to where the mare was tied. "Hey, girl," he whispered to her, "you're okay." His eyes were constantly combing the area around them as he reached up to pull off her halter and set her free. At first, Sloppy didn't know whether to stay or go, so Shane slapped her on the hindquarters to send her galloping in the direction of the other mustang's repetitive calls.

"All right, you piece of shit, where are you?" Shane whispered to himself, still looking around as he made his way back to Tory.

Hawk, JB, and Tara were just getting to the canyon and were carefully working their way along the high side of the east canyon wall.

"Look, there's the mare," Tara pointed below, as they watched her run in a wide-open sprint toward the rest of the herd. Now that they knew the mare was safe, JB saw no reason to stay quiet.

"Shane!" he hollered. "It's JB, are you okay?" Although they weren't in sight, JB's loud echoes reached Shane down on the canyon floor.

He quickly answered, "I'm all right."

"Have you seen the Arapaho?" JB yelled back.

"No."

"There's a trail that leads up to us, about a hundred yards east of where you are. Hawk and I will meet you halfway down." JB looked at Tara and told her sternly to stay up on the ridge. He handed her a pistol, and said, "If that Arapaho comes for you, don't hesitate to use it." Tara nodded as she watched JB and Hawk start down the steep trail toward Shane.

At the bottom, Shane rode east, like Hawk had told him to do, and soon found the way up. He knew Jack was out there somewhere. He just hoped the sound of his friends calling would be enough to scare him off. Shane had made it up to a level spot about fifty feet above where he had started. The fog had cleared, so he turned to see if he was being followed. Hawk and JB were still several hundred yards up the winding trail and were just now coming in sight above him.

Then, out of nowhere, he heard the sound of Jack's voice. "Hey, asshole," the Arapaho hollered. Jack moved from behind a tree about forty feet down the trail from Shane. "Damn, I must have ridden right by him," Shane murmured.

Jack was on foot as he moved into the open with his rifle pointed at Shane. During their descent, Hawk and JB lost sight of Shane for a few minutes. The slow, winding trail had taken them behind some large rocks and trees, which obstructed their view below. "Drop your rifle now," Jack yelled.

"Well, at least you didn't shoot the defenseless horse," Shane retorted, trying to stall for time. He knew JB and Hawk were not far away and would soon be able to help.

Jack laughed, "I could care less about that damn horse. It's you I'm after. Besides, I may still go out and shoot the mare after I'm done with you."

Shane looked Jack square in the eye, pointed at him angrily, and yelled, "There was no reason to rough that kid up like you did."

Jack laughed again. "I did that just to piss you off. I heard you'd been helping him with his horses."

Shane, still stalling for time, replied, "You're a tough guy when it comes to beating up young boys and women, aren't you? Why don't you put down that gun and let's see how you can do with a grown man?"

Jack sneered as he shook his head. "I know your friends are coming down the trail to meet you. I figure they'll be here in about five minutes. That doesn't give me enough time to kick your ass before I shoot you." Suddenly, the look on Jack's face turned to pure evil. The next sound Shane heard was the clicking noise of a rifle as Jack cocked the lever and took careful aim. "This is for my partner, Thomas," he yelled as he started to squeeze the trigger.

At that same instant, a shot rang out from above. The bullet that came from behind Shane tore into Jack's right shoulder, knocking the rifle out of his grasp. The Arapaho scrambled to his horse which he'd tied nearby, and took off.

JB and Hawk had come around the bend of the trail just in time to see what was happening, and Hawk had squeezed off a quick shot at Jack. Neither Hawk nor JB were about to let Jack get away. JB screamed out one of his crazy war cries as they rode past Shane in hot pursuit of the Arapaho. Shane knew that his two friends hadn't noticed he was hit.

Tara didn't stay at the top of the ridge like she'd been ordered. As soon as JB and Hawk disappeared around the first bend, she started following them down. She heard the shot and was now riding toward Shane and Tory at a fast trot. He was still sitting on his horse, with his back toward her, as she rode in close. It took her a minute to realize what was going on, but she soon grasped the terrible truth. Shane was beginning to slump over his saddle horn with his open hand pushed into his stomach, as blood oozed through his fingers.

It sounded like only one shot had been fired, but in reality, Jack fired his rifle simultaneously with the shot Hawk had got off from the trail above.

"Shane," Tara yelled. "Oh God, NO!" Before she could get to him, Shane had fallen off his horse and was tumbling down the ridge to the bottom of the steep trail fifty feet below. She screamed his name out again and again as she helplessly watched him plummet down across the pounding, punishing rocks until he finally landed hard at the bottom.

Shane lay broken, mangled, and bleeding at the base of the steep slope, barely conscious. He was too far gone to feel any pain. Tara urged her horse down the long sloping trail at a dangerous pace, hoping and praying that somehow he would be all right.

The ride down only took a minute, but to her, it felt like an agonizing eternity. She frantically jumped off her horse and knelt by his side, tears streaming down her cheeks. Tara picked up his hand, put her face close to his, and looked into his eyes for what she feared would be the last time. He struggled to stay conscious, but as hard as he tried, he could not speak the words that he desperately wanted to say to her. With blinding tears, she gently kissed his lips, held his hand tightly, and slowly inhaled his final outward breath. Then his body went limp, and he closed his eyes forever.

Tara moved her quivering lips to his ear, exhaled the breath she had taken in from him and whispered, "You go to them, *Tahotay*. Your family is waiting."

She kept her composure for a short while, but the reality overwhelmed her, and for the first time in her adult life, Tara broke down and sobbed uncontrollably. Now she felt the pain and loneliness Shane had been through. A pain that could only be understood by losing someone whom she had loved with all of her heart.

*   *   *

Suddenly, something caught her attention. It was a cloud of dust and the sound of thundering hooves heading in their direction. It was Naatea with the herd coming toward them, hard and fast. Then, for no apparent reason, the mustangs slowed down and came to a sudden halt, only fifty yards away. With the herd calmly settled, only Sloppy separated herself out and continued to come closer. Tara, still kneeling at Shane's side, watched as Sloppy moved toward them. In her shaken state of mind, it took her a moment to realize the horse was actually trotting up to them, in some kind of suspended slow motion. Although the morning fog had lifted a while ago, a strange mist surrounded the mare. She stopped only a few yards away and nervously pawed the ground. The mare's eyes were wide open, and her nostrils flared as she inhaled the mist that surrounded her, and then anxiously snorted it back out.

Tara gasped as she caught a glimpse of something else in the cloud-like mist. Something that sent chills up her spine and made her heart race wildly. With an unsteady, blood-stained hand, she wiped the tears out of her eyes to see more clearly. It was then that she saw an outline of a man. The silhouette looked faint to her at first, but it gradually grew more defined. As the image moved through the misty haze and closer to the fretful mare, the horse began to calm down. Then Sloppy let go one last snort and, in an instant, became totally relaxed.

Tara struggled to gain control over her emotions as she saw the shadow reach out for the mare's mane, and gracefully swing up on her back. Seconds later, the mist slowly began to clear away and the figure became recognizable to her. Even before she could make out the features of his face, she knew it was Shane by the way he sat on the horse. He turned and looked into her eyes, and deep into her soul. Although no words were spoken, she knew he was telling her good-bye, and that she would always be in his heart. Tara remained speechless as she noticed him smile while the outline, that a minute ago was so clear, began to fade. Shane turned and looked ahead just as the odd mist smoothly drifted back in and enveloped him.

Tara stood up and said under her breath, "Go to them." Then as if someone had given the horse a perfectly timed cue, Sloppy backed up three steps, rolled over her hocks and raced off to join the herd. As the mare reached the other horses, Naatea screamed one of his loud, echoing screams, and the mustangs banded together in a stampede that soon disappeared through an open field and into the dusty horizon.

Tara closed her tearful eyes and a scene became vividly clear in her mind. She envisions the herd running at full speed, charging wildly to the top of a high, grassy hill. Passing over the peak, Shane looks down and sees his family in the meadow far below. Tina and Jacob are laughing and playing by a stream, while Jen sits nearby, watching over them. The horses stop where the top of the ridge meets the clear blue skyline, and only Sloppy and Shane continue down into the meadow. Jen and the kids look up to see Shane coming and begin to wave excitedly as he gallops toward them. Suddenly, the mare drops her haunches and slides to a smooth stop. This is as far as she's allowed to go.

Shane slowly climbs down off her bare back and proceeds to rub her affectionately on her muzzle. He leans in close to the mare's ear, and whispers to her softly, "I brought you to yours, now you've brought me to mine." Then, with a gentle slap on her hip, he sends his old friend off in a slow trot, back to her waiting herd.

He turns to face his family just in time to have Jacob and Tina jump into his arms, with Jen soon joining them in the embrace.

The clear vision in Tara's mind brings a smile to her weeping face. She knows Shane has finally played out his destiny, and the spirit horses have taken him to where he belongs. He is now in a place where sadness will not exist for him anymore.

EPILOGUE

Hawk and JB had no idea Shane had been shot when they rode by. Even if they'd realized it, they couldn't have saved him. It was the bullet from Jack's gun that killed him, not the fall.

They did catch up with Jack. He had eventually collapsed off his horse and passed out due to the massive loss of blood from his shoulder wound. He bled to death before they could get him out of the valley.

Later that day, Tigee received the news that Jack had shot and killed Vince Nethers earlier that morning. He apparently had come from Nethers's house before beating up young Tommy, and sending the boy to Shane with the note. Jack had demanded money from Nethers or he threatened to testify against him. Vince pulled a gun on Jack. The Arapaho showed no hesitation when he pulled out his own pistol and blew a gaping hole in Nethers's chest.

He had told others he blamed Vince Nethers for his best friend's death, just as much as he blamed Shane. No one ever found Thomas's body. This ended up as a very interesting story, written by Chad Dunning, the investigative reporter.

In time, the Shoshone tribe prospered from the oil in the valley. Because of the oil money, Tara's dream of a better education for the children on the reservation, along with college scholarships did come true. Shane's idea of building a resort eventually did happen. The Spirit Horse Resort and Lodge stayed booked up year around. It provided a good income for the tribe and kept a healthy public fascination for the mustangs as well as the valley they live in with all it has to offer.

Tommy became a respected clinician and took ole Tory with him on the road until the horse grew too old to haul.

The two wolves, Butch and Jessie, ended up as JB's sidekicks, and whenever you saw JB, you were more likely than not to see them, too.

It was several years before Tara met another man to whom she could give her heart. She did eventually end up with a family, which included two strong and healthy sons. Her oldest boy was already five years old when she married. He was born a little less than nine months after Shane's passing. She named him Jacob, and from the time he was old enough to walk, all he ever wanted to do was to ride horses with his Uncle Tommy.

Author's Note

The word *Tahotay* along with the myth it represents, as well as all of the other tribal spiritual beliefs in this story, came solely from the imagination of the author. The other Native American words used in this book and their translated definitions, came from research on the Shoshone Web site dictionary. The combination of some of these Shoshone words was formatted to fit this fictional story, therefore they may have been used out of context to the actual Shoshone language.